The
Tierans

Book One – The Citizens

The
Tierans

Book One –The Citizens

Randy Ellena

The Tierans: Book One—The Citizens

Forest of Grativy Publications
Fresno, California

ISBN: 978-0-578-56971-0 paperback
ISBN: 978-0-578-56973-4 ebook

LCCN: 2019912957

This one is for my parents,
Jack and Doris Ellena,
with love and thanks.

Contents

Contents

Preface

The *Trasceran Chronicles* is an anthology comprised of two distinct but related series of novels. Like its sister series, *The Kylgahran*, book one of *The Tierans* is set in the lands surrounding the Middle Sea on the two-mooned world of Trascera. Magic, the mystic power of the Yir, stirs on Trascera—wondrous and ominous in equal measure.

As the story opens, the Tieran Empire, long the dominant military and economic force in the region, remains mired in a civil war, known as the War of Houses, that has been grinding on for decades. The outcome of this struggle appears fated to determine the way ahead not only for Tier but for all the kingdoms and nation states bordering the Middle Sea.

Situated along the northern shore of the smaller, thumb-shaped Myr Sea, bounded by the Escalon Plateau to the north, the Syrus River to the west, and the River Poe to the east, the Three Rivers Territory marks the northwestern frontier of the Tieran Empire. Nearly two generations' worth of civil war has loosened imperial ties there and given rise to a dangerous murmur—that of freedom.

During these troubled times, three friends—Mat, an apprentice blacksmith, his intended, Bodewhin, who longs to become a singer, and Jaryd, an ambivalent student of the law—come of age to face an uncertain future. Mat will be summoned by a call to duty, and for Bodewhin and Jaryd, the twin coils of witchcraft and sorcery await.

Jaryd is destined to meet Dyrileah, a young woman hailing from a different culture, a world apart from his. Mat and Bodewhin's love will be tested by separation, trial, and, ultimately, the insurmountable, while for Jaryd and Dyrileah, forces beyond their control will rise, threatening to tear them apart.

Meanwhile, a sudden and unexpected end to the War of Houses sets into motion a sequence of events none could have foreseen. At the forefront is a battle-weary Tieran soldier, Quintus Glabrio Jens, who strives to reconcile duty and conscience, which seems simple enough for a thoroughgoing professional—until he encounters a black-eyed beauty and the unthinkable.

Citizens of the empire find themselves poised on the precipice of a new era, a time of rapid and widespread change. Choices matter amid the ensuing tumult, more than in less turbulent days, and some will bear hard edges, propelling those who make them into the most daunting of consequences.

Author's Note

Those who have read the first book of *The Kylgahran* will note that the opening paragraph of *The Tierans* is virtually identical. It's a thing.

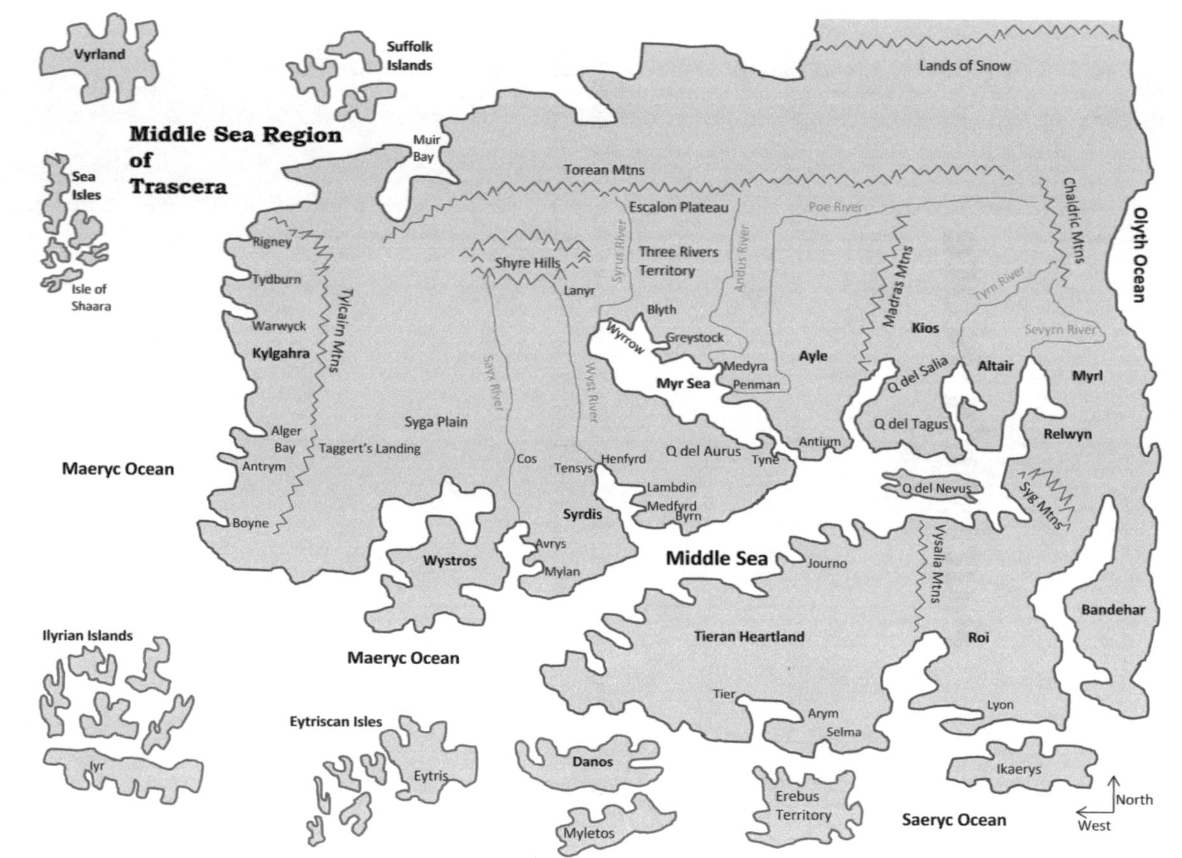
Middle Sea Region
of
Trascera
Vyrland
Suffolk Islands
Sea Isles
Isle of Shaara
Muir Bay
Lands of Snow
Torean Mtns
Escalon Plateau
Poe River
Chaldric Mtns
Olyth Ocean
Rigney
Tydburn
Warwyck
Kylgahra
Tylcairn Mtns
Shyre Hills
Lanyr
Syrus River
Three Rivers Territory
Andus River
Madras Mtns
Tyrn River
Sevyrn River
Kios
Blyth
Greystock
Wyrrow
Medyra
Penman
Ayle
Q del Salia
Altair
Myrl
Myr Sea
Q del Tagus
Relwyn
Syga Plain
Sayx River
Wyst River
Antium
Q del Nevus
Alger Bay
Taggert's Landing
Cos
Henfyrd
Tensys
Q del Aurus
Tyne
Syg Mtns
Antrym
Lambdin
Medfyrd
Byrn
Vysalia Mtns
Maeryc Ocean
Boyne
Syrdis
Middle Sea
Bandehar
Wystros
Avrys
Mylan
Journo
Roi
Ilyrian Islands
Maeryc Ocean
Tieran Heartland
Tier
Arym
Selma
Lyon
Iyr
Eytriscan Isles
Danos
Eytris
Erebus Territory
Ikaerys
Myletos
Saeryc Ocean
North
West

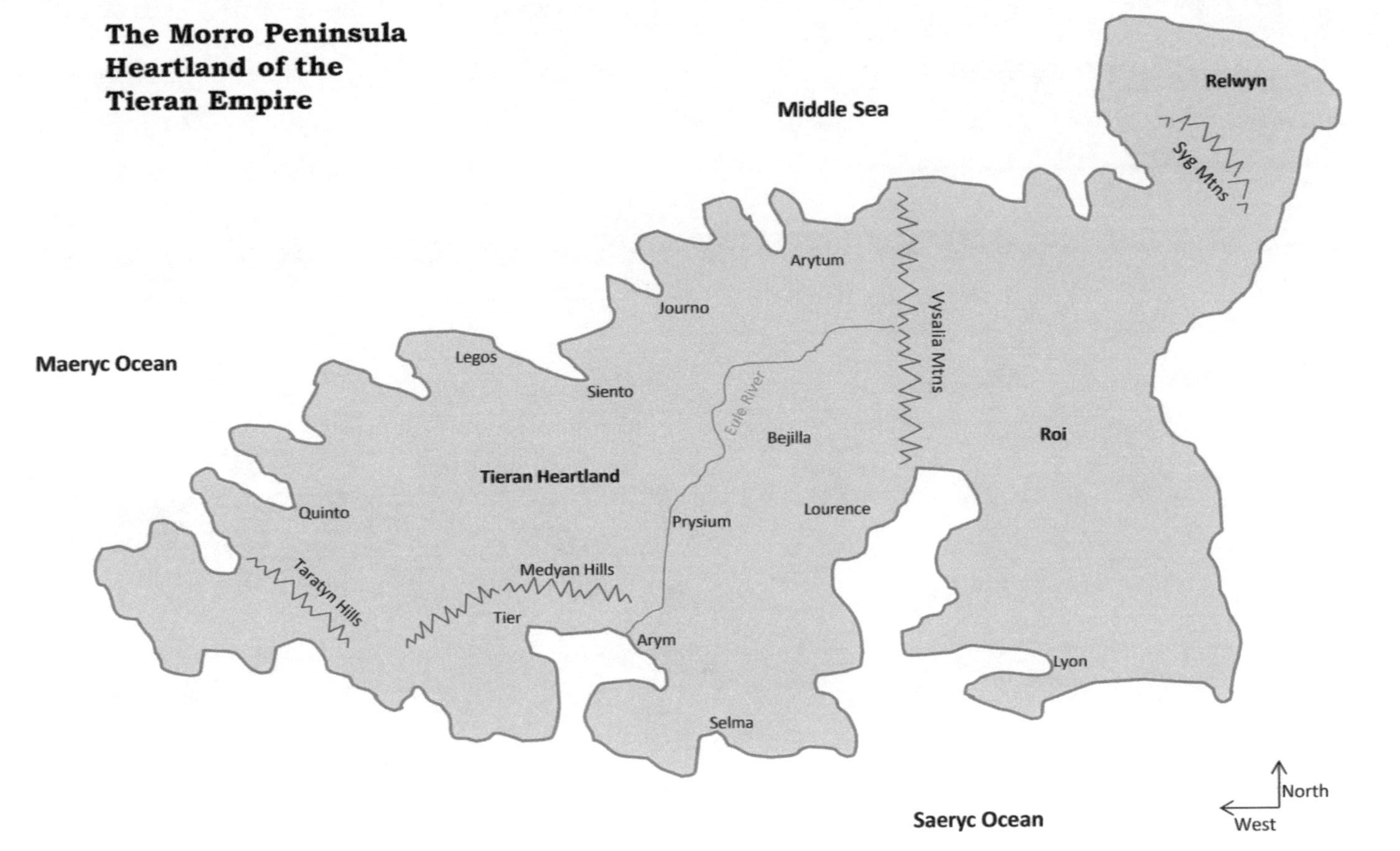

The Morro Peninsula
Heartland of the
Tieran Empire
Middle Sea
Relwyn
Syg Mtns
Maeryc Ocean
Arytum
Journo
Vysalia Mtns
Roi
Legos
Siento
Bejilla
Eule River
Tieran Heartland
Lourence
Quinto
Prysium
Medyan Hills
Tier
Arym
Taratyn Hills
Selma
Lyon
Saeryc Ocean
North
West

The
Tierans

Book One — The Citizens

1

Heckisyah's Point

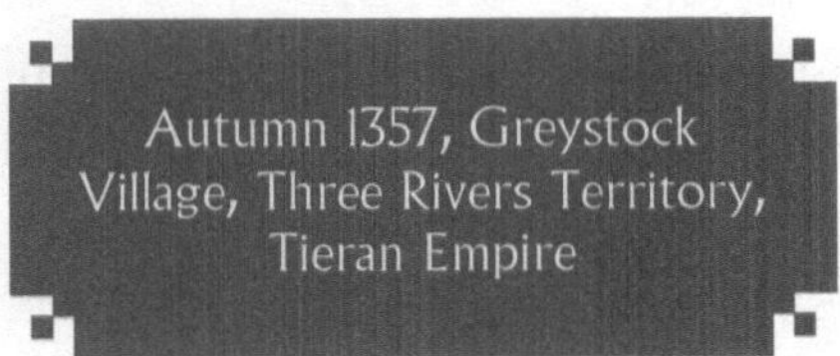

Dawn came softly to the Three Rivers country as if the light of day waxed reluctant to intrude upon night's inky presence. The twin Trasceran moons had long since set when the first stir of waking rippled through a land still steeped in darkness. The night wind shifted and then faded as stillness descended. The first tendrils of sunlight furtively crept into the waiting silence. Having begun as a pale crescent low along the eastern horizon, the gathering light surged like a slowly rising tide, gradually drowning out the stars until the deep velvety black of the nighttime sky gave way to the soft purple hue of early morning.

Mathias Bayrd knelt beneath the spreading branches of a massive oak. The tree stood upon a small rise at the edge of the Great Wood overlooking the northern shore of Deben Bay. Across the narrow expanse of water called the Neck, which marked the opening of the bay, Mat could barely discern the ridge lines and the tall stands of spruce that mantled the far shore.

Thumbing his watch cap a little further back on his forehead, Mat climbed to his feet. Made of wool stitched to a broad leather brim that warded against both sun and rain, the watch cap helped keep the wearer cool in summer and warm in winter. The woolen cover showed gray, as did his waist-length coat. Beneath the coat he wore a cream-colored woolen shirt.

Designed to be pulled on over his head, the long-sleeved shirt fell well past mid-thigh. Three buttons carved from rosewood fastened it at the neck. A wide leather belt buckled at his waist. Sturdy leather sandals encased his feet along with a pair of woolen socks that reached nearly to his knees. Otherwise, his legs were bare. Though the autumn morning air bore a crisp chill, it would be a couple of months before winter properly settled in along with the first snows.

Early morning had long been Mat's favorite time of day, especially amid the lush forest surrounding his home village of Greystock. Dark blond hair curled about Mat's ears. Green-eyed, he stood a couple of finger widths above medium height for a Three Rivers lad, with the broad shoulders and barrel chest of a blacksmith. Well, an apprentice yet, but Mat felt sure he'd be raised to the black apron soon. Master Logan had said as much, and he was not a man given to idle talk.

Smithing came naturally for Mat, if not always easily. The ringing of hammers and the smell of hot iron seemed as much a part of home to him the now as the lowing of cattle or the scent of apple blossoms on his family's farm half a day's walk outside of Greystock. Learning the blacksmith's trade had taught Mat patience and the importance of paying attention to detail. A forging was easily ruined, and even small mistakes were rarely simple to put right. Similarly, hasty words or thoughtless deeds, especially those spurred by anger, could cause hurt not intended or readily mended, particularly so when you had arms as thickly muscled as his.

He supposed working the farm would have taught the same lessons, or maybe just living. Mat liked to think things through. Sometimes that took a while. Bode said that was because he did most of his thinking with the hair on his chest. Mat pretended not to understand her, claiming he could no more think with the hair on his chest than he could breathe through his ears. Saying it always seemed to make Bode smile.

Bodewhin Ware was a slender, brown-haired young woman lacking a year and a day of Mat's own age of nineteen. Bode had kissed him for the first time on his thirteenth birthday. The gentle, feather-light brush of her lips against his, full of promise and mystery, had laid claim to his heart. Mat had known from that moment he and Bode would marry. Bode was lovely. The contours of her face curved, subtly heart shaped, accentuating large gray eyes the color of a storm-tossed sky and every bit as tempestuous, aglow with warmth and wonder one moment, burning with cold fury the next. She possessed an engaging self-assurance that seemed to come as naturally to her as breathing.

How so marvelous a creature could care for the likes of him fell beyond his ken. According to Bode, green eyes were lucky. Kneeling on the soft, loamy soil of his homeland, Mat felt as if he'd used up whatever luck he possessed. Bode was leaving this day, aboard a ship bound for the city of Antium.

Known for its library and the Hall of Learning associated with it, Antium lay at the far end of the Myr Sea. Bode was journeying there to return to the Hall for a second year of instruction. Mat struggled to see why she needed more than the one year she'd already spent there, especially as it was music that she studied.

"You could play and sing better than anyone in Greystock even before leaving for the Hall." He'd said those words to her two evenings earlier as the pair of them stood in the side parlor, a small room off the main hall of her parents' home.

In response, Bode flashed him one of those slantwise looks that warned of trouble if he persisted. "Not that I know anything about singing," Mat hastened to add. "Everyone who has heard me try says I sound like a stepped-on frog or some such."

"That's not fair," Bode protested stoutly, "to the poor, wee froggy."

"Aye, well, that's just," Mat started, hunching his thick shoulders, "about true, I reckon."

Bode laughed. The sound of it rang pure, as melodious as a bell, nearly as infectious as her smile. She stepped across the small room and into his arms. She smelled of soap with a hint of cinnamon and felt like a slim bit of heaven in a pale-blue gingham dress.

"One more year it's to be, then," Mat conceded.

"One more year," Bode affirmed, "and then we'll see."

One more year then at least is what you mean, Mat thought. He said, "I'll miss you."

Bode kissed him then, her lips soft and sweet and warm as life itself, and for a few moments, nothing else mattered. Bode pulled her mouth gently away from his. "You could come along, you know."

"To Antium City? And what would I be doing there?" Mat demurred, knowing what was to come.

"Of course to Antium City," Bode flared, peering up at Mat from within the circle of his arms. "You're not nailed down, are you? The place is fair brimming with blacksmith shops."

"And thousands of people, strangers all," Mat countered, "living behind doors with key locks in them. That's no place for the likes of me."

"Having never been there," Bode said, sounding vexed, "how would you be knowing that?"

"I'd have to start all over again," Mat contended, "as an apprentice."

"Not with a proper letter of introduction from Master Maywell," Bode shot back. "My father would write as well, and my uncle will vouch for you too."

"Master Maywell is a truly fine smith." Mat trod as carefully as he could. "Why should I travel clear across the Myr Sea to enter the employ of a stranger when, if I study as hard as I am able, in twenty years or so, I might learn half what he can teach me right here in Greystock?"

"So it is right for you to stay in pursuit of your dream..." A truly dangerous light flickered in the storm-cloud depths of Bode's eyes the now. "...but wrong for me to go in search of mine?"

"I did not say that," Mat averred.

"That's what you meant." Mat thought Bode was about to push him away. Instead, she pressed closer. "I cannot shelter in your arms forever, Mat. I need to find my own way. Surely, you can see that."

"It is welcome you are here, lass." Mat squeezed her gently. "Forever." Bode made a soft sound deep in her throat and hugged him back. "Seeing is one thing, I suppose," Matt continued. "Understanding is another."

"I love you, Mat Bayrd," Bode declared. "Do you doubt it?"

"I love you too," Mat replied with equal intensity. But doubt he did. *What if you have outgrown your love for me?* A child's love for a backcountry blacksmith could fade in comparison to being part of a wider world filled with music and magic and all that life in a great city like Antium had to offer. His heart thudded hollowly in his chest at the thought.

"I have given you my whole heart," Bode vowed softly, fiercely.

"Glad I am of that," Mat said. "I just wish the rest of you came along with it."

Bode stiffened. Rearing back in his embrace so she could see more directly into his face, she glared at him, flat eyed. "Is that all you want, Mat Bayrd? A woman in your bed?"

"I didn't say that either," Mat hedged, knowing he stood near a precipice deep and forbidding. In an attempt to lighten the mood, he japed, "Comes to it, I'd settle for a wee slip of a girl like you."

The glare vanished, and Mat saw Bode's smile bloom first in the depths of her eyes. "I think of that, too." She kissed him lightly. "This matters to me, Mat."

"I thought we mattered," Mat retorted without thinking.

"We do matter," Bode insisted. "You matter."

"Just not enough." Even as he spoke the words, Mat wished he could call them back.

Hurt flooded the thundercloud recesses of Bode's eyes, followed almost immediately by a flash of anger. Bode lit into him then. At some point, Mat lost his temper and growled something even stupider in rebuttal. They parted with heated words hanging between them.

The following evening, Bode's father, Eddard, had staged a small gathering to honor her departure and that of Mat's friend Jaryd Hume, who would accompany Bode, returning, like her, to the Hall in Antium to continue his studies. Eddard Ware was a successful merchant who owned the largest general store in Greystock and a goodly warehouse as well. Bode and Mat had been able to spend very little time alone together at the gathering, and what conversation passed between them seemed stilted and strained. Even their farewell embrace felt hurried and a little awkward. The distance that suddenly loomed between them, however small, concerned him more than the anger of the previous night.

Pushing worry aside Mat resumed his journey. He did not have far to go. As he cleared the tree line, he could feel a breeze freshening. The wind blew seaward—a lubber's breeze, the sailors would call it. In his left hand he carried a hunter's bow. Adjusting the quiver of arrows slung across his shoulders, Mat hefted the oil lantern he'd brought with him in his right hand. His walk had begun in full darkness, and though the path Mat trod wended a familiar way, he'd welcomed the lamp light.

Striding along a narrow pathway to the edge of a rocky promontory named Heckisyah's Point, Mat clambered onto a large anvil-shaped boulder overlooking the Neck. In full sun, the stone, he knew, would appear blue-gray in color. Bathed in the faint light of dawn, it looked black and felt smooth to the touch. Mat couldn't help wondering how many bottoms had graced this perch over the years. It seemed darker somehow on the lonesome point at the edge of the bay than it had a few moments before. Nothing there was to do the now but wait.

2

Deben Bay Farewell

Aboard the twin-mast schooner *Sly Cat*, Bodewhin Ware stood at the rail on the port side of the vessel. The spot she'd chosen, just forward of the mainmast, proffered a location where Captain Jynks Warrow had assured her she would not be in the way. The tide flowed swiftly outward through the Neck, and aided by a following breeze, *Sly Cat* loped along.

The wind bit just deeply enough to make Bode glad of the cloak she wore over her traveling dress. Fashioned of winnowed wool, sky blue in color, the cloth proved both remarkably soft and warm for its weight. Her mother, Annelle, said it went well with her eyes. The clover-shaped polished brass clasp she wore at her throat to fasten the cloak had belonged to her grandmother.

The weave of her linen frock showed a slightly darker shade of blue. The hem of the dress fell to mid-calf. A broad, brocaded belt of waxed linen, called a kyrobi, adorned her waist. Homespun woolen socks and closed-toe leather shoes, sturdy and comfortable, covered her feet. Under it all she wore a new silk shift, one of three in her possession.

The shifts were a parting gift from her father. Silk was dear. When she'd remarked at the cost, he just smiled and told her they'd had a good year. Papa would have said the same regardless. Unmatched for comfort whatever the price, silk served well through a long day of travel, so practical consideration framed her acceptance of his gift. If she succeeded, if her dreams could be realized, then she would be able to match her father's generosity and mayhap a little more in return.

She wore her hair in a thick, single braid that reached the small of her back. Brown her hair was—such an ordinary color, or so it seemed to her. Both her mother and her younger sister had rich, honey-blond hair. Try as she might not to be jealous, that felt a little unfair. Mat said what mattered resided within your head, not upon it. *Mat*, she sighed, *the great looby.*

Water hissed along the hull of the ship, whose every movement seemed smooth and sure. Experience had taught her that however tame the sheltered waters of the bay might appear, the Myr Sea stirred just beyond, a much larger and wilder creature. *Sly Cat* was well made, though: lateen rigged, Captain Warrow had explained, with both the main and foresails running fore and aft. In addition to the fore and main courses, she carried topsails on both masts and a large jib at her bows. Outfitted with sweeps, *Sly Cat* could be rowed, but as Warrow described her, she stood wedded to the wind.

Sleek and sound *Sly Cat* put to sea eager as a fractious colt. Jynks loved his ship, as any good captain would. A rascal he might be ashore, but at sea, Jynks Warrow knew what he was about. Pretty much everyone in Greystock said so. Her father told her Warrow was a man you could trust when it counted. Perhaps because of that trust, Bode had the feeling that this morning, the Myr would remain calm. Its fury banked like a forge fire at the end of the day, caged and unbowed, ready to roar back to life but only at some later time. They were off to a good start—or should have been.

Mat had looked so hurt. Not that he had any right to, him and his pride. She had broken no promises. He had not seen her off nor even said good-bye, not really. She should have been angry with him. A couple of nights before, he'd made her mad enough to spit.

Today, amid the sting of parting, she couldn't even work up a proper miff.

Mat embodied all she loved most about Three Rivers folk. Mat was stronger than any two men had a right to be and yet so gentle. He could not tell a lie to save his life, not that he'd try. Slow to anger, Mat was kind and generous and steady as the pulse of a sleeping child. Some thought Mat not as bright as he might have been. Bode knew better. He might talk slowly, but his mind worked quickly enough. Brave he was too, endowed with the kind of stubborn courage that would hold fast through hard times. His eyes lit when he smiled, which he did often. Green they were, with flecks of gold in the depths of them.

If only he could see, with those splendid eyes of his, just a little further. For Mat, life in the Three Rivers encompassed all he needed or wanted. He knew it without questioning. That kind of certainty she found impossible to understand. *How could he be so complacent?* It was not that he couldn't conceive of a broader existence elsewhere; he simply felt no need. *Is there something lacking in Mat,* she wondered, *or in me?*

"You haven't run across my sea legs anywhere hereabouts, have you?" Jaryd Hume asked. "I could use 'em just the now." Bareheaded, Jaryd was otherwise clad in a waist-length woolen coat typical of the Three Rivers, butternut brown in color. He wore an oatmeal-colored linen shirt beneath his waistcoat that fell nearly to his knees. A sturdy leather belt girded his waist. Jaryd was wearing boots, she noticed, not the more usual sandals. He had a paper-wrapped bundle tucked under one arm.

Jaryd Hume was Mat's age, his best friend, and about as different from him as night compared to day. Well, not quite, actually; they had a shared sense of humor. Burn the pair of them. Jaryd was joshing the now. He'd turned out to be a good sailor, better than her.

"I thought you'd be looking farther aft," she responded, nodding toward the rear of the vessel, in the general direction of the Clegg sisters.

Jaryd smiled. *He has a good smile,* Bode thought, though small compensation for the unfortunate thatch of red hair atop his head. He came by it honestly, Jaryd did. His father and two of his brothers were redheaded as well. A couple of finger widths taller than Mat, Jaryd had the lean, angular build typical of the Humes. His eyes were gray, a mirror of her own. At least he didn't have too many freckles, and his cheeks dimpled when he smiled. Jaryd didn't take anything too seriously, himself least of all. Good company, Bode had decided, when he wasn't trying too hard to be clever.

"Tempting, but truth to tell, there's at least one too many Cleggs back there," Jaryd said in a conspiratorial whisper, even though, with the rising wind, he would have had to shout to be heard aft of the mainsail.

Plump, pretty blondes in new, city-made clothes, the sisters Clegg, Dara and Valene, were making their first trip to Antium. An outing, they called it. When asked, they were a little vague as to just what an outing might entail. What they lacked in purpose, however, they more than made up for in enthusiasm, fairly bouncing all over the place. Their older brother Daryl was along as well. *To contain his sisters' more natural inclinations, no doubt.* Bode turned back toward the rail.

"Ran into a fella yesterday," Jaryd was saying, "curly-haired, broad as an axe handle, he talked kind of slow. He asked if I would pass this along to you." Jaryd proffered her the bundle. "He said to mind the note."

Taking the package and tossing decorum overboard, Bode plopped down on the deck and carefully tore into the paper wrapping. The bundle contained a fine winnowed wool cloak, hooded with a deep cowl, dove gray in color. Also included she found a polished brass clasp, shaped into a pair of doves facing one another, eye to eye and heart to heart. Doves, Bode knew, mated for life and were a symbol of fidelity.

Affixed to the pin of the clasp she found a small folded piece of heavy vellum paper. Opening the paper, Bode eagerly scanned the words written in simple block letters.

Bode,
For one year or a thousand.
Mat

"Not one to waste words, is he?" Bode observed, handing the note to Jaryd.

"You know Mat," Jaryd said after glancing at the missive, obviously choosing his words carefully. "When he says a thing, he means it. It just doesn't occur to him that some things, once said, bear repeating."

"H'yar helm," Captain Warrow shouted through a speaking tube from up toward the bow of the ship, where he was standing in the lower rigging on the port side abreast of the foresail, his voice slicing through their conversation like an axe. "Wear one point ta starboard, if ye please."

"Aye, Captain," came the helmsman's reply, fainter than the captain's bellow but still clear enough for both Jaryd and Bode to hear. "One-point starboard."

The Neck was narrow with some shoals to snag the unwary. A deep channel that sailors referred to as the upper course ran along the northern shore of Deben Bay. The closest approach to land lay just off Heckisyah's Point, a distance of about four hundred paces. Despite the fair weather and favorable wind and tide, Jynks Warrow clearly intended to keep *Sly Cat* squarely in mid-channel until well past the point.

"He couldn't see his way clear to give this to me himself?" Bode asked, climbing to her feet to reclaim the note and making no attempt to hide the tears welling in her eyes.

"I think he was a little worried about gettin' yelled at with half of Greystock within earshot," Jaryd replied.

"He didn't even say a proper good-bye." Bode spoke softly.

So softly she wasn't sure Jaryd had even heard her until he pointed landward. "Not yet, maybe."

Blinking back tears and trying to follow his indication, Bode took note of what appeared to be a man standing on a rocky outcrop atop the point of land they were nearing. Bode squinted for a long moment into the soft morning light and then looked up at Jaryd. "Is that Mat?"

"Unless gray bears have taken to toting long bows, I think it must be," Jaryd opined. "There can't be two pairs of shoulders like that within a day's walk of Greystock."

The burly fellow on the point bent at the waist, extending the arrow set in his bow toward something at his feet. In a moment, he straightened, the arrow ablaze. Pressing the bow, he loosed, and the flaming shaft sped skyward. With the first arrow still in flight, he lit, drew, and released a second. The pair of them arched gracefully through the rose-colored morning air to land hissing one after the other in the bay off *Sly Cat*'s port bow.

"What's he about," grumped Jynks Warrow as he walked to where Bode and Jaryd were standing, "flamin' arrows in salute!" The captain placed his hands on his hips. "We're an honest trader, not some bloody war galley." Jynks was a wizened little leather strap of a man with a voice like a rasp. He was slightly taller than Bode, who stood only to about Jaryd's chin. What scant hair he had left on his head showed iron gray, and his eyes were ice blue. His glare, when he chose, glinted hard enough to crack walnuts, or so it seemed to Bode.

"Your pardon, Miss." Jynks thumbed his forehead in deference to her. Whatever the circumstance, Bode always felt better in his presence. She responded with a brief smile.

"The custom may have been stretched a little past the occasion, Captain," Jaryd put in. "But it's still good luck, isn't it?"

"Aye, 'tis that," Jynks mused. Cupping his hand, Warrow let loose a prodigious shout aft. "Boson, answer him, three long on the horn."

"Aye, Captain, three long it is," the boson replied. Moments later, the ship's trumpet sang three long notes, returning the salute. On the point, the archer raised his bow high over his head and stood unmoving as the schooner glided by.

Warrow stumped away aft, still all business. The ship's boy, though, following in his wake with the speaking tube, was grinning.

So too, Jaryd noted, was a whipcord-lean top man as he clambered aloft. He watched the youthful sailor climb swiftly and surely into the rigging for a few moments before turning back to the young woman at his side.

"Proper enough as good-byes go, don't you think?" Jaryd asked, to no avail, as Bode stood unhearing. With the small vellum note clutched like a talisman in her right hand, her gaze fixed upon the lone figure standing still as a stone on the rocky point.

3

Aboard Sly Cat

Figuring he had at least temporarily worn down his welcome, Jaryd ambled across the deck away from Bode and settled himself on a hatch cover. His voyage the previous year had taught him he could while away an hour or two perched there without running afoul of one of Captain Jynks Warrow's glares.

Slipping out his belt knife, Jaryd pulled a small piece of drift-wood, fine grained and almost black, from his wallet. He did not recognize the wood he had found a few days before while walking on the beach near the Greystock docks. As he held it in his left hand, the knife in his right, Jaryd let his mind wander.

Often, the shape of a thing would come to him this way. Carving a piece mostly boiled down to discovering what dwelt within to begin with and then not doing more than necessary. For a small piece, his hand sometimes felt what was and wasn't there more readily than his eye could see.

He thought of his belt knife as a miniature version of the Hawken packed away in his satchel back in the rear of the ship. His satchel and the rest of his belongings were stowed in one of the small passenger cabins built along the sides of *Sly Cat*'s aft section. *Passenger box more like.* Jaryd smiled at the notion. However tiny, his cabin kept the wet out, and the mattress on the folding bed inside was clean and soft. Not a bad place to sleep, even if he couldn't quite stretch his legs full out while lying on it.

Idly, almost without thought, Jaryd pressed the edge of his belt knife against the dark grain of the driftwood, slowly scraping away a long, narrow slice. The piece in his hand felt hard and looked shiny as if it were not wood at all, but the knife cut easily enough. One stroke led to another, and soon Jaryd lost himself in the work.

So engrossed was he that Jaryd started slightly at the gentle touch of Bode's hand upon his shoulder. "Would you mind some company?" she asked.

Scooting over to make room, he responded, "Not so long as it is the cheerful kind."

"Not sure I'm up to that," Bode said, taking a seat beside him, "but I'll do my best." Peering around, Jaryd noticed they were well out to sea, heading southeast. Bode looked tired. He knew without asking that she had maintained her vigil until Heckisyah's point, or at least the young man standing upon it, was lost to sight.

"Someone should have warned you about blacksmiths," Jaryd observed.

"And farmers' sons." Bode gave Jaryd a direct look. "And men in general. Someone has, repeatedly." She lowered her eyes. Long lashes brushed the supple curve of her cheeks.

Light, she's beautiful, Jaryd thought. He had known Bode all his life, but in that moment, he seemed to see her if not for the first time then in a different way. Bode smiled wanly. "It didn't take."

"You and Mat," Jaryd began and then paused. "For years, that's how I've thought of you—as a pair. The two of you together seemed sure as summer. Lately, you're beginning to worry me."

"Mat wants to be married," Bode said softly, "to make a home and have children."

"And you don't," Jaryd prompted.

"I want those things to be part of my life, Jaryd," Bode asserted, "not the whole of it. You can understand that, can't you?"

The thing was, he could. Jaryd said nothing.

After a bit, Bode glanced up at him. "You're staring."

Jaryd smiled. "I'll take no blame for that. You're turned out mighty pretty."

Bode's chin dipped demurely. "Thank you."

Jaryd cocked his head to one side. "Must be the dress."

Bode punched him on the arm. Some things never changed. She took comfort in that. "You think I'm doing wrong?"

Jaryd shrugged. "Can't say. I admire you for it, though."

"Admire me," Bode exclaimed. "For doing the same thing you are?"

"What we're doing, Bode, is nothing like the same thing." Jaryd's voice took on a serious tone. "You are pursuing a dream, doing something you love, knowing it might cost you. That takes courage and confidence. As for me…" He sighed. "I'm returning to Antium from Greystock not so much because I've found a reason to go as that I lack a reason to stay."

The Hall of Learning in Antium, capital city of the Kingdom of Ayle, and its counterpart in Tyne, capital of the Tieran province of Quistyn del Aurus, counted as the most renowned institutions north of the Middle Sea. Tyne and Antium were similar in size and, given their proximity just across the Donn Narrows, a channel connecting the Myr Sea with the larger Middle Sea to the south, vied with one another as more or less friendly rivals in many things. In addition to the Halls, both cities featured Gyft Rylls, special schools dedicated to the education of initiates, students who sought to master the Yir, magic's Hidden Source, and become sorcerers.

Jaryd had chosen the Hall in Antium over its counterpart in Tyne mainly because his father had a friend living there, willing to offer room, board, and part-time employment. In Bode's case, her mother's family hailed from Antium. While attending the Hall, she stayed with her Uncle Haryld Tucker, who still lived in the city.

Bode's eyes crinkled slightly at the edges. "You are just determined to get out from behind a plow."

"Desperate is more like it." Jaryd's smile returned. "I've discovered knowing what you don't want falls a long stride short of finding what you do."

"I thought you'd settled on law," Bode stated.

"Mostly by process of elimination," Jaryd affirmed. "It seems I have no talent at all for music or singing."

Bode laughed outright. "You are the only person I know what sings worse than Mat."

"I wouldn't go that far," Jaryd replied. "I'm interested in mathematics, but I'm no theoretician. Engineers tend to spend way too much time off in the boondocks building roads and bridges and such."

"Have you thought of becoming a surgeon?" Bode inquired.

Jaryd looked askance. "My impression is that people are bloody messy on the inside. I have no desire to spend my time poking and prodding, wiping up, and generally dealing with all manner of slippery, smelly stuff on the outside of sick or injured folks that, under normal circumstances, is supposed to stay inside. Aside from a few highly skilled surgeons, I understand the best healers are those touched by the Yir. The only magical ability I have is to make pumpkin pie disappear."

"Your prowess in that regard is the stuff of legend," Bode acknowledged readily.

Though the occasional Yir-capable healer and a few Hall-trained physicians were available in the larger communities, most Three Rivers folk relied upon midwives and apothecaries for their doctoring. Shaking his head, Jaryd continued. "As for natural philosophy, students there always seem to wander about with chapped hands and stained fingers. And have you noticed some of the smells emanating from that wing of the Hall?"

"You do have an ear for languages," Bode said, trying a different tack.

"No more than most folks," Jaryd countered. His native tongue was Lynium, the language of Tier. Like most living in the region of the Myr Sea, he was fluent in Aylitic, the chief language of Ayle and many of the lands north of the Middle Sea. He also spoke a little Glaylic, the lilting speech of Kylgahra far to the west.

Bode tossed her head, teasing a little. "So a lawyer you are to be then, is it?"

Jaryd sighed. "I reckon." A law degree from Antium Hall, which he could earn in two more years' time, would enable Jaryd to practice virtually anywhere in Ayle or the Three Rivers or even within the Tieran province of Quistyn del Aurus, which bordered the Myr Sea along much of its southern shore. While starting his own office right away didn't sound too practical, obtaining a position clerking for some magistrate or as an employee of an established lawyer seemed reasonable enough. "At least I won't be digging potatoes or shearing sheep."

Glancing down, Bode noticed Jaryd's hands, large, sun browned, and strong. Mat had big hands too, broad as a bear's paw. Jaryd's showed a different, more tapered shape, long-fingered, archer's hands, she supposed. Jaryd was a fine archer, like his father and brothers, for that matter. The Hume boys all had the knack.

Bode laid her fingers atop his. "Perhaps it does not matter what you do so long as you do it in your own way."

Jaryd turned toward her, his features settling into a bemused expression. "That sounds clever. Do you reckon it might be true?"

"I hope so," Bode said fervently. Releasing his hand, she fell silent for a moment and then asked suddenly, "Did you never wish you'd been born with the Gyft?"

"No," Jaryd said emphatically. "That's not for me." He did not have the Gyft, the capacity to draw upon the Yir. Like most children in the lands surrounding the Middle Sea, he had been tested twice a year until his eighteenth birthday. The local caestor, who served as a school administrator, Gyros Claudius Ban, kept a magic talisman, one he called a seeking charm. Physically, the charm consisted of a small glass figurine shaped like a dolphin, of all things. No one in the Three Rivers, to the best of Jaryd's knowledge, had ever seen an actual dolphin.

Held in the hand of someone with the ability to invoke the Yir, the seeking charm glowed, emitting a soft blue light. Conducted in private, testing involved only the minister, the child and his or her parents or guardians, and a witness. The witness was usually a member of the village council or one of the local ship captains.

The Gyft typically manifested early in adolescence. A few children developed the ability at an earlier age. Testing began at age twelve and stopped at eighteen. None of his close friends had shown the ability to invoke the Yir, including Bode and Mat.

"You've never dreamt of setting a candle alight with a glance or healing the sick with a touch?" Bode pressed.

"Or tossing lightning bolts at people?" Jaryd countered.

"Aye, well," Bode allowed, only slightly abashed, "maybe the occasional Clegg."

"Or a rampaging witch," Jaryd interjected.

"Like in the adventures of Sebastyn Card, do you mean?" Bode queried.

"He was always my favorite," Jaryd allowed. The sorcerer Sebastyn Card, who had roamed all over the Middle Sea region two centuries before, was still spoken of in tones of awe and disbelief and was prominently featured in children's stories to this day.

"He was a rogue," Bode scoffed.

"To some," Jaryd argued. "To those better informed, he was a hero." In truth, accounts sometimes depicted Sebastyn Card as a hero and sometimes as a rogue. By any measure, Card's adventures were manifold. Among the more well-known was his long-running battle with the dreaded white witch Lylith Caddow. Some said they struggled for dominion over men. Others claimed their dispute revolved around possession of powerful magical talismans. Oddly enough, given their notoriety, the ultimate fates of both Card and Caddow were unknown. The sorcerer and his witch nemesis appeared to have faded into the mists of time.

"I wonder if Lylith Caddow really tried to conjure a talisman with the power to stop time itself," Bode mused.

Talismans were magic devices that came in many types and physical forms. Most had been produced in antiquity. The art of making them having largely been lost in modern times, talismans had become rare and mysterious things shrouded by the arcane. Those few who still produced them jealously guarded their secrets.

"My mum says witches are capable of anything," Jaryd reported. According to the doctrine of the Penitent faith, the principal religion across all lands encompassed by the Tieran Empire, witchcraft was inherently tainted, a foully distorted form of magic laced with evil. "My da says the real trouble with witches pertains not so much to what they do as where they hail from." Witchcraft was the dominant form of magic practiced within the Kingdoms of Roi and Kios. The Kiosans and, in particular, the Roi were among Tier's oldest and most formidable adversaries.

"Your da is full of odd ideas," Bode put in, "at least according to Mistress Mayhew." Adeline Mayhew ran the Wayward Fox, one of Greystock's more popular inns. The food at the Wayward Fox was supposed to be as good as the gossip was plentiful.

"I think Mistress Mayhew is sweet on my da and just won't admit it," Jaryd retorted.

Whether attributed to differences in culture, doctrine, or merely geography, rivalry between the practitioners of sorcery and witchcraft, extending to the societies that sponsored them, had endured for centuries to the present day.

While a student at the Hall in Antium, Jaryd had seen a few sorcerers, both men and women, visiting one speaker or another and at the library located near the Hall grounds. At a distance anyway, they appeared ordinary enough. The Initiates, as they were known, those studying to become sorcerers, were rarely seen outside the tall, white, stone walls of the Gyft Ryll itself.

"Do you know of Speaker Allus?" Jaryd asked. Allus taught oration at the Hall in Antium. "Speaker" denoted the formal title given to instructors there.

Bode nodded. "Don't tell me he reminds you of Mistress Mayhew."

"Well…" Jaryd drawled. "Come to think of it, they do both have a bald spot."

"Jaryd Hume, shame on you," Bode chided but could not keep the smile from her face.

"Anyway," Jaryd continued, "Speaker Allus maintains that inanimate objects bear no intrinsic characteristics unto themselves. Weapons, for example, are merely tools. A sword or a knife can as easily be used to murder the innocent as to defend them. All that matters are the actions taken by the wielder. I told Mat that when I got home this summer."

"What did Mat say?" Bode asked.

"Nothing." Jaryd grinned. "For two days running. On the third, he told me he doesn't see it that way." Bode's delicately shaped mouth curved into a small smile, and her dove-gray eyes went soft and still. She knew as well as he that Mat liked to think things through. "Mat said he believes the maker's intent is indelibly infused into the tool or the weapon as it is crafted. If the sword-smith intended to forge a weapon for use in a just cause, a righteous spirit would inhabit the blade. If, instead, the maker sought to pillage and burn, Mat's belief is that the blade would take on an aspect as dark as the soul of the weapon-smith himself. Actions count in the world of men all right enough, but to God the All Father and in the realm of Spirit, intent weighs more heavily than anything else."

"That sounds like Mat," Bode murmured.

"Mat Bayrd, the religious philosopher," Jaryd proclaimed. "You wouldn't know it to look at him or to hear him swear at a recalcitrant sway joint."

Bode blinked, gray eyes gone stormy. "What in the world is a sway joint?"

"You girls don't know anything useful, do you?" Jaryd remarked.

"I knew enough to stay out of Mistress Mayhew's pumpkin patch." Bode sniffed. Mistress Mayhew's pumpkin pies were widely admired. When they were children, Jaryd speculated that there must be something special about her pumpkins. He and Mat, age eleven, and Bode, then ten years old, debated the matter at some length. Jaryd and Mat's subsequent foray into Mistress Mayhew's pumpkin patch to obtain proof blossomed into one of their more noteworthy misadventures.

"That didn't end well," Jaryd admitted. Bode looked as if she was about to cry. Setting aside his belt knife, Jaryd took her hand. "Hoi," he said gently, "let's have none of that."

"Jaryd, I don't know what to do," Bode said miserably. "Half the girls in Greystock would marry Mat in an eye blink, and I..." She swallowed hard. "What if he—" Her voice trailed away.

"Your passage is paid, is it not?" Jaryd spoke as firmly as he dared. Bode raised her eyes to his. "As much as he dotes on you, I doubt Captain Warrow would turn around even if you asked him." Reaching out, Jaryd tapped Mat's note, still clutched in Bode's free hand. "If Mat Bayrd says he'll wait a year, then a year from the now, sure as I'm sitting here, you'll find him waiting, half the girls in Greystock or no." Jaryd took a breath. *Here goes.* "If I were you, I'd return to Antium, pour myself into my studies, my music, come to grips if I can with what is and isn't possible, and then decide."

Bode stared at him, wide-eyed. She appeared so startled that, for a moment, Jaryd feared she'd topple right off the hatch cover. Finally, she said, "That sounds like good advice."

Releasing her hand, Jaryd sat straight up. "You needn't look so surprised."

Bode laughed with relief. "Mat is lucky to have you for a friend."

"As are you, Bode Ware," Jaryd told her. "As are you."

Leaning forward, Bode bumped her shoulder against his arm. "What is that?" Bode asked, pointing at the bit of driftwood in his lap.

"It is *going* to be a carving of a Fey rune," Jaryd informed her.

"A rune," Bode surmised, "from the picture writing of the Elves. The Fey rune stands for freedom, does it not?"

"That's what I hear," Jaryd concurred. Taking up his knife, he went back to work. Bode remained at his side. Together, they sat in companionable silence as *Sly Cat* ran before the wind.

4

The Gambit

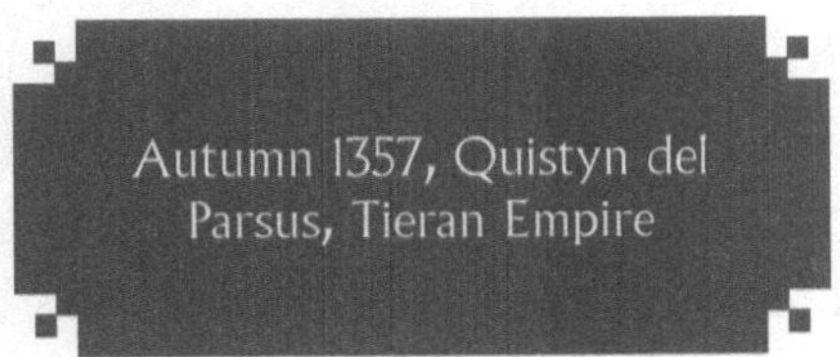

Quintus Glabrio Jens gambled, at stake, the lives of his best men. It was almost always so. In all but the most extraordinary circumstances, Victory demanded that in battle, a commander place the lives of his warriors at hazard. Sometimes the cost of winning settled feather light and at others crushed mercilessly downward, too heavy to bear. Either way, goddess Victory required the wager.

The Penitent faith maintained a firm grip upon the Tieran soul, as it had for generations. For all that, soldiers clung still to the old gods. As superstitious as they were pragmatic, not a man stood among them what didn't carry some bit of something to guard his luck: an old coin, a new pair of socks, a lock of his sweetheart's hair, or maybe a child's tooth. The ancient ones demanded a personal token, a private thing potent enough if not to curry favor then at least to deflect their wrath. A teardrop-shaped bit of amber his younger sister had bestowed upon him when they were children nestled safely in Quintus's tunic pocket.

A cruel mistress, Victory, capricious and intoxicating, lured her suitors. Many a battle leader had succumbed to her wiles, among them even those who knew full well her inconstant nature. For himself, well, he was a professional. He courted Victory out of necessity. This time, however, he feared he had blundered. If that fellow across the little valley below didn't do what Quintus wanted him to, Victory would turn her face from him, and Mayhem would rend the two regiments of regulars and the company of archers he'd placed there—and perhaps the rest of his command as well.

That fellow. Quintus shook his head. Even after all the years and all the blood spilled, the men over there never quite seemed the enemy. Tierans they were, as was he. The warriors approaching from the other side of the valley fought under the Golden Lion of House Gracci. The banner his men carried was emblazed with the White Rose of House Sylas. Though the combatants shared a language, a common history, the same laws and customs, and the same sense of loss, the war went on and on, seemingly without end. The War of Houses, it had become known as. A struggle destined to either destroy the Tieran Empire forever or give rise to its rebirth.

A form of retribution, some said, the War of Houses was for Tieran hubris. Hubris meant exaggerated or false pride. This implied, of course, that there must also be such a thing as true pride. *And how*, he wondered, *does one tell the difference?* The night before the Battle of Prysium that past spring, Gaius Sylas Endryk, the young patriarch of House Sylas, told his gathered officers, Quintus among them, "It is hubris only if you lose." They won the following day. Gaius Endryk was lucky. All great generals were.

Quintus's official rank was kernyl, or regimental commander per Tieran military hierarchy. His current orders placed him in charge of a brigade-sized unit, a mix of heavy infantry, auxiliaries, and Tieran cavalry. Quintus had no illusions about being a great general. He would, however, need to be lucky today.

"The Gracci are taking their sweet time," Jon Tiberius Elder, Quintus's chief scout, grumbled. A veteran, Elder had refined grumbling to an art form.

On the far side of the valley in front of them ran a creek called Dog Run. The creek coursed through the southern portion of the

Tieran province of Quistyn del Parsus. Located in the central region of the Morro Peninsula, Quistyn del Parsus had long been a stronghold of House Gracci. They were about to fight what some chronicler would insist upon calling the Battle of Dog Run. *For every grand engagement like Prysium, there must be a dozen Dog Runs.* The thought made Quintus smile but left a bitter aftertaste he knew well—that of fear.

Quintus noted, "Whoever is in charge over there may be smarter than I gave him credit for." The real fighting, Quintus knew—a struggle bearing the weight of another Prysium—would take place soon but well to the south in Quistyn del Byrn. His mission here embodied a diversion, or at least that is what House Sylas intended. It was a diversion that would draw troops from and/or delay supplies to Gracci forces in the south in numbers sufficient to justify any losses he, Quintus, incurred.

"Leaving the lower ford unguarded is like hanging a 'free samples' sign on the front door of a brothel," Jon opined. "They'll be along all right enough. I just wish they'd hurry it up some."

Little more than a stone's throw wide, Dog Run flowed over a man's head deep in most places, and the water ran cold and swift. Two fords crossed the creek in this area, five kylos apart, about an hour and a quarter's march. Quintus had placed two regiments of regulars, the Third Regulus and the Fifth Minoa, in position opposite the upstream crossing. He and his men had come from that direction, and it was that ford they had encountered first. The second ford Quintus had purposely left unattended. He hoped his Gracci opponent would seize upon that and divide his forces, sending a portion of his command to the second ford.

"You like to fight that much?" Quintus inquired mildly. He wouldn't have known of the second ford except that Elder and the small band of mostly poachers, woodsmen, and horse thieves who rode for him were very good at what they did. Quintus himself had crossed the upper ford for the first time the day before in the late afternoon. Stark in the long shadows, he had seen in the lay of the land a possibility. That possibility had blossomed into the gambit he would play out this day.

"What I'd like is to get this business over with," Jon replied. "Waitin' is hard on my digestion."

Quintus could have laid an ambush at the second ford. The Gracci would expect that, though, and move accordingly. Besides, even without their heavy cavalry, the Gracci outnumbered him nearly two to one. To win in the manner he needed to, Quintus would first have to break them.

"Most of the killing happens," General Nyus Sylas Cain told Quintus years earlier, "only after most of the fighting is done." Nyus Sylas Cain, uncle to Gaius Sylas Endryk, had been Quintus's mentor and remained a cherished friend. Quintus wondered what Nyus the Fox would think of his plan this day.

"Waiting is what regulars do second best," Quintus observed. If the Gracci commander split his force, those marching east to west over the downstream ford would encounter a cart path running through the valley alongside a bend in the creek. The path led up a gentle rise in the vicinity of the upstream ford. They would not be able to see the first ford until reaching the top of the rise. At a distance of about half a kylo, the Gracci would find themselves looking down on the flank of the Sylatic units guarding the upper ford. As they topped the rise, they would become visible to the House Sylas troops.

"I suppose you are about to tell me what it is we do best?" Elder prompted.

"In your case, I'd say complaining tops the list," Quintus remarked.

After catching sight of the Gracci coming down on his flank, Quintus had instructed Kernyl Davyd Claudius Ban, in command at the upper ford, to do the sensible thing: run. Run back across the valley toward a boulder-strewn, rocky outcrop. The valley narrowed there, and the rock-covered slope defined one end of a gap, while a thick stand of pines shaped the other. Quintus had placed the lion's share of his missile troops, two hundred Danoan archers and three hundred slingers from the province of Quistyn del Pydras, on the far side of the gap. Their left flank was protected by the rocky slope.

On their right, Quintus had stationed the six hundred marines under his command.

Seagoing infantry normally assigned to man the war galleys of the imperial fleet; the marines were equipped in the same manner as his regulars. The primary weapon of the Tieran regular was a thrusting spear, called the croix. Tipped by a wicked, triangularly shaped spearhead forged of pressed steel, the croix measured eight span in overall length, about the distance the average soldier could reach up to standing flatfooted with one arm fully extended over his head.

For defense, regulars bore a large semicylindrical shield, the sutra, constructed of cross-grained strips of hard wood layered to the thickness of about a man's thumb, faced with bull hide and reinforced with a sturdy steel center boss. Each soldier was equipped with an open-faced steel helmet featuring hinged, thickly padded cheek guards. Body armor consisted of a chainmail vest fitted over a short-sleeved, padded leather jacket known as a jaltryn. As a secondary weapon, the regulars carried a short, heavy, double-edged straight sword named the Glavius, after the smith who first produced the weapon.

Like his regulars, Quintus wore chainmail armor over a jaltryn. Underneath the armor, he was clad in a knee-length, blue woolen tunic. Closed-toed sandals covered his feet. His helmet plain and unadorned, Quintus wore no badge of rank. His neck cloth was made of white, sweat-stained cotton. His spada, or cavalry sword, was attached to the broad leather belt around his middle on his left side, in the cavalryman's fashion. Well-muscled and fair-skinned like many of his countrymen, Quintus stood to average height. Unlike most Tierans, though, he was black-haired with hazel eyes.

In addition to the infantry, Quintus had stationed one hundred of the Danoan archers at the upper ford. They were equipped with the Danoan long bow, the stave carved from a single piece of golden yew. Nearly as tall as most of the bowmen themselves, the islanders' longbow proved a fearsome weapon.

The men standing at the upper ford were veterans all, infantry and archers alike. Tough and battle-hardened, they were as good as any he'd seen. They'd need to be. Withdrawing in the face of the enemy embodied a task not well suited for amateurs. Too often a feigned rout became the real thing. Upon reaching the gap, his regulars would need to turn and reform, presenting a solid wall of spears to their pursuers, with the archers ranged behind. They would become the anvil.

Once within range, his concealed missile troops would strike the Gracci's right, raining arrows and slingshot down on the side opposite to where most men bore their shields. With luck, the Gracci would slam into his regulars piecemeal, their flanking force well ahead of those who needed to cross the now-abandoned upper ford. The spears of the anvil force, supported by the marines, would stack them up, and the missiles would thin them out, and Quintus would then turn loose his cavalry and light infantry, his hammer.

Sometime ago, a scout, carefully concealed atop the rise at the base of the valley where he could see across the upper ford and watch for the approach of a Gracci force from the second crossing, had flashed a message using a signaling mirror. The Gracci were in position on the far side of the creek from the upper ford. They had so far made no attempt to force a crossing.

"You know the marines are pissed off," Jon said. The pair of them stood near the edge of the wood, at the base of a towering pine. Lean with long, ropey muscles, Elder stood half a head taller than his commander. A year older than Quintus, with reddish-brown hair thinning at the back and keen and intelligent green eyes, the lanky scout moved easily, exhibiting a canny fighter's grace. Clad in a light, boiled-leather cuirass over a faded blue tunic, Jon wore knee-length soft leather boots instead of sandals. Elder was armed with a pair of infantry short swords, one sheathed on each hip. Disdaining a helmet, he had a floppy-brimmed leather hat on his head.

"Are they, indeed?" Quintus asked, never taking his eyes off the clump of bushes where the scout lay hidden.

"Aye, they think it ent right that the Beagles should have all the fun down there"—the chief scout thrust his chin toward the formation of regulars near the upper ford—"while they are tucked away up here like Granny's best linen."

Why marines referred to regular infantry as small, floppy-eared dogs posed a question the answer to which, Quintus suspected, not even they knew. Of course, being a Beagle himself, he could only speculate. His response was a noncommittal, "Hmm."

"Marines are bloody crazy, the lot of them," Jon observed.

"They have a peculiar notion of fun; I'll grant you that," Quintus said. "Marines fight hard because, being marines, they are incapable of doing anything else. They'll fight even harder if they are irritated."

"You're a sly bastard, Kernyl," Jon spoke fondly. Glabrio was an ancient if not prominent House, having long ago won the garland of nobility. In Jon's experience, most nobles were stiff-necked whoresons unable to see beyond lineage and birthright. Quintus took a man for what he was.

In truth, Quintus had held his marines in reserve because, per his reckoning, six hundred alone at the ford were not enough, and some reserve was essential because only the All Father knew what would happen once the enemy hove into sight. There, he'd managed to think of the Gracci as the enemy, not merely the opposition, a good thing that, as he intended to kill them all.

Glabrio had entered the military academy in the city of Quinto in the province of Quistyn del Orro at eighteen, just after his final examination had revealed no capacity to invoke the Yir. Having completed a course of study in engineering at the Hall in Quinto nearly two years younger than most prior to entering the academy, he had an early start on a military career. If he lived another two months, Quintus would be thirty-five years old. Most of the time he'd spent in the army had centered on service for the Sylatic faction in the War of Houses.

The civil war ebbed and flowed with the course of time. On occasion, some external threat, in the form of an Eytriscan incursion or aggression on the part of another traditional enemy such as the Kingdom of Roi, would demand attention, and the factional Tieran dispute would wane for months or even years. Sometimes one faction or another would take the offensive, and the fighting would rage. Over the past five years, three Houses had emerged as dominant: House Sylas, the faction his own family served, and those of two principal adversaries, House Gracci, and House Dyraii.

Quintus was glad of Elder's presence. The man's competence brought with it an air of calm. It was Jon who had recommended the scout that Quintus ordered to monitor the Gracci's approach.

"The best pair of eyes in the bunch," Jon had said.

Still, no further sign had been displayed from that scout on the rise across the valley. Quintus glanced briefly at the sun, nearing midafternoon. If the Gracci had sent troops to the lower ford, they should have crossed over some while ago. Even moving cautiously, wary of ambush, they should have come within view by the now.

"Signal, sir," his aide, Tynan Valerius Glans, spoke urgently. "Two short and one, two, three long," Tynan counted. "I make it two short and three long, sir."

Quintus had seen the mirror flashes himself. The signal meant that the Gracci had crossed the lower ford with three of their four available infantry regiments. Turning to his aide, Quintus ordered, "Report to Claudius. Tell him to hold fast until he sees them topping the rise and then move like a hare before hounds."

"Aye, sir," Tynan responded, banging his right fist against his left breast in salute. Moving quickly to his horse, the young officer swung into the saddle and galloped away.

5

The Battle of Dog Run

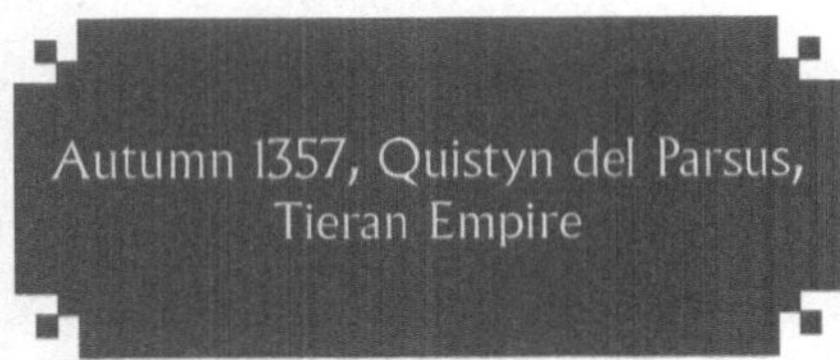

Of course, nothing happened as Quintus had envisioned it. The Gracci approaching from the second ford had light cavalry among them. The Gracci horsemen raced forward to harass the Sylatic infantry with missiles, hurling throwing spears from their saddles. The Danoan archers responded, and arrows flashed out from amid the withdrawing infantry. A few riders tumbled from their mounts, but the retreat slowed. Moving more quickly than Quintus could credit, the Gracci light infantry, unencumbered by heavy armor, rushed in, spears leveled. To the rear of the skirmishers, the Gracci regular infantry deployed, three regiments going into a line abreast formation, with crossbowmen arrayed behind them.

Davyd Claudius Ban was forced to halt short of the gap. The Sylatic infantry whirled into a defensive stance. The Danoan archers accompanying them loosed shaft after shaft at the approaching Gracci, darting for cover amid the Sylatic spearmen at the last possible moment. With a roar, the Gracci infantry closed.

The Gracci line overreached that of the Sylatic troops, threatening especially the left flank of the House Sylas warriors. Seeing their

Beagle compatriots were in trouble, the Sylatic marines charged without orders, howling down into the Gracci right. Moving too fast for their own good, the marine formation lost cohesion in the charge. They compensated for what they lacked in precision with sheer ferocity. The marines were soon heavily engaged, holding an entire regiment of Gracci heavy infantry and another of light infantry at bay.

The Sylatic missile troops clambered out of their places of concealment and took up loose formations at the crest of the rock-covered slope, raining slingshot and arrows down upon the onrushing Gracci.

Knowing he could wait no longer, Quintus ordered his Megyar light infantry forward. "Take out their crossbowmen," he directed their commander, a long, lanky cutthroat named Erastus. The Megyars, mercenaries from the Kingdom of Relwyn, faced a longer run than he'd intended, much longer, but they were fresh and fast, and the wild call of battle spurred them. Released, the Megyars streamed forward, screaming like souls in torment. Quintus led his cavalry out behind the Megyars. Already arrayed line abreast four ranks deep, the lancers quickly formed after exiting the trees and then advanced.

Veering right to stay clear of the charging Megyars, Quintus took his cavalry to the trot. He urged them forward, aiming for the Gracci light horse, reforming on the far-left flank of the Gracci line. He needed to engage the Gracci cavalry before they, in turn, could come down on the Megyars' flank. At his signal, the buglers behind him sounded the charge. Crouching in their saddles behind kite-shaped shields, the troopers swept down their spears. Menacing as death itself, Quintus's horsemen thundered forward. At close quarters, the Gracci light cavalry could do little against the more heavily armed and armored Sylatic lancers. They broke and raced away as quickly as they might, leaving nearly a quarter of their number dead or wounded upon the field.

Refusing to pursue them, Quintus stood in his stirrups, waving his spada high above his head and shouting for the recall. His buglers responded, and most of his lancers swung back into formation. Wheeling his cavalry about, Quintus reversed course. Angling slightly to his left, Quintus launched them a second time, his target the exposed flank of the first Gracci infantry regiment.

Quintus knew this was the moment when Victory hung in the balance, if only his cavalry could close before the Gracci were able to punch through his hard-pressed infantry. Dust swirled about him as sweat stung his eyes. Physical fear receded, banished by an overwhelming sense of urgency. He could feel the charge gaining momentum about him. *Not far to go the now, please God, not far.*

The crash, as the Sylatic lancers smashed into the rear ranks of the Gracci infantry, could be heard by archers and slingers alike atop the rocky crest. Soldiers were knocked sprawling, and horses tumbled, men and beasts screaming in a cacophony of red rage and terror.

"At them!" Quintus cried over and over. "At them!" Assailed front and rear, the left-most regiment of Gracci regulars collapsed. The Gracci infantrymen scrambled away as best they could. Relentless, the lancers pressed on, hacking down with their spadas tracing crimson arcs in the afternoon sun.

The carefully formed ranks and files of the lancers separated in the melee. The fighting tended to cluster in smaller and smaller groups. Out of the dust, just to Quintus's right front, stepped a Gracci spearman. The Gracci had lost his shield and was holding his croix across his chest like a quarterstaff. Most times, a cavalryman would slash downward with his spada at a man on foot.

Quintus had spent so many years in the infantry that his instinctive reaction was to thrust his sword at the Gracci. Rolling his hips and shoulders forward to lend power to the strike, Quintus aimed at the man's neck. The Gracci regular caught sight of Quintus and his mount an instant too late. His spear swung upward but not in time to parry. Quintus felt his sword bite. The Gracci fell away, blood spewing from the wound in his throat.

The Megyars had made short work of the Gracci crossbowmen. Racing around the Gracci left flank, the Sylatic light infantry flung their javelins into the ranks of the crossbowmen and then charged home, their sedyars, sickle-shaped swords, wreaking bloody havoc.

The crossbowmen had virtually no defense at close quarters against the Megyar swordsmen and so ran for the safety of the Gracci spearmen pouring onto the field at the upstream ford. Seeing the gleaming croix points before them, the wily Megyars turned, looking for more likely prey, and fell upon the rear ranks of the Gracci light infantry.

Pushing his tiring horsemen to his right, Quintus drove them into the second Gracci infantry regiment. The Gracci broke more readily this time, streaming away across the valley. Quintus allowed the pursuit, and his cavalry harried the fleeing Gracci, cutting them down from above. Seizing the opportunity, Davyd Claudius Ban hurled both regiments of regulars under his command at the remaining Gracci troops entangled with the Sylatic marines. Outnumbered, the third Gracci regiment of heavy infantry and the tattered remnants of their militia fell back in good order toward the upper ford, intending to link up with the fourth regiment of Gracci regulars, which had deployed west of the creek.

Determined to cut off the Gracci infantry, Quintus galloped toward the ford. "Recall, sound recall!" he shouted. The bugles trilled, and his weary horsemen broke off their pursuit and were turning toward him when he was struck by the crossbow bolt. He knew not where the dart had come from since most of the Gracci crossbowmen were down. Perhaps a wounded man had shot at him. He supposed he would never know.

Fortunately, the bolt only glanced off his helmet. However, the strike was solid enough to cause him to reel in the saddle, his ears ringing. He felt his sword slip from suddenly nerveless fingers. He would have fallen from the saddle except Tynan, appearing at his side as if conjured from thin air, grasped his arm, swinging his mount and his own body into position to shield Quintus.

"Hang on, sir," Tynan called.

Tynan on his right side and one of his buglers on his left guided Quintus to the rear, where he dismounted, slumping against the remains of a low stone wall. He imagined the wall must have come from some long-abandoned farm. He had not noticed it before.

"Sir, are you all right?" Tynan asked anxiously. Tynan was an ensign, a junior officer from a House nearly as old and even more impoverished than his own. Blond, blue-eyed, with a slightly pug nose and a perpetually cheerful disposition, Tynan had served as his aide for the past four months. "Shall I send for Demetrius?"

Demetrius was a physician endowed with a healer's touch assigned to Quintus's command.

Still a little groggy, Quintus responded, "If they wanted to do serious harm, they should have shot at something other than my head. I suspect Demetrius has more pressing concerns." He loosened his chin strap, pulling off his helmet. He saw no obvious signs of damage.

Looking up at the younger man, Quintus said, "Help me to sit on top of this little wall instead of in front of it. It's more dignified."

"Only if you manage not to fall off," Jon Tiberius Elder said, swinging down from his horse. "You know, you might be getting a little too old for this."

"Orders, sir?" Pavyl Tevius Drachi inquired as he reined his mount to a halt nearby.

"What are they up to?" Quintus asked.

"They're regrouping, sir, what's left of them, just west of the ford," Pavyl said.

"Who have they got on their left?" was Quintus's next question.

"The Askante," Jon answered.

The Askante were good soldiers, highly trained skirmishers, but as light infantry, they were vulnerable to cavalry, especially those that could hit as hard as the Sylatic lancers. "Take command of the cavalry. Rearm your lancers and form on our right," Quintus instructed Pavyl, pointing to a dell, a dip in the valley floor to the south of their current position. "Wait there until you hear from this reprobate." Quintus jerked a thumb at his chief scout.

"Aye, sir, and thank you," Pavyl responded before galloping away.

"Jon," Quintus said, "I need you to find us a way round their left, along the creek bed. We'll need a track wide enough for the lancers to fight effectively."

"Ent sure there is such a thing," Jon replied, cautioning.

"If there isn't, we'll see if we can't come up with something else to annoy them," Quintus stated, rubbing his temples with both hands. "Whatever you find, see me first."

"We could send our cavalry across the lower ford and come down on their supply train," Tynan offered speculatively. When he saw both Jon and Quintus staring at him, he ducked his head in embarrassment.

Quintus was reluctant to send his cavalry that far afield this late in the day. What he said was, "If you are not careful, Tynan, one of these days you might make a soldier after all." Tynan smiled as if he'd been handed something precious.

"Do you mind if I take this budding military genius with me?" Jon asked, nodding his head toward Tynan. "He's well mounted."

"Go ahead," Quintus said. "Be careful." Turning to the bugler, whose name, Quintus was ashamed to admit, he could not recall, he ordered, "Find Kernyl Ban and bring him to me." Sitting quietly as his men hurried off, his head throbbing, Quintus tried to empty his mind. It was too soon to think yet—and too late.

A short time later, the bugler returned, leading his horse with Davyd Claudius Ban following. The young kernyl had his helmet tucked under one arm. Dried blood smeared the infantryman's face, and he was limping noticeably. Davyd's expression showed wan but determined. Like Quintus, Ban was a professional, aged thirty-two, a leanly muscled man with brown hair and eyes.

"How do you fare, Kernyl?" Quintus inquired.

"I fear this job is tougher than I am, sir," Davyd said, his smile cracking the rivulet of clotted blood mantling his left cheek.

"A hard day today," Quintus agreed, "and not over yet. I need you to form your men for an attack, regulars out front with what's left of the marines in reserve. Center them there." He pointed to a withered fig tree that stood about three hundred paces in front of the Gracci position at the upper ford. "Order the missile troops in and have them shoot whatever they have left. Jon is looking for a way round the Gracci left. If he can find one, you'll need to pin them until the cavalry hits their flank. Wait until you hear from me before advancing. Questions?"

"None, sir," Davyd responded, saluting.

Watching his infantry commander limp away, Quintus suddenly felt too tired even to breathe. Maybe he was getting too old for this—not yet thirty-five, but perhaps age had little to do with it. Turning his gaze back to the Gracci, he saw movement among their regulars. He watched for a few moments, staring dully until he realized that they were withdrawing, pulling back across the ford.

"Davyd," he shouted, "they're pulling out." Lurching into a run, he caught up with Claudius. As he overtook the young kernyl, Quintus skidded to a halt. He had to pause a moment, breathing deeply to ward off a sudden wave of nausea. "Time to hit them. Have your infantry advance the now, directly behind the missile men."

"Aye, sir," Davyd said as he donned his helmet, eying the Gracci retreat. "We'll move on them immediately."

The Gracci commander pulled his most valuable troops, the heavy infantry, out first, leaving the Askante, some slingers, and what remained of the lightly armed militia to act as a rear guard. The Gracci light troops, militia included, made a gallant but futile stand against the Sylatic regulars. Overmatched, the Gracci were pushed back and systematically cut down by Quintus's hard-eyed professionals. Fleet of foot, most of the Askante escaped, racing back over the ford on the heels of the Gracci regulars.

The militia and the slingers were not so fortunate. Farther from the ford to begin with, most of them were cut off and fell like leaves in autumn before the machinelike croix thrusts of the Sylatic spearmen.

Davyd Claudius Ban sent a runner inquiring as to whether he should push across the ford. Quintus sent the runner back with instructions to resume their original defensive position on the western side of the ford, using the surviving marines to fill any gaps in the lines from the day's losses to the Third Regulus and the Fifth Minoa.

Resuming his seat on the low stone wall, Quintus allowed the events of the past couple of hours to wash over him. They'd won, that was clear. It was not the rout he'd intended but a decisive victory nonetheless. If the goddess Victory had not truly smiled upon them, she had at least relented.

Quintus was too tired to think more on it. His primary objective required that he move farther east to destroy a Gracci supply depot in the town of Bejilla while causing as much mischief en route as possible. With the Gracci forces in the area much reduced, his chances of success had improved. *Or at least,* he thought wryly, *the likelihood of failure has diminished.* That thought was impertinent, perhaps even insubordinate. *I am tired.* He'd see what his scouts had to tell him the next day and then decide.

It had not taken long for Demetrius to catch up with him. He could vividly recall the intense tingling throughout his body that he felt as Demetrius placed his hands on either side of his head. Delving, Demetrius called it. Though it was not the first time he'd experienced it, Quintus supposed he would never become accustomed to the eerie sensation, somewhere between pleasure and pain, that accompanied being the subject of a healer's touch.

"You're hardheaded enough for soldiering," Demetrius growled after a brief examination. The slender, dark-haired, dark-eyed healer was hard to live with for a while following any day of battle on which he had to mend rent flesh and shattered bone. Yet it was a small enough price to pay for the lives he saved.

Quintus downed a draught of something truly vile that Demetrius foisted upon him. "To ease your pain, if not your conscience," the healer informed him. The worse it tastes, the better it works, the old saying went. If true, he'd be doing handsprings in a few moments. Looking up, he noticed Jon Tiberius Elder approaching.

"Tynan is dead," the scout said without preamble. "He was riding on a steep slope near the creek bed when his horse lost its footing. Tynan tried to jump clear but was caught between his mount and a pine tree when the animal toppled. His neck broke. There was nothing we could do for him."

Soldiering tended to be hard on junior officers. Tynan was not the first aide he'd lost. Still, Quintus felt the boy deserved a better death than that—assuming there existed such a thing for someone who would never see his twenty-second winter. Noting the expression on his commander's face, Jon said, "Sorry, Quintus, I know you liked the lad. We all did."

Quintus waved his hand, a vague, weary gesture. "Tynan was a good man. He deserved better." Pointing out across the now-silent battlefield, he spoke softly. "They all did."

"Aye, well," Jon acknowledged, clearing his throat, "a few mayhap. Past caring the now, the lot of them. You really put a twist on the Gracci today," he went on, his voice brightening, "Whipped them right proper. Here, this'll cheer you up." He extended a leather-bound flask of something or other.

Quintus declined, saying, "Demetrius warned me to drink no alcohol after swallowing that concoction of his."

Slipping the flask into his belt, Jon snorted, "That little squint is even less fun after a fight than you are." He wandered off after a bit, seeking more cheerful company.

Darkness settled about the encampment, gentle after the hard, sharp slaughter of the day just gone. The stars shone bright in a sky so clear it seemed heaven itself bent toward them. Quintus had ordered that his tent remain packed away. He would have no need of it this night.

Sat propped against the little stone wall, a blanket wedged behind him, his cloak wrapped about his shoulders, Quintus would not sleep. He never could after a battle. He was going to need a new aide. Aides, actually—he'd been making do with only Tynan. He could make good use of three. The fact they kept dying on him constituted a poor excuse for inefficiency.

"It is hubris only if you lose," Gaius Sylas Endryk had said. He meant it as a joke to lighten the mood on the eve of what he and his assembled officers all knew would be a hard fight. Was it true? What did it say about the man? Quintus's father, Deryk Glabrio Jens, had long ago told him that a wise man discounted words spoken in anger but paid heed to all that was said in jest. Gaius Endryk of House Sylas was courageous, daring, and very probably brilliant. Was he just? And if unjust, what were the implications in this world and in the next for Quintus and all those who served, and warred, and killed for House Sylas? To a just God, would not what one fought for matter more than for whom?

Quintus felt a kinship with all soldiers, especially those slain on either side in a battle in which he had taken a hand. While some were his compatriots and others at least temporarily his adversaries, the souls of all would become his brothers in the next life. He wanted nothing so much in this one as to earn their respect.

"Does it matter, Tynan, after all, any of it?" Quintus reached out with his mind, stretching for the heavens. He heard no answer, only the long, low sighing of the night wind coursing down through the pines. His eyes slid shut. Hot tears welled, leaking down his cheeks. "God rest you, Tynan," he prayed, "and all those too soon fallen, whatever their cause."

6
Return to Antium Hall

Misfortune shrouded Jaryd Hume's return to Antium. The Twin Pines Inn, his lodgings and source of part-time employment while in attendance at the Hall, had burned to the ground during the time he and Bode were at sea. No one had been hurt in the fire, but the building was a complete loss. The proprietor, Jakyb Deal, and his family were staying with friends when Jaryd caught up with them. Jakyb still seemed to be in a state of shock. His wife, Layris, told Jaryd that they would rebuild. Until then, Layris informed him, Jaryd would have to fend for himself.

Uncertain as to what he should do, Jaryd made his way to the Hall, carrying his luggage, a pair of leather satchels draped over one shoulder, and a large canvas bag slung across the other. The Hall grounds occupied three small hills and the saddle-shaped dell between them about a kylo from the harbor.

The perimeter of the Hall grounds was not walled and melded directly with the rest of the city. Adjacent to the Hall stood the Gyft Ryll of Antium. Unlike the open access of the Hall, a tall stone and brick wall some twelve span in height surrounded the Ryll. Massive granite blocks formed the base of the wall. The upper reaches were made of red brick and concrete, a Tieran invention, but the volcanic sand so key to its constituency was readily available in Ayle, and many regarded the Aylitic formulation superior to the original Tieran mixture. Granite foundation stones and brick upper works were both painted a brilliant white, and the shining walls of Antium's Ryll had won renown as a landmark of the city.

An array of buildings of various types comprised the Hall complex. The oldest, constructed of sandstone blocks, occupied the campus center, while the majority—classrooms, dining halls, kitchens, stables, and dormitories—were more recent and predominately made of brick. Open spaces between the buildings featured an array of gardens and treelined walkways. Though no physical barrier existed, Jaryd could almost always tell as soon as he crossed from the city proper to the grounds of the Hall.

He went first to the lodgings of Hyram Regys, who served as first speaker of mathematics at the Hall in Antium. Jaryd appreciated Regys's open-handed style of teaching; for all his vaunted reputation as a mathematician, Jaryd found nothing haughty or standoffish about him. Jaryd felt he could rely on whatever counsel the man could provide.

The speaker's quarters were located on the second floor of one of the new brick buildings; new in this case referred to a cluster of six two- and three-story buildings constructed of brick and concrete nearly a century ago. The buildings were arranged in a rectangular formation with a grass-covered courtyard between them. They housed the school of mathematics and natural philosophy.

When he arrived, two others, an old man and a young woman, waited ahead of him. Jaryd had seen the young woman before. Enrolled in the Hall, studying mathematics, he recalled. Tall for a girl, blond-haired, and full-breasted, she was, Jaryd recollected, highly intelligent. Seated on a chair nearest the door to the office, she wore a conservatively cut, long-sleeved, gray linen dress called a jupon. Her honey-colored hair was done into a pair of braids, one tossed over each shoulder, but Jaryd couldn't for the life of him remember her name. Deeply engrossed in whatever was written on a sheaf of papers held in her lap, she didn't even glance at him when he stepped into the sitting room.

Although other chairs were available, the old man leaned casually against the far wall. Shorter than Jaryd by about a hand span, the oldster looked lean and fit, deeply tanned with a full head of close-cropped white hair. The man stood clad in a faded green cotton tunic belted at the waist. His legs were bare except for the sturdy pair of sandals covering his feet. He held a potted plant of some kind in his hands. Selecting an empty chair on the opposite side of the room, Jaryd set down his baggage. Glancing up, he saw the old man looking at him with eyes that were vivid blue.

"Good afternoon," Jaryd said, nodding.

"Come a long way, have you?" the white-haired oldster inquired, speaking Aylitic with a slight accent that Jaryd couldn't place.

"I'm from the Three Rivers," Jaryd responded, "off a farm just outside the village of Greystock."

"Greystock is adjacent to Deben Bay, is it not?" the old man asked.

"It is," Jaryd confirmed. "Most people have never heard of it. My name is Jaryd Hume. I am a student of law here at the Hall."

"I'm fond of maps," the old fellow said, smiling. "I am a gardener, one of many employed by the Hall. Everyone calls me Uncle Spats. Do you speak Lynium?"

"About as well as I speak Aylitic," Jaryd answered in the language of Tier. "Or as poorly. Take your choice."

"Have you any Glaylic?" Spats asked, using the Kylgahran tongue.

"I do," Jaryd responded in kind, "but only just. One of my father's farmhands is from the Highlands out west. I learned a bit from him growing up."

The office door swung open, and Hyram Regys ushered a pair of finely dressed merchants out. Of middle years, his dark-brown hair balding on top, the speaker wore a simple, porridge-colored tunic with the usual waist belt. Regys was a handsome man, just starting to jowl, with a pair of merry green eyes. Hyram Regys qualified, in Jaryd's estimation, as the smartest human being he'd ever met.

"Thank you, gentlemen, I will consider it," Regys declared

cheerfully while practically shooing the pair across the waiting room floor.

Seeing the old gardener, Speaker Regys said, "Uncle Spats, there is no need for you to wait out here."

"I don't mind," Spats said. "It was a choice of waiting a while or trimming hedges. With enough luck, somebody else will have attended to the trimming by the time I get back. Did you know this young fellow speaks Glaylic?" He thrust his chin at Jaryd.

Regys looked toward Jaryd. "Jaryd Hume, is it not?"

Pleased that the speaker remembered his name, Jaryd said, "It is, sir. Thank you."

"What are you doing here?" Regys inquired. "I thought you settled on law. How is it you speak Glaylic?"

"Bit of a long story, sir," Jaryd said. "And I believe I'm third in line."

"What? Oh, yes," Regys said, turning to the young woman seated to his left. "What is it, Dara?"

Dara Thresher, that's her name. Jaryd felt relieved at the recollection.

Upon being directly addressed, the young blonde finally looked up from her notes. Jaryd saw that her eyes were large and brown. He had not noticed them before. "Speaker Regys," she said, "I think I've come up with a systematic elimination process for solving a linear system. It's quite simple really."

"The best ideas usually are, my dear," Speaker Regys enthused. "Let's have a look. Be with you shortly, gentlemen. Young Dara here does not believe in wasting time." Stepping aside, he waved Dara into his office.

As she walked past, Dara asked, "Why would anyone be interested in wasting time?"

"Because, young lady," Hyram Regys said in a firmly authoritative voice, "it goes down easier than trimming hedges." The door closed behind them.

"Theoretical mathematicians," Uncle Spats observed, "should not be allowed to roam about unsupervised."

True to forecast, Speaker Regys's discussion with Dara Thresher did not take long. His office door swung open once again, and the Hall instructor stepped out, saying, "Brilliant, Dara. Write this up just as you have it outlined the now. Be sure to include the example we talked about, and then you can present it at the forum next month."

"Present?" Dara sounded shocked. "Me? At the mathematics forum? I couldn't do that."

"Why not? It is your idea and a good one." Regys paused when he saw the panic-stricken look in the young woman's eyes. Patting her arm, he said reassuringly, "We'll work on it together and then decide how best it should be presented. All right?"

"Thank you, Speaker Regys," Dara said quickly, bobbing a curtsey to the speaker and again to the gardener. "A pleasure to meet you it is, sir," she said to Spats, "and to see you again, Jaryd Hume, even if you are studying law." Nodding to Jaryd, she practically bolted from the room, clutching her notes to what Jaryd couldn't help noticing was indeed a fetching bosom.

"Been a long time since anyone called me 'sir,'" Spats commented.

"Dara Thresher is a sweet girl with a first-rate intellect. It is a pity…" The speaker's voice trailed away into thought. He stood scratching his chin. After a moment, his gaze settled on the gardener. "What do you want?"

"I brought you the Roselle you were asking about," Spats replied, holding up the plant. "Good for flavoring tea it is."

"Tea?" Speaker Regys sounded perplexed. He stepped back into his office with the gardener on his heels. "I don't even like tea."

"That's why you wanted it flavored, you great looby," Spats grumped as the door swung shut.

Unlike a new elimination process for solving a linear system, which only took a few moments to discuss, flavored tea apparently required a much more detailed conversation. The speaker and the gardener had been at it for quite a while when Jaryd gave in to boredom and fished the rune carving out of his wallet. He'd nearly finished putting the final touches on the thumb-sized carving, turning a piece of black driftwood into the rune symbol Fey. Taking a small leather case from his wallet as well, he opened it and selected a fine-bladed chisel. Concentrating thoroughly on the detailed work that remained on the miniature, he didn't notice the office door opening.

"What is it you are working on there?" Uncle Spats asked. Jaryd looked up to see both Speaker Regys and the gardener staring intently at the tiny carving in his lap.

"It is rune symbol. Fey, it is called," Jaryd answered.

"May I see it?" the gardener inquired, holding out his hand.

Passing the carving along, Jaryd watched as Spats squinted closely at it before handing it to the speaker. "Where did you come by the piece you are carving?" Spats asked.

"I found it lying on the beach, near the Greystock docks in Deben Bay," Jaryd responded. "Do you know the wood? I don't recognize it."

"It is not wood," Speaker Regys informed Jaryd as he returned the carving to him. "It is rather a form of resin, quite rare."

"Why Fey?" Spats wanted to know.

"Fey symbols are common in the Three Rivers," Jaryd told them. "My father has one carved from oak hanging over our farmhouse door. Folks there say the Fey stands for freedom."

"Do they now?" Spats seemed intrigued. "In the Three Rivers you say, the Fey rune stands for freedom. Interesting that is."

Speaker Regys waved a hand at Jaryd's baggage. "Are you planning to move in here?"

"I may have to, sir," Jaryd explained. "I lost my lodgings and, with them, my employment to a fire a few days ago. I need to find a place to stay that does not cost too dear. I was hoping you might be able to advise me."

"Mistress Rawlins handles student housing on Hall grounds," Hyram Regys said. "We could speak with her."

"I think I can make good use of a farmer's son," Uncle Spats said with a mischievous glint in his eye. "If you don't mind getting your hands dirty while poring over your law books, we'll make a place for you in the gardeners' quarters. You'll have a room of your own. The pay is scant, but the lodgings will cost you nothing, and you can take your meals in the Hall kitchens or with me if you can mind your manners."

"What say you, young fellow?" Speaker Regys asked.

Glancing out the window, Jaryd reckoned there were still a few hours of sunlight left before evening. "I'd say odds are I'll be trimming hedges before sundown," he observed.

Both older men grinned like a pair of boys. "He's no dullard," Spats remarked, "despite his chosen field of study."

"Thank you both," Jaryd said seriously. "Without a place to stay, I'd have been in for it."

"Think nothing of it, lad," Spats said, hoisting Jaryd's large canvas bag easily onto one shoulder. "Come on. Those hedges won't tend to themselves."

7

To Envy Not

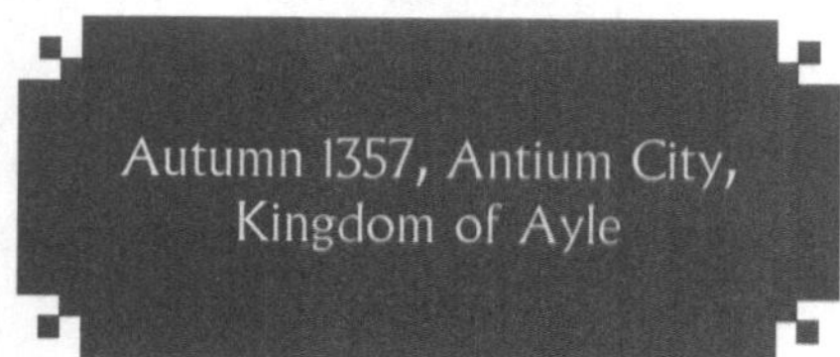

Jaryd had not realized just how extensive the green space, as Spats called it, was on the Hall grounds. In addition to ornamental gardens, other areas were devoted to growing vegetables for the Hall kitchens, and there existed several experimental plots as well. Some contained plants from all over Trascera, and in others, hybrids developed at the Hall had been planted in hopes of producing better yields or strains less susceptible to disease.

Bode found him the next afternoon, weeding a patch of cabbages. "I thought you traveled across the sea to escape hoeing cabbages?" she asked by way of greeting.

Bode was wearing a sleeveless, light-blue frock, belted at the waist, and had a woolen shawl of a slightly darker shade draped over her shoulders. Pinned at the sides, just behind her ears, Bode's lush, light-brown hair framed her face before falling loosely about her back and shoulders. Her gray eyes twinkled with amusement.

"I needed lodgings and a job of some kind," Jaryd said in return, "and they needed a gardener. Turns out farming is similar, you know."

"I should have known you would land on your feet." Bode

50

smiled, and the light in her eyes softened. "I thought you might come to see Uncle Haryld and me."

"I went first to Speaker Regys. He and Uncle Spats, the head gardener, helped me out," Jaryd said. "If I'd come up empty after seeing the speaker, you were my next stop." That wasn't true, strictly speaking. It had not occurred to Jaryd to ask Bode for help, but he supposed that if things had not gone well, he would have gotten around to it sooner or later.

"How are the Deals taking it?" Bode asked, sobering.

"They are determined to rebuild," Jaryd responded. "They own the property. I don't know if they'll need a loan to cover the cost of building again or not."

"I'll ask Uncle Haryld to stop by," Bode said. Her uncle was well off. The Twin Pines inn had been prosperous. Maybe Bode's uncle would be inclined to provide financing for more than generosity's sake alone.

"Are you studying law too?" Uncle Spats asked Bode as he sauntered up, crossing over from an adjacent garden. Spats wore his usual faded green tunic and sandals. A battered straw hat was clamped atop his head, and a broad leather belt wound about his waist, from which dangled a couple of different types of shears in canvas sheathes. The gardener held a hoe canted over his right shoulder and carried a bright yellow rose blossom in his left hand.

"No, I'm studying music," Bode said, trying not to stare. Jaryd made the introductions.

"Instrument or voice?" Spats inquired.

"I play the lyre and the harp," Bode answered him. "And I sing."

"I would have wagered you were a singer by the tone of your voice alone." Uncle Spats bowed gracefully and presented the rose to Bode with a flourish. "To the loveliest blossom this old garden has ever seen."

Bode accepted the gardener's gift with a curtsey, blushing. "Why, thank you, sir."

Taking a few steps away, Spats paused suddenly as if remembering something he'd forgotten, looked back over his shoulder, and asked, "Would you two care for some tea and biscuits?"

Delicately sniffing her rose, Bode looked over the top of it at Jaryd, leaving the decision to him. "Tea always tastes like boiled weeds to me," Jaryd pronounced. "But Spats's biscuits are something to behold." He'd sampled some the night before.

"We'd be honored, Master Spats," Bode said graciously. "Please forgive Jaryd's manners. He was raised in a barn, practically."

"Well, come on then," Spats said, leading the way.

As they passed out of the garden, Bode nodded at Spats and whispered to Jaryd, "He thinks I'm lovely."

Slinging his hoe over his shoulder, Jaryd observed, "What he actually said was that you are prettier than a patch of cabbages." Laughing, Bode punched his shoulder and then latched onto his arm. They walked together back to the gardeners' quarters.

To Bode, the gardeners' quarters looked like a cluster of small cottages taken out of a children's tale, constructed of stone with thatched roofs and chimneys made of red brick. The door to Spats's cottage was painted bright green. Inside, there were three rooms: a kitchen, a bedroom, and what Spats called his sitting room. The furnishings were old and mismatched, but the overall feel of the place was tidy and snug. Bode felt as if she'd stepped into a doll's house brought somehow to life size.

"This is so quaint," Bode exclaimed, looking about.

"Don't know about that," Spats said, busying himself in the kitchen. "But it keeps the rain out."

"Are your quarters so grand?" Bode asked Jaryd.

"Only two rooms," Jaryd had to admit, "but I get to share the privy out back, and there are communal baths just across the yard."

"You'll be putting on airs," Bode teased.

As it turned out, Spats's biscuits were delicious. The tea, despite Jaryd's joshing, was excellent as well, a fine black leaf. Spats flavored it with honey and regaled them with tales of old Antium in the time of kings before the Tieran invasion of Tyne across the Narrows. Spats spoke in a rich, mellow voice that ebbed and flowed with the tenor of the tale he told. The Madryn Kings ruled in Tyne at that time, and even though they shared a common tribal ancestry, the rivalry between the kingdoms of Ayle and Madryn raged fierce and bloody. In addition to the Madryns, the rulers of Ayle warred also with the old Kingdom of Kios to the east.

The Kingdom of Ayle writhed in desperate straits when the Tierans invaded the lands of the Madryns. King Symon, second of that name to rule in Ayle, was quick to seek an alliance. The Tierans agreed. With Aylitic lancers warding their flanks, the vaunted Tieran infantry routed the Madryn forces in the field and lay siege to Tyne itself. Eventually, the city fell, and the last of the Madryn kings died in the fighting. Once the Madryn scourge had been crushed, Symon II was able to throw the full weight of his army against that of Kios. The battle ended in a bloody stalemate that cost Symon II of Ayle his life, but his kingdom was saved. From that time until the present, the Symonic Alliance with the Tieran Empire had held.

Spellbound until Spats had finished his discourse, Bode had lost all track of time. She gasped softly, startled, when Jaryd announced the setting sun. Spats wouldn't let her go without promising a return visit. "To make the Hall's masons and carpenters properly jealous," he said. Jaryd insisted upon walking her home. Spats stepped into his bedroom, returning with a long walking stick for Jaryd to take along. Hefting the stick, Jaryd observed that it weighed more like a quarterstaff. "Which is why you carry it while escorting a pretty girl down darkening streets, you ninny," Spats huffed, winking at Bode.

"I've never actually met a Hall gardener before," Bode said a short while later as she and Jaryd strolled across the campus. "Are they all like Spats?"

"I don't think there is anyone else like Spats," Jaryd commented. "I doubt the first speaker of history at the Hall could have matched the lecture we just heard this afternoon. There is much more to Spats than what meets the eye, Bode."

"He might have made the whole thing up," Bode speculated.

"At a minimum, that makes him a remarkably talented storyteller," Jaryd responded. "He called the first speaker of mathematics a great looby yesterday." A looby was a mythical bird, popular in children's fables for its size and stupidity. "What's more, the speaker treated him as an equal. Hyram Regys is known for being open-handed, but still I can't help wondering what Spats is doing working as a gardener. He works, that much I can tell you. Trying to keep up with him this morning nearly wore me out."

"You like him," Bode said, smiling.

"I do," Jaryd confirmed. "I suspect not nearly as much as he likes you."

"As well he should," Bode announced, brandishing her rose. "It isn't every day you meet someone prettier than an entire patch of cabbages."

Jaryd walked her to the door of her uncle Haryld Tucker's two-story wood and stone-built home. Located in an affluent section of the city, the house stood not far from the Hall grounds. Her cousin Michaela answered Jaryd's knock. Bode invited Jaryd in, but he declined politely, saying he had a big day ahead tomorrow, fertilizing pear trees or some such. Nodding to Michaela, Jaryd bade Bode goodnight and walked off, absently twirling the enormous walking stick Spats had given him.

Bode stood with her cousin at the head of the stairs and watched until Jaryd rounded a corner, disappearing from sight. Michaela pressed down on the latch, and the door swung silently open. No sooner had the two of them stepped through the front door than Michaela rounded on Bode.

"Really, cousin," Michaela sounded exasperated. "How are you ever going to meet a better class of people if you insist upon associating with yokels like that fellow?"

"That yokel is a friend of mine, Michaela," Bode said firmly.

"Your loyalty does you credit, Bodewhin." This observation came from her Aunt Rayleen, who stood at the far end of the front parlor. "But there is truth in what Michaela says as well. No one can climb without first reaching up."

"Speaking of which," Michaela practically gushed, "we've been invited to a dance at Lord Bly's residence. The invitation makes special mention of you."

Bode had met Eddard Bly, Lord Hemish Bly's second son, after singing in the Hall choir at the citadel closing ceremony late last spring. They had spent some time together during the two weeks or so before she left for Greystock. Eddard was tall, dark-haired, and blue-eyed. He insisted she call him Ned, a nickname her father, also named Eddard, detested. Ned was an officer candidate at the citadel, Ayle's equivalent, she supposed, of the Tieran military academy in Tyne. Hemish Bly occupied a well-established position among what in Ayle was known as the lesser nobility. In addition to a city residence, the Blys also held title to a large estate somewhere east of the city. A military career constituted a likely choice for young Ned as a second son of the lesser nobility; it was one of the few acceptable careers for someone of his social status.

She hadn't given much thought to Ned Bly in the weeks that passed since she'd last seen him. She couldn't have without feeling disloyal to Mat, but any excuse to dance qualified as a good one. What could she wear without looking like a backcountry schoolgirl? That question warranted some consideration. Appearance counted, after all; she'd learned that much. She wanted to rise, true enough, and stood determined to do so in a manner that left her unashamed of her origins.

Full dark it was by the time Jaryd returned to the gardeners' cottages on the Hall grounds.

"Your girl is a rare beauty," Spats informed him as Jaryd handed over the gardener's walking stick.

"Bode is a beauty and a rare one, I'll grant you that, Spats," Jaryd told him. "But she's not my girl. In fact, she is betrothed to my best friend."

Maybe Spats heard something in Jaryd's voice—something the young man had not intended to reveal—or maybe Spats just imagined that he had. At any rate, he said, "Sorry I am to hear that, lad." The gardener reached out and patted Jaryd on the arm. "Except for the alternative, I can't much recommend getting old. Sometimes, though, I don't envy you young folks a bit."

8

The Black Apron

Mathias Bayrd reckoned on killing some time, mostly. As was his custom, Logan Maywell had closed his smithy at noon on Solstice Eve. By midafternoon, only Mat still occupied the shop. Winter Solstice, the shortest day of the year, was also the most joyous of holidays in the Three Rivers, denoting, as it did, the turning point of the seasons. The lengthening days that followed led jubilantly on toward spring. Though deep in the early throes of winter, the Solstice gave rise to fresh hope and new beginnings, proving once again the Creator's promise of renewal.

At least that was what Father Vars Nebus Bayu said at temple on First Day last. Within the Penitent Church, Vars Bayu of House Nebus held the rank of axton, or senior priest. To the people of Greystock, the kindly, gray-haired prelate would forever be known simply as Father Vars. Mat figured he couldn't argue with the sentiment. Not that he'd get far if so inclined. Arguing with the endlessly patient, relentlessly persistent Father Vars usually proved about as fruitful as trying to catch raindrops with a fishnet.

For this season and the last, however, the Winter Solstice, with its emphasis on family gatherings, religious service, and the exchange of gifts, served only to heighten Mat's feeling of loneliness. Bode loved the Solstice celebrations and the singing and dancing that were so much a part of them. Mat felt her absence most keenly during the days leading up to the winter holiday—in part because much of the activity that so occupied people most other times of the year was set aside during the Solstice season to savor the bounty derived from simply spending time with loved ones.

With Bode gone, Mat couldn't help feeling his plate stood half empty. Selfish, he figured that was, and unfair to his family and friends. Even so, the feeling lingered, as real and every bit as oppressive as the overcast sky above. No snow had there been in a week, but the low clouds, roiling gray and restless overhead, threatened—or promised, rather. Three Rivers folk regarded fresh snow on the Solstice as a sign of good fortune to come.

Mat had nearly finished the head of the gardening hoe upon which he labored. He'd already shaped the blade, tempered the leading edge, and welded it to the tang. All that remained was to punch a pair of rivet holes into the flattened portion at the butt of the tang.

In midwinter, customers weren't exactly clamoring for garden hoes, but spring would come round sooner or later, and Master Maywell always liked to have a good stock of staples like hoes, shovels, and garden rakes on hand ahead of time. Judging by the amber hue of the heated metal, Mat reckoned the tang end had reached the right temperature. He used a pair of heavy tongs to lift it from the forge.

Placing the hoe head into the jaws of an iron helper, an adjustable wrought-iron rack featuring a series of groves and clamps situated alongside the anvil he was using, Mat positioned the tang over the hardy-hole of the anvil's flat iron. Taking up a steel punch, Mat aligned it and, using a long-hafted hammer, struck two sharp blows. Shifting the tang, he repeated the process, punching out a second rivet hole. Using the tongs, Mat lifted the hoe head and examined the two openings. Satisfied, he plunged the flattened end of the tang into the saltwater barrel. The hot metal hissed and steamed for a moment and then fell silent.

Mat hung the hoe head in the ready rack on the wall near the grinding wheels. One of the junior apprentices would later sharpen it and attach the ash wood handle. Mat took another look out the window. Afternoon shadows were lengthening. He could still see the shadows, so the overcast hadn't thickened much. Good omen or no, he could do without a snowfall that night or the next morning.

He was due at the Maywells' for supper this evening and was expected home before noon the following day to partake of the Solstice meal with his family. Mat's father owned a farm outside of Greystock—well outside. It was a good half-day's walk—longer than that should there be a heavy snow. Judging by the shadows, he had a little time left, enough for something simple. He could hammer out a barrel scrape or maybe a drawknife.

"Mat, are you still in there?" Logan Maywell called from just outside the smithy. Before Mat could respond, the big smith stepped through the entry door. Logan had a brown winnowed wool wrap wound about his shoulders, worn over a fleece-lined leather vest. Beneath the vest, he was clad in a blue woolen shirt that fell to his knees. Thick woolen socks of an indistinct earthen tone and a pair of leather sandals covered his lower legs and feet. Bare-headed and dark-haired, a trace of gray just showing at his temples, Master Logan's towering form filled the doorframe at his back. The smith's eyes were blue. "It's Solstice Eve, lad. What in sweet blazes are you doing still dancing round a forge?"

"Small work mostly," Mat replied quietly. "Just trying to keep my touch."

Logan glanced at the ready rack. He saw a freshly made scythe blade, a pruning hook, and a hoe head suspended from the pegs.

Maywell shook his head. "Ellah sent me to fetch you. If we're late returning, she'll likely get sore at the both of us. Do me a favor, will you? Knock off the now and wash up a bit. I'll still that iron oven, and the pair of us can clear out of here." Ellah was Maywell's wife, a buxom, blond-haired woman with eyes as green as Mat's.

Mat had been apprenticed to Logan Maywell at age twelve. He'd lived in a spare room in what had once been a storage shed adjacent to their house ever since. Though firm, Mistress Maywell also exuded patience and kindness and had always treated Mat as if he'd been born one of her own. Mat could not have been fonder of Ellah Maywell if she had been his mother.

Hanging up his apron and vest, Mat sponged himself off in a washroom adjacent to the central bay. With practiced ease, he and Logan finished banking the forge. Closing the shop, they left together. On the way out, Mat donned a fleece-lined, gray woolen waistcoat, leaving a pair of mittens in the pockets, and clapped his watch cap onto his head. A cobblestone street ran in front of the smithy, winding its way up a gentle hill that led away from the waterfront.

The Maywells' home stood upon the crest of the hill at the intersection of a second stone-lined roadway. Most of the streets in Greystock were paved with stone. This better served the villagers, especially in winter, and provided a source of considerable pride. Most of the houses in Greystock were constructed of stone or brick as well and featured slate roofs. Slate was abundant nearby and so not as dear as in most places and virtually fireproof. It wasn't far, and as was usually the case, Mat and Master Logan made the walk sharing an easy silence.

Master Logan preceded him through the front door of the Maywell house at the top of the hill. By Greystock standards, the Maywells owned a large home. A two-storied affair, the house had walls constructed mainly of brick supporting a wood frame and featured a fine slate roof and a pair of stone-lined chimneys. Dominated by a large sitting room that connected directly to the kitchen, the first floor also contained smaller front and side parlors. The upstairs stood devoted to a quartet of bedrooms. With three boys of their own ranging in age from ten to sixteen years, the Maywells made good use of them.

No sooner had Mat stepped across the threshold than he heard Ellah Maywell cry, "Hooray!"

Mistress Maywell's shout was echoed moments later by those gathered round the main fireplace in the sitting room. Startled, Mat looked up to see his parents, Ruhl and Myriam Bayrd, smiling at him from where they were standing just in front of the hearth. His two younger brothers, Bart and Donner, and his little sister, Belle, were also present, fresh scrubbed, he noticed, and wearing their First Day best. Byan Hume and his tall, slender wife, Annette, were there too, as was Father Vars and the school master, Gyros Claudius Ban.

The Maywell boys waved at Mat from one corner of the room, while lithesome, brown-eyed, and recently married Lesalle Bowdry, a longtime friend of Bode's and his and Jaryd's, also smiled at him from another, her arm wound firmly about that of her husband, Warren. Standing on Lesalle's other side, lanky Danel Owen grinned and nodded. A few years older than Mat, and long a good friend despite the difference in their ages, Danel was a lumberjack by trade. Justyn Graves, owner of the Greystock boatyard, waved a mug of cider at him, and even the usually dour lawyer Titus Wilkes gave him a warm smile.

Looking about the room, Mat saw neither Eddard Ware nor his wife, Annelle. Their absence didn't constitute much of a surprise. Eddard was ever affable with Mat but never particularly friendly, and Annelle had always been a little standoffish whenever Mat came calling, as if she feared he might track something on her carpet.

Logan Maywell handed him a bulky paper-wrapped package. "Before you open that, lad," the big smith said loudly enough for everyone to hear, "there are a couple of things I'd like to say. You've always been a good boy, Mat, and you've grown into a fine young man, an artisan worthy of the name. I'm proud to know you and even prouder to call you my friend."

"Before his head swells too much to hear right," Byan Hume called out, "there are a few things I'd like to say too." Byan, Jaryd's father, regaled the gathering with a tale regarding a couple of Jaryd and Mat's more spectacular misadventures from their youth. Byan was a gifted storyteller, and he stretched the truth just enough to delight the crowd and embarrass Mat something fierce.

One or two others followed, saying nice things about him. Mat's father, Ruhl, spoke last. Ruhl was about Mat's height and nearly as thick through the shoulders. A man of few words, he said simply, "You're a son to be proud of, Mat. May God love you as we do."

Maywell nodded after that, and Mat carefully stripped away the paper wrapping. In his hands he held a thick, black leather apron, the mark of a fully fledged journeyman smith. He'd expected this, the black apron anyway. Some while ago, Master Maywell had told him it was about his time. Still, firmly gripping the supple, well-oiled leather, Mat felt a surge of emotion. To anyone who knew what it involved, achieving the rank of journeyman while still shy of twenty counted as no small thing.

Clearing his throat, Mat looked out across the room. "I never realized until just the now, after listening to you all, what a fine fellow I am."

It wasn't much of a joke, he reckoned. Jaryd or Bode would have said something really clever, but the room was suddenly full of warmhearted laughter anyway. "This," he continued, waving one hand to indicate all those present, "all this means more than I can say. Thank you."

"All right then, everyone," Ellah Maywell hollered happily, "let's eat."

The meal that followed was truly sumptuous: roast turkey with all the fixings. Having eaten his fill, Mat found a place to himself on a settle located beneath the window adjacent to the front door of the Maywell home. He idly ran his fingers over the marbled texture of the black apron he held folded in his lap. Mat had long viewed attaining the apron as the cornerstone of the life he envisioned. He had cause to wonder the now. Bode had not answered any of his letters. She had not written once since departing for Antium in the fall. She'd corresponded regularly the year before. This wasn't like her. If she wanted him to clear off, she would have told him so in no uncertain terms—at least the old Bode would have, the Bode he knew, the girl he loved.

Looking back over his shoulder, Mat gazed up at the window. The interior of the house was well lit by oil lamps augmented with an array of candles and the fire burning in the sitting-room hearth. He could see nothing through the frost-rimmed glass except for the looming dark. A knock sounded at the front door. As he was closest, Mat answered. He opened the portal to find Eddard Ware standing before him, bundled in a brown woolen coat and scarf with a rabbit-fur cap tugged firmly down about his ears.

"Happy Solstice, Mat," the square-shouldered storeowner greeted him. "Sorry to be so late. We couldn't seem to close up tonight."

Eddard Ware was Bode's father. A sturdy, handsome man of middle years, he owned the largest and best-stocked general store in the area. The bustle of the Winter Solstice season entailed a busy time for him.

"Happy Solstice, sir," Mat replied. "Please come in."

"I hear congratulations are in order," Eddard said as he stepped past Mat into the front parlor, offering his hand.

"Thank you, sir," Mat said. They shook; Eddard Ware had a strong grip. A wealthy merchant he might be the now, but Ware had worked hard most of his life.

Patting his pockets, Eddard extracted a small, paper-wrapped package. "I have a Solstice gift here for you from Bode. She picked it out before taking ship last fall." Eddard squinted at him. "She writes sending her love along with best wishes for the Solstice. I should warn you she also complained some about your not writing often enough."

She did, did she? Mat thought. *The little mort. How many letters does a fella have to pen to earn one from her in return, I wonder?* All he said was, "Thank you, sir. I'm not much of a letter writer."

"It is not so much what you put down, lad," Ware advised him quietly, "as letting her know you took the time and the care to do so."

"I have a Solstice gift for her as well," Mat told him. "Would you mind posting it for me?"

If Eddard Ware thought there was anything strange about Mat's request, he gave no sign of it. "Of course not," Ware replied. Breathing in deeply, he grinned. "Roast turkey, is it?"

"Aye, sir." Mat smiled back. "With all the trimmings. Let me take your coat. The kitchen is right through there." Mat pointed.

Slipping free of his coat and scarf, Eddard passed them, along with his cap, to Mat and headed down the hall.

As Eddard hurried off to the kitchen, Mat took the merchant's outer garments into the small parlor adjacent to the entryway on the right. Ellah had strung clothesline across the room to hang her guests' coats, hats, and cloaks. Draping Ware's over a bare strip of line, Mat shrugged into his own coat and made his way out through the front door, Bode's gift clutched in his hand. A pair of oil lamps suspended from wrought-iron stanchions above the door on either side illuminated the front porch and the steps leading up to it.

Mat carefully unwrapped Bode's gift to him. The package contained a small, hinged wooden box sanded smooth and well lacquered. Inside, he found a straight razor, folded. Opening the razor, he saw scrollwork of some kind etched onto the blued steel of the blade. The handle was made of bone or ivory. The soft, flickering light of the lamps wasn't strong enough for him to be sure, and neither could he make out the images depicted by the engraving on the blade. The heft of the razor in his hand and the smooth action as he opened it spoke of fine craftsmanship. It was beautiful.

Something cold and wet lightly stung his cheek. Gazing upward, Mat saw snowflakes swirling down from above. Only a few at first, in moments, the snowfall thickened considerably. A White Solstice it appeared there would be this season in Greystock. Her love she sent, Eddard Ware had said, along with her Solstice wishes. Snow fell steadily the now. Mat looked out across the street already dusted with fresh white powder and felt his heart lift. Maybe he had some luck left after all.

9

A Storm-Tossed Sky

Bodewhin Ware tugged open the door of the wardrobe in her room on the second floor of her aunt and uncle's house in Antium City. Bode's cousin Michaela had warned her to dress warmly. The four of them—Bode; Uncle Haryld Tucker; his wife, Rayleen; and their daughter, Michaela—were bound for a Solstice Eve dinner party hosted by one of Tucker's business associates, a merchant named Tobyas Blair. The dinner was to be a private affair with only the Blairs and the Tuckers attending. As Aunt Rayleen and Uncle Haryld's niece, Bode supposed she rated Tucker enough. She'd been invited anyway.

After only a moment's hesitation, Bode chose Mat's parting gift, the gray winnowed wool cloak. The outer garment would go well with the conservatively cut, gray silk evening gown she was wearing, an early Solstice present from her aunt. Slipping the cloak about her shoulders, Bode took a final peek at her reflection in the polished brass mirror above the dressing table. Her long brown hair coiled about her head in the fashion Michaela swore was all the rage in Antium this Solstice season. Bode hoped the pins would hold.

64

She hurried down the stairs, relieved to discover she was the first to reach the front parlor. Her uncle Haryld descended next. A nice-looking, heavyset man, Uncle Haryld wore a simple but well-tailored gray woolen coat with matching shirt and trousers. He had a winnowed wool cloak similar to hers draped over his arm. Michaela came down soon after, clad in a cream-colored silk gown with a light-blue winnowed wool wrap wound about her slender shoulders.

A vivacious girl, Michaela, aged seventeen, was graced with a rich mass of medium-blond hair offset by a face a touch too round and bright blue eyes slightly too close together for her to ever be more than almost pretty. Michaela stood full bosomed, though, and slim hipped, with a knack for putting people, especially young men, at ease. Bode couldn't help thinking Michaela's charm came a little too easily, something she slipped on and off as readily as a pair of old shoes.

Aunt Rayleen brought up the rear. Her silk dress was of a similar cut to Michaela's but a shade darker in color, and the wrap she wore was a deep blue. Rayleen looked like her sister, Bode's mother: comely with honey-blond hair, a heart-shaped face, and wideset blue eyes. Bode shared a smile with her Uncle Haryld. Whenever they were to go out, Aunt Rayleen was always the first to start clamoring about the need to get ready and almost always the last one down.

The sun was just going as they stepped out the front door. While they clambered into the waiting carriage, Bode noticed the storm clouds looming low above. The instant she settled onto the seat, lightning seared a ragged tear in the gloaming, and moments later, thunder rumbled in the distance.

The carriage pulled away from the curb, swaying gently, and Bode could not help remembering another thunderstorm, years ago, back home in the Three Rivers. Early summer it had been then; school was just out. Bode had been tutoring Mat Bayrd for several months by that time.

Despite an initial reluctance, she'd become increasingly taken with the muscular young apprentice. Mat had entered service with Logan Maywell, the blacksmith, as soon as the school term ended. When school resumed in the fall, Mat would continue his studies but only on a part-time basis. Though Mat was soft-spoken and closemouthed to the point of being laconic, it had not taken Bode long to realize he was no dullard. She found him to be unfailingly honest with a fetchingly wry sense of humor. He was hopelessly immature, however—not nearly as interesting as some of the older boys.

Bode and her friend Lesalle Dent had decided to go berry picking. They weren't really supposed to be doing so. Rather than risk having permission denied, they left a note for Lesalle's father, a widower who owned a bakery just two doors down from the Wares' general store, before departing. The weather gloomed, cloudy but seasonably warm, as they started out, heading into the Great Wood just north of the village. The best berry picking nearby would be found on the east side of Owain's Meadow, located less than an hour's walk to the northwest. Equipped with a large wicker basket apiece, both girls wore lightweight cotton frocks. Bode's showed blue and Lesalle's green, and each had a pair of leather sandals covering her feet. Lesalle insisted upon wearing a broad-brimmed straw bonnet to keep the sun off her face, she said, and had prevailed upon Bode to do the same. Bode had no bonnet of her own but was happy enough to borrow one of Lesalle's.

Bode felt tremendously fond of Lesalle. A month younger than Bode, Lesalle, a pretty, brown-eyed little thing with long, lustrous, medium-blond hair, had become a bosom friend, or so Lesalle said. Ever kind and never cross, Lesalle was not overly bright. She remained, however, as steadfast as she was sweet tempered. A friend stayed a friend in Lesalle's book. Gossip never swayed her.

By the time they reached Owain's Meadow, it was nearly noon, and the day had become oppressively, soggily hot. Bode knew Sager's Creek ran west to east a kylo or two farther to the north, feeding a pond near a tangle of large boulders that Three Rivers youths had been using as a swimming hole for generations. It took only a little cajoling for Bode to convince Lesalle some wading was in order before getting down to the business of berry plucking.

When they arrived at the pool, Bode was surprised to find no one else there. After peering carefully about just to make sure, she stripped off her clothes and dove, bare as an otter, into the pond.

Some time passed before Lesalle overcame her mortification, but then she, too, peeled off her clothes and stepped daintily into the cool water. The two of them splashed happily about for some time, reveling in the freedom and daring of skinny-dipping. Finally, they emerged cooled, refreshed, and emboldened.

Dressing hastily, they then carefully combed and braided one another's hair to avoid the inglorious tangle that would otherwise inevitably ensue. While only partway back to Owain's Meadow, they stumbled across a large berry patch at the edge of the wood, fairly brimming with ripened elderberries. The humidity intensified, unrelenting. Their baskets about half full, Bode and Lesalle decided to rest a bit.

Having kicked off their sandals and set aside their bonnets, Bode and Lesalle sat barefoot, side by side, under the shade of the trees, giggling as eleven-year-old girls are sometimes wont to do, when a voice called from out of the woods nearby.

"Hoi, a pair of wood nymphs you said they were," Jaryd Hume announced, stepping into the clearing. "Looks to me to be only Lesalle Dent and knobby-kneed Bode Ware."

Jaryd's red-haired head was covered by a leather-billed watch cap canted at a jaunty angle across his brow. He carried a long bow in his left hand. A quiver of arrows slanted down his back one way, while a blanket roll wound round a leather strap looped over it, going the other direction. A canteen dangled from the lower end of his blanket roll. Both the blanket and the canteen looked brand new, as if they'd just been lifted from a store shelf. Jaryd wore a gray cotton shirt that reached nearly to his knees. His feet were shod in a pair of sturdy sandals, closed at heel and toe. A broad leather belt girded his waist, and Bode saw a long-bladed Hawken resting in a sheath suspended from it over his left hip. His gray eyes glinted with amusement.

"That's Bodewhin to you, mister," Bode sallied.

"I only caught a glimpse of them. Couldn't be sure," Mat Bayrd explained, striding out of the wood just behind Jaryd. The boys were about two months shy of thirteen, almost exactly one year older than Bode, and very nearly the same height. Mat appeared noticeably wider through the shoulders and more heavily muscled. He also carried a bow with quiver and bedroll strapped in a crisscross fashion over his back. Like Jaryd, his canteen and blanket looked brand-spanking new. Similarly attired, Mat wore a butternut-brown cotton shirt, his watch cap fashioned of gray wool, while Jaryd's showed a dark forest green. Mat, too, had a Hawken knife sheathed at his waist.

Lesalle hastily tucked her bare feet under the skirt of her dress, instantly managing, Bode thought, to appear as demure as she was pretty. Determined to brazen it through, Bode crossed her legs and stretched them full out, wriggling her toes in the process. "As if a pair of wood nymphs would deign to speak with a couple of miscreants such as the two of you."

"I thought wood nymphs were fond of miscreants," Mat observed.

Jaryd knelt in front of Lesalle, within easy reach of her basket. "Let's not be too hasty," he warned, speaking to Mat. "This one," he thrust his chin at Lesalle, "is pretty enough to be a wood nymph, and that other," Jaryd said, jerking a thumb negligently in Bode's direction, "does have something growing between her toes. It might be a bay leaf." Wood nymphs were supposed to sprout bay leaves from their feet and toes. Winking at Lesalle, who was smiling at him shyly, Jaryd pilfered a berry and popped it into his mouth.

"Try stealing anymore of our berries, Jaryd Hume, and you'll find whatever is between my toes resting halfway up your fundament," Bode challenged.

"I am going to try and communicate with the pretty one here," Jaryd told Mat, peering intently at the brown-eyed girl before him, "which leaves you free to deal with the surly little critter over yonder." He briefly nodded Bode's way before returning his full attention to Lesalle Dent.

"Thanks," Mat answered shortly. Stepping over, he took a knee alongside Bode. "Feeling ornery, are we?" Mat asked.

At first glance, Mat's eyes appeared to be a clear light green. Upon close examination, however, Bode had discovered there were flecks of gold in them as well.

"I suppose you'll be wanting to filch some berries too?" she inquired.

"Fair exchange," Mat offered. "I'll replace any I eat and then help you fill that basket of yours."

Before Bode could respond, a burst of brilliant white light exploded into the clearing, followed almost immediately by a tremendous roar. Lying nearly prone, Bode could feel the thunderclap reverberate in the pit of her stomach. She knew with complete certainty that it was the loudest sound any of them had ever heard. Bode found herself stunned into silence. Lesalle screamed.

Slinging his bow across his shoulders, Jaryd clasped Lesalle's hand. There was nothing coy in the gesture. Reaching across, he handed the young, doe-eyed girl her sandals.

"Best put these on," he directed, releasing her hand. Gazing at the sky above, Jaryd shook his head. "That sure came on fast."

Bode snatched up her sandals. Mat, too, scanned the swirling storm clouds overhead. "In about two shakes, it's going to be raining buckets."

Straightening, Jaryd again grasped Lesalle's hand in his. Helping Lesalle to stand, he took hold of her basket with his other hand.

"Follow me," Jaryd ordered and set off back through the wood.

Mat looked at Bode, who had risen to her feet. Their eyes met. "At least let me carry your basket," he requested. Bode didn't argue, and the two of them followed Jaryd and Lesalle into the Great Wood.

Mat's prediction came true. Within moments, the temperature plummeted, and rain soon hammered down in torrents, lashed by a furious, swirling wind. Bode could scarcely see. She stumbled and fell to her knees. Mat was there in an instant, his arm around her. Helping her up, Mat guided her onward. Lightning flashed again and again, and thunder bellowed. Jaryd led them quickly and unerringly to a huge deadfall.

An enormous pine had fallen across a gentle rise in the forest floor, crashing down upon a gaggle of large rocks. The great trunk settled atop the rocks, forming a snug enclosure. Jaryd was woods wise, Bode had to give him that. But how he managed to find the deadfall amid the tumult that surged about them she couldn't imagine. Jaryd ducked quickly inside and emerged a moment later to usher Lesalle within. Bode and Mat hurried after.

While offering not enough headroom to stand upright, the enclosure afforded sufficient space to easily accommodate the four of them. Setting aside his bow, Jaryd slipped free of his quiver and unfurled his bedroll. He sat and, putting one end of the blanket over his shoulders, gently pulled Lesalle down beside him, wrapping the blanket around her as well. Soaked to the skin, Bode sank down upon the pine straw covering the floor of the enclosure and looked up at Mat. He had removed his quiver, leaning it and his bow against the side of the treefall-formed cave. Wet as she, Mat proffered her his bedroll. Taking it, Bode shook out the blanket, wound one end about her, and then opened her arms to him. Mat hesitated.

"Don't be daft," Bode chided. "You're wetter than me."

Mat took a seat facing her. Scooting close, he wrapped the blanket about the both of them and put his arms around her. "Mat Bayrd," Bode exclaimed a little breathlessly, "what are you doing?"

"You can be as riled as you like later," Mat assured her, "just as soon as you warm up enough for your teeth to stop chattering."

Dismayed by the realization that she was indeed shaking like a leaf, Bode relented. "All right," she said, pressing close to him, "but you had better behave."

"I am being-have," Mat replied. Bode could hear the smile in his voice.

Outside, the storm continued to rage. The warmth of Mat's body registered immediately. Bothered only slightly by the feeling she was asking for trouble, Bode rested her head against his shoulder, savoring the nearness of him. Some time passed, and Mat said quietly, "You know you are as pretty as any wood nymph too, despite whatever it is that's growing between your toes."

Instead of replying, Bode punched him in the short ribs. Sturdy as he was, she hit hard enough to make him grunt. He didn't let go, though, and neither did she.

A few moments later, Bode whispered, "Thanks for coming after us."

"Stuff," Mat scoffed. "We were out after jackrabbits."

"Carrying bedrolls and canteens fresh from my father's store?" Bode surmised. "Not bloody likely."

"Clever girl," Mat said fondly. "How do you like being rescued?"

"I don't mind," Bode murmured. "But don't let it go to your head."

"Your father and Lesalle's are combing the woods just east of Owain's Meadow," Mat informed her.

"Oh, no." Bode stiffened. "We should go."

"This blow won't last long," Mat soothed. "We'll catch up to them soon enough after."

Unable to refute his logic, Bode relaxed against him once more. "How did you find us?" she asked.

"Jaryd thought he saw a pair of fresh tracks leading away from the meadow in the direction of Sager's Creek," Mat explained. "He figured you were just contrary enough to go swimming in a thunderstorm."

"We never noticed the weather closing in on us," Bode admitted reluctantly.

"Smart as paint you are." Mat chuckled. "And thick as pine tar."

Bode hadn't quite decided whether to punch him again when she heard Lesalle laugh softly from the other side of the enclosure. "Sounds like they're having fun anyway," Mat remarked.

"I suppose you'll be wanting to trade partners the now?" Bode inquired a little defensively.

Mat gave her question some consideration. "Nay," he finally answered. "Snuggling under a blanket with Jaryd Hume ent any fun; he's all elbows and knees." Bode couldn't help but laugh at that.

The storm passed soon thereafter. Jaryd and Mat escorted Bode and Lesalle back to Owain's Meadow. Her papa, Eddard Ware, was so relieved at the sight of Bode safe and unharmed that he forgot entirely to be angry with her. The same turned out to be true of Lesalle's father, so much so that he allowed Lesalle to sleepover that evening at the Wares'.

Bode found herself jolted back to the present as the carriage came to an abrupt halt in front of the Blair house in Antium. Bode's sudden return left her feeling restless and irritable. The Solstice was upon her, and Mat had yet to reply to any of her letters. He'd written regularly last year. She couldn't understand what could have happened. Unease growing, she stepped down from the carriage. Michaela at her side, Bode followed her aunt and uncle up the steps leading to the portico of the Blairs' home.

The dinner party turned out to be a pleasant, if uneventful, affair. Aware that the Blairs were important suppliers for her uncle, Bode determined to display only her best behavior. Tobyas Blair's eldest son, Devin, sat between Bode and Michaela while at dinner. He was a tall, slender young man, brown-haired and brown-eyed with an Adam's apple nearly as pronounced as his nose. Michaela described him as scholarly. Bode thought him prim. Devin proved to be an attentive, if pedantic, dinner partner. For some reason, his knee kept brushing up against Bode's during the meal. They did not stay long after, Uncle Haryld citing the worsening weather.

Bundled into the carriage for the ride home, Bode found her thoughts slipping once again into the past and the close of that stormy summer day from her youth. She and Lesalle had settled into Bode's bed. An oil lamp turned down low bathed Bode's bed chamber in a soft, golden light. Lesalle wore one of Bode's nightgowns, a slightly newer version of the shift Bode was wearing.

"Today turned out to be more of an adventure than we bargained for, wouldn't you say?" Bode asked quietly.

Lesalle nodded. "I've never been skinny-dipping before," she whispered.

"Neither have I," Bode confessed.

"Wasn't it positively scandalous?" Lesalle enthused softly.

"Positively," Bode concurred. In Lesalle's world, there were very few shades of gray. She dwelled in a place where events tended either to be thoroughly splendid or completely devastating. She was an angel.

"That first thunderclap…" Bode's voice sounded hushed and timorous to her own ears. "I never imagined there could be such a sound."

"I know what you mean," Lesalle murmured and then tossed her head in vexation. "I behaved so dreadfully, wailing like a baby."

Bode had been too frightened even to squeak. She clasped Lesalle's hand reassuringly. "Perfectly understandable under the circumstances." Bode paused a moment. Lesalle didn't seem reassured, so Bode changed the subject. "You certainly managed to charm that rascal Jaryd Hume."

"Just because he gives as good as he gets when you tease him doesn't make Jaryd a rascal, Bode," Lesalle said staunchly.

"Do you remember the time he claimed to have seen the old man in the tree?" Bode pressed the point.

"Jaryd does have an active imagination," Lesalle acknowledged. "He kissed me, you know, under his blanket," she added so softly Bode could barely hear her.

"Rascal enough Jaryd is," Bode retorted, "as evidenced by his kissing ways."

"I like boys," Lesalle announced suddenly, "rather more than I did last year."

"Lesalle Dent." Bode feigned astonishment. "You're becoming a flirt."

"As if you had any room to talk, Bodewhin Ware," Lesalle volleyed right back. "I heard you laughing under Mat's blanket." Lesalle fell silent, waiting. Bode said nothing. Lesalle levered herself up on one elbow so she could look Bode square in the face and arched one delicately shaped eyebrow in anticipation.

Finally, Bode shrugged. "Mat didn't kiss me." She couldn't quite keep from smiling as she went on. "He did hold me close, though, and he said some things that were nice to hear."

"Mat Bayrd would walk through fire for you, Bode," Lesalle admonished, "and well you know it."

Bode didn't want to talk about her feelings for Mat Bayrd. They were all jumbled but warm and sweet and private. "There will be no living with the two of them now that they've rescued us."

Lesalle flopped back down, sighing blissfully. "Weren't they wonderful? So brave and sure."

"The little darlings did come in handy today." Bode hugged her friend close. "I'll grant you that."

"Jaryd told me I was pretty," Lesalle recounted.

"I heard," Bode replied.

"He was teasing then," Lesalle stated softly. "Later, with his blanket wrapped about us." She paused, giving her shoulders a little shrug. "The way he spoke to me, so gently, I think he meant it." She took a breath and then added, "He told me I was sweet tempered."

"And so you are," Bode affirmed. "Mat said I was clever and pretty too," she put in for good measure.

"I wish I was clever," Lesalle said wistfully.

"You are plenty smart," Bode assured her, "with a good heart, the truest of friends. I wouldn't change you, Lesalle Dent, not one wit."

Lesalle hugged her back. "Still, it would be nice to have gray eyes, the color of a storm-tossed sky."

"And I would like to have blond hair." Bode gently stroked Lesalle's soft tresses. "A burnished amber gold."

"Your spirit," Lesalle offered.

"Your patience," Bode countered.

"If they could smoosh the two of us together," Lesalle said, smiling, "we'd make quite a girl."

Bode smiled in return. "With our luck, we'd wind up with four ears and two noses." Lesalle giggled. Then Bode giggled. And suddenly the two of them couldn't seem to stop giggling. Finally, Bode's mother, Annelle, swept into the room to shush them.

Upon returning to her aunt and uncle's house, Bode went straight to bed. No snow fell that Solstice Eve in Antium City in the Kingdom of Ayle, but there was rain aplenty with some thunder and the occasional splash of lightning. Bode went to sleep thinking of days gone by back in the Three Rivers and of Lesalle and Jaryd and Mat and feelings still jumbled and warm.

10

A Call to Arms

Word reached Deben Bay and the village of Greystock with the arrival of a Tieran warship. A sleek, twin-mast bireme sailed gracefully through the narrow channel of the Neck without requesting a pilot. The name *Falcon*, stenciled across the stern and at both bows, announced her presence. Square-rigged, with two banks of oars and a deadly bronze-covered ram at her prow, the galley looked like the predator she was.

The message she carried to Greystock two weeks following the Winter Solstice in the early days of 1358 came in two parts. The first confirmed rumors that had been flying for weeks; the Tieran civil war, the so-called War of Houses, was over. A great battle fought at a place called Arym on the Morro Peninsula between the Gracci and Sylas factions had proved decisive. Forces under the command of Gaius Sylas Endryk, head of House Sylas, had crushed the Gracci. The Gracci faction leader and two of his three sons lay dead upon the field.

With the Gracci broken, House Dyraii, the only significant contending faction remaining, sued for peace. Terms were swiftly agreed upon, and Gaius Sylas Endryk marched unopposed into the capital. Upon establishing possession of Tier, Gaius lost no time in convening the Chamber and having himself elected emperor.

Seemingly overnight, nearly four decades of internecine warfare ceased. A vast silence had descended. Some said victory celebrations were muted with purpose, out of respect for the fallen. To others, it seemed the empire was holding its breath, waiting to see if the peace, so long sought, would hold.

The second part of the message entailed a more direct concern for the people of Greystock. The territorial militia were to be mustered, some three hundred archers from the vicinity of the village itself, for transport next spring to Tyne City in the province of Quistyn del Aurus. The militiamen were to commit to a one-year term of service that would commence upon their departure for Tyne. The muster order said nothing about what the militia would be doing during its twelve-month deployment.

Aboard the *Falcon* were three veteran sajars, Tieran army regulars, noncommissioned officers, who would oversee training of the militia scheduled to commence as soon as the three hundred archers could be assembled. Also on board was a Tieran army officer, one Barnabus Valarius Glens, a senior regent who would assume overall command of what would become three one-hundred-man companies of auxiliary troops. Local authorities, in this case the Greystock village council, were responsible for filling the muster roll. In addition to the three hundred archers, the muster call required three junior officers, one to command each company.

The method of troop and officer selection was also left to the village council. Village council meetings were usually held in the tap room of the Oak Hill tavern. Due to the short notice, a storage room at the back of Eddard Ware's general store would have to serve for that evening's special session. The people of Greystock had elected Eddard first councilman, and as such, it was his responsibility to chair the meeting. Though he often made light of the council's activities for the amusement of his family around the dinner table, he took his responsibilities seriously. Bickering over the location of a new well in the village might seem like a small thing until a fire broke out. However mundane their usual agenda might be, the decisions they made this night would directly impact the lives of three hundred and three of their friends and neighbors, many of whom were also relatives.

Eddard Ware had attained forty-six years of age. He stood to medium height with a stocky build. He'd spent his youth working in his father's warehouse or pulling an oar on one of the Myr Sea fishing boats. His wife, Annelle, insisted he remained as handsome as ever. While grateful for his wife's good opinion, Eddard knew his light-brown hair was thinning in back and graying at the temples. His wideset gray eyes didn't see as well as they once did close up, and he was beginning to jowl. He could not deny that his age showed. His wife, on the other hand, six years his junior, appeared still as slim hipped as a girl, without a trace of gray in her honey-blond hair, and her captivating blue eyes sparkled more brightly than ever when she smiled.

Eddard had asked Gyros Claudius Ban to attend the meeting as well. In his capacity as an imperially appointed minister, Gyros was not, strictly speaking, a member of the council, but his knowledge of the empire's laws and customs had proven useful on more than one occasion.

Eddard closed his store early this Fourth Night of the week to prepare for the council meeting. Per the Tieran calendar, a week comprised eight days, named simply First Day through Eighth Day. He and his chief clerk, Jakyb Beam, laid a spare sideboard atop some crates in the storage room to use as a table and brought in a few benches that normally sat just outside the main entrance of the store for seating. His wife, Annelle, placed a pair of large earthenware jugs containing apple cider on a shelf under the window along with a bunch of wooden cups. Soft apple cider it was. Eddard wanted none but clear heads this night. Annelle lit two oil lamps, bathing the room in a soft amber light.

Eddard sat on an overturned barrel at the head of the table as the council members filed into the room. Logan Maywell, the smith, came first, followed by Byan Hume and another farmer, Huell Dowtry. The two fishermen on the council, Cable Dallyck and Morgyn Rees, entered next and then the apothecary Dydius Varo Higgs. Gyros Claudius Ban and the lawyer Titus Wilkes were the last to join and walked in together.

With the men gathered, Annelle kissed Eddard lightly on the cheek and walked out, closing the door behind her. "Not very elegant, gentlemen," he said, indicating their surroundings, "but it will have to do."

"The cider's good," the squarely built, mostly bald Huell Dowtry commented, holding aloft one of the wooden mugs, his brown eyes twinkling.

"As we're all here, we may as well get started," Eddard said by way of convening the council meeting. "We've been tasked with selecting three hundred archers and three officers for what this says"—Eddard waved the copy of Barnabus Valarius Glens's orders the senior regent had given him that morning at his fellow council members before laying the paper on the table—"is deployed service."

Eddard swept the room with his eyes, gauging every man. "I've asked Gyros here," he pointed at the caestor, "to answer a couple of questions." His comment engendered a round of hullos and howdys directed at the schoolmaster. "First off, I'd like to know, Gyros, if this action is legal."

"Why would you suspect it is not legal, Eddard?" Titus Wilkes demanded.

"I want to make certain we all understand just what our obligations are here," Eddard replied matter-of-factly. He paused a moment to see if there were anymore questions. Hearing none, he said, "Go ahead, Gyros."

"The short answer to Eddard's question is that, in my opinion, the action is legal," Gyros said gravely. Slightly built, Gyros's hair had gone gray, but his lively brown eyes shone with a keen intelligence.

"I suppose that means we are about to hear the long answer?" Byan Hume asked, to the general amusement of the gathering. Byan stood tall for a Three Rivers man, a fine archer, redheaded and hazel eyed, with a farmer's lean, ropey-muscled build.

"He is the schoolmaster, after all," observed Morgyn Rees.

Morgyn was blond with blue eyes, a hand span or so shorter than Byan but thicker through the shoulders.

Well-known and well-liked by the men present, Gyros, a gentle, urbane scholar, had spent the past twenty years dwelling among hearty frontiersmen.

"Bear with me, gentlemen," Gyros said. "As you know, the Territorial Charter allows the raising of a militia to provide for what is referred to as common defense. This means that per Tieran law, territorials may organize under arms as militia for the purpose of defending their homes and property. This is how militia is traditionally used. However, the charter also stipulates that in the time of war, or should a general emergency be declared, the cognizant imperial authority may deploy militia in support of operations both civil and military at his discretion."

Gyros extracted a sheaf of papers from his tunic pocket and placed them on the table next to the orders Eddard had displayed. "This document bears the seal of the Imperial Chamber, declaring that until rescinded by subsequent action, a general state of emergency exists in all Tieran provinces and territories north of the Middle Sea."

Laying his hands atop the two documents on the table, Gyros concluded, "These documents combine with the Territorial Charter to make the action assigned to you legal. In my opinion, you are obliged by law to comply."

"'Cognizant imperial authority'...I wonder just who it is what wants three hundred odd of us to go traipsing off to Tyne," Byan Hume inquired.

"According to the copy of his orders that Regent Barnabus Valarius Glens left with me, the imperial authority cited is one General Segus Gracci Versi," Eddard answered. "Commander of something called the Northern Expeditionary Force."

"A Gracci general," Cable Dallyck exclaimed. "That don't seem likely the now, does it?"

"It may be," Gyros responded, "merely an indication that the Tieran civil war is indeed over. Assigning Tomas Gracci's only remaining son to a key military role might well be viewed as a gesture of good will." Gyros scratched an ear. "Or perhaps it is a move on our new emperor's part to send a potential political rival as far away from Tier as possible while at the same time giving him something useful to do."

"I thought you were supposed to keep your enemies close," Cable remarked.

"That is certainly conventional wisdom," Gyros agreed. "If nothing else, however, I think our new emperor has demonstrated he is not a conventional thinker."

"This conversation avails us nothing," Titus Wilkes interjected. "And it may be considered impolitic by some." Titus was a tall, homely, narrow-shouldered man with piercing black eyes and iron-gray hair. "As there is no dispute that the action assigned to us is legal, I suggest we get on with it."

"How many Greystock men are currently enrolled in the local militia?" Dydius asked.

"Six hundred and forty-four are on the scroll." Forty-four-year-old Logan Maywell spoke for the first time. The smith was the biggest man in the room, as tall as Byan with wide shoulders and a deep barrel chest with arms nearly the size of Titus's legs. Logan had gentle blue eyes—that is, until he got angry. Fortunately, it took a lot to make Logan Maywell mad. Logan commanded the Greystock militia with the rank of regent.

"Why not simply ask for volunteers?" Titus suggested.

"I'm against that," Eddard said quietly but firmly.

"If," Titus sounded incredulous, "three hundred want to go, why not let them?"

"I have several reasons, Titus." Eddard looked first to the lawyer and then let his gaze sweep the table before continuing. "Principally, I am opposed to asking for volunteers because we do not know where this call to arms will lead. With luck, whatever threat has prompted this action will dissipate soon, and the boys will be home in time to help with the spring planting with nothing more exciting to talk about than the boat ride to Tyne and back. But if the worst happens and what we are met here tonight to discuss is only the first peal of thunder in a tempest soon to be raging about us, we'll need some of those who would volunteer to stay close and help weather the storm that follows."

"We cannot simply pick and choose," Dydius stated. "The officers maybe but not all three hundred."

"We haven't the right to do that," Eddard agreed. He found himself thinking of his son, Ayden, drowned—sweet God, could it be—nearly seven years ago. Ayden had been his eldest, his only son. Sometimes the now, he would go an entire day and not think of him. When recall he did, the pain he felt and the sense of loss never seemed to fade, not a jot. Eddard knew all too well what they, what he, might be asking of others.

"Each man on the muster scroll is a qualified archer," Logan said. "We could draw lots among them. The three hundred selected will stand for deployed service."

"Those on the muster roll have already sworn to serve if called," Morgyn commented. "That sounds fair to me."

"Most of them are scarcely more than boys," Cable Dallyck noted.

"As is ever the case with war or the threat of war." Eddard rubbed his hands together. "Shall we put it to a vote?"

The results, much to Eddard's relief, were unanimous. The three hundred militiamen Greystock stood obliged to supply for deployed service would be drawn by lot from among those currently enrolled on the muster scroll. The lottery would be held the following day at sundown in the temple courtyard.

"I'll speak with Father Vars," Eddard said. "But I'm sure it will be all right with him. The courtyard is large enough to accommodate any who want to attend in person." He introduced the next topic of discussion. "We still need to choose three officers."

"I'll go," Byan Hume declared without hesitation. In answer to the looks cast his way, Byan continued, "Someone from the village council should go. An older man among them will help steady the boys, and I'm the best archer in the room."

"You're the best archer in the Three Rivers," Logan said flatly.

"We'll need to raise and train more men, more bowmen, to replace those called for deployment. You'd come in handy for that."

Smiling at the big smith, Byan replied, "A man can be taught how to properly press a bow in an afternoon. Most of the lads around here know that much before they start school. From there, it is a matter of practice. What counts is learning how to stand together. You are the man to teach them that, and we all know it."

Looking about the room, Byan added, "Besides, I've never been to Tyne. I'd like to have a look. My eldest, Jaryd, is attending the Hall in Antium just across the Donn Narrows. With luck, I'll be able to arrange a visit."

"Soon as she hears, Nan is liable to skin you," Huell Dowtry remarked. "And then come looking for the rest of us." Annette Hume was Byan's wife. Everyone called her Nan.

"She won't like it much, I guess," Byan agreed. "But she'll see the sense in it, boys. It makes sense for me to go."

"Two left to choose," Eddard said, sealing the discussion. They settled on two current militia officers, Lyjah Bowen and Gyl Tanner. Both were farmers in their late twenties, married, with plenty of family close by to help while they were away.

"I'll notify them first thing in the morning," Logan said.

As the meeting broke up, Byan turned to his neighbor Huell. "You'll look in on Nan and the boys while I'm away?" While his firstborn, Jaryd, attended the Hall in Antium, Byan's three younger sons were still at home. Micah, nearly eighteen and lucky enough to look like his blond-haired mother, was his second son. Branyck, sixteen, and Oryn, the youngest at fourteen, had hair as red as his own. Good lads they were and farmers all. Jaryd the now, he was meant for something else. Nan saw that before he had.

"Those boys of yours can handle your place and mine too." Huell grinned. "But you know I will visit now and again. Nan's a fine cook."

It was late by the time Byan Hume got home. When he entered the house after putting his horse up in the barn, he found Nan still awake, waiting for him. Nan was long-legged and tall for a woman, too tall to be fashionable. She remained slim hipped despite having born him four fine sons. Nan had green eyes to go along with her sandy-blond hair. They'd been virgins, lying together for the first time a few months before they were wed. She remained the only woman he'd ever been with. At thirty-nine, she was three years younger than he. They'd been married for twenty-one years. Byan figured she knew him better than he knew himself.

By the light of a single candle in their bedroom, he told her of the village council meeting and what had been decided. Nan sat at the edge of their bed and listened quietly until he finished. Then she began to cry.

Sitting by her side, he put an arm around her, saying, "Easy there, gal, take it easy."

After a bit, Nan drew still and wiped her tears, scrubbing a hand across her face. "You are a good man," she told him. "I love you, and I've always been proud to be your wife, never more so than the now. But…" She took a deep, ragged breath. "Damn your eyes, Byan Hume, damn your eyes."

He kissed her then, and passion flared between them. Their lovemaking was more intense than it had been in a while. Together they lay afterward, arms and legs entwined beneath a pair of quilted blankets that had both been wedding presents. They talked softly of small things, the boys, the farm, and their parents, as if, by invoking shared memories of the sweetest parts of their life together, they could forestall the coming dawn.

At sundown the following day, Father Vars Nebus Bayu said a brief prayer before beginning to draw numbered bits of clay from a large iron kettle set upon a sturdy wooden table at the foot of the steps behind the temple. The backside landing, or portico, as it was formally known, of the temple overlooked the courtyard, a large, lawn-covered park with trees lining its perimeter. Often the people of Greystock employed the space to stage picnics, outdoor dances, and wedding celebrations. The courtyard was full this day. Nearly the entire village had turned out to observe the lottery. Some had come from pure curiosity. Most, he knew, were there to honor those who would be called to serve. An array of standing torches spread throughout lit the courtyard's green space.

Vars wore his robe of office made of dove-gray winnowed wool with the symbol of his Penitent faith, an all-seeing eye, embroidered on the back over a pair of linen tunics cut in the Tieran style. Even so, he could still feel the chill at the close of this winter's day. *I'm likely getting old,* he thought. He smiled wryly. *Old indeed.* For twenty years, he served the church in this quiet village that showed such promise, waiting and watching for a spark, one that could be fanned to a mighty flame. So far, he had watched in vain. Had he misjudged yet again? Twenty years was too long in one place. He would have to move on soon.

Slightly built, Father Vars was of medium height. Largely bald the now, he kept the hair that remained to him—across his temples, above his ears, and around the back of his head—neatly trimmed. His fringe, as he'd come to think of it, showed stately gray in color. His dark-blue eyes were wideset, kind, and crinkly, or so he understood fair, young Bodewhin Ware had described them. About his neck on a silver chain dangled a medallion also emblazoned with the Eye of the All Father. He had purposely curtailed the invocation before beginning, saying only a few words in prayer. The air teemed this night with too much feeling for overlong speech of any kind.

Reaching into the kettle, he withdrew the first clay shard. Logan Maywell and Eddard Ware sat at a second table next to the one bearing the kettle with the militia scroll spread out before them. Each name on the scroll had a number assigned to it.

Vars looked down at the shard in his hand. "The first number is one hundred sixty-seven."

Logan ran a thick finger down the scroll, and Eddard double checked him. Drawing a breath, Eddard pitched his voice to carry across the courtyard. "Mathias Bayrd is the first called."

11

Acquaintances

Jaryd Hume relished time spent with Uncle Spats, the head gardener at Antium Hall. Spats could be cranky, and he didn't suffer fools with any sort of grace. The other gardeners and staff, including, Jaryd noted, the speakers themselves, tended to walk softly around the old man. While mistakes were quickly pointed out, and any necessary correction came short and sharp, Jaryd found Spats equally quick to praise a job well done.

Bode seemed to enjoy the rascally gardener's company as well. She visited often, and the three of them shared several evenings talking. Topics were wide-ranging, and if anything, Spats appeared more interested in learning their perspectives than in conveying his own. Spats would usually close out the visit by regaling them with some tall tale or a bit of history with a twist or two they'd never heard about before passing along his heavy walking stick and sending Jaryd off to escort Bode home.

One day, Spats surprised Jaryd, appearing as if conjured, carrying a pair of quarterstaffs. Busy pruning roses, Jaryd failed to hear Spats's soft-footed approach.

Tossing one of the oak staves to Jaryd, Spats said, "It's about time I found out if you know how to use one of these things, just in case, for Bode's sake, that is."

Like most boys and young men in the Three Rivers, Jaryd had sparred with a quarterstaff. In addition to arming themselves with long bows, the Greystock militia also carried an array of short-hafted pole arms such as pole axes or halberds should they be called upon to engage at close quarters. Learning to handle a quarterstaff proved good training for wielding a short-hafted pole arm as many of the basic strikes and parries were similar.

At first, Jaryd engaged Spats with some reluctance, but after quickly being thumped a couple of times, he discovered the old gardener made deft use of the weapon.

Seemingly in defiance of his age, Spats remained remarkably quick and supple. His technique was much superior to Jaryd's. *It looks like Spats has something else to teach me,* Jaryd thought. *At least we're doing this in private. It's embarrassing getting whipped this badly by an old codger.* After working up a mutual sweat, which resulted in Spats giving Jaryd a couple of bruises, the gardener called a halt to the proceedings.

"Well," Spats commented, "you're quick enough and stronger than you look. With a little practice, you might become someone to reckon with."

The next day, after Jaryd returned from attending lecture, Spats met him at the door of the cottage, saying, "Come on. There is something I want to show you." Spats led him a short way down one of the garden paths to a small, gray, stone building. Jaryd recognized the structure as one of the oldest on the Hall grounds, dating to a period well before the founding of the Hall itself. The rectangular building was constructed of stone blocks apparently fitted together without the benefit of concrete or any form of mortar at all. A small portico fronted the building, shading a wooden door. Much newer, obviously not part of the original construction, the door was equipped with a modern keylock. Extracting a ring of keys from his tunic, Spats fitted one into the door lock, turned the key, and then opened the portal.

Sunlight flooded the interior of the building, which turned out to be a sparsely furnished room that reflected the rectangular shape of its exterior. A pair of oil lamps sat on a wooden table near the door, and in the center of the room, a low, three-sided stone wall girded the opening to a stairway leading downward into darkness. Lighting a bit of tender using flint and steel from another pocket of his tunic, Spats used it to set alight one of the lamps. Motioning Jaryd to follow, Spats started down the stairs. The steps were cut and lined using the same gray stone as the outer structure and spiraled downward to a depth that Jaryd estimated must be two or three times his height.

At the base of the stairway stood a second locked wooden door bracketed by a pair of torches set into the wall on either side. Taking a taper from a wall-mounted shelf, Spats set it alight using the flame of the oil lamp and then lit the torches.

Handing one of the brands to Jaryd, Spats took the other and, setting the oil lamp aside, remarked, "We're almost there the now."

The second door opened into a short corridor that led to a third locked portal, this one crafted from what appeared to be heavy iron bars. Passing through the third door, Jaryd accompanied Spats into a large subterranean chamber, bigger than the stone building above. Surprised, Jaryd discovered the room partially lit. Sunlight from without must have been channeled into the enclosure by some means. Spats busied himself lighting several large candles fixed to sturdy iron stands spread throughout the storage compartment. In the soft light, Jaryd saw that the chamber stood filled with shelves and cabinets, iron-bound chests and wicker baskets all stuffed with books and clothing, tools and pottery, carvings of wood and stone and ivory, and small statuaries, most of which looked as if they had been hewn from marble. Maps covered one wall nearby, and Jaryd noticed a large gathering of weapons in racks or suspended from pegs lining a second.

The array of weaponry included a collection of swords and knives, pole axes, spears and halberds, and a number of long bows. One in particular immediately drew Jaryd's attention. Unstrung, the bow hung suspended from a set of pegs in the wall. It appeared to be constructed of laminated wood in the manner of a Three Rivers hunter and featured the distinct curved shape at both ends of the bow stave. What attracted Jaryd's eye, however, was not the familiar shape but rather its color: rich ebony strains ran through the wood. Most hunters showed a light, tawny blond reflecting the natural color of the ash and golden yew from which they were made. This bow displayed black swirls threaded throughout the deep, honey-colored hue of the stave flowing with the grain of the wood.

Following the younger man's gaze, Spats smiled and said, "Beautiful, isn't it?"

"It looks like a Three Rivers hunter," Jaryd observed.

"If you say so." Spats chuckled. "I assure you it is not." He selected a quiver full of arrows with gray goose feather fletching from an adjacent rack. Handing the quiver to Jaryd, he continued. "You'll find suitable bowstrings in the pockets of this quiver. I think you should give that bow a try as it obviously suits your eye. See how it draws in comparison with one of your vaunted Three Rivers weapons."

"Are you sure it is all right that I do so?" Jaryd wondered.

"I am steward of this chamber," Spats assured him. "One of what Speaker Regys calls my irregular duties. It functions as an archive of sorts. I think the bow will serve a better purpose in your hands than it will sitting hidden away down here. Just to play safe, don't tell anyone where you got it. If anybody asks, say it belonged to your grandpa or some such."

Jaryd nodded and lifted the bow from its pegs. The weapon felt as if it were made to fit his hand.

"Do you see anything else that catches your eye, lad?" Spats inquired.

Jaryd ran his gaze along the weapons wall. Knives there were aplenty, but he didn't think a better one in the world existed than the Hawken that had been his grandfather's, stowed away in his quarters at the gardeners' cottage. Swords, of course, were not unknown to Three Rivers folk, but they held little appeal for him. Pole axes, bills, and halberds all looked familiar. Those displayed before him appeared to be finely crafted.

His eye fell upon a strange-looking spear—at least that is what he thought it was—left simply leaning against the stone wall. Instead of a more typical leaf-shaped or triangular spearhead, the dark-hafted weapon featured a large single-edged blade, gently curved in a concave fashion, nearly a hand's span wide at its broadest point. About two span in length, the blade reminded him somehow of a sickle, although it was not as deeply curved as the farming implement and was tapered to a well-defined point perfectly aligned with the haft. Ebony black, the haft seemed to absorb the candlelight. He noticed a spiked tip riveted to the butt end. The butt spike looked to be fashioned from the same gray-toned steel as the blade at the head of the weapon.

"What is that?" Jaryd asked.

"Ah," Spats responded. "It is called a styaxe, an elegant weapon of ancient origin, once wielded by the Guidons of old. Elite warriors, the Guidons were sworn to uphold honor and protect the lives of sorcerers with which they were paired. Sorcerers being sorcerers, doing both jobs simultaneously must have been quite a feat." Spats pointed to the elegantly curved length of steel that formed the head of the styaxe. "The blade and butt spike are power wrought, the Yir infused into the metal while being forged. Power-wrought steel will never rust, and while a sorcerer well-schooled in battle arts may ward against it, doing so is draining, even for those highly skilled."

"How can you be certain this is one such weapon?" Jaryd questioned.

"To a knowing eye, the gray cast to the finished steel is unmistakable," Spats answered. The white-haired gardener scratched his chin. "Power-wrought steel is also the bane of dark spawn, wyrbeasts and such, creatures born of the twisted arts."

"I thought wyrbeasts were the stuff of nightmares," Jaryd exclaimed.

"So they are but no less real for all that," Spats said evenly. "Here, let me take those," he indicated the bow and quiver, "and see how it feels."

Handing the bow stave and quiver to the old gardener, Jaryd grasped the black haft of the styaxe. About six span in overall length, the pole arm weighed less than he expected, and the balance felt perfect. Two hands would be necessary to wield it properly.

"The styaxe handles like a quarterstaff," Spats continued. "You can both cut and thrust with the blade, and the butt spike makes a reverse stroke equally deadly."

"A bow can be employed to feed your family," Jaryd spoke softly. "A knife or an axe has many uses. But this"—he held the styaxe aloft—"is meant for only one purpose: to kill men. It is beautiful and terrible."

"An apt description of mankind itself, don't you think?" Spats said just as quietly. "I believe the men who forged that weapon were determined to fight for something they loved more than life. I suppose that makes it no less terrible. But intent must count for something, if not in this world then in the next."

Jaryd grinned. "You sound like a young blacksmith I know back home."

"Smithing is hard, hot work," Spats remarked.

"While trimming hedges, on the other end, is pure joy?" Jaryd grinned.

Choosing not to respond directly, Spats said, "Talking philosophy makes me hungry. Bring the styaxe with you, and let's go see if we can find something to eat."

The following week, after their third practice session with the styaxe, Spats sent Jaryd to the Antium library to find, if he could, the medicinal purposes of the herb patchouli, a green, leafy plant that originated in the Elven Isles. Jaryd headed for the library on a bright but brisk midwinter afternoon. He was clad in a cream-colored, long-sleeved linen shirt over which he wore the distinctive green woolen tunic of the Hall gardeners. Both garments reached a hand span or so below mid-thigh. The outer tunic bore, embroidered on the breast, the crossed lightning bolts that symbolized the Hall of Learning at Antium.

He supposed he could have changed but decided the gardeners' tunic, both warm and reasonably clean, suited well enough. No formal attire was required to enter the library, and as he intended to walk straight there and back, it seemed simpler just to go dressed as he was. A pair of thick, homespun, woolen socks and sturdy Three Rivers sandals covered his feet. A broad leather belt girded his waist, while a gray wrap knit from winnowed wool draped over his shoulders. A matching gray woolen scarf wound loosely about his neck, and he had a woolen mitten stuffed into each of the pockets of his outer tunic.

Attached to his belt on the left side, Jaryd carried his Hawken, sheathed. A full span in length and three fingers wide at the base, the Hawken blade may have stretched the definition of a belt knife some, but no one had ever said anything to him about it on previous trips into the city. Over his shoulder, Jaryd had slung a leather satchel containing pen, ink, and some writing paper.

The library basked in the wan winter sunlight near the Hall grounds, so he didn't have far to travel. The day before, Jaryd had taken one written and one oral examination. Both tests were in courses pertaining to civil law. He thought he had performed well on the oral exam. At least the speaker seemed satisfied with his responses, most of them anyway. He was less certain about the written test. With some effort, he had managed not to think too much about the exam questions in the time since turning in his paper. As he could do nothing about it the now, Jaryd wanted to put the exam out of his mind until the graded papers were returned.

Founded nearly fifty years prior to the opening of the Hall and almost a century before construction of the Gyft Ryll, the great Library of Antium sat atop its little hill with quiet dignity, a massive, three-story rectangular building faced in white marble. Most of its inner walls framed open-air courtyards, the enclosed book wells that surrounded them fashioned of brick. The oldest portion of the library, known as the Stone Rook, encompassed entirely by more recent construction, was built from beautifully carved sandstone blocks so closely fitted that even a piece of vellum could not be slipped between them.

Striding quickly across the lobby of the Stone Rook, Jaryd climbed a flight of stairs leading to the second floor of the main building, where he knew materials pertaining to the study of natural philosophy were kept. As he entered one of the book stalls, the so-far suppressed memory of a written exam question popped unbidden into his mind along with what he felt certain composed the correct response. Unfortunately, his submitted answer did not match it.

Bending over a battered wooden table in the center of the book stall, he gripped the edges with both hands and muttered, "You remember the now, for all the good that will do."

"Do you always talk to the furniture?" An amused voice, softly feminine, greeted his pained utterance.

Jaryd looked up to see a fair-skinned young woman standing near the back of the stall with a pair of books hugged close to her chest. A window set high in the wall above allowed the weak winter sun to light the chamber. The girl wore a dress of a type he had not seen before: a snug-fitting, short-sleeved bodice above a full skirt that fell to about mid-calf. The garment appeared to be made of cotton, a light green in color. He found himself gazing into a pair of large, slightly tilted brown eyes. Her hair shone a lustrous honey blond, arranged in an elaborate single braid, the tail of which she had looped over one shoulder. The books she clutched in her arms obscured a direct view of her upper torso. Slender she was, though, her features fine and regular, with a small, straight nose and a full-lipped mouth. She smiled at him, and the warmth of the expression lit her eyes.

"Tables mostly," Jaryd said. "Chairs are not nearly as sympathetic. I suppose that comes from being sat on all the time." He ventured a return smile.

"Do the tables and chairs talk back?" she inquired, arching one golden eyebrow as she did so.

"So far, the conversation has been pretty one-sided," Jaryd allowed. "There is the occasional creak but not much else."

"So I should not be concerned that you are standing between me and the exit?" the blonde asked.

"Left to my own devices, I'm harmless enough," Jaryd responded.

"That is reassuring." She set the books down on the table and turned to fetch a cloak she had draped over the back of a chair standing nearby, revealing clear evidence, Jaryd thought, of a pleasingly well-rounded bosom in the process.

"My name is Jaryd Hume," he said to forestall her departure.

She did pause, holding the gray woolen cloak in her hands. "Mine is Dyrileah Quirow. It was a pleasure to meet you, Jaryd Hume. I think."

Searching for something to say that might extend their conversation a bit, Jaryd informed her, "I am attending the Hall."

"You attend the Hall while wearing a gardener's tunic?" She sounded surprised.

"As a matter of fact, I do," Jaryd answered. He then asked, "Are you a student there as well?"

Dyrileah straightened as suddenly as if he'd pinched her bottom. Quickly wrapping the cloak about her shoulders, she picked up the books and started to walk past him. "Good day," she said in a voice as stiff as her posture.

Stepping in front of her, with his hands held at shoulder height in supplication, Jaryd implored, "Wait, please. Don't go. If I've offended you, it was not my intent."

Dyrileah stopped and stood looking up at him. She was, he decided, about Bode's height and very nearly as lovely. "I am Elsacian." She spoke as if that declaration would explain everything. "Please step aside."

"I've only ever met one Elsacian," Jaryd told her, speaking sincerely but without moving. "She is very pretty but tends to get mad in a hurry, and I'm afraid I still don't know why."

Dyrileah's eyes locked onto his. "There are only the two of us here. Why would you mock me, Jaryd Hume?"

"I'm a farmer's son from the Three Rivers." Jaryd spoke gently as if he were trying to calm a fractious mare. "I may still have hay in my hair, but I was raised to mock no one."

"The Three Rivers." Dyrileah mulled that piece of information over for a moment. "This is a Tieran possession out west, is it not?"

"The Three Rivers is a Tieran territory," Jaryd confirmed. "My home is near the village of Greystock on the northwestern coast of the Myr Sea."

"According to the laws of Ayle," Dyrileah said, her voice softening, "no Elsacian may attend Antium Hall." She hesitated a moment and then went on. "The library, on the other hand, is open to all, even one of my blood."

"Hay in hair and, it appears, foot in mouth." Jaryd spoke in a self-deprecating tone. "Not the impression I was hoping to make. I am sorry."

"You truly did not know?" Dyrileah queried softly. Jaryd shook his head. "Then it is I who should apologize," she concluded.

"That is so, isn't it?" Jaryd's smile returned.

"You needn't look so pleased." Dyrileah dropped her eyes. He spied the corners of her mouth tug slightly upward.

"Do you know anything about herbs?" Jaryd asked hopefully.

"I have a great interest in herbs," Dyrileah declared briskly. "Why do you ask?"

"The head gardener at the Hall dispatched me here—to the library, that is—to see if I could discover the medicinal properties of an herb called patchouli," Jaryd explained. "You wouldn't know where I might look, would you?"

"Patchouli is a tender, aromatic herb that has upright, square stems with soft, oval leaves and whorls of whitish flowers on spikes." Dyrileah spoke as if informing him that the summer sun was hot at noon. "In Ilyria, the Elves use it as a stimulant and an antiseptic, an insect repellent, and as a remedy for venomous snake and insect bites. It is given for headaches, flatulence, vomiting, diarrhea, and fever. The essential oil has a penetrating cedar-like smell. The Elves incorporate it into both incense and perfume."

"Would you mind writing that down?" Jaryd hoped he sounded suitably impressed. "I lost you at flatulence."

Dyrileah laughed briefly and hesitated only a moment before slipping out of her cloak to take a seat at the table. "I'll talk. You write. How's that? You do have something to write with, don't you?"

"I do indeed," Jaryd said, happy to occupy a seat beside her. Dyrileah repeated her description of the herb and its uses. When she'd finished, Jaryd read his notes back to her to confirm their accuracy and then asked, "You wouldn't be pulling my leg, would you? If I show up with this, and it turns out patchouli is only good for flavoring stew or something, Spats will box my ears."

"The information I've given you is accurate, farm boy," Dyrileah quipped. "Any decent apothecary should be able to tell you the same. I doubt patchouli will grow here. The winters are too cold."

"Spats intends to try to grow the herb indoors in something he calls a glass house, city girl," Jaryd replied. "I haven't seen the thing yet, this glass house, so I have no idea what he's talking about."

"Who exactly is this fellow Spats?" Dyrileah wondered. This provided Jaryd with an opportunity to launch into a couple of his favorite Spats stories. His rendition left Dyrileah laughing out loud.

Not wanting to anger her or dampen her mood but feeling that he had to know, Jaryd took a breath and then posed the question, "Just who are you Elsacians, and why is it against the law for you to attend the Hall?"

Dyrileah gazed for a long moment into his eyes before looking off into the middle distance and answered, "Those who rule here in this place they have renamed after themselves are not the first inhabitants of this land. The Ayle are descendants of the Gehdai, a northern tribe who also gave rise to the Madryns of Tyne. My people, the Elsacians, are also immigrants, although we came across the Middle Sea from the Basyr Peninsula, not as conquerors but as artisans by invitation of the Dalwhin, who governed here in the time of the old kingdoms."

Dyrileah's voice was soft and sad. She peered again into his eyes. "You are taking no notes, Jaryd Hume."

Listening intently, Jaryd responded, "I've a feeling I won't be able to forget the tale you tell even if I wanted to."

Nodding but without looking away, she continued. "The Ayle came down from the northeast like ravening wolves. In that time, they were known as the Horse Lords. There was war and slaughter. Many of my people were spared in the end. After all, we were glassmakers, apothecaries, and silversmiths, not warriors. Over time, the Dalwhin who survived were absorbed into the general population. We Elsacians remained apart, separated by our ethnicity and our faith. We are Diadyms out of the east, followers of the Trascera

Mother." She paused and stared deeply into his eyes as if searching for something. He kept his gaze steady on hers. Seek first to understand, wasn't that something Spats had told him recently? Her eyes, so sad and so wary, compelled him to listen. He wanted with a sudden sense of urgency to comprehend not only what she was trying to tell him but why.

"Please go on," Jaryd prompted gently.

She did so while continuing to look only into his eyes. "For generations, my people lived and labored under the Ayle as they had the Dalwhin. The Penitent reformation changed everything. Before that time, those who ruled here were pagans, believers in many gods. Our God, Almyr, numbered but one among a pantheon. The Elsacian belief that she stands the only true God was considered nothing more than a benign aberration. Afterward, there remained room for only one god, the Penitent god, this All Father of yours. Today, we are heretics in this land that has so long been our home. Our faith is unclean, and so we are banned from holding public office or attending the Hall. Some guilds will still accept us; others will not."

She finally looked away, and her voice strengthened. "We have become highly skilled, however; the goods and services we proffer are more valuable than ever. And so we are tolerated, at least for the time being, provided we are willing to live in the shadows and stay silent." Dyrileah could not keep the bitterness from her voice as she said, "Invisibility is our best defense because even the devout find it difficult to be offended by something or someone they do not see."

Jaryd did not know what to say and so remained silent. "Is it I who have the now offended you, Jaryd Hume?" Dyrileah asked.

"No, I am not offended," Jaryd assured her. He took one of Dyrileah's hands in his own. Her hand felt small, soft, and fine boned. Holding it reminded him of clasping an injured sparrow he'd picked up once as a boy. She did not pull away, and he went on. "I am of the Penitent faith. Back home, we have Redeemers and Brynnai among us and even some Saryns." Redeemers were an offshoot of the Penitent faith who believed a place in heaven could only be won by experiencing redemption while living. The process of redemption culminated in a ceremony Redeemers called Rebirth. Redeemers believed the All Father would one day send a Messenger, a High Holy One, to redeem the sins of man.

Jaryd paused, searching for the right words. "They're just people, like us I mean, except that we and they go to different temples on First Day. I guess I've never thought much about it—other faiths, that is—until the now."

Dyrileah phrased her next question quietly. "Have you reached any conclusions?"

"Back home, Father Vars says you cannot separate love and faith and that both should be leavened with tolerance and mercy." Jaryd fancied he could hear Father Vars Nebus Bayu speaking in that light, clear voice of his. "I'm opposed to anything or anyone who would seek to make you invisible," he added with conviction.

Dyrileah dropped her eyes and blushed, which pleased him mightily. She at last seemed to become aware that he was holding her hand. She gently disengaged. "That last bit does not sound particularly logical."

"It's honest anyhow," Jaryd retorted. "Do you frequent the library?"

"I do," Dyrileah affirmed. "I'm here most every Third Day afternoon."

"Would it be all right with you if we were to meet here again, accidently say, in order that we may speak some more?" Jaryd asked.

"Somehow I doubt my people would think that a very good idea." Dyrileah's voice again sounded suddenly soft and sad. "Most would say foolish, even."

"That isn't what I asked," Jaryd pressed firmly.

Smiling, Dyrileah looked him squarely in the eye once more. "I suppose it would be all right as long as it is by accident. My mother says most of the best things in life happen by accident."

12
Gone a-Dancing

Soft music filled the candlelit hall. Stars sparkled without, amid a chill winter night, as frost rimmed the windows and icicles clung to the iron railing of the balustrade that surrounded the building. Located on Dowd Street in one of Antium's more affluent neighborhoods, the Builders' Guild Hall often served as a public gathering place. The Builders' Gala had become a featured part of what city dwellers referred to the now as the midwinter festival.

From her seat at a table beneath a corner window, Bodewhin Ware of Greystock Village in the Three Rivers glanced up into the sky-blue eyes of Eddard Bly. She saw them crinkle with amusement.

"I insist," Eddard reiterated. "You must call me Ned." Tall, dark-haired, blessed with a firm, square jaw, a generous, full-lipped mouth, and an unmistakable air of self-confidence Eddard climbed to his feet and extended his hand. Wide-shouldered and athletically built, he moved effortlessly. Clad in a finely tailored woolen waistcoat and trousers of pearl gray worn over a cream-colored silk shirt, Ned looked every bit of him like the young scion of Ayle nobility that he was. Bode rose and slipped her hand into his.

"My father's name is Eddard," Bode informed him. *Papa can't abide being called, Ned.* The thought rippled through Bode's mind as Eddard Bly released her hand only to then place his at the small of her back, guiding her gently but surely toward the dance floor.

"And what do people call him for short?" Ned wondered.

"Eddard," Bode replied, gray eyes twinkling as she peered up at him over her left shoulder.

"He sounds formidable." Ned's answering smile seemed familiar to her, reflecting as it did the same mischievous aspect as one of Jaryd Hume's smiles, except none of Jaryd's smiles ever caused the nervous flutter just the now rippling through her stomach. "An option I'm afraid not available to the second son of a minor noble." Ned's mouth twisted slightly into a wry cast. "Superfluous is more my style."

Bode stepped onto the polished hardwood dance floor. "I doubt any of us are completely necessary."

"True enough, I suppose," Ned allowed, "but not exactly comforting."

Still smiling, Bode turned to face him. "You certainly are decorative."

Ned's smile stretched easily into a grin. "Look who is talking."

Bode said nothing, but her chin dipped demurely. Dressed as she was in a pale-green cotton frock that featured a velvet bodice of a slightly darker shade, with her long walnut-colored tresses piled atop her head, Bode could not help but feel the neckline plunged in a manner slightly too daring. According to her aunt, both her hair and the cut of Bode's dress reflected only the latest fashion.

Placing his right hand at her waist, Ned took her right in his left. His fingers felt calloused and strong wrapped about hers but gentle for all that. With a slight nod of accord, they stepped together into the flow of the dance.

"What do they call you for short, I wonder?" Ned speculated. "It wouldn't be Bodewhin, would it?"

"You know very well my friends call me Bode," she chided. They whirled in time with the music.

"And if my ambition is to be more than friend," Ned inquired gently, "what then?"

"Start with Bode," she replied firmly, "and mind your manners."

"Would it be impolite," Ned started as he led her adroitly into the next turn, "to ask after that blacksmith of yours. Metteos Bird, was it?"

"Mathias Bayrd," Bode corrected him. "Truth to tell, I've not heard from him in some time."

Bode had received no letter from Mat since her return to Antium in the fall. A couple of weeks after the Winter Solstice, she had received a package from her father. A note accompanying the package apprised her that Mat had been recently raised to the black apron, and the brief message also said enclosed she would find a Solstice gift for her from him. Inside, she discovered a pair of ear fobs. Fashioned of silver, they were crafted in a gentle swirling shape with a small sapphire at the center of each. *Simple*, Bode thought, *but beautifully wrought. How like Mat.* She'd received no word from him, though, not a line. *How unlike Mat.* The thought rankled. *Why had he not written?*

"I trust he is well." Bode detected a serious note threaded through Ned's jocular tone.

"Well enough, I'm sure," she replied. Her father's letter clearly indicated Mat fared well in health and with respect to his employ under Master Maywell.

"If he has become inattentive to you," Ned proclaimed, "he's a dunderhead."

"He is anything but," Bode countered.

As the music faded, Ned escorted Bode back toward her seat. Glancing up, she saw her cousin Michaela being returned as well, accompanied by a slender, dark-haired young man in a finely tailored, brown silk suit. She noticed her Aunt Rayleen looking on with an air of approval. *Michaela must have latched onto a good 'un.* Bode promptly regretted the thought, however accurate it might be.

"This is intolerable," Ned announced. "If you are seen in my company looking so careworn, my reputation will be ruined."

Bode's eyes warmed. "How may I make amends?"

"By accompanying me into yonder alcove," Ned replied immediately. He pointed toward a series of arched window enclosures lining the far side of the room. "I have arranged for some biscuits and a passable bottle of wine."

In no hurry to rejoin her aunt, Bode stopped and turned, laying a hand lightly on Ned's forearm. "That sounds delightful."

Ned's smile teased. "A note of caution," he warned. "Slipping unescorted into one of those alcoves with the likes of me, while not entirely scandalous, is liable to raise a few eyebrows."

"Just as well." Bode's eyes took on a determined cast. "Raising a few eyebrows would suit me fine."

"As daring as you are lovely," Ned enthused. "Luck seems to be with me this night." He offered her his arm. Bode slid the fingers of her left hand inside his right arm and placed them at the bend of his elbow.

"Charm is your principal advantage, sir," Bode informed him.

"That sounds bloody improbable," Ned responded, "but I'll not dispute ye." Together they made their way to a curtain-shrouded window alcove at the near end of the ballroom.

A stocky-looking fellow in a plain brown broadcloth jacket and trousers standing to one side of the arch greeted Ned with a smile. "Good evening, sir."

"So far, Jackson, an enchanted one," Ned replied with an answering smile and slipped a silver coin into the man's wide palm.

Ned swept aside the curtains, and Bode stepped within to find a small wooden table placed beneath a large, multipaned window. A bottle of wine and a wicker basket loaded with small golden-brown cakes drizzled with honey sat atop the table along with a pair of tall-stemmed glasses.

"Confident were you, sir?" Bode leveled a direct look Ned's way.

Gazing into those thundercloud depths, Ned smiled once more. "Only of making the attempt, my lady."

"You appear to be well prepared," Bode noted.

"Nothing ventured, as they say." Ned shrugged. "I figured if worse came to worst, I could take on a bit of wine and a few biscuits and rest my feet awhile."

Bode walked to the table and stood gazing out the window. Ned joined her, standing at Bode's side.

"Someone should have warned you about blacksmiths," Ned proffered.

"I've heard that before, those very words." Bode's smile appeared shadowed, touched by sadness. "Too late then as the now." She laid her hand on his arm. "But no less appreciated for all that."

"If old Matted Beard manages to break your heart," Ned vowed, "I'll gut him like a fish."

"Mathias Bayrd," Bode said automatically and then raised her eyes to his. "You're a fraud, Ned Bly."

Ned put his arms around her. "Aye, well, I'll give him a bloody good talking to anyhow."

"That's not what I meant." Bode accepted his embrace. "Everyone says you are a rogue, a beguiler of young women. You are too kind by half for such as that."

"I wouldn't be too sure," Ned demurred, "and the now, by your own admission, you can't claim not to have been warned."

Taking her gently by her upper arms, Ned leaned Bode away just far enough to bring his mouth down upon hers. His lips felt warm and surprisingly soft, his kiss more tender than passionate, offering more than demanding. Bode's eyelids slid shut as if of their own volition. She'd had been kissed by a few young men along the way. None but Mat's kisses had ever caused her to want more. Ned lifted his mouth away. His kiss had filled her with longing, swathed in layers of guilt, not so much wanting as wondering, *is there something here?*

With some difficulty, Bode pushed the thought aside. She opened her eyes to find Ned's beaming down intently. "Now there," he breathed, "is a sight to see."

Bode felt the blush color her cheeks. "There may be a bit more rogue in you than I thought after all," she allowed.

Ned's eyes glimmered. "This would nay be half the fun if that were not the case."

Later that same evening, Bode and her cousin Michaela met in Bode's bedroom to discuss the events of the day.

"Isn't Ned Bly handsome?" Bode's blond-haired cousin fairly gushed.

"I think we've established that, Michaela." Bode smiled into the mirror affixed to the wall at the back of her dressing table. In its reflection, she saw her cousin, clad only in a white silk shift covered by a thin cotton robe.

"His friend Jehan is rather good-looking too," Michaela put in slyly, fiddling with the sash of her robe. "Don't you think?"

Bode's smile stretched. *So that's the way the wind blows the now, is it?* "I think so," Bode affirmed. "And if what I've heard is true, young Jehan Broward is even wealthier."

"But not of noble birth," Michaela lamented.

A determined lass, my cousin, Bode thought. "A common affliction," she teased. "One we share."

"Curable, though," Michaela volleyed in return, "at least in your case, with a little effort."

"If we are still discussing Eddard Bly," Bode retorted, "I fear the cure may prove worse than the disease." Clad in an old cotton shift with a wrap of winnowed wool draped over her shoulders, Bode continued to run the brush through her hair. Her mother and aunt had warned her that constant attention was required for her hair to look its best. She'd lost track of the number of brush strokes.

Michaela laughed and plopped down upon Bode's bed. "You've changed...from last year, I mean."

"How so?" Bode wondered.

"Back then you were a little starry-eyed but content." Michaela's features sobered. "This year, I don't know...you seem more knowing but restless."

"I spent last year fascinated by the realization that the world was wider than ever I imagined," Bode allowed. She could not deny the disquiet in her heart. The previous year, her study of music—the lyre and harp and, in particular, singing—had brought Bode both joy and fulfillment. While music and singing continued to enthrall, time spent away from the music rooms and the Hall theaters left her feeling hollow and restless indeed. "More recently, I suppose I've begun to consider what that might mean."

"Joining the big world requires leaving your little one behind," Michaela surmised. "Is that it?"

"Not little," Bode demurred, "so much as different."

"I cannot imagine you in love with a blacksmith," Michaela proclaimed.

"That is because you cannot imagine my blacksmith," Bode contended. Did she love Mat Bayrd? Yes, of course; that was never the question. Did she want to share his life? That was harder to answer. If she married Mat, she could see their life together in Greystock laid out before her with such surety of mind it seemed to her already a memory. There would be hard work and children. She blushed a little at that thought. Bode envisioned a snug house someplace overlooking the bay, not too far from the boatyard. There would also be Winter Solstice celebrations and soft summer evenings and the love of a good man to sustain her—more than enough, she knew, for most women. Was it enough for her? The truth was she didn't know.

"You are very talented," Michaela was saying. "Everyone thinks so. You could join a choir, perhaps even a touring group. Of course, Ned might not approve of such in a prospective bride."

When it comes to me, I suspect marriage is not at the top of Ned Bly's list of priorities. Bode smiled at the thought but kept silent.

"You know you will have to break off your betrothal if you expect Ned to court you formally," Michaela advised.

Private alcoves aside. Bode's smile broadened.

Michaela's eyes narrowed. "Just the now you look like the tabby what got into the cream. What is behind that smile?"

"Nothing," Bode hedged, "except the thought that life is full of possibilities."

This spring, Ned would graduate from the citadel and take up a commission in the Aylitic Army. His father would purchase at least a senior ensign's rank for him; Bode's Uncle Haryld told her that at supper yesterday.

As a second son, Ned would not inherit his father's title or estates. He would have a stipend in addition to his army pay, a combined income that far exceeded what a Greystock blacksmith would earn. Did that matter? Not much, at least she didn't think so.

"Are you thinking of breaking off your betrothal?" Michaela demanded.

"I am not ready to do that," Bode said firmly. She was not a complete fool. Ned's reputation, she suspected, was well earned. Still, he stood freer to choose a bride than most men of his station. His family enjoyed considerable wealth, and so a modest dowry on her part posed no impediment. As he would not inherit, even her status as a commoner would not mar their relationship or his standing in society. This bit of information she had from her Aunt Rayleen. Bode was aware that her marriage into a noble family would do her aunt and uncle's status in Ayle society no harm either.

Michaela merely shrugged. "So tell Ned Bly one thing and your blacksmith another."

"You mean lie," Bode exclaimed.

"I mean," Michaela replied, unconcerned, "allow Ned Bly the opportunity to pursue you in earnest. If he doesn't, what's the harm? So long as you do not compromise yourself. If, on the other hand, Ned proposes, well, do you really want to be the wife of a blacksmith that badly?"

Bode stared for a moment into the apparently guileless depths of Michaela's slightly too close-together blue eyes.

"For his sake," Bode commented, "I hope young Jehan Broward appreciates who he is up against."

Michaela's smile returned. "He'll never know what hit him." She pouted slightly. "If only *he* were of the nobility." Heaving a sigh, Michaela rose from the bed to plant a kiss on Bode's cheek before slipping out of the room.

On the dressing table in front of her lay Mat's note dating to the day of her most recent departure from Greystock. The small bit of heavy vellum looked a bit tattered. She carried it with her everywhere. He had not written since. She had penned eight letters to him. The last was pretty short and pretty sharp. She regretted the tone of her most recent writing. *Why has he not responded?*

Last year, she had regularly received letters from him. She'd saved those letters, and rereading them had taken some of the edge off her loneliness even the now. She knew Mat. This was not like him. If he were angry with her, even if someone else had come into his life, he wouldn't simply stop writing to her. *Would he?*

Perhaps she could write her friend Lesalle Dent. Lesalle was Mistress Bowdry the now, having recently wed Warren Bowdry. Lesalle proved as faithful a correspondent as she was a friend. What could Bode write, though? *How do you fare, Lesalle? Has that scamp Mat Bayrd taken up with some light skirt from Herryn's Crossing?* Bode had heard about the girls from Herryn's Crossing, a two-day ride southeast of Greystock.

She had read Lesalle's last letter eagerly, searching for some hint of what Mat might be up to but found nothing concerning the young blacksmith. Lesalle's missive brimmed with other news. She and Warren had just moved into a small home his parents had built for them with a view of the bay. Lesalle closed her letter, as she usually did, with a gentle query as to how Jaryd Hume fared. It didn't seem fair that Lesalle could ask about Jaryd if she couldn't inquire after Mat, but then their circumstances were different.

Bode recalled the night Lesalle had told her she intended to marry Warren Bowdry. Warren stood tall and handsome. Half the girls in Greystock had their hopes pinned on him. Bode was a little surprised that the blond-haired, blue-eyed fisherman had sense enough to seek out Lesalle. Despite her best intentions, as soon as Lesalle spoke of her betrothal, Bode couldn't help asking about Jaryd Hume.

"Jaryd will never be happy in Greystock, Bode," Lesalle answered in a soft, sad voice, "and I will never be happy anywhere else."

Life would have been much simpler, Bode thought at the time, *if Lesalle loved Mat and I loved Jaryd.* Bode tossed her head; life, real life, never seemed to work that way.

Lesalle was a dear friend, but Bode didn't want to explain that she hadn't heard from Mat in months. Mat and Jaryd stayed in touch with each other. Climbing into bed, she blew out the side table candle and decided she would speak with Jaryd Hume. Bode fell asleep still trying to determine just what she would say.

13

Accidental Encounters

Just before noon the following day, Jaryd Hume began his third accidental encounter with Dyrileah Quirow at the Antium library by asking if she would walk with him onto the Hall grounds. Dyrileah had at first demurred, saying no Elsacian would be welcome there. Jaryd persisted, pointing out that while she was not allowed to attend the Hall, there was no law against her simply walking the grounds. Their only stop would be at the gardeners' cottages to visit Spats, and he, Jaryd assured her, would be delighted by her presence. Her cloak would cover her uniquely Elsacian dress, known, she'd informed him, as a keppi, and if she kept the cowl drawn, no one passing would even be able to see the distinctive cast of her eyes.

"You will be suitably invisible," Jaryd concluded, knowing the remark would strike a spark.

Dyrileah responded by sticking her tongue out at him. "We may be violating no laws, Jaryd, but we will be breaking the rules. There will be consequences."

"If nothing is wagered," Jaryd retorted, "why toss the dice?" Seeing by her expression that sally had gained him nothing, he implored, "The grounds are beautiful, even in winter. I'll show you where my cabbage patch will be next spring and some exceptionally well-groomed hedges. I'll even throw in a visit to a glass house that will one day soon be producing bushels of patchouli."

"You are such a fool, Jaryd Hume," Dyrileah began but could not suppress the laugh that bubbled up from within her. "All right, I'll walk with you onto the Hall grounds. Let's go the now before my courage fails."

With Dyrileah on his left arm, cloak and cowl firmly in place, Jaryd stepped through a side door of the library and headed down a path that led to the Hall campus. The day sparkled bright, and the winter air hung nearly still, though tingling with cold. Dyrileah clung to his arm, fitting, he thought, very nicely there. He sensed her excitement. She didn't seem frightened in the least.

Before leaving for the library, he'd warned Spats he was going to try to talk her into visiting. He had been careful to mention her Elsacian lineage. The news didn't appear to faze Spats a bit. His only question had been whether she was pretty. Jaryd had responded by saying he thought it best Spats judge for himself. On his way out, Spats asked if Jaryd had ever finished the Fey carving he'd been working on the day they'd met. Jaryd replied that he had some time ago but could not decide what to do with the thing. Spats said he had a notion and asked if he could borrow the miniature for a time. Jaryd had handed over the small rune carving, wondering what Spats intended. He didn't ask.

Bathed by the soft winter sun, the Hall grounds appeared lovely indeed. The lawns and walkways were carefully manicured with snow swept from the walks into gently sloped mounds on either side. The evergreen trees and shrubs, and the winter blooms of holly, provided splashes of color, and even the bare-branched, broad-leaved trees proffered a stark beauty all their own. Walking with Dyrileah, Jaryd felt as if he were somehow seeing the parklike vistas all over again, if not for the first time then at least from a new perspective.

Upon their arrival at the gardener's cottage, Jaryd knocked on the door. Spats opened it, smiling, and waved them through into his sitting room. When he introduced her, Spats bowed over an extended left leg in a manner Jaryd had never seen before, saying to Dyrileah, "Welcome here you are, lass."

Apparently charmed by his gesture, Dyrileah curtseyed in an equally unusual fashion by sweeping her straightened left leg to her front while gracefully bending her right knee. "Thank you, sir, and may I offer a prayer of blessing on all who dwell here."

Taken a little aback, Jaryd drawled, "Well, howdy to the both of you." Just to show he wasn't completely lacking in manners, he asked Dyrileah if he could take her cloak and scarf to hang near the fireplace.

A little later, as they were seated comfortably at a table with mugs of steaming tea and a platter of biscuits laid out before them, Spats observed, "You are the most fortunate of fellows, Jaryd. Never do I see you except in the company of beautiful young women." Spats's smile had a definite "take that" aspect to it. Sipping her tea, Dyrileah raised one golden eyebrow upon hearing the head gardener's comment but said nothing.

Looking directly at her, Jaryd replied, "Never more fortunate than the now, I'll grant you." Dyrileah smiled at that and complimented Spats on his biscuits. She asked after his glass house, which led to an animated discussion of various plants and herbs. This evolved into a conversation about seaweed, and that, in turn, culminated in Spats's rendition of a fishing story just slightly naughty and so improbable that it left Dyrileah laughing hard enough for her eyes to tear. Spats had managed to make the young Elsacian girl feel at ease without giving the impression he was even trying to do so.

"I wonder if things turn out the way they're supposed to or if they merely reflect the choices, good and bad, that people make?" Jaryd did not realize that he'd spoken out loud until he noticed both Spats and Dyrileah staring at him.

"Where did that come from?" Spats asked.

Embarrassed, Jaryd raised both hands as if in surrender. "I was just thinking of home and choices."

"My people believe that is why we are here." Dyrileah spoke softly, and her eyes reached out to Jaryd as gently as a caress.

"We live so that we may experience firsthand the dread power of choice."

"And the tangled web of consequence that inevitably ensues?" Spats inquired.

"Yes." Dyrileah looked to Spats before returning her gaze to Jaryd. "Choice to consequences intended and unintended, leading in turn to more choices and further consequences, our lives fashioned from the decisions we make."

"The doctrine of free will," Spats put in. "The notion that each of us, no matter what the circumstances of our birth, who our parents are or our forebears were, has the ability to shape our own destiny."

"Or are we empowered only to accept the inevitable?" Dyrileah queried.

"Even the inevitable must bend before the irrevocable power of change," Spats noted. "That is why the future is always so full of possibilities."

"So long as I can shape my destiny just enough to avoid having to shear sheep, I'll not complain," Jaryd said fervently. "Well, not much, that is."

Dyrileah uttered a soft laugh. "My poor farm boy," she said fondly, possessively, as she rose and walked to Jaryd's side to run her fingers lightly through his red hair. "Will you never get the hay out?"

Smiling up at her, Jaryd was about to respond when a knock sounded at the door to the cottage. Spats answered the knock, and Bode stepped into the room. She wore Mat's parting gift, a dove-gray winnowed wool cloak with a clasp fashioned into a pair of doves placed heart to heart. She had apparently been walking with the cowl flung back as her face was flushed, and her rich, brown hair, tied into a loose ponytail, looked slightly disheveled. *The wind,* Jaryd thought, *must be rising.* She was lovely. Bode's wideset gray eyes swept the room, settling upon Dyrileah.

"No one would credit it," Spats fairly crowed. "The two prettiest girls in all Antium, and both of them are in my sitting room."

"I'm sorry." Bode looked uncomfortable. "I did not mean to intrude."

"Nonsense," Spats scoffed. "Come in and sit yourself down. I have it on good authority that the biscuits are better than usual, and dinner is on the stove."

"Thank you, Spats," Bode intoned. "But I really can't stay."

"Let me take your cloak," Jaryd said, rising from his chair. "You should sit at least long enough to warm up a bit." He introduced Dyrileah. The two young women gazed at one another. *Appraising,* Jaryd thought. The very air between them in the room seemed charged, like it sometimes felt just before a lightning storm.

"Have we met?" Bode asked, peering intently at Dyrileah.

"No, I don't think so, Bodewhin," Dyrileah replied. "I am certain I would have remembered."

"You seem so familiar," Bode remarked. "It is as if I must know you from somewhere."

Beneath the cloak, Bode was dressed in a forest-green frock with a slightly daring neckline and belted about the waist by a matching silk sash. Her shoes and socks both looked damp. "Come sit by the fire," Jaryd directed her, positioning a chair in front of the hearth. "You know it is winter out there. Your shoes look like you've been skipping through puddles again."

Slipping her shoes off, Bode placed them near the hearth to dry. "The Hall grounds are well maintained, a wonder considering who they've taken on as under gardeners." She cast a level look at Jaryd. "But the roads between the Hall and my uncle's house are something of a mess." She sank gratefully down upon the chair.

"I'll get you some dry socks," Jaryd said, walking to the door. "I'll be back in a moment."

After Jaryd left, Bode turned to Dyrileah. "Please forgive us. We grew up together. That is I grew up; Jaryd just got larger."

Dyrileah smiled. "He's told me of you and his friend the blacksmith and your village. He speaks of both of you with such warmth and pride. He said you were comely." Dyrileah paused a moment, looking carefully at Bode. "It appears Jaryd has a gift for understatement."

"Thank you." Bode smiled in return. "He has very carefully not mentioned you. Don't worry," she hastened to add. "That's a good sign. He must be smitten."

When Jaryd returned from his quarters next door a short while later bearing a pair of woolen socks, a winnowed wool scarf, and some mittens for Bode to wear on the walk home, he found the two young women sitting side by side on the hearth, talking about dresses. Bode looked up as he approached. "Jaryd, may I speak with you? It's about Mat."

"If you will excuse me," Dyrileah said, standing, "I'll go see if Spats needs any help in the kitchen."

Bode pitched her voice low as the slender young Elsacian girl stepped out of the sitting room. "She's a dear. And very nicely put together, I see."

"I noticed that myself," Jaryd agreed.

"Have you heard from Mat?" Bode sounded anxious.

"Yes. I had a letter from him last week." At his response, Bode looked stricken. Jaryd went on. "He closed the letter by saying he had not heard from you. He has written a dozen times and has received not even one letter in reply. He asked if I would speak with you." Jaryd's voice hardened a little. "What are you playing at? He deserves better than that."

"But I have written," Bode exclaimed. "I've penned at least eight separate letters. I've received none from him. I don't understand what could have happened."

"They're mustering the Greystock militia, apparently for deployed service," Jaryd commented. "Mat's was the first name called. Since there is nothing he can do about it, Mat writes to say he's interpreting that as a good omen."

"The militia," Bode was incredulous. "But why? If what we've been hearing is true, the War of Houses is over. Deployed where, does he say?"

Reaching into his shirt, Jaryd extracted Mat's letter. "Here. Why don't you read it for yourself?" Jaryd returned to the table, leaving Bode the privacy of her seat by the fire.

The four of them ate an early supper of beef stew and flatbread. Spats served up a pudding for dessert that both girls made much of, to the old gardener's evident delight. After supper, Bode asked if she could borrow pen and ink to write Mat a brief letter.

She did not take long to finish her correspondence and soon thereafter asked Jaryd if he would post it for her. Mail ran regularly via packet boats between Antium and the coastal settlements all along the shores of the Myr Sea. The occasional letter might be lost, but, overall, the system had long proved to be prompt and reliable. Jaryd promised to see to it first thing in the morning.

The sun was setting as Jaryd, equipped as usual with Spats's heavy walking stick and his Hawken, escorted the two young women off the Hall grounds. After seeing Bode to her uncle's house, Jaryd insisted upon walking with Dyrileah at least as far as the Porter's Gate, which marked one of the entry points to the Elsacian quarter of the city.

As they passed the library, Jaryd paused beneath a bare-branched beech tree and looked up at the two Trasceran moons. Both shone full this night, and hanging low on the horizon, they bathed the city in a soft white light. "What did you think of Spats?" he asked.

Dyrileah's eyes sparkled as brightly as the stars overhead. "Spats is elemental, a force of nature. I like him immensely."

Jaryd smiled. "I won't mention that to him. He's hard enough to live with as it is." He hesitated a moment, shifting his feet and causing the snow beneath his sandals to crunch softly. "And what of Bode?"

"Next time I'll know better what to expect when you tell me a female friend of yours is nice looking." Something in Dyrileah's tone reminded him of sighting shoal waters from the deck of a Coaster caught on a lee shore.

Tucking Spats's walking stick under one arm, Jaryd cupped hands before his mouth and exhaled to warm them. He'd forgotten his mittens. "That's what comes of using you as a standard of comparison." *It's worth a try*, he thought.

"Clever farm boy," Dyrileah observed archly, "but not particularly convincing." She looked away for a moment and then said suddenly, "She has a secret. I wonder if she knows it."

"We all have secrets," Jaryd said to fill the silence that had sprung up around them, wondering what she meant.

"I like her better knowing that she truly cares for a betrothed," Dyrileah said, eyes fixed on his, "who is not you."

Driving the butt of Spats's walking stick into a small mound of snow, Jaryd placed one hand on either side of her waist. Even through the cloth of her cloak, he thrilled at the supple feel of her beneath his fingers. He murmured, "That's encouraging."

"It was meant to be," she whispered back, sliding her arms up to reach around his neck.

A first kiss under the light of two full moons was supposed to be lucky. He hoped so. Despite the cold, Dyrileah's lips were soft and warm and sweet with promise. After a bit, he reluctantly withdrew his mouth from hers and looked down into her eyes. "I sure hope your mama likes me."

Dyrileah hugged him tightly for a moment and then leaned back slightly so she could see his face. "My maman," she said distinctly, "and my patua will see in you the same strength and kindness that I do and be glad of you for it."

"You failed to mention my charm and dashing good looks," he said helpfully.

"Did I?" Dyrileah's smile took on an impish quality. "I wonder why?"

"That stings, girl," Jaryd grumbled, thinking that never in his life had he been happier than at that moment.

Turning her face to the side, Dyrileah pressed her cheek against his chest and spoke softly. "My maman says I blossomed early. Young men have been trying with varying degrees of success to kiss me since I turned eleven. Yes?"

Nodding, he remarked, "You should be careful of young men, scoundrels and blackguards most of them."

Tightening her embrace, Dyrileah went on. "I felt nothing, a mere pressing of flesh. I was beginning to think there was something wrong with me. Now I know all that was wrong was that none of those young men were you."

Fearing that anything he might say would break the enchantment her words had sent whirling and tumbling about them into the crystal-clear winter night, Jaryd bent without speaking and kissed her a second time.

14

Hindrance Resolved

Bode sat waiting quietly in her Aunt Rayleen's sitting room, still clad in the winnowed wool cloak that Mat had given her, when the door opened, and the older woman stepped through. Her aunt looked like her mother, blond and blue-eyed, perhaps a touch heavier.

"Dehlia said you wished to speak with me," Rayleen announced by way of greeting. Dehlia was her aunt's principal maid, a servant of long standing within the Tucker household.

"I've written a number of letters to my parents and friends, including Mathias Bayrd, in Greystock village." Bode had decided to get right to the heart of the matter. "In all cases, I've passed my letters on to Dehlia to have them posted. Those I addressed to Mathias have apparently not been delivered. I would like to know why."

Without hesitation, her aunt responded, "Letters never posted are impossible to deliver."

"How can you be certain of that?" Bode asked.

"Dehlia has ever been most scrupulous about following my instructions," Rayleen answered.

"How could you?" Bode was aghast. "And why would you?"

"For your own good, my dear," her aunt spoke reassuringly. "Your mother and I have had a long correspondence about your infatuation with this…blacksmith." Rayleen said the word "blacksmith" as if she was referring to something unpleasant. "If you are to rise in society, Bode, you must overcome the hindrance of your past. You are possessed of sufficient intelligence and beauty to do so, but some ties must be broken."

"I cannot believe my mother agreed to this," Bode stated firmly.

"She is not aware of my actions in this regard," Rayleen affirmed. "But she is convinced that for you to attain the status you deserve and to advance the cause of our family in the manner you are obliged to, any thought of marriage to this Mathias Bayrd must be set aside. You are not a child, Bode. Surely you realize this?"

"Advance the cause of my family," Bode parroted, "through a suitably affluent marriage, you mean?"

"Why not?" Rayleen seemed puzzled. "Each of us has an obligation to lift ourselves and, by extension, our family to greater heights as each generation passes. You could have your pick of any number of very suitable young men, even noblemen of Ayle. Is this such a burden? Think of the life you will lead and of the advantages your children will have."

Bode was astonished. Her aunt seemed incapable of even seeing the wrong she had done. She could not remember her mother, Annelle, ever voicing any objection to her marrying Mat. Bode did recall the now that the prospect of their marriage was ever a topic her mother seemed reluctant to discuss, referring to it as a someday thing. Outrage flared within her, awash in a flood of relief. Mat had not simply abandoned her. Whatever the future held, the care they'd nurtured for one another, the joy they shared, would always have meaning.

"I am not a child, Aunt," Bode affirmed, her voice taut with anger. "My ambitions and my obligations are my concern. Do you have my letters to Mat Bayrd? And what of his addressed to me?"

Seeing the fire in her niece's eyes, Rayleen relented with what grace she could muster. "As you are set upon it, I'll see your letters to him are returned to you and his to you delivered into your hands."

Her aunt's voice echoed concern that Bode felt certain was genuine. "We have but one chance at life, my dear. Some choices have hard edges, and some mistakes can never be overcome. Be wise in this, Bode. I pray you, be wise."

A short while later, sitting alone in her room with her letters to Mat piled on her dressing table and his to her stacked in her lap, Bode wondered where wisdom lay. She had begun to read Mat's first letter, written the day after she had sailed for Antium last autumn. Tears blurred her eyes almost immediately. She'd set the letter aside. For the now, just having it in her hands was enough. In the morning, she would read them all.

Reading the letter Mat had written to Jaryd earlier in the day had been like hearing his voice again. Mat's letter had said that if what they had been told turned out to be true, the Greystock militia would be deployed to Tyne City in the spring. Tyne lay less than a day's journey away, just a short boat ride across the Donn Narrows from Antium. Mat hoped he would be able to visit. As she read the words penned by his hand, Bode knew that she loved Mat still. But that knowledge availed her nothing. She would post her letters to him on the morrow—except for the last. That short, sharp missive would need to be rewritten. What could she say? She was no closer to an answer. Her heart remained just as torn as it had been at their last embrace months ago.

15

A Conciliatory Gesture

General Segus Gracci Versi, aged twenty-five, counted himself no fool. Some thought his assignment as commander of the Northern Expeditionary Force represented an exceptionally conciliatory gesture on the part of the new emperor, Gaius Sylas Endryk, an attempt to bind the deep wounds of civil war. Others believed it embodied a clever ploy on the emperor's part to remove the new head of House Gracci, a potentially dangerous political adversary, to a distant part of the empire where he could be isolated, quietly surrounded by those loyal to House Sylas. Segus knew the true purpose for sending him to the frontier was to provide an opportunity for him to die bravely in service to the new empire, an edifice founded on the bloody remains of House Gracci.

If he died victorious, advancing the banner of empire in the process, so much the better. Should he perish courageously in defeat, well, then his passing would become yet another shining example of self-sacrifice in the name of duty and honor, a rallying point to spur subsequent Tieran military action. In return for a suitable death, his family name would survive. House Gracci would retain the garland of nobility. His twin sons, five years old the now, would live, as would his wife and baby daughter. In time, perhaps some grandson or great-grandson he would never know might even succeed in returning his house to some semblance of its former glory.

Segus breathed deeply. The air at sea stirred cold and bracing. Clad in a white, flannel, knee-length inner tunic over which he wore a heavier gray woolen outer garment cut to match, gray woolen socks, ankle boots of fine Tieran leather, and a sturdy, military-blue woolen cloak, he stood at the rail of a sleek bireme called the *Ranger*. The ship was Gracci-built with a slightly longer keel, taller masts, and, therefore, more sail area than most dual-oar-banked Tieran war galleys. Both the main mast and the foremast were squared rigged and carried topsails in addition to their primary courses.

Segus's eleventh-hour decision to ship aboard the *Ranger* instead of the ballanteen transport originally planned had been a test designed to gauge the reaction of his second-in-command, General Leptavius Nervi Jute, a man devoted to House Sylas.

"It is your prerogative, General," was all Leptavius had said in response. "Would you like me and the rest of my staff to join you aboard the *Ranger* as well?"

Segus had declined, observing that however swift and seaworthy the bireme may be, quarters were going to be cramped enough with just his immediate staff aboard. When he sailed the following day, only the four junior officers serving as his aides were with him aboard the *Ranger*. He had been allowed to choose all four of his aides. Segus had served with each of them fighting for the Gracci faction in the War of Houses. Despite this, he would have wagered half of what remained of his family fortune that at least one of them was a spy.

Though he had no direct control over its composition, especially the assignment of senior officers, his was to be an independent command. So far, it had proven so. Segus sailed with only a portion of the Northern Army. He would not refer to his command as the Northern Expeditionary Force, an appellation that, to him, sounded ridiculous. Newly named general Quintus Glabrio Jens had departed three weeks prior with three regiments of infantry.

Four more would disembark at the port of Tyne with Segus himself. Two additional regiments waited already in place there. He hoped additional reinforcements were on the way. He intended to push for them. Segus suspected he would fare better shoving a rope, but it was worth a try.

Tall though he stood for a Tieran and well built, Segus also knew few would have described him as handsome. His nose was a little too prominent, his mouth a trifle too thin for fashion. His hair curled naturally and showed a deep walnut brown in color. He wore it trimmed conservatively short. His eyes were blue. His wife said he had a noble face. Julyah was careful to offend no one, him least of all.

The operational scenario originally envisioned for the Northern Army incorporated nothing less than an invasion of Syrdis. Driving west and then south out of Quistyn del Aurus, the plan called for the Northern Army to close on the port city of Tensys approaching overland. In concert with the land-based assault, a second seaborne force under the personal command of Gaius Sylas Endryk was to smash its way ashore just west of Tensys and move on the city from there. It was a strong pincer movement designed to ensure the capture of Tensys and establish a firm toehold from which the combined Tieran armies would then march on Avrys, the Syrdisian capital. The emperor subsequently changed his mind, deciding he would need the forces intended for the seaborne strike to fend off the Roi.

The task of the Northern Army had been scaled back to seizing the newly discovered silver mines at the foot of the Shyre Hills near a town called Lanyr. The silver mines were in a border region between Syrdis and Quistyn del Aurus. Officially, from the Tieran perspective, this border region remained tribal land, belonging to a people called the Chyrchroni. The Chyrchroni of old had allied with Tier when the southerners first invaded the Chestyre Peninsula to battle the Madryns. The Chyrchroni were allied still, at least in theory. In practice, there had been little contact between them and the Tieran Empire since the onset of the War of Houses.

Time, the rampant spread of diseases with which they were not familiar, and encroachment of both Tieran and Syrdisian settlers had not been kind to the Chyrchroni, and their numbers had steadily declined. In recent times, the Syrdisians, under King Dardan, had been particularly ruthless in driving the Chyrchroni into the northernmost reaches of their traditional homeland. Farther south, Dardan had conquered Tuchyck tribal land, proclaiming it rightfully part of his kingdom. So far, however, Syrdis had stopped short of formally annexing the Chyrchroni lands. Segus's mission mandated he strike first, occupy the border region containing the new silver find, and ward off any subsequent incursion on the part of the Syrdisians. Recent border skirmishing initiated by the Syrdisians might well complicate matters—something to consider.

The young head of House Gracci journeyed alone. His heirs, twin sons, and a younger daughter, would never be allowed to leave Tier while he, Segus, lived. He wondered if it might be possible to arrange for his wife to join him. The former Julyah Semprano Reed was three years his junior. Not particularly beautiful, Julyah managed still to entice, sweetly made with blond hair and bright blue-green eyes. Her family fairly reeked of fabulous wealth, and Segus's father had insisted upon the match. Segus had been nineteen at the time. Julyah was naturally quiet and just intelligent enough to know when to keep her mouth shut altogether.

He enjoyed mounting her. She didn't seem to mind being mounted either. Over time, he had developed a certain fondness. Thoughts of her had set his loins to stirring. He was going to have to find a woman or two in the hinterland where fate had cast him. He doubted he would discover anyone truly refined, but for his basic needs, that was not necessary.

Segus smiled grimly, pulling a pair of fleece-lined leather gloves from his outer tunic pocket. His enemies and, in particular, that butcher Gaius had miscalculated. He was young enough to sire more sons whether by Julyah or someone else. He would not play the emperor's game. How to turn the tables represented the real challenge. He could easily understand the emperor's interest in the silver mines that would soon pockmark the border region at the base of the Shyre Hills. House Sylas and, by direct extension, the resurgent Tieran Empire reeled, deeply in debt. If Segus Gracci Versi could take control of the border region and the newfound wealth it contained, perhaps the game could change. Donning the gloves, he clasped his hands behind his back and began to pace the deck. *Patience for the now,* he decided.

16

Learning to Soldier

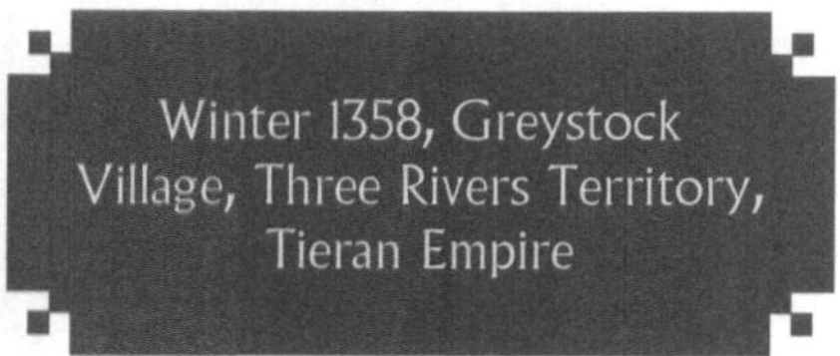

The hard part about soldiering, or at least training to be one, Mathias Bayrd had decided, boiled down to putting up with the chicken shit. According to Nathyn Biddle, Sajar First of Third Company, 133rd Regiment of Auxiliaries, Northern Expeditionary Force, Tieran Army, a certain amount of chicken shit was necessary because soldiering did not come naturally. Soldiering wasn't like fighting. Next to fornicating, fighting formed as much a part of human nature as lying, cheating, and stealing. Soldiering, however, had to be learned. To do so correctly, a recruit first had to learn to follow orders. Wallow around in chicken shit deep enough, long enough, and even the most contrary, wrongheaded, stubborn-assed hayseed would eventually learn to keep his mouth shut and do what he was told.

The trick when dealing with chicken shit, Mat had discerned, was to realize that it could not be avoided entirely. When encountered, the best course entailed keeping your mouth closed and moving as quickly and unobtrusively through it as possible. Third Company, Nathyn Biddle's responsibility, formed one of three being raised in

Greystock Village during the winter of 1358. About Mat's height, in his mid-thirties, balding with dark-brown hair and steel-blue eyes, Biddle looked like a man best left alone. A provincial hailing originally from a small village in Quistyn del Aurus, the sajar stood not as broad through the shoulders as Mat or as deep in the chest—few men did—but exhibited a lean muscularity, a feral quality to his way of moving that warned of trouble if you started something.

"What's hard about soldiering?" Sajar First Nathyn Biddle rhetorically asked the assembled recruits of Third Company at the close of their first full day of training. "Most times, it's less physical work than smithing or farming, so that ent it." The sajar's hard blue eyes raked the group. "Is it that you will be asked someday to kill somebody? Take it from me: any damn fool can kill. Killing comes easy enough for most men. I never met a man yet who wouldn't kill if doing so meant the difference between him living and dying. It ent that." Biddle paused, clasping his hands behind his back. "Is it standing up to danger?" The sajar shook his head. "Nah, if you reckon the average lumberjacking is more dangerous, and so is plying the seas fer fish."

Biddle looked directly at Mat. "What makes soldiering hard is that someday you're going to be told to do something, and the doing is going to cost the lives of men around you. Men you've come to know better than your own kin are going to be dying right alongside you. Some are going to die real hard, screaming for their mamas or calling out to God, spouting blood and pissing and shitting themselves while they are about it. A soldier has got to stand that kind of dying and still do what he was told. To do it, a soldier has to learn to forget about himself when in action and instead become part of a unit, Third Company for you bastards, and stay a part of it no matter what. That ent natural, and it ent easy." Biddle broke eye contact with Mat and again swept the assembled company with a stone-hard gaze. "My job is to teach you miserable whoresons how to soldier." He smiled, but there was no hint of mirth in the expression. "If I can't do it one way, I'll find another. You'll learn whether you want to or not. That I promise you."

Regent Barnabus Valarius Glens held charge over all three companies. A handsome, blond-haired, green-eyed man of thirty-four, the regent, like the sajar, also served Tier as a professional soldier. Unlike the sajar, Glens had graduated from the Tieran military academy in Quinto some twelve years prior. A regent typically stood second in command of a regiment. Kernyl was the rank assigned to the officer in charge of a regiment. Just who their regimental commander might turn out to be, Mat had no idea. A regiment of auxiliaries generally numbered one thousand men, not counting officers, the same as for a regiment of regular Tieran infantry. Mat had been told that auxiliary units were often deployed in much smaller numbers and sometimes larger. Whether or not anyone in addition to the three hundred Greystock archers would join the ranks of the 133rd Auxiliary Regiment remained yet another open question.

A naturally garrulous man, Valarius spent much of his time assuring the good people of Greystock that the young men placed under his charge would be well looked after. Most evenings the commander devoted to squiring a young Greystock widow named Belinda Myncks. Belinda had two children, both daughters, by her husband, a fisherman lost two winters past in a storm on the Myr. Belinda clerked in a store owned by Cassius Glegg. At thirty years of age, she was a handsome little woman, standing a couple of finger widths under the regent's chin, buxom with light-brown hair and dark-brown eyes.

The regent regularly inspected the three companies of archers he would lead once they were deployed later that spring, looked to their provisions and pay, but left virtually all the actual training to the three veteran sajar firsts assigned to him. Sajar First was the rank ascribed to the senior non-commissioned officer in a company of Tieran soldiers, regulars and auxiliaries alike.

"I'm the hardcase you need to worry about while training," Nathyn Biddle had assured Company Three recruits. Nobody much liked Nathyn Biddle. Profane, irascible, and impatient, the sajar first was not one to suffer fools with any sort of grace. Mat had to admit that characteristic tended to cut down on foolishness. Biddle was an asshole but, in Mat's opinion, one that shat on everyone equally in a manner that, however harsh, remained also scrupulously fair.

Mat was grateful that the company commander assigned to them turned out to be Byan Hume, Jaryd's father. Byan entered the auxiliary regiment's scrolls with the rank of altyrn, or company commander. Everyone knew Byan was the best archer in the territory, or at least anywhere around Greystock. Even-tempered with an easygoing sense of humor, Byan had long since earned a reputation for fairness among his friends and neighbors. The recruits of Company Three soon learned, however, that Byan was as strict a disciplinarian as the sajar first. While no one thought of Byan Hume as an asshole, his unwavering support of the sajar first's training methods sent a clear message. They were to be forged into soldiers. Discipline and drill would serve as the hammer and anvil that shaped them.

Archers they were, and archery practice encompassed part of the daily routine. After watching them loose arrows at the targets laid in the new range carved out of the woods near Owain's Meadow for a few days, Biddle quickly concluded they could shoot.

When it came to handling their pole arms, however, the sajar first was much less complimentary. "You assholes are only a danger to yourselves."

Practice at close-quarter fighting began by working with quarterstaffs, executing evermore complicated series of strikes and counterstrikes. This was followed by sparring, first with oaken staves and, eventually, with hooded pole axes, the steel head of the weapon and the butt spike covered by thick leather sheaths. Getting whacked by a quarterstaff, let alone a hooded pole axe, was no picnic, and soon every member of third company sported an array of bruises to prove it.

On the afternoon that marked the close of their fifth week of training, Biddle had singled Mat out as a sparring partner. They were both armed with staves. The rawboned sajar was handy with a quarterstaff and proceeded to give Mat a thorough thumping. Mat's temper slipped at the last, and he powered through the sajar's guard to land a solid blow to Biddle's shoulder. The sajar wore both cuirass and jaltryn. Though not injured, Biddle was staggered by the blow. The sajar backed away a couple of steps, and his hard blue eyes locked on to Mat's. Mat stood blowing like a winded racer, gripping the oaken staff so hard his hands and fingers began to ache.

A long moment passed, and then Biddle hollered, "All right, knock it off. That's enough for today."

Biddle then assigned Mat to the firewood detail for the remainder of the afternoon. Swinging a maul to split logs at least provided Mat with an outlet for pent-up anger. The maul was nothing but an oversized hammer, and he took comfort from the familiar heft of it in his hands. He went to work with a vengeance despite his bruises and sore muscles. Driving the maul with brutal efficiency into a set of steel wedges, Mat smashed log after log.

"I doubt you'll ever make a soldier, Bayrd." Biddle originally hailed from the east coast of Quistyn del Aurus and spoke with a slightly nasal accent typical of the region. "But you sure are useful around a woodpile, burn me if you ent."

Mat paused at his labors and stood silently, the maul held lightly in his hands while he regarded the sajar first. Biddle held a packet of letters. "It's a little early for mail call," the sajar observed. "From the looks of this, I'd say you've got some catching up to do. Don't know who she is, but it seems the lass who penned these has a fair amount to say. I figured a head start might do you some good." Biddle tossed the letters, bound together with twine, to Mat. Snatching the bundle out of the air, Mat could only stare mutely at the package. He recognized Bode's hand immediately. He hadn't heard from her since she departed for Antium in the fall. In desperation, he'd written to Jaryd just after being called up for auxiliary training, asking his friend if he would speak to Bode.

"Thank you for this, Sajar," Mat said, meaning it.

Biddle waved his hand in dismissal. "You're done here. Might as well get started on them letters. Reading always gives me a back-ache." Turning on his heel, the sajar first marched briskly away.

Unable to wait, Mat sat down immediately on a nearby stump and carefully untied the twine. Doing that took a while. The twine was finely wound. He had big fingers, and they were trembling for some reason. With equal care, he opened the first letter, noted that it was dated months prior, and began to read.

Bode constantly teased him, almost as often as Jaryd Hume did. Like his best friend, Jaryd, her play remained ever gentle with never a hint of meanness. He loved her for many reasons, this not least of all. Her letters were like that, like her. Bode's writing washed away his heartache and his loneliness. He might lose her in the end to this other world she'd discovered. She cared for him still, however, and that meant more than he could put into words.

A week later, he received a short note from Bode explaining that she'd written numerous times but that her letters for some reason seemed not to have been delivered, nor had his to her. Somehow the packet of letters she'd forwarded soon after reached him first. This wasn't unusual. Most mail traveled to and from the Three Rivers by ship, and some sailed faster than others or by more direct routes. She promised to write again soon and closed the brief missive with a simple "I love you." He carefully folded that letter and placed it in the band inside his watch cap.

17

A Command Decision

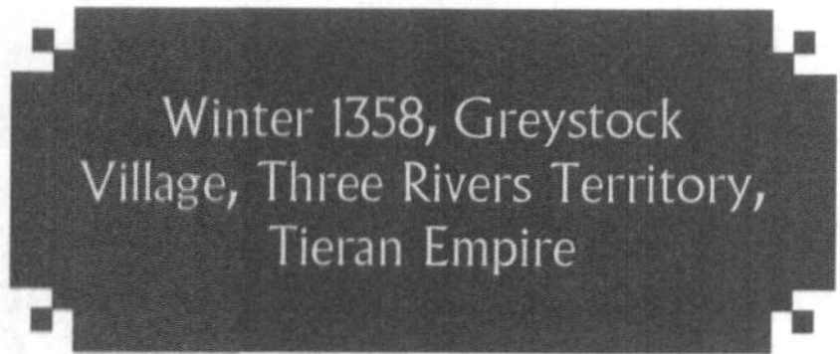

Byan Hume was apprehensive about becoming a company commander. He'd been a member of the Greystock militia for twenty years but never as an officer. Three times he'd joined expeditions to track down Indiquoi raiders. The Indiquoi were a tribal people, often warlike, whose lands extended into the northern reaches of the Three Rivers. On the first and third sorties, they came up empty, returning without ever catching sight of the tribesmen. The second time, however, they managed to close with them. Volleys of arrows were exchanged. Byan's first shot went wild; he'd rushed it. He killed two men with this next pair of arrows. He didn't like to think about that day. Nothing about it qualified him for command, at least nothing he could discern.

Byan knew most all the boys in Third Company. Boys they were. Tall, lanky Danel Owen stood the oldest at twenty-four. More than half had yet to see twenty. Many of them he knew well. A few, Mat Bayrd in particular, were very close. The burly young blacksmith was like a son to him.

His soldiers made evident early on their trust and respect for him. This added to his burden while somehow simultaneously making it easier to bear. He was determined not to let them down. They worked hard; that was clear enough. Even Biddle the leather-lunged veteran seemed impressed.

"They form well," Biddle told him about a month into the training cycle. "There is a natural bond between them. That's good 'cause while a man might march into battle for flag and country, he only fights and dies for the men standing at his side. This lot will stick together, and that's the main thing."

The junior officers, the two ensigns who would round out his company, would join once they reached Tyne in the spring. Five sajars were typically assigned to each one-hundred-man company, the most senior designated as sajar first. In Lynium, the term "sajar" literally meant "leader of twenty." As company commander, it fell to Byan to select the junior sajars, four of them, who would serve under Biddle. A training sajar was not normally assigned to a company once it deployed. Biddle expected to be transferred in the spring but could not say for sure.

At the start of the sixth week of training, the time had come to select the four additional sajars from among the other members of the company. Hume had asked Biddle for his recommendations. Looking at the list Biddle had placed in his hand, Byan registered some surprise not to find Mat Bayrd's name among them.

"I expected to see Mat Bayrd on this list," Hume remarked.

"Bayrd is steady, no dullard, and if it comes to a fight, I'll be mighty glad he's on our side," Biddle responded. "He is every bit as strong as he looks and a lot quicker." Nathyn Biddle paused long enough to look his commanding officer in the eye. "There is more loner than leader in him, though. He is liable to go his own way despite orders. He'll be a handful, sir, for any junior officer placed over him."

"I trust Mat Bayrd, both his judgment and his courage." Hume directed, "I want him on this list."

Biddle made no further argument. "You're the boss, Altyrn. Whose name do you want stricken?"

"I'll leave that to you, Sajar First," Hume replied. "The others you've recommended are all acceptable to me."

"Very well, sir." Biddle saluted in the Tieran fashion, swinging his right fist up to his left breast with his right forearm held carefully parallel to the ground.

The next day, Mat Bayrd was mildly astonished and then a little dismayed to discover that the three stripes of a junior sajar were to be sewn onto the left breast of his tunic. As the weight of his promotion settled upon him, Mat felt that the responsibility out-matched any benefit his newfound authority represented. The sajar first made this abundantly clear in the weeks that followed.

"You don't know shit," Biddle growled at his four junior sajars. "It is important, by God, for you to realize you don't know shit. Do-ing so might just keep the poor bastards who'll have to follow you alive long enough for you to learn something."

Biddle didn't know who the little piece was what wrote Mat Bayrd all those letters, but whoever she might be, he blessed her sweet ass for it anyhow. Her writing took the bit out of Bayrd's teeth. The rage Biddle saw brewing in the young man dissipated. Whereas before, the muscular young blacksmith was just going through the motions, after her letters arrived, Bayrd settled down to soldiering proper. Bayrd embraced his new responsibilities as sajar instead of shirking or bucking against them. While Biddle still felt there were better choices for promotion as the time for their embarkation drew near, he had to admit Hume might have been right about Bayrd after all.

Byan Hume was no soldier; of that, Biddle had no doubt. Hume was a good man, though, and sometimes that would be enough, for a while anyway. Maybe they'd get lucky. Biddle hoped so.

Hume gave the company three days' leave starting the fourth day prior to their scheduled departure. He did not ask permission of Regent Barnabus Valarius Glens before doing so. Lyjah Bowen, the altyrn in charge of First Company, and Gyl Tanner, who com-manded Second Company, followed suit. Biddle would not have done such a thing but couldn't really disagree with the decision. The boys would climb onto the transports with their sweethearts' kisses still fresh on their lips and home-cooked food in their bellies. That would do them more good than a couple of extra days' drill. Biddle had heard there were some sporting women in the village at a tavern called the Blue Duck. He decided to take what money he had and spend his leave seeing if he couldn't ruffle a few feathers.

18

A Proper Volunteer

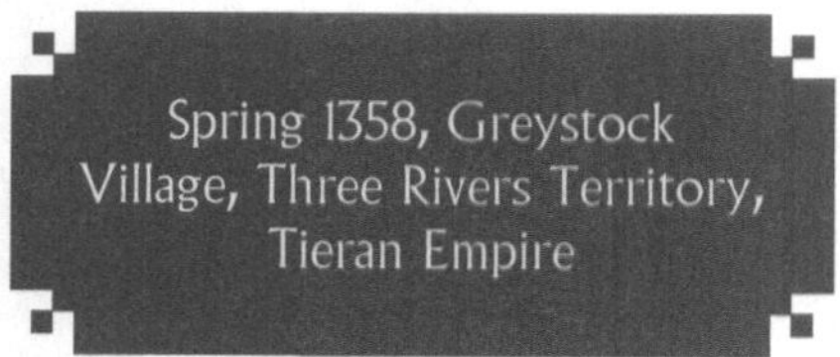

Sajar First Nathyn Biddle called Third Company together at the end of their last full day of training, some three months and three weeks after they started. Leave would begin at sundown, this being the third day of the week, and run through nightfall at the end of Sixth Day. They would board the transport ships starting at noon on Seventh Day and sail with the evening tide.

His message rang short and simple. "When push comes to shove, they's only two things what kills soldiers: bad luck and stupidity. Every man is lucky until the day he ent. There's no point in worrying about that. Best you can do is make damn sure you don't die of stupidity. I reckon you'll do. Good luck to ye."

During the time the Greystock militia had trained as Tieran auxiliaries, Byan Hume spent most days from dawn until dusk at the camp in Owain's Meadow. He participated in as many of the training exercises as he could, including pole-arm sparring and the interminable marching. He loosed his share of arrows too. The time spent on the archery range represented the one aspect of auxiliary training he truly enjoyed. Strictly speaking, he wasn't required to do so. The regent-in-command, Barnabus Valarius Glens, rarely took part in the direct training of the troops he would lead once they were deployed. Byan did because he'd feel like he was shirking if he didn't and because he felt obliged to try to set a good example for the boys.

He also figured the marching would help toughen him up, his feet anyhow, and working with the pole axe in particular, he thought, wouldn't do him any harm, either. Any improvement in skill with the weapon might save his life someday. He and the other two company commanders, Lyjah Bowen and Gyl Tanner, regularly met with Valarius to discuss training schedules and logistics for the voyage to Tyne. Valarius had little to tell them regarding what they might expect once deployed. From Tyne, Valarius thought it likely that they would be sent west to the borderland of Quistyn del Aurus. Exactly where and for what purpose were questions their commander was unable or unwilling to answer.

Nan had moved from the farm to stay with her older sister, Myrin. Myrin was married to a potter named Olvyr Dowd. Myrin and Olvyr's two sons were both grown, married, and living in homes of their own. They had put Nan up in one of the boy's old rooms on the second floor of the Dowds' two-story house, which could be accessed by an external staircase. This enabled Byan to join his wife there nearly every night since Nan had begun her stay. The Dowd home, situated on the southwestern edge of the village, stood only about a third of an hour's horseback ride from the training camp. Byan felt a little guilty sleeping each night warm in his wife's arms while his men took what comfort they could in thin canvas-walled tents. Nan's loving embrace and the sweet passion rekindled between them since his appointment as altyrn quickly stamped out any substantial feeling of remorse.

He'd granted leave to as many of the men as he could on the eve of their departure. He knew full well the professionals, Valarius in particular, did not approve. *Their approval be damned*, Byan thought. His men weren't professional soldiers. They'd do their part, and with any luck, most would return home to take up their lives once again without being scarred too deeply either physically or emotionally by the experience. For many of the militiamen, this was their first good-bye from family and loved ones. Unless they were extraordinarily lucky, for some, this first good-bye would also be their last. Even if they saw no fighting, disease or accidents were liable to claim at least a few of them. He would not deny his men the chance to spend an evening or two with those they loved to say and do the things that ought to be said and done.

Byan couldn't give everyone leave. The training ground was a Tieran military facility and would remain so until their departure. As such, it had to be guarded. This made sense as both weapons and material would be left at the camp until the three companies of archers embarked for deployment. Byan felt he had to stay at the camp. He'd warned Nan in advance of his decision. It was only fair, after all. He and Nan had had plenty of time to say their farewells. Byan needed a few men to stay posted until the leave ended and the full complement regrouped for departure. He'd asked for volunteers. Not surprisingly, Mat Bayrd had stepped forward. A few others had as well—not enough for a proper guard detail, but Byan decided not to push it. A token guard would keep up appearances.

He'd left his mount, an easy-gaited gelding named Nix, with Nan at the Dowd place. He wasn't going to take the horse with him. Auxiliary officers were not obliged to provide their own horses, and if the army wanted him to go about on horseback, the army could bloody well supply him with one. Most of the men cleared out of camp as soon as the leave period began. To the handful left behind, the first day of leave stretched on endlessly. Near sundown, Byan was surprised to hear a familiar voice call out to him as he sat on a camp stool just outside his tent, trying with paltry success to concentrate on a supply list spread out before him on an overturned crate.

Nan reined Nix to a halt a few paces away and cried, "Hullo there, Altyrn, sir. Could you stand another volunteer?" She sat astride the gelding, her upper body swathed in a sturdy woolen wrap. Her skirts were hiked up, however, and he could see her feet and lower legs were covered by sandals and socks. A tantalizing glimpse of shapely upper thigh was also visible. He found himself pretty much equal parts pleased and scandalized.

"Don't see how I could turn away such a stalwart as yourself, ma'am." Byan grinned. "For the next couple of days anyway, we're liable to be a little shorthanded."

"Help me down off here then," his wife cajoled, smiling, "and I'll volunteer properly."

Nan brought with her a goodly supply of fresh-baked bread, beef sausage, and cheese. These he doled out to the members of his guard detail. Nan insisted on spending a little time with his troopers. Byan suspected that the few moments spent in her company amounted to a greater boon to their spirits than the food she'd brought. Nan asked Mat Bayrd to join them for supper. The meal was a simple affair held in Byan's tent, and Nan did most of the talking. She congratulated Mat on his promotion to sajar and asked after Bode. She managed to get him to converse a little and smile more.

When the meal finished, Mat climbed to his feet. "I'd like to thank you, sir, and you, ma'am, for the meal and the hospitality." Looking to his commanding officer, he added, "I'd best take a turn round the perimeter, sir, and make sure the boys are on their toes."

Byan nodded. Mat saluted, rendering the honor formally, standing straight and bringing his clenched right fist to his left breast. Byan's return salute was considerably more casual.

Before Mat could leave, Nan embraced him and kissed the broad-shouldered young smith on the cheek. "God bless you and keep you, Mat. Come back to us."

Hugging her back briefly, Mat grinned. "I'll sure do my best, ma'am. Thank you."

Watching Mat go, Nan wiped a tear from her cheek. "He's always been such a gentle boy." Turning, she glared at her husband, green eyes flashing. "And you all want to turn him into a soldier and set him to killing."

Byan rose to his feet and went to her. Slipping his arms about his wife, he said, "Mat's a man grown, Nan, with a man's duty before him."

Their lovemaking that night was tender to the point of being tentative. It left him feeling restless. "We've never done this in a tent before," Nan observed, pressing close to him under a pair of Tieran-issue blankets and a quilt she'd brought along with her.

"Nor on a cot neither," Byan concurred gently, brushing a strand of sandy-blond hair from her forehead. "Bide a while, and maybe we can work in a little more practice."

"Belinda Myncks is with child," Nan offered suddenly. "And that *fellow* Valarius is going to just sail off and leave her." The way Nan pronounced the word "fellow" left no doubt as to her opinion of the regent.

"How did you come to know this?" Byan asked, thinking that of all the things they could be talking about, this particular subject would have been pretty far down on his list.

"Hester Riggs told me," Nan replied. Hester was a midwife, married to Jon Riggs, an apothecary. Having devoted their lives to the well-being of their fellow villagers, the Riggs were highly regarded throughout Greystock. Hester and Nan were like sisters. They'd been the best of friends since childhood. Still, it seemed to Byan that Hester had no business discussing so private a matter concerning Belinda with anyone, including his wife.

"Belinda is no child, Nan," Byan commented softly.

"Belinda is a sweet little thing," Nan whispered fiercely, "desperately lonely the now, and you can be sure Valarius took full advantage. Any man who would do that is not to be trusted. You watch yourself around him, Byan Hume."

"I will," Byan agreed readily, not wanting to argue. Something clicked in the back of his mind. "What were you doing talking with Hester Riggs? She lives all the way over on the east side of town."

"I had a few questions. It's been a while." Nan smiled, a slow, private smile for his eyes alone, as bright as dawn spilling over into a soft spring morning.

"Nan, are you pregnant?" Byan's voice sounded strange in his own ears, thin and reedy and a little ridiculous.

Nan nodded, laughing like a girl. "Oh, Byan, you should see your face." She hugged him close. "If you ask me how this could have happened, I'll box your ears."

Byan had a pretty good idea how this had happened. Ever since coming home that night some four months ago to tell Nan that he would be accompanying the Greystock militia once it deployed, they'd been going at it like a couple of newlyweds. Their youngest, Oryn, was fourteen. Byan had thought he and Nan were through with all this. "Are you all right? I mean considering, well, it has been a while."

"Byan Hume," Nan growled with mock severity, "if you are suggesting that I might be too old to bear your child, I really will box your ears. Lysa Devers just gave birth to a fine, healthy girl not two months ago, and she's five years older than I am."

Lysa Devers was a fine woman, Byan thought, who also happened to be built like a lumberjack. Nan was slim hipped. She hadn't had too much trouble with the boys, but, still, fourteen years spanned a long time. Determined not to scare her, he gave way to the joy budding inside him and smiled back.

Seeing the worry flicker across his face and knowing his first thoughts were for her, Nan felt her heart swell. She thanked God not for the first time for allowing her to love a good man. Too many women loved those who weren't and paid a terrible price.

Byan laid his hand on her belly. He had big, strong hands, farmer's hands, well suited for gripping a plow or drawing a bow and for touching her gently. "Hullo there," he said quietly. "This is your papa talking. We might not have a chance to get acquainted before you get here. Just in case, I'd appreciate it if you would take it easy on your mother. You'll like her, I promise. I can't wait to meet you. Remember, I'll love you always."

Nan's tears came unbidden, and she pulled her husband into her arms, smiling through them. "You mustn't worry for me. Hester says I'm fine, and I'll be fine. With your bairn growing in me, it will be as if I can hold you close even though you are away." She kissed him. "I won't be so lonesome this way, at least not quite so much."

Byan kissed her back. Nan and Hester were as close as two women could be. If needs be, Nan would fight to bring his child into the world with a calm courage he could never match, and Hester would help her. He felt the fear, which was knotting his insides since her pronouncement, begin to ease. "I hope it's a girl," he whispered into her ear so the baby wouldn't hear.

"You always say that," Nan teased. Running her fingers through his hair, she said, "I'll settle for hale and hearty."

Their lovemaking the second time around was anything but tentative. Nan never cussed—well, hardly ever—except during coitus with climax close upon her. Byan had her going a blue streak there for a little while just before a release that rocked them both. After, lying together warm and close, he thanked the All Father not for the first time for allowing him to love a good woman. Too many men loved those who weren't and paid a God-awful price.

19

Heron in a Duck Pond

Byan Hume didn't much like boats. While not prone to seasickness, he wasn't much of a swimmer either, and the bloody thing kept bobbing about as if, given half a chance, it might slip right out from under him. To a bird in flight, the Donn Narrows measured twenty-four kylos across. The actual distance from Tyne harbor to the Antium docks ranged a few kylos farther. A good day they had for traveling at least. The rain that had plagued them the past week seemed finally to have dissipated, and although the weather remained cool, the sun as it rose climbed into a clear blue sky.

In the four weeks since their arrival in Tyne, the archers of the 133rd Auxiliary had done little but continue to drill in the manner they'd become accustomed to while training back in Greystock. Word of desultory fighting along the Syrdisian border drifted in, but so far, no formal declaration of hostilities had been announced. "We're going to war in dribs and drabs," one wit described the news. After some wrangling, Byan had managed a pair of two-day passes, one for him and another for Mat Bayrd.

The coaster named the *Maya*, aboard which he and young Mat

booked passage, proved swift enough, and according to the captain, they had a good wind for an eastern crossing. Altogether, sixteen human passengers, four pigs, two large dogs, and a crate full of chickens made the morning voyage aboard the *Maya*. The coaster was rigged for oars and carried a single, large, square sail. Under sail alone, it completed the crossing and glided up to a quay in Antium harbor at the start of the first hour after noon.

Mat was never very talkative, but the burly blacksmith-turned-sajar scarcely said a word during the crossing. Once ashore, Byan and Mat made directly for the campus of the Hall at Antium. The Hall grounds themselves were easy enough to find, but locating the gardeners' cottages turned out to be a little more challenging. Adhering to their second set of directions led them to a cluster of neat, white-painted buildings with bright-green doors and window trims.

A young woman answered Byan's knock. Slim she was and pretty with large, slightly tilted brown eyes and long, honey-colored hair bound up in a ponytail. She wore a green cotton dress with a snug-fitting bodice of a type he'd not seen before. A white cotton apron draped about her slender hips. Pulling his watch cap from his head, Byan noticed that, apparently, she'd been baking as a smudge of white flour adorned one cheek just below her eye.

The moment she opened the door, Dyrileah Quirow knew she stood in the presence of Jaryd's father. Jaryd had told her that he would likely be visiting sometime soon, and the family resemblance was unmistakable. Byan Hume's eyes were hazel colored, whereas Jaryd's were gray, but she recognized the same light in them, radiating kindness and strength, that so strongly attracted her to this man's son. The father had the same hair, the same bearing and build as his son. The broad-shouldered young man standing at Byan's side could only be Mat Bayrd, the blacksmith who was Bode's intended.

Both men were similarly attired in watch caps and bluff blue woolen cloaks. Each had on a woolen tunic that looked to be of Tieran design. The tunics were medium blue in color. Byan's was adorned by a brass pin affixed to his left breast, while Mat's had a trio of white linen stripes sewn above his. Broad leather belts were fastened about their waists, and both bore large knives sheathed over their left hips that reminded her of the one Jaryd often carried. Each also had a small axe fitted through a loop in his belt on his right side. Thick woolen socks and leather sandals covered their feet.

Dyrileah smiled. "You must be Byan Hume, Jaryd's father."

The smile transformed the pretty young girl before them. Her face lit, and her large brown eyes, the color of polished maple shone, taking on a beauty all her own.

"And you are Dyrileah Quirow," Byan said. At her nod, Byan returned her smile. "My son's letters do not do you justice. He said only that you were the prettiest girl in the city." He extended his hand, and Dyrileah grasped it in both of hers without the slightest hesitation.

Dipping her lashes briefly in response to Byan's compliment, Dyrileah shifted her gaze to his powerfully built young companion.

"Mathias Bayrd, is it?" Dyrileah asked.

Belatedly snatching his cap from his head, Mat replied, "Yes, ma'am. Been warned, have you?"

Dyrileah laughed. "Jaryd said only not to get between you and the table come dinnertime."

Mat grinned, and Dyrileah noticed the dimple in his cheek. Though he was far too muscular for her taste, she had to admit that Mat Bayrd was actually quite handsome.

"That's fair enough," he acknowledged.

"Jaryd will be so happy to see you," Dyrileah announced. "He and Uncle Spats are out planting fruit trees. I'll take you to them."

She started to remove her apron when Byan stayed her by observing, "You must have been baking."

"I was just rolling some dough." Dyrileah paused, and then realization dawned. "Oh, no," she cried, raising her hands to her cheeks.

His smile gentling, Byan took a step closer, saying, "Hush the now. You couldn't be any prettier if you tried." Pausing before her, he asked, "May I?" Byan extracted a handkerchief from his tunic pocket. Dyrileah nodded briefly, and Byan wiped the trace of flour from beneath her right eye. "There. All right the now, let's go find that rascal son of mine."

Dyrileah removed her apron and tossed it just inside the cottage door before closing the portal and stepping off the porch.

"Do you think we might catch sight of Jaryd actually working?" Mat wondered out loud as she led them away.

They heard Jaryd and Uncle Spats before laying eyes on them. The rapid staccato *clack, clack, clack* of quarterstaffs sparring announced their presence. Stepping around the corner of a large hedged enclosure, in its center a statue of a woman holding two small children by the hand, Byan caught sight of his son squared off against a wiry-looking white-haired man, each armed with an oak quarterstaff.

"Quit mooning over Dyrileah, or I'll thump you proper," the old man growled. The two of them were positioned just in front of the statue, which looked to be carved from granite. A small array of gardening tools, shovels, and pickaxes leaned against the base of the fountain.

"I wasn't mooning," Jaryd retorted, "not exactly." Both Jaryd and his sparring partner were clad in simple, light-green tunics cut in the Tieran fashion, belted at the waist, with knee-length socks and leather sandals on their feet.

"Again," the oldster hollered and whipped his staff down toward Jaryd's left shoulder. Jaryd warded the first blow with his staff and then a second. A flurry of strikes and counterstrikes followed, the heavy staffs whirring and humming like a pair of large, angry bees. Byan glanced at Mat, who nodded in return. The two sparring before them showed a remarkable expertise, the quarterstaffs blurred almost too fast for the eye to follow. The match ended when the old man succeeded in driving the butt of his staff into Jaryd's chest.

"Ow," Jaryd cried, lowering his guard. "What was that for?"

"You had me twice and would not strike." The old fellow leaned on his staff, breathing deeply. "That was to teach you to stop showing off."

"You are old and doddering." Jaryd rubbed his chest. "I didn't want to damage you."

"And here I told your father that you would be working," Dyrileah called. At the sound of her voice, Jaryd turned toward them.

"Da," he cried, tossing his quarterstaff to Uncle Spats. Jaryd rushed up to his father and embraced him. Looking to Mat, Jaryd grinned. "What did you bring him for? In two days, we won't have anything left to eat."

"We can only stay the one. We'll need to start back by noon tomorrow," Byan informed his son. Jaryd released him long enough to give Mat Bayrd a hug. Returning to his father's side, Jaryd flung an arm about him and smiled at Dyrileah.

A laugh arose from within the young girl, and she clasped her hands. "Oh, what a happy day this is, yes."

Letting go of his father, Jaryd scooped Dyrileah up in his arms, lifted her easily from the ground, and whirled about. He lowered her gently to her feet and looked his father in the eye.

"She's the one, Papa," he proclaimed.

Embarrassed, Dyrileah pressed her face into Jaryd's chest. "You shouldn't say such things."

"It's true," Jaryd replied earnestly. "I'll keep saying it until I can convince you." For a moment, he looked deeply into the eyes of the girl in his arms. It was only a moment but long enough for Byan to see that the two were in love. Without taking his arms from about Dyrileah, Jaryd nodded at the old man with the quarterstaffs. "Father, Mat, I'd like you to meet Uncle Spats. He is the chief gardener at Antium Hall. Uncle Spats, this is my father, Byan Hume, and my best friend, Mat Bayrd."

"A pleasure," Mat said.

Byan stepped over and extended his right hand. "A chief gardener who handles a quarterstaff like a weapons master, I see."

Shaking Byan's hand, Spats replied, "Aye, well, I was young once and foolish." He grinned. "I got over the one and used to the other."

The five of them gathered in Spats's cottage for a brief visit. Mat was anxious to push on to Bode's uncle's house in hopes of seeing her.

"Are you sure I can't walk you over?" Jaryd offered.

"No, thanks," Mat demurred. "You've got some visiting of your own to do. If Bode is willing, maybe we could come back here?"

"Sure thing." Jaryd grinned. "Tell Bode that Spats has put some biscuits on, and you'll likely have to trot to keep up with her." Jaryd's expression sobered. "I know she is as anxious to see you as you are to see her. Beyond that…" Jaryd paused. "Well, you'll have to see for yourself. Good luck." Using a pen borrowed from Spats, Jaryd drew Mat a map on a scrap of paper.

His friend's parting words ringing ominously in his ears, Mat hurried off across the Hall grounds. Jaryd's directions were clear enough, and he had no difficulty finding Bode's Uncle Haryld and Aunt Rayleen Tucker's home. A large two-story structure half again the size of any in Greystock, the Tuckers' house was not far from the Hall grounds. A serving woman answered his knock, took one look at him, and sniffed. At least she didn't slam the door in his face. He asked politely if Bode was home. She informed him that the Tuckers and Mistress Bode were attending an afternoon tea at the promenade. Having no idea what the promenade might be, or its location, Mat asked for directions. The woman, who gave her name as Dehlia, complied but then informed him that dressed as he was, he would never be admitted.

"I've traveled a long way, ma'am, and have only this one chance to see her," Mat said in reply. "I'm bound to try. When she comes home, would you tell her Mat Bayrd called and that I'm staying at the gardeners' cottages on the grounds of Antium Hall? I'll be there until noon tomorrow."

Dehlia surmised that the broad-shouldered young man standing before her must be Bode's blacksmith. He certainly looked the part. There was something about him, though: the way he pulled the cap from his head, holding it before him in those large, work-roughened hands; the tousled, curly hair that was not quite blond; and his eyes, green and genuine. She felt herself softening toward the burly youngster despite Mistress Rayleen's well-founded objections. One glance was enough for Dehlia to see this fellow stood no proper match for Mistress Bode. Still, if someone like him had come court-ing her a few years back…well, she had promised him to tell Bode of his visit and knew she would do so.

The promenade turned out to be a park of sorts located along a canal. A wrought-iron fence enclosed a portion of the park that included an outdoor theater and a stone platform that could be covered with a removable wooden floor, evidently for dancing. As he approached, Mat could hear music playing. He paused down the street from the main entrance of the enclosed area, marked by a large arched gateway, and watched as a pair of young men clad in Tieran naval uniforms were quietly but firmly refused admittance by a trio of muscular fellows wearing red waistcoats, black three-cornered hats, and close-fitting black trousers. Each redcoat was armed with a sturdy wooden truncheon.

Deciding Dehlia had been right, he turned and walked along the edge of the park down toward the canal. Outside the fenced enclosure, an array of tables had been positioned on a large lawn. Around each table, four or five rather flimsy-looking white wicker chairs were placed. A number of people were already seated at the tables, being served by waiters dressed in white waistcoats and black trousers similar to what the redcoats out front were wearing. The waiters came and went from a brick building inside the enclosure. He could see that they passed from the closed-in area to the table-filled lawn by an open side gate located at about the midway point of the wrought-iron fence. A bored-looking redcoat was stationed at the side gate as well.

Having so little time, he hated to just leave. Mat supposed he could wait at the main entrance and attempt to contact Bode when she exited. *How long,* he wondered, *would an afternoon tea last?* The wrought-iron fence of the enclosure stood none too tall. Mat could climb over it easily enough, and those redcoats didn't seem to be watching the fence line itself. One look at him in his Tieran militia-man's uniform and it would be evident to all he did not belong. He had no right to just barge in either.

No redcoats appeared to be guarding the perimeter of the lawn outside the enclosure. He spotted a couple of boys dressed in work clothes fishing in the canal not a stone's throw from the outermost row of tables.

Then he saw her. Bode wore a cream-colored silk gown bound at the waist by a kyrobi, a broad belt fashioned of brocaded linen. Bode's rich, brown tresses were piled atop her head in some odd manner, but it was her all right enough; he would have known her anywhere. She walked onto the dance platform inside the enclosure on the arm of a tall, dark-haired young man elegantly dressed in a waistcoat and trousers and wearing white gloves, of all things.

Dodging through an intervening rose garden, Mat started across a section of lawn, threading his way between the tables set with glass wine goblets, plates, and silverware and surrounded by the delicate-looking white wicker chairs. He'd made it nearly to the wrought-iron fence, when an officious-looking little man in a white waistcoat and black trousers stepped in front of him with his hand extended, palm facing Mat.

"Just where do you think you are going?" the white-jacketed fellow asked.

"I've come to see Mistress Bodewhin Ware," Mat answered quietly, pointing toward the dance platform. "She's right over there. I won't bother her but a moment."

"You will not bother her at all," the little man said firmly. The fellow in the white jacket was a couple of years his senior, Mat figured. He was a full head shorter, fox-faced, and skinny to boot, but his voice rang with authority. "You have no right to be here. Leave immediately, or you shall be forcibly removed."

"This is a public venue," Mat protested, hoping he was right about that.

"And a very private affair." Fox Face cut him off. "Do you have an invitation?"

"I've come all the way from the Three Rivers." Mat implored, "If you'll only let me say hullo, I know she will recognize me. She's just over there."

The man had curly brown hair and brown eyes that narrowed the now in righteous indignation. "I've warned you. You must leave immediately."

"Please," Mat entreated. "I mean no trouble." He started to push past the little fellow, who suddenly raised his white-gloved hand in a clenched fist. The scrawny bastard directed his gaze over Mat's shoulder, evidently signaling someone. Turning his head, Mat saw a pair of redcoats running toward him, truncheons in hand.

Uncertain where he stood and angry because of it, Mat grasped the unctuous little whitecoat, latching one hand onto his lapel and looping the other round the leather belt at his waist.

"Unhand me, you bugger," Whitecoat hollered. Gauging the approach of the two redcoats, Mat hoisted the white-jacketed runt into the air and flung him at their feet. The three of them sprawled in a tangle of arms and legs.

"Bounder," someone shouted to his left. Mat pivoted just in time to slip a punch thrown by a paunchy fellow in a silk coat who must have been at least fifty. Not wanting to hurt the man, Mat side-stepped and caught sight of a third redcoat swinging a truncheon at him from the right. Reacting instinctively, Mat raised his arm to block the blow while simultaneously ducking under it. The redcoat's fist smashed down on his forearm, but he avoided the truncheon strike. Trapping the redcoat's right arm against his side with his left, Mat twisted about and threw the man over his right hip. The fellow crashed onto an unoccupied table, smashing it and flinging glasses and silverware all over the place. Somewhere, a woman screamed.

One of the two charging redcoats regained his feet and rushed Mat, jabbing with his truncheon. Thoroughly angry the now, Mat deflected the baton with his left hand and punched the guard in the face with his right fist. The redcoat dropped as if pole axed. Something smashed down on the top of Mat's head, knocking his watch cap to the ground. He whirled to confront the little white jacket who was holding one of the wicker chairs in his hands. The white-jacketed fellow raised the chair for a second strike. Mat snatched it out of his hands and tossed it away, absorbing a punch to the short ribs from the little git in the process. Mat grabbed the puny bastard by his coat front, hauling him off his feet.

"Mathias Bayrd!" Bode's voice rang as clearly as a bell. "Put that poor man down."

Mat complied, none too gently sending the little whitecoat tumbling onto the lawn. "What are you playing at?" Bode sounded angry. Mat turned. She was making her way toward him, holding her skirts in her hands and stepping daintily across the lawn. Her eyes raked him, wide, gray, and furious. Her hair, a rich walnut brown, coiled on top of her head and held in place by pins, he imagined, in a manner he'd never seen before. *Strange that, but beautiful too.* The cream-colored gown she wore was made of silk, and it clung to her slender form cunningly, in all the right places. She looked lovelier than ever he could remember.

"That little squint just hit me with a chair," Mat pointed out as reasonably as he was able.

"Master Hodges, is it?" Bode inquired of Mat's diminutive white-coated nemesis.

"Yes, Miss," Hodges replied, climbing to his feet. "I'm the chief usher here."

"Mat is notoriously hardheaded," Bode explained. "If you intend to damage him next time, I would recommend aiming somewhere else." She laughed as if taken by surprise, a delighted, lyrical sound. *She mustn't be too mad,* Mat concluded.

"Bode," a sturdily built man of middle years wearing a gray silk waistcoat called out from the crowd gathered about, "do you know this ruffian?"

"This ruffian, Uncle," Bode replied, "is Mat Bayrd. He's a blacksmith from Greystock Village in the Three Rivers. I've known him most all my life. Mat is my..." Bode paused, her gray eyes searching Mat's for a moment. "Childhood friend — he saved my life when I was twelve. Remember?" She looked up at Mat. "I fell through the ice at the duck pond on the Hume farm."

"You were trying to reach a heron trapped when the pond froze over," Mat recalled. "Friend" she had named him, not "betrothed." He supposed he couldn't blame her. "I feel like a heron in a duck pond about the now, all right enough."

Bode stepped up to him; she smelled like strawberries. Her anger had melted away altogether, and she smiled. She seemed about to say something, when her eyes suddenly widened. "You're bleeding," she cried.

"Well," Mat growled, "if you'd just been clouted over the head by a piece of"—he wasn't sure what the bloody wicker chairs were called—"lawn furniture," he improvised, "you'd be bleeding too."

"You're too tall. I can't see." She sounded as if he'd managed to make her mad again. "Sit down," she directed. He straightened one of the little wicker chairs and sat down gingerly. Bode removed a handkerchief from a small leather purse she wore suspended from a narrow strap about her wrist. Gently parting his hair behind his right ear, she briefly examined his scalp and then pressed the cloth against his head. "It doesn't look too bad," she informed him.

"Easy enough for you to say," Mat grated through clenched teeth.

"Honestly, Mat." Bode couldn't keep the smile out of her voice. "Tossing people about like sacks of grain. What will your mother say?"

Mat noticed Bode's uncle, Haryld Tucker, walking up to them. Raising his eyes to her uncle, Mat said, "I'm sorry, sir. I didn't mean to cause a ruckus. I'm with the Tieran militia forming just outside of Tyne, and I have only a few hours' leave. I didn't know if or when I'd ever get a chance to see Bode again. I was going to just wait by the main entrance in the hopes of catching her when she left here, but when I saw her on the dance floor, I stepped across the lawn without thinking. I never meant to intrude."

"Strictly speaking, Master Tucker, the lawn is public space. He has a perfect right to be here," the tall young man at Bode's side observed, earning, Mat noticed, a grateful smile from Bode in the process. Mat decided he didn't like the handsome bastard. The dark-haired fellow was about his age, maybe a bit older, good-looking, and wearing what must have been some sort of uniform. Unlike Mat's company-issued hodgepodge, Bode's dancing partner's uniform appeared finely tailored: a dark-green waistcoat with dove-gray trousers and knee-length leather boots.

Tucker harrumphed. "That is a rather generous interpretation, my Lord Bly," he replied, speaking to the tall fellow with the fancy clothes. It took a moment for Mat to realize that Bode had been dancing with a lord. The implication settled about him like a lead weight.

"Is Collins hurt?" Tucker asked, looking back over his shoulder. A couple of other redcoats had the man on his feet, standing a little unsteadily between them.

"He's still a little wobbly, sir," one of the redcoats answered, "but I reckon he'll live."

"You have business with my niece, sir?" Haryld Tucker inquired of Mat.

Mat looked up at Bode's uncle and then the people standing about, including the young, athletic-looking Lord Bly that Bode had been dancing with. His gaze came to rest on Bode. She suddenly looked uncomfortable, embarrassed, maybe even frightened a little.

Mat cleared his throat. "Mistress Bodewhin has always been very kind to me and my folks back home."

Mat reached into his tunic pocket and took out the letter to his parents that he'd been trying to finish. He handed it to Bode. "I brought you this, from your parents," he lied around the lump formed all of a sudden in his throat.

Bode was ashamed of him. He wanted only to get out of there and back to where he belonged before he caused her anymore hurt or harm. "I'll tell them how fine you look…my folks, I mean," Mat said to her. "And how well this new world you've found here suits you. I'm not sure how I'll explain it to them. I couldn't have understood myself without seeing with my own eyes."

Something in her eyes flickered, pulling at him, but he was unable to see past his own hurt far enough to divine any meaning from her gaze. He couldn't say what he wanted, not in front of a bunch of strangers, lords and all. Mat stood to his feet. "I'll tell them you've somehow become even prettier. I know they won't believe how that could be possible. I wish you"—he paused, blushing—"that is, we all wish you only happiness."

Mat turned to Bode's uncle as he seemed to be in charge. "May I go, sir, the now?" he asked quietly. "I won't trouble you further." He pointed at the broken table. "If you'll let me know where to send the money, I'll pay for that. It might take a while. Pay has been a little spotty lately."

Tucker sighed. "I think our people," he directed a glare toward young Hodges, "may have overreacted a bit. As no real harm has been done, let's call it even." Bode's uncle pursed his lips for a moment. "I don't want to see you again, young man. If I do, you'll not find me so tolerant."

"I understand, sir. Thank you." Mat looked at Bode a final time. "Good-bye" was all he trusted himself to say. Returning her handkerchief, Mat picked his watch cap up from the ground, where it had fallen during the tussle, and started to walk away.

"Mat," Bode cried out to him. He stopped and looked back toward her. "Thank you for this." She held up the letter never intended for her. A quick glance at the missive was all she needed to know what he'd done and why. "God bless you." Her voice faltered only slightly in her own ears, surely not enough for anyone else to notice.

Mat nodded, and the look in his eyes, a mix of bewilderment and hurt, flayed her. He turned away and slipped through the crowd, headed for the street that fronted the promenade.

"So that's Mat Bayrd, is it?" Ned Bly inquired of her; his blue eyes crinkled with amusement. "He certainly makes an entrance; I'll give him that." Ned paused just slightly. "I thought he was your intended."

"So did he," Bode said quietly.

"Well…" Ned's smile broadened. "That's the best news I've had in quite some time. Shall we finish our dance?" He offered her his arm.

Bode nodded a little absently. They were just about to step back onto the dance floor, when a quiet voice emanating from just behind stayed them.

"Excuse me, Miss Bodewhin," Hodges, the chief usher, spoke deferentially. "That big fellow dropped this. I believe he had it tucked inside his hat. I thought perhaps you should have it."

Looking embarrassed, Hodges proffered a tightly folded piece of paper. Bode took it and immediately recognized her writing. In her hand, she held the note she'd so hurriedly penned to Mat the day she'd discovered his letters to her were being intercepted. She remembered how she'd signed it. "Thank you, Master Hodges." She looked gratefully into the little man's deep-brown eyes. "Thank you very much."

"You will excuse me please, Ned," she said to Lord Bly and headed toward the pavilion.

"Bode, where are you going?" Ned called after her.

"To the ladies' necessary," Bode lied in a manner designed both to avoid the need for further explanation and to prevent him from following her. Her ruse apparently worked as Ned only shrugged and turned to Hodges, asking where he might find something decent to drink.

Bode made her way quickly through the pavilion, a brick structure at the front of the enclosed terrace that housed a large reception room, kitchens, and, indeed, a lavatory dedicated to women's use. A similar room for men was located at the opposite end of the hall.

She flagged down one of the ushers standing near the main entrance. "My name is Bodewhin Ware. Please inform my uncle, Haryld Tucker, that I'm not feeling well and have gone home. Please ask him to pass my regrets on to his guests."

The usher, a slight little man who looked like he could be related to the chief usher, Hodges, assured Bode he would. Walking through the main gate, Bode stood in the street for a moment, clutching her letter to Mat in her hand. Where had he gone? She looked up and down the street and could not see Mat. She started down the roadway in the direction of her uncle's house. Antium Hall lay in that direction as well. She didn't know where Mat was staying while in Antium but guessed it would likely be with Jaryd.

20

Together

Bode hurried at first, walking rapidly. Her pace quickened. She was wearing a fashionably high-heeled pair of shoes, difficult enough to dance in let alone run. But run she did—as fast as she could. She passed one side street and then another. Mat could have turned down either. She still had not seen him. She gripped the letter tightly in her right hand as if it might provide some means of guiding her steps. She turned down the third side street; it angled away to her left. Bode thought it was not the most direct route, but something compelled her to turn anyway. Doing so felt right somehow.

She was tiring. The street narrowed and curved to her right. Rounding a bend, she thought she caught a glimpse of him, a familiar cast to a pair of broad shoulders, lost to sight behind a passing wagon.

"Mat!" she shouted. "Mat, please wait." Bode put on a burst of speed, running as fast as she was able, calling Mat's name. Her heel caught in a crack between cobblestones, and she fell. Pitching forward, she managed to twist to her side, landing mostly on her left hip and shoulder. She skidded into a mud puddle. Her dress, the finest she owned, was ruined. Aunt Rayleen would skin her. Gasping for breath, she looked up but couldn't see him.

"Are you all right, miss?" a slightly slurred voice inquired of her. "Let's help you up out of there." She felt a strong hand grip her arm, not hard but firmly enough to help lever her to her feet. A young man stood at her side. Of medium height and build, he was brownhaired, blue-eyed, and nice-looking, with a deep cleft in his chin. His mode of dress indicated some form of uniform—Tieran Navy, she thought. Tieran soldiers and sailors seemed to be pouring all over Antium those days, mostly on leave, as Mat was, from the forces being assembled in Tyne. She'd heard some of the locals grumbling that the Tierans acted as if they owned the place.

"I'm fine, thank you," Bode answered. She attempted to withdraw her arm. "I must be going."

"What's your hurry?" the young sailor asked, still clinging to her arm. His breath smelled of sour wine. "I'll be happy to escort you anywhere you'd like to go. These streets aren't safe, you know, not for a wee, pretty thing like you."

"Oh, please," Bode said, trying to be polite, "I'm in a terrible hurry."

She tried again to pull away, but the sailor held fast, smiling just a little nastily. "You're not very well equipped for wrestling, darlin'. I reckon you're much better suited fer other things." The confidence in his voice irked her. Bode didn't feel frightened until she looked into his eyes. Something hard and predatory leered back at her from within the sky-blue depths.

"Take your hand away, mister," Mat spoke quietly, not one to raise his voice. Bode turned her head. He stood only a pace away.

"Bugger off, mate," the sailor growled. "I saw her first."

Mat reached out and grabbed the seaman's arm. Her blacksmith had big hands, Bode knew, and they were massively strong. Long hours spent swinging a hammer or pulling at an oar had made them so over the years. *Her blacksmith.* The thought made Bode's heart throb.

Mat tightened his grip. The sailor blanched; twisting toward Mat, he tried to punch him using his free hand. The sailor released his grip on Bode's arm as he did so. Jaryd had told her often Mat was quicker than most everyone gave him credit for. His strength alone would have been easy enough to counter, Jaryd said, except that when combined with his quickness, the power Mat could draw upon was remarkable, frightening even, when fully unleashed.

Mat slipped the punch, pulling his head aside, and pushed the sailor. It was a short, sharp shove that didn't look like much, except the force of it sent the brown-haired Tieran tumbling into the street.

The fellow rolled quickly and gracefully to his feet. He assumed a fighter's crouch, fisted hands held up in front of him. Mat stepped toward him, a growl in the back of his throat. Bode slipped between them. Mat grabbed her and instinctively pulled her to his side, positioning his body to shield her from the sailor. Peeking around Mat's thickly muscled arm, Bode smiled sweetly at the blue-eyed seaman.

"This is Mat Bayrd," she called, "a gentle lad unless you rile him. I wouldn't if I were you—rile him, that is." Bode clung to Mat's arm. He froze in place, and she could feel the hard, round muscle tense beneath her hands.

The sailor glared at Mat for a long moment and then relaxed, slowly straightening. "Maybe you're right," he allowed. Tipping his hat, the Tieran turned on his heel and strode away.

"I haven't seen you in a fight since you were twelve years old," Bode scolded Mat gently. "And the now, out of the blue, I find you involved in two altercations in a single afternoon. What are they feeding you in that army you've joined?"

"As I recall, all three fights were over you." Mat looked down at her. His eyes were warm and green and suddenly as gentle as ever.

"The first incident and just the now, I'll grant you." Bode smiled up at him. "But that business at the promenade I claim no responsibility for whatever."

The first fight, when he was nearly thirteen, happened because two fifteen-year-old boys in Greystock had been taunting her about her older brother, Ayden. Ayden had taken a bad fall some months earlier and lingered near death afterward, unconscious for days. He recovered eventually, at least partially, but suffered ever after, plagued by sudden fits and seizures.

The older boys' japes had been cruel enough to make her cry. Mat took on the pair of them, bloodying both their noses. He'd received a black eye and cuts to his face and lips in return. She kissed him for the first time as soon as his lips healed, on his thirteenth birthday. That still counted as the happiest day of her life. Mat had asked if she would marry him, and she'd said yes. They found her brother drowned in a creek just outside of the village a few days later. He'd been fishing when, everyone assumed, a seizure must have claimed him, and he fell into the water. That was the saddest day of her life. Forever linked in her mind, those two days remained happiest and saddest, like two sides of the same coin.

"Are you all right?" Mat asked, an anxious cast clouding his eyes.

Bode felt giddy, lightheaded, and a little dizzy. In part, she knew it was from the sheer joy of finding him. She sensed there was something else to it, though, likely nothing more than the aftereffect of her hard run. Whatever the cause, it concerned her not—not any longer. She stepped into his arms. "I ran as quickly as I could. When I fell, I thought I'd lost you." Her voice shook, and she could feel tears rising.

Mat enfolded Bode in an embrace and hugged her briefly. "C'mon." In Bode's ears, his voice sounded a little shaky too. "Let's get out of the street." Even with his arm about her, Bode wobbled when she stepped on the foot encased in the shoe with the broken heel. "Are you sure you're not hurt?" Mat asked again.

Bode nodded. "I broke the heel of my shoe running on the cobblestones, that's all."

Mat scooped her up in his arms and carried her quickly round the bend in the street. "Mat, put me down. You can't carry me all the way to my uncle's house," Bode exclaimed.

"That sounds like a fine idea to me," Mat countered but swung her carefully to her feet regardless. "Do you have a better idea?"

Holding him close, Bode whispered, "I don't know. I seem to be having some difficulty concentrating right at the moment."

Gently tilting her head back, Mat kissed her, and for a long, blissful moment, nothing mattered except the warm press of his lips against hers.

Mat was the one to break off the kiss. He slowly pulled his mouth away from Bode's. When she opened her eyes, she saw him smiling down into hers. "You taste," he said in a very private tone, "just exactly the same as when you were eleven." She did too—like sunshine on molasses.

"I was only one day short of twelve," Bode replied tartly, "and much more grown-up than you were." She pressed close, feeling safe in his arms. Still, her voice trembled when next she spoke. "I never expected to see you today. And, suddenly, there you were."

"Breaking furniture," Mat put in with a wry twist to his voice.

"Holding your ground," Bode countered and hugged him tighter. "It was as if I couldn't believe my eyes. I was just so surprised." Her voice faltered.

"And ashamed," Mat concluded for her. "I can't say that I blame you."

"No," Bode shot back as if by reflex. Then she paused. "Well, yes, but not of you, Mat—never of you." She leaned back so she could look again into his eyes.

He shook his head slowly, not in disbelief—Bode would not lie to him—but because he truly didn't understand.

Bode wondered how to explain what she didn't really comprehend herself. Knowing she had to try, she forged ahead. "Coming here to this city, to the Hall, was like stepping into a different world. Every day felt like a new beginning. I wanted so much to find a place for myself here, to embrace all that it meant to me." He nodded, and that gave her courage. "I spent last year remaking myself, becoming someone new. When I went home this past summer, everything was so unchanged; there seemed no place for this new me. It was easier just to be the old me."

Mat disagreed. The change in Bode the previous summer was so profound, so evident, he struggled to see how she could not have been aware of it. However much he might long for her, the old Bode was gone forever—that, he knew. Mat said nothing, though. He saw the turmoil roiling in the depths of her luminous gray eyes. He wanted to hear her out and to understand, if he was able.

"It seemed like an easy solution: be my new self here and my old self back home," Bode continued. "Simple except for you, for us. When I looked up this afternoon and saw you, it was as if my old world and my new came crashing together. I had to choose."

Bode paused, and the silence grew, stretching thin. Mat spoke quietly. "And so you chose to be who you have become." The worst part of it all was that Mat did understand. She'd found something here, something he couldn't share. He'd seen with his own eyes how she fit into this new world of hers, a world with no place for him. "I understand the now; I didn't before. You belong here. I don't."

"No." The anguish in Bode's soft, tremulous voice sounded as if he'd stabbed her. "I was afraid—afraid they would see that all the time I've spent here was a lie." Tears welled in her eyes, and she clung to him. "Don't you quit on me, Mat Bayrd," she sobbed. "Please don't quit on me."

"Our promise is an old one, Bode." Mat gave voice to his greatest fear. "You were but a child; we both were."

"No." Bode stamped her foot, looking so much like a frustrated little girl that he had to smile despite the pain bedded so deeply in his heart that he could scarcely breathe. Drawing a ragged breath of her own, Bode spoke slowly but urgently. "When you turned to look back at me on the promenade just before walking away, I could see how badly I'd hurt you. I could feel my heart breaking. I wanted to run after you, but I couldn't. I wasn't brave enough. And then you were gone, and I thought I'd lost you." She touched his cheek. Her eyes probed his. "I knew then what fear really was. I came after you as quickly as I could. When I fell in the street and couldn't see you…oh, Mat, I couldn't bear it. And then you were there. You were there, and I wasn't afraid anymore. I love you so much."

Mat kissed her, lightly brushing his lips against hers. She tasted salty sweet the now. He clasped her close to his breast once more. The supple feel of her slender body in his arms was like taking hold of life itself. His fear and pain receded, washed away by her words, her presence.

"I need to hear you say that you love me," Bode whispered.

"I love you," Mat said automatically. He looked down at Bode. She was shaking her head. Her eyes were closed. "I love you," Mat said again and let the truth of the words fill his voice. Bode stilled. Her eyes opened, and she looked at him. "I love you," Mat said a third time, feeling the full power and the promise of the simple phrase.

Bode smiled, a radiant smile that sprang from someplace deep within her. "I'll never be afraid again, not that way, not alone, ever again." Reaching into the small leather purse she wore, Bode extracted the note she'd written to him, the one he had carried in his hat band. "You dropped this. Hodges returned it to me."

"Small compensation for the trouble he caused," Mat grumbled, accepting the note.

"I take better care of your correspondence," Bode announced, removing a worn piece of vellum from her purse.

Examining it, Mat recognized the brief note he'd attached to his parting gift to her this past fall. "A fair exchange then," he said, handing back her letter but keeping his note. "This will fit more easily in my cap anyway."

Removing his watch cap, he slipped the bit of vellum into place. The words written upon it, he knew, were simple enough:

> Bode,
> For one year or a thousand.
> Mat

Bode accepted the exchange without comment, slipping the letter back into her purse. Mat lifted her in his arms once more and strode off, headed for her uncle's house. Bode protested but weakly. She was still lightheaded and drained, not only emotionally but physically as well. Mat felt so strong and sure; she twined her arms about his neck and closed her eyes.

While running desperately after Mat, she'd forgotten to pray. She prayed the now to the All Father, the one God. She gave thanks and then asked for His blessing and His mercy, for Mat and herself. She prayed for all she was worth.

21
Father and Son

As soon as Mat departed, Spats and Dyrileah both headed for the kitchen in the gardener's cottage, he to get started on some biscuits and she to finish preparing a peach pie for baking. Jaryd couldn't help teasing his father about becoming a parent for the fifth time.

"Aye, well," Byan replied, "some of the best things in life happen by accident."

"That's what Dyrileah says," Jaryd observed fondly.

"Do you really intend to marry that girl?" Byan asked softly.

"I've asked her twice," Jaryd responded. "She hasn't exactly said no."

"I'd keep at it if I were you." Byan laid a hand on Jaryd's shoulder in encouragement, wondering just when his son had grown up. "She loves you; that's plain enough. Just why she'd do a fool thing like that is a might harder to understand."

Jaryd smiled and then excused himself long enough to step into his own quarters and fetch the bow and quiver of arrows Spats had given him. "Spats says she's not a hunter," Jaryd noted, referring to the weapon he handed over to his father. He'd strung the bow in his quarters before bringing it to the gardener's cottage. In addition to thirty-two arrows, twenty heavy broad heads, and twelve lighter needle-tipped flight arrows, a pocket on the quiver also contained a pair of leather bracers for protecting the archer's forearm and several spare bowstrings.

"He's right," Byan agreed, examining the bow. Doubly curved like a Three Rivers hunter, the weapon was beautifully crafted of laminated wood—golden yew mostly, Byan thought—but with long black strains running the length of the grain. He had never seen the like. "The belly is shaped differently. See here? And she tapers a bit more at the bend too. She's a beauty, though; that's certain."

"Spats told me she's a named weapon," Jaryd told his father. "Dark Hope she's called."

In days of old, smiths would occasionally name a weapon that was intended to be the first of a type or one that was of unusual quality. More often, the warrior who wielded it would bestow the name, generally a reflection of purpose or pride. Once thought to imbue mystic power, the practice had long since gone out of style.

"Strange name. I wonder what it means," Byan commented. Testing the flex of the bow by pulling firmly at the string, Byan whistled softly. "No toy is she."

"Pressing her has near worn me out," Jaryd admitted. "Would you like to give her a try?" Byan's grin provided answer enough. About to call out, Jaryd saw Dyrileah step through the kitchen door, wiping her hands on a towel. She'd left her apron behind.

"We're headed to the range to loose a few before supper," Jaryd informed her. "Would you like to come along?"

"Come on, lass," Byan entreated. "What's the point of showing off without a pretty girl to watch?"

Dyrileah smiled. "Jaryd is a lot easier to understand now that I've met you, Master Byan."

With a shouted farewell to Spats, the three of them set out for the archers' practice field. The archery range at Antium Hall lay adjacent to a strip of woods along the far western portion of the grounds. The wood paralleled a canal that marked the boundary of the Hall property. Large wicker targets were placed at marked distances. A painted sheet showing concentric white and black circles was affixed to each target. The smallest circle, a white one at the very center of the sheet, measured exactly one-third of a span in diameter. The buck's eye, it was called.

Jaryd had made the walk from the gardener's cottage holding the bow in his left hand and Dyrileah's left hand in his right. Passing the bow to his father, he turned to place the quiver easily within Byan's reach.

"In deference to your advanced age," Jaryd quipped.

Byan selected an arrow, a broad head with a razor-sharp triangular point forged from fine steel. Nodding in approval as he examined it, Byan chose a target at the fifty-paces mark. He let fly, pressing the heavy bow in an easy, fluid motion. The arrow thunked solidly into the heart of the buck's eye.

"She draws as sweetly as she looks," Byan commented.

Jaryd took his turn and placed an arrow alongside that of his father. He winked at Dyrileah. "It's always good to put the first shot behind you." She smiled encouragement. The next round proffered Jaryd the choice of target. He shot at one standing on the one-hundred-paces mark. His arrow struck well within the buck's eye.

"Been practicing, have you?" Byan asked and sent his next arrow to within a finger's width of Jaryd's, slightly closer to the center of the target. The two of them repeated the process at one hundred and twenty paces, both arrows striking just inside the buck's eye. Dyrileah clapped her hands in delight, brown eyes shining.

"All right," Byan said finally. "Let's have a go at a mark suitable for grown men. Do you see the used target just to the right of the range boundary?" Following his father's gaze, Jaryd took note of a much-used wicker target, its sheet holed countless times standing just outside the range boundary. The worn target sagged slightly, not placed near any particular range marker, but Jaryd estimated the distance to be a bit more than two hundred paces.

"I can barely walk that far without a nap along the way, and you expect me to hit the thing?" Jaryd protested.

"Sooner or later, we're going to prove to Dyrileah we're naught but poor mortals anyhow, and I'm getting hungry," Byan replied. "Of course, if you're willing to concede, we can start back the now."

"My pride's worth the hike, I suppose." Jaryd gauged the wind. The breeze was slight and felt as if it was blowing directly into him. He fixed one of the flight arrows to the bow and took his stance. The flight arrow was lighter than the broad heads they'd used earlier and would carry farther. The flight arrowhead had a sharply pointed pyramidal shape well suited for piercing mail.

Jaryd raised the bow and pressed using the muscles of his back and belly in addition to those of his arms and shoulders. Byan had taught him to bend the bow not by merely pulling at the chord but by also pressing his whole body forward into the draw. Simple enough in concept but subtle, it took hours of practice to master the movement. Done correctly, the result combined grace and power, adding both range and accuracy. Even with a bow as heavy as Dark Hope, he would have to put a fair arch on a shot at this distance. He loosed, and the arrow leapt away, flashing through the soft light of an early spring afternoon. It plunged home, striking a hand's span outside the buck's eye.

"Well done, lad." Byan slapped his son on the shoulder. "Somewhere along the road, you've learned to shoot."

Immensely relieved that he'd actually hit near the target center, Jaryd handed the bow to his father and teased, "My da is a fair hand with a bow. At least he used to be before slipping into his dotage."

"Dotage my ass, boy," Byan growled. He pressed Dark Hope, moving as gracefully as any dancer despite the strength required. The slightest pause at full draw, followed almost instantaneously by the deep thrum of the bow, announced his release. Moments later, the flight arrow drove home, just inside the buck's eye.

"With a bow in your hands, Papa, you're barely human." Jaryd smiled ruefully and extended his hand.

Shaking his son's hand briefly and firmly, Byan grinned. "Right living and the love of a good woman is what does it, lad." He returned Dark Hope to Jaryd.

"I could come with you when you go." Jaryd blurted the words softly, but the tightness in his voice spoke volumes.

No, Dyrileah's mind cried out, torn by a longing she'd never known before. *Don't take him from me.* She bit her lip and remained silent.

"No, lad." Byan's calmly stated response came nearly as quickly as Dyrileah's tortured thought. "This is not your time."

"You can't have many along who are better with a bow," Jaryd pressed, his voice rising.

"That's true," Byan said without hesitation and with no change in tone. He had been expecting this, after all. "And there is no one that I would rather have at my side."

"Then why can't I come with you?" Jaryd had not planned to talk about this in front of Dyrileah, but the words wouldn't stop.

"Your number was not called, Jaryd. You have different obligations. Completing your studies, for one." Byan glanced at Dyrileah. "And others, I think." He paused for a moment before continuing, his voice still calm and measured. "We could stand together, son, and if things go wrong, we could fall together too. That would be hard on your mother, and there is no need. Your number was not called."

"If I had been selected in the lottery, what then?" Jaryd asked.

"You would have been given dispensation as you were away at school, as some were for one thing or another." Byan placed his hands on Jaryd's shoulders. "But your number never came up, so there was no need."

"If I volunteered," Jaryd insisted, meeting his father's eyes, "what then?"

"You would have been turned away, as were a number of others in Greystock Village. You still would be," Byan assured him.

"Why?" Jaryd pleaded. "I don't understand."

"We don't know what the future holds, Jaryd," Byan explained patiently. "With luck, the worst danger we'll face over the next few months is army food. But if war results, and the worst along with it, you will be needed then. Your mother will need you, your brothers, the little one coming, and all those back home who give our lives meaning." Byan tightened his grip on Jaryd's shoulders. Dyrileah saw his knuckles whiten with the strain. "I don't know if that day will come, son. I pray God it will not. I know it has not come yet, not yet."

Jaryd reluctantly nodded his understanding and his unspoken consent. Byan stepped back. "I could have sworn I just won an archery match."

Jaryd smiled a little wanly and, having lost the bout, trotted away to gather up the arrows. "Best shot I ever made," Byan confessed to Dyrileah, pointing at the worn target so far away. "Good time for it too. The lad really can shoot."

Standing near Byan's side, Dyrileah kept her eyes fixed on Jaryd. "Jaryd always speaks so fondly of his home and his family. Having met Bode, I could understand a little." Meeting Byan's gaze, she said softly, "I see more clearly the now."

"You know he's in love with you," Byan said as seriously as Dyrileah had ever heard him speak.

Dyrileah nodded mutely in affirmation.

"Asked for your hand, has he?" Jaryd had told him so, but Byan wanted to hear Dyrileah's response.

Dyrileah's eyes were remarkable: large, golden brown, and slightly tilted. She held his gaze. "Twice he has asked," she confirmed.

"And you have said no," Byan remarked, not judging but clearly wondering.

"I have not said yes." Dyrileah dropped her eyes. "It is complicated; there are things about me and my family he does not know."

"Do you love him?" Byan asked bluntly.

Dyrileah's chin raised defiantly, her splendid eyes flashing. Byan forestalled any immediate response from her by saying quietly but forcefully, "I love my boy. That makes it my business. I'm leaving in the morning, so I don't have time to go up and around with you."

Her look softened. "I love him," Dyrileah declared and smiled the smile that transformed her from merely pretty to beautiful.

"You're a good lass; any fool can see that, and Jaryd's no fool. Tell him, Dyrileah," Byan enjoined softly but intently. "Tell him all. Trust your love and, for pity's sake, say yes the next time he asks you to marry him."

Tears washed her eyes then, and Byan gathered Dyrileah into

his arms. "Some fool will tell you that a man can love a woman and not need her. Bunk that is. A man needs a woman like yonder oak needs water." He nodded at a massive tree standing at the edge of the wood. "Women are life bringers. Without a woman at his side, a man turns inward too much. He becomes a hard, brittle thing, and sooner or later he cuts himself off from life itself. He'll go blind and never notice the growing dark." He tightened his arms, giving Dyrileah a brief, encouraging hug. "A good woman can help a man hold fast to life and to his courage when he needs most to be brave. No matter what happens, good and bad, she will become his joy and his solace. I know. Be good to my son, and you'll be good for him." Releasing her, Byan stepped back. "He won't quit on you, lass; you can count on that."

Smiling through her tears, Dyrileah nodded. "I know that. In my heart, I've always known it."

On the way back to the gardener's cottage, Byan insisted upon carrying the bow and its quiver. He strode along a few paces ahead of Jaryd and Dyrileah, offering the gift of privacy. Jaryd slipped his arm about the young girl at his side and glanced down. "You've been crying." The concern in his voice soothed the raw surge of emotion that still churned inside her.

"I'm full of tears this day," Dyrileah acknowledged, "happy ones mostly. Your father is rather wonderful."

"I'm partial to him," Jaryd allowed, "even if he doesn't want me for company."

"I should hate to lose you." Dyrileah's soft plea warmed his heart.

"You wouldn't have lost me, lass," Jaryd asserted. "It will take more than a puny thing like war to keep me from your side. No worries the now anyway."

"Do you know how big a fool you sound?" Dyrileah seemed only a little cross with him.

"Whatever happens, we'll figure something out." Jaryd's voice rang with confidence. "My girl is a clever little thing." He squeezed her tight for a moment without breaking stride. "You are my girl, aren't you?" he asked a little less confidently.

"I can't seem to help myself." Dyrileah sighed. "I think it is time for you to meet my father."

It took a moment for the significance of her words to sink into his consciousness. "I've heard," Jaryd said slowly, "that when an El-sacian girl asks you to meet her father, it's time to cut and run."

"Just you try it, boyo," Dyrileah said, echoing a term she'd heard Jaryd use a time or two, and took her turn squeezing him, "and see how far you get."

22

An Antium Farewell

Bode slipped off both her shoes and ran up the stairs to the front door of her uncle's house. At his insistence, Mat waited outside. True to her word, Bode was gone only a short while. When she returned, she was wearing the same pearl-gray frock she'd worn at her going-away gathering back in Greystock last fall. Over the dress, she had on the dove-gray winnowed wool cloak that had been Mat's parting gift. She'd let her hair down, wearing it loose about her shoulders. Bode smiled down at him from the head of the stairs and rushed to his side.

"Dehlia nearly went into hysterics at the sight of my gown. I told her we were going to visit Uncle Spats on the Hall grounds and that I wouldn't be back until morning. She was positively scandalized."

"If you're going to get into trouble," Mat said slowly, reluctantly, "we don't have to go."

"Hang trouble." Bode laughed. "You're actually here, and I still can't believe it." She flung her arms around Mat's neck and hugged him tightly. "Let's go. I'm starving."

Mat offered her his left arm, and they began the walk back to

170

the Hall. "The army seems to agree with you," Bode observed and pointed to the stripes on his tunic. "What do those stripes mean?"

"One is for being stubborn," Mat replied, "the second is for pure foolishness. They gave me the third one 'cause I'm so good-looking." The comment earned him a slantwise look that he'd learned long ago could lead to trouble. He briefly explained his sajar ranking and his duties. "This deployment is supposed to last one year. I've heard that depending on what happens, we could be released much sooner or perhaps much later. No one seems to know."

Bode tightened her grip on his arm for a moment to acknowledge his words and remained silent, waiting. She'd learned long ago that if you wanted Mat to say anything, you needed to give him time. "When it is done, whenever that is…" He looked about them and sighed. "I suppose there must be a blacksmith's shop around here somewhere. I was raised to the black apron, you know, just before the Winter Solstice."

Bode's heart swelled at his words. She knew how much they cost him. She also knew he wouldn't have said them if he didn't mean them. With equal certainty, she knew that such an arrangement would never work. "Lately," she replied, "I've found myself thinking a good deal about a snug little house overlooking Deben Bay, not too far from the boatyard."

Mat stopped and looked down at her. The light in his eyes warmed her to her toes. "Thank you for that," he said quietly. Then he shook his head. "I'll not ask you to be less than you are." He kissed her then, and she felt that down to her toes as well. Mat held her close. "Where does this leave us, I wonder?"

"I don't know," Bode replied. His body pressed against hers, large and hard, warm and welcoming, all the home she would ever really need. "I care not so long as it leaves us together."

"Glad I am to hear that," Mat intoned. "It's a little short of being practical, mind, but I am glad to hear it."

"We have the rest of our lives to be practical," Bode murmured. "Tonight, I just want to be in love."

It was nearly dark by the time they reached the gardener's cottage. Lamplight spilled through the windows, and they could hear laughter emanating from inside. In answer to Mat's knock, Dyrileah opened the door. She and Bode stared at one another for a moment and then embraced.

"Are you well, little sister?" Dyrileah asked, concern and tender regard weighting her words.

Fighting tears, Bode replied, "I'm awfully lightheaded." She jerked a finger back at Mat. "It's all his fault." She laughed, and the tears spilled onto her cheeks. Sliding an arm around Bode, Dyrileah steered her toward Spats's bedroom. Looking back over her shoulder at Mat and Jaryd, Dyrileah sniffed. "You two, stay out." Guiding Bode into the bedroom, she slammed the door.

"I'd say the pair of you," Byan Hume indicated Jaryd and Mat, "are either luckier than you deserve or," he added slyly, "in more trouble than you can handle."

"With women involved," Spats put in with a wicked smile, "both are possible at the same time." He chuckled gleefully.

"Do you have anything useful to offer in the form of advice?" Jaryd asked a little pointedly. He'd discovered teary-eyed women were enough to crack even the stoutest of hearts.

"Nay," Spats replied immediately. "Biscuits and brandy are the best I can do."

The four men had barely dug into the food and drink when the bedroom door swung open, and Bode and Dyrileah emerged, arms twined around one another.

"How much trouble are we in, do you think?" Jaryd asked, speaking around the remains of a biscuit he'd been chewing.

"Is it anything we can't fix with biscuits and brandy?" Mat wanted to know.

The muscular smith sat at table opposite Jaryd in Spats's sitting room. Bode slipped free of Dyrileah's grasp and walked over to Mat to lay a hand upon his shoulder.

"We've decided to forgive you," she declared, smiling sweetly.

Dyrileah strolled to Jaryd's side to run her fingers through his red hair. "We won't forget, though," she declared, smiling tartly.

Gauging the expressions on the two young men's faces, Byan could contain himself no longer and burst out laughing. Spats rose, chuckling, from his place by the fire and offered each of the young women a mug of brandy. The supper that followed was a simple affair. More of Spats's biscuits with cheese slices were served first and, after, ham with a porridge flavored by bits of bacon and fried onions, a mixed bowl of raisins and salted almonds, and peach pie still warm from the oven for dessert. After the meal, Spats and Byan declared they needed some air. The two sauntered out, leaving the sitting room and the fire to the four young people.

Jaryd did most of the talking and all the teasing, although it was Mat's brief, sardonic rejoinders that most often set the two young women to laughing. An hour or so passed, and then Dyrileah rose to her feet, tugging on Jaryd's arm. "Come and help me in the kitchen," she entreated.

"I'll be happy enough to join you in the kitchen," Jaryd responded. "When it comes to actually helping, I'll make you no promises."

Bode watched as Jaryd and Dyrileah made their way into the kitchen. "You like her, don't you?" Mat asked. Bode nodded, and Mat inquired, "She called you 'little sister' earlier. What was that about?"

Bode shrugged. "I think she thinks I need some mothering or at least some elder sistering. I can't imagine why. I'm usually so levelheaded." She looked at him, smiling fondly. "I was a little dizzy when we got here. I had been ever since falling in the road. I don't remember bumping my head, but maybe I did. When we stepped into the bedroom, she asked me what had happened." Mat was seated on a floor rug near the base of the hearth he'd occupied while the four of them were talking. Bode slid off the chair she sat on next to him and joined Mat on the rug. She peeked up at him through long, brown eyelashes. "I told her…well, mostly, that is. She put her arms around me and hugged me tight for a few moments. And just like that," Bode snapped her fingers quietly, "my dizziness was gone. I feel fine the now."

"Is she a healer?" Mat queried.

"No, she couldn't be. She's over eighteen. There is something about her, though, a connection I don't understand," Bode said softly, speculatively, hugging him. "I know I can trust her," she continued more assertively.

Bode kissed him. "I want to go someplace private," she announced. Rising, she pulled Mat to his feet. Bode drew a taper from a clay jar on the mantle, held the long, wooden sliver over the fire until it ignited, and then used it to light an oil lamp. She led him out the front door and turned to the right. The cottage that Spats occupied was the largest in a cluster of similar white-painted, thatched-roofed structures. The next one over contained Jaryd's quarters.

By the light of the lamp, they walked hand in hand to Jaryd's cottage. She unlocked the door. Upon entering, Bode placed the lamp on a table in the middle of the room. Mat closed the door and set the latch. His hand trembled. He turned to see Bode standing near the fireplace. The pit gaped cold and dark; the room swathed in the soft amber glow of the lamp. Saying nothing, Bode held out her arms. Mat could not recall crossing the room. He must have, though, for, all of a sudden, he was holding her close.

They kissed the first truly private kiss they'd shared that day. Bode's mouth was soft and warm beneath his and sweetly responsive. Her lips parted, and he felt the shy touch of her tongue. He responded in kind, and when their tongues met, he could feel her body shiver. Bode made a subtle noise deep in her throat and pushed closer. His arms tightened about her, taking her slight weight. Pulling her mouth from his, she turned in his arms and swept aside her hair, revealing the row of buttons running down the back of her dress.

"Help me," she whispered.

His hands and fingers seemed too large and cumbersome for the task, and Mat slowly undid the top two. Bode reached around her back to deftly unfasten the remaining three. With a supple shrug of her shoulders, she slipped free of the dress, letting it fall about her ankles. She'd taken off her shoes. He hadn't noticed that. Wearing only a white silk shift, Bode stepped back into his arms. "This tunic of yours is scratchy, Sajar," she complained, tugging at his belt.

The belt fell away, striking the floor with a soft thud. He pulled both tunics upward over his head. He got them tangled for a bit, which made Bode laugh. He could tell she was nervous. Dragging the garments free, he tossed them aside and stood naked before her except for his loin cloth, socks, and sandals. Mat felt a little ridiculous wearing his sandals. He forgot all about them when Bode slid her arms about his neck.

Her body under the thin silken sheath of her shift moved against his. He could feel the press of her thighs. Seemingly of their own accord, his hands found her breasts. Through the slight barrier of the cloth, her nipples rose. He kneaded gently, not really knowing how to touch her. Impatient of even the flimsiest of obstructions, Bode pulled her shift down, and Mat found bare flesh beneath his hands, firm but incredibly soft. Her mouth plied his, hungrily searching. He paused long enough to look at her. Her eyes were closed, her lips slightly parted. The sweet swell of her breasts caught his eye, high and full, pink nipples taut above the startlingly white flesh beneath.

A blanket, a sturdy comforter from the look of it, covered a settle near the fireplace. He grasped it with one hand and spread it roughly on the floor. Easing Bode down atop it, he cradled her in his arms. His mouth found her right breast, his tongue rasping over the budding rise of her nipple. Bode whimpered, a low, urgent sound.

His right hand reached down under the hem of her shift to slide upward over the velvety skin of her inner thigh. As gently as he could, he placed his hand over her most intimate flesh, parting with his fingers the soft folds of skin he found there, seeking. His middle finger pressed inside her, enveloped by the moist heat of her inner core. Bode gasped at his touch, her thighs parted, and she stirred beneath his hand. Her hips began to move in a rhythm as old as man and woman, slowly increasing in frequency and urgency. He probed, trying to please, guided by her response. Her body strained, swept up in a rising tide of passion. Finally, she cried out, wracked by a spasm that seemed to grip her entire being. Her head snapped to the left, and with each subsequent breath, she uttered a softer moan, fading after a bit to silence.

Removing his hand, he wrapped his arms about her, wanting to touch her everywhere. He settled for watching her face. Her cheeks were flushed. He could see that even in the faint light of the lamp. Bode's eyes opened. He'd never seen her look so vulnerable or half so beautiful.

"Don't stop, Mat," she pleaded. "I don't want you to stop."

Gazing deeply into her eyes, Mat slowly shook his head. "I'll be leaving in the morning. I don't know when I will see you again."

"All the more reason for us to be together the now while we can," Bode interjected.

"I can't take the chance of walking away and leaving you alone and pregnant, Bode." Mat's voice was pitched low and thick with emotion. "I won't do that to you. I can't."

Bode saw tears in his eyes. Mat never cried. She couldn't remember ever seeing him cry. Very carefully, she reached up to brush away a tear from his cheek. "All right." Bode nodded. "Lay on your back," she commanded him. Mat complied, and Bode rid herself of her shift, setting it aside. Completely naked the now aside from a very sensible pair of woolen socks, Bode pulled at his loin cloth.

"Bode," Mat started, reaching for her hand.

"Hush," Bode growled at him quietly. "I've known your touch, and you must know mine the now. Fair is fair, after all." Tugging away the cloth, she took his engorged penis gently in a slim-fingered hand. "Well, hullo there," she murmured. Slipping astride him, she pressed her sex against his organ. He could feel the wet heat of her. He wasn't inside her so much as alongside her. "Mat," she whispered, her voice trembling. "I don't know what to do."

"You're doing fine," Mat whispered back, gritting his teeth. Taking hold of her hips, he thrust his pelvis upward against her.

Bode's stormy gray eyes widened and then slid shut. "Oh," she protested softly, "that's not fair." He moved beneath her, grinding their loins together. He could feel Bode responding, rocking her hips forward and back to meet him. She groaned and crooned his name over and over so quietly he could barely hear her but with an intensity that spurred him. Mat cried out as climax consumed him, and he rose to a sitting position, crushing Bode to his chest heedless of the hot pulsing of his manhood as it surged between them.

Mat eased his grip on her. He ran his hand down her back beneath the silken fall of her hair, stroking gently, marveling at the feel of her in his arms. "Are you all right?" he asked. Bode nodded, snuggling close.

"Am I still a virgin, do you think?" Bode spoke in a whisper, sounding, he thought, younger than she had in a long while.

"Yes," he assured her without hesitation, "you are a virgin still."

"Oh," Bode sounded disappointed. "I thought so. We are lovers the now, though, are we not?"

"Yes," he said again, "and what a joy you are."

"Really," she breathed, looking at him anxiously, "and truly, you think that?"

"Like a dream come to life in my arms you are," Mat assured her.

Bode relaxed against him. "I'm so glad to hear that." She wriggled a little after a bit. "This is messy business."

Mat grinned. "That is your fault entirely."

Kissing him briefly, Bode climbed to her feet, an easy, graceful movement. "Bide a moment," she enjoined. "I'll be right back." She walked to the bedroom. Mat's eyes were drawn as surely as if enchanted to the supple movement of her hips as she did so. Bode wasn't all that tall, but her legs seemed remarkably long in proportion to the rest of her. He could hear water splashing into a basin. She returned after a short while with a white cloth in her hands.

Kneeling beside him, she announced, "This is clean and damp. The water was a little cold." Without further warning, she pressed the cloth against his groin.

Mat started at the chill touch of the wet rag. "Hoi, girl." He gasped. "You'll shrivel my pod with that thing."

Giving his penis a friendly pat, Bode cooed, "I'm sorry, little fellow. I didn't mean to startle you."

"Must you call him little?" Mat grumbled.

"No offense was intended." Bode giggled. Mat sighed.

"I think you're just splendid, all of you, if a bit hairy," Bode told him. She continued to bathe him, wiping his belly and upper thighs as well. Her gentle ministrations soon had the opposite effect of shriveling, something Bode noted with delight. "Hullo again," she murmured throatily, giving his manhood a light squeeze. Looking up at Mat, she smiled. "I think he's looking for mischief."

"It's the company he's been keeping lately," Mat replied. He kissed her tenderly, careful not to spark to life a flame neither of them could control. Assisting Bode back into her clothes was, Mat felt, every bit as intimate a gesture as helping her to undress—intimate and sad because dressing her felt like parting.

Upon joining Dyrileah in Spats's kitchen, Jaryd put his arms around her, asking, "You don't really have any work to do in here, do you?"

Settling into his arms, Dyrileah told him, "There is always something to do in the kitchen, but nothing that can't wait."

"It's getting late," Jaryd observed regretfully. "I'll walk you back."

"I can stay over until morning," Dyrileah responded, laying her head against his chest.

"Your parents will worry," Jaryd objected. "They'll skin me on sight."

"My father knows," Dyrileah murmured. "He will tell my mother."

"How could he possibly know?" Jaryd queried. "Mat and my da blew in this afternoon with no more warning than a spring shower."

"Well…" Dyrileah hesitated just a little. "He doesn't know exactly, but I warned him I would soon be staying over."

"And he is all right with this?" Jaryd sounded skeptical. "He's never even met me."

"He knows all about you." Dyrileah hugged him tightly. "Don't worry."

"That's easy for you to say. They love you, after all," Jaryd responded. "It's my hide they'll be peeling."

Changing the subject, Dyrileah said, "I gave Bode the key to your quarters. I hope you don't mind."

"Good thing I changed the bedclothes this morning," he commented.

"Jaryd," Dyrileah chided him, "that's awful."

"It's about time is what it is. Speaking of which," he went on, "I asked you the first time kneeling. We were seated for the second go. I'll ask you standing this time round." He looked into her eyes, thinking he'd never seen anyone so lovely. "If you refuse me again,

I'll be down to standing on my head for the next try. After that, I'm going to get a little desperate."

"Yes." Dyrileah interrupted him.

"Yes?" Jaryd echoed, cautiously hopeful. "'Yes' what, exactly, I'm wondering?"

Dyrileah's eyes glowed. "Yes, I will marry you."

Jaryd whooped, and Dyrileah clasped her hand over his mouth, whispering furiously, "Hush, you fool. Everyone will hear you."

Jaryd quieted, and Dyrileah removed her hand. "I don't care if everyone hears. In fact, I'd like to shout it from the rooftops." His voice swelled a little more with each word.

Dyrileah's eyes searched his. "I love you so much. More than I thought I could ever love anyone." She touched his cheek, her fingers feather light, her eyes never leaving his. "I want nothing more than to be your wife. You must believe that."

"I do," Jaryd replied fervently. "Why can't you believe that I do?"

"We have much to discuss." Dyrileah sounded anxious, frightened even.

"I wish you would tell me what troubles you so," Jaryd urged.

"I will tell you all, after you meet my family," Dyrileah promised. "I want you to see us, to know us a little first, please."

"You are never going to talk me out of loving you," Jaryd vowed. "When can I see your parents? Tomorrow?"

"Tomorrow is too soon," Dyrileah replied firmly. "My father will be leaving tomorrow evening. He'll be gone for nearly a month. When he returns, on First Day soonest, please come for supper."

"Next month," Jaryd mused. "I suppose I can hold out that long if supper is in the bargain." He smiled, and Dyrileah could only shake her head.

"You must promise me," Dyrileah said seriously, "not to tell anyone until after we've spoken to my parents."

"May I tell my father?" Jaryd pleaded. "In the morning? Only my father?"

Dyrileah took a breath. "Yes, your father should know." She sighed. "In the morning. You must tell no one else, though; for the now, our betrothal must be for us alone."

Gathering her into his arms, Jaryd held Dyrileah as gently as he knew how. "Sounds a fine idea to me that does."

Upon their return to the gardener's cottage, Bode and Mat found that Spats and Byan Hume were nowhere to be seen. Jaryd and Dyrileah occupied the settle near the fireplace and sat with their arms around one another. Jaryd looked up. "We didn't expect to see you two until morning."

Bode slipped her arm around Mat's waist and pressed close to him. "We took care of everything that needed doing."

Glancing down at her, Mat shook his head and asked of Jaryd, "Has your father gone to bed?"

Jaryd thrust his chin toward the bedroom. "He and Spats are in there. If you listen carefully, you can hear them snoring in unison."

Hand in hand, Mat and Bode walked to the fireplace. Mat took a seat on the floor in front of the hearth. Bode settled beside him.

"Jaryd says there has been some fighting in the borderlands, men killed, entire villages burned," Bode said, her voice just loud enough to be heard above the soft crackle of the fire.

"Sometimes," Mat growled, "Jaryd talks too much." He glared at his friend.

Jaryd met his gaze. "Just trying to keep things balanced," he replied evenly. "Some compensation for those times you don't talk at all."

Mat reclaimed Bode's hand. "Elven mercenaries have been raiding along the western border of Quistyn del Aurus. Word is they do so at the behest of King Dardan of Syrdis. Small and sporadic at first, the attacks began last winter. With the spring, they appear to be growing in size and frequency. Still, the raids are hit-and-run affairs, something like what the Indiquoi used to do in the Three Rivers. There has been no sign of an invasion, at least not to this point. Just what old Dardan is up to is anybody's guess so far as we've heard." By Mat's standards that was quite a speech.

"I don't understand," Bode broke the brief silence that followed. "If Dardan wanted to attack, wouldn't it have made more sense to do so during the War of Houses and not after?"

"I'm only a part-time soldier." Mat shrugged. "But it seems like Dardan is poking a bear with a stick, doesn't it?"

"Maybe," Jaryd mused, "as the bear is no longer otherwise occupied, Dardan figures it is about to turn on him and has decided to get his licks in early."

"You sound like your da the now," Mat replied.

Jaryd smiled. "That ought to worry at least one of us."

Shifting position, Mat continued. "Up until now, the only thing of military significance we've done is to guard a bunch of tents just outside Tyne City."

"Tents are valuable things," Jaryd put in helpfully, "waxed canvas and all. I suppose they need careful looking after."

Mat grimaced. "The tents only need guarding because we've taken the trouble of setting them up in the first place. We took no casualties at all during the stalwart defense of our tent city until they started handing out passes. A couple of the fellows got themselves banged up pretty thoroughly fighting with the locals in Tyne."

"Greystock boys," Bode exclaimed, "involved in physical altercations while on leave? I can't imagine." Her eyes widened, and she gazed up at Mat in carefully posed amazement.

Mat looked to Dyrileah. "Do you see what I'm up against?"

"I understand completely," Dyrileah replied, smiling.

"I suppose," Bode said carefully, her countenance sobering, "with summer coming, they'll have you guarding tents someplace farther afield?"

"Garrison duty, the rumor is," Mat confirmed. "Someplace farther west, most likely. The Tieran professionals in charge apparently have some reservations about auxiliary troops in general and militia in particular as we are only amateur soldiers, after all, with a reputation for being somewhat unreliable." He bent to briefly touch his forehead against Bode's. "Frontier garrison duty will, I suspect, have a lot more to do with keeping our feet dry and our bellies full than fending off Syrdisians."

"Asking you to be careful sounds so silly," Bode started and then let her voice trail away to silence.

"They's only two things what kills soldiers," Mat declared, doing his best to emulate Nathyn Biddle's slightly nasal twang. "Bad luck and stupidity." He went on to recite the sajar first's lecture on stupidity. Bode and Dyrileah were laughing openly by the time he finished.

"May I trouble you for the blanket?" Mat asked Jaryd, pointing to a quilt folded over the back of the settle. Jaryd reached around and passed the blanket over to Mat, who handed it to Bode. "We'll leave you two the fire," Mat told Jaryd and Dyrileah. Catching Bode's eye, he whispered, "It is liable to be a little chilly over there by that window, but it will give me a chance to look at you by moons' light."

Lifting Bode in his arms, he carried her across the room to the corner window. Bode made no protest. Taking a seat on a rug underneath the window, Mat helped Bode drape the blanket over them and then collected her in his arms. Looking at her, he said, "You get prettier with every breath you take. How is that possible?"

Bode laid her head on his shoulder. "I promised you not to cry anymore. You are not helping."

"I'll make you a promise," Mat said with quiet determination. "I'll be back. I promise I will be back."

"You'd best keep that promise, Mathias Bayrd," Bode told him. She pressed her face against the cloth of his tunic so he could not see the tears trickling down her cheeks.

Mat cradled her to his chest. Bode felt small and soft in his arms and warm with life. Feeling welled within him, a mix of desire and affection and something more—a small piece of forever, maybe. Mat feared he had not heart enough to hold it all. Bode drifted off to sleep. Mat gazed through the window into the darkened sky above and prayed to the All Father, asking Him to allow a way to keep his promise and to watch over Bode until he could hold her safe once again.

Byan and Spats arose just after dawn. They stepped quietly into the sitting room to find the two young couples asleep. Mat and Bode were huddled together beneath a blanket on a rug under the window, while Jaryd and Dyrileah nestled on the settle by the hearth, covered by Jaryd's cloak.

"I hate to wake them," Spats intoned.

"I don't suppose another hour or so will hurt any," Byan whispered back.

"C'mon," Spats said, pointing to the kitchen. "Let's get a kettle on the stove."

Jaryd awoke to the smell of bacon frying. He sat watching Dyrileah until her eyes opened. "Hullo there," he said quietly, a note of wonder in his voice. Dyrileah smiled and stretched as lithely as a cat.

"Hullo yourself," she murmured sleepily. Looking about, Dyrileah suddenly turned to him and clasped his arm. "Your father…what he must think."

"I know he thinks I'm luckier than I deserve." Jaryd folded his hand over hers. "I've noticed every now and again that the old man is right about one thing or another."

The morning seemed to fly by. Class sessions at the Hall were scheduled only between Second Day and Sixth Day; as it was Eighth Day, neither Bode nor Jaryd had classes to attend. Breakfast was followed by a brief tour of the Hall grounds. Bode and Mat touched constantly and said very little.

Just before the time came for Byan and Mat to leave, Jaryd pulled his father aside. "Looks like the third time was the charm."

"She said yes?" Byan asked, grinning.

"Aye," Jaryd affirmed. "Our betrothal is a secret for the now—something Elsacian, I imagine." He met his father's eyes. "I owe you, I think, more than I can repay."

"Ah, it was only a matter of time, lad. She loves you, she does." Byan grasped his son's hand. "Treat her right, you hear." Jaryd nodded. Enfolding Jaryd in his arms, Byan said, "I love you, son."

Holding tight to his father, Jaryd replied, "I love you too, Papa."

With Bode and Dyrileah there, Spats's quarters always before seemed full. Once Byan and Mat left, however, Jaryd could not help but feel a sense of emptiness. Bode looked bereft and worn out. Jaryd walked the two girls home early. As usual, he and Dyrileah parted company at the Porter's Gate that opened into the Elsacian Quarter of Antium City. Jaryd watched until she rounded a corner and disappeared from sight.

23

A Matter of Perspective

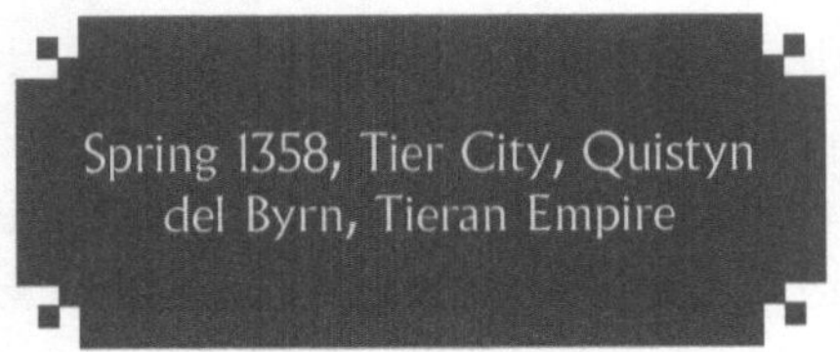

"The real danger"—Gaius Sylas Endryk made no attempt to hide the contempt in his voice—"is that soldiers will become used to anything. Once they grow accustomed to sitting on their butts all day, chasing whores, and fighting among themselves all night, that is all they'll be good for until someone reminds them what duty means."

"The Gracci has learned caution, Gaius," Nyus Sylas Cain observed mildly. "As it was you who administered the lesson, that should not come as a surprise."

"Being cautious is one thing, Uncle," Gaius remarked. "Young Segus has practically become catatonic."

Nyus laughed dutifully, thinking it was hardly fair to blame a walking corpse for exhibiting a lack of enthusiasm. Gaius, he knew, had a remarkable capacity for appearing sincere. *Easy the now*, Nyus thought. *I'm being unfair to Gaius.* His nephew's sincerity was genuine, merely subservient to his ambition. In the event one became an impediment, Gaius would not hesitate to cut one's throat. While doing so, he would honestly regret the inconvenience incurred, but one would wind up with a second smile, as soon as may be, all the same.

Nyus watched as Gaius drained his cup of some heavily watered wine and then set the finely wrought silver goblet down atop the map table beside which the two of them were standing. The table sat squarely in the middle of Gaius Sylas Endryk's study. The room stood but one of thirty-three in the two-storied villa located immediately below the crest of Edeon Hill just south of the city center. The house and grounds were located in the most affluent section of Tier. Constructed of red brick and white marble, the villa had been built by one Jervys Sylas Endryk over a century ago, long before the conflagration known as the War of Houses had erupted. The Gracci faction had occupied the home during most of the civil war. Its reclamation by House Sylas represented one of the few obvious garlands of victory that Gaius allowed on display.

While a boy, Gaius didn't look much like his father, Albys Sylas Endryk. As he grew older, the resemblance became more and more pronounced. An impartial and discerning eye would not describe Gaius, aged thirty-four, as a handsome man. His nose jutted a bit too prominently, as did his cheekbones. This lent his countenance a permanently gaunt cast. It might be said that Gaius Sylas Endryk possessed a noble face, if not a kind one. Gaius's hair looked more like his mother's, thick, light brown, and wavy, worn short in the military tradition.

Gaius's eyes were his most striking feature. Black they were, not simply dark brown but a deep, glossy black. Intense, intelligent, and ever perceptive, they were his father's eyes and projected the visage of a man not to be trifled with, one well suited for command. Tierans of old used to say it took a hard man to make hard choices and a harder one still to make them stick. Gaius's smile saved him from looking too severe. He had good teeth, white and even. The young emperor rarely smiled these days, and it was even more unusual for the expression to warm his black-eyed gaze.

Tall for a Tieran and spare of flesh, Gaius looked lean and fit. A sheathed dagger affixed to the belt on his right side. At least a span and a half long, the blade curved gracefully, crafted from the finest steel of Roi. Gaius had taken to wearing it constantly as if he needed yet another reminder of just how potent a threat the Kingdom of Roi posed to the resurgent Tieran Empire.

A hand shorter than his nephew and fourteen years his senior, Nyus still looked the soldier despite a lame left leg. His knee had been shattered by a Gracci spear two years earlier. The healers had managed to mend the wound, but the knee remained ever stiff. The older scion of House Sylas had hair the same shade as that of his nephew, still thick and equally wavy, and eyes of blue.

"Resurgent" might be too strong a word regarding the state of the empire, Nyus corrected himself; perhaps "recovering" was more accurate. This bit of knowledge represented something Nyus felt certain that King Mymnon, third of that name to rule in Roi, also knew. Mymnon III would not wait for the Tierans to bind the wounds of civil war and regain their full strength and, more importantly, their sense of unity before striking at them. So far, however, that is exactly what wily old Mymnon had done: wait. Not knowing the reason for this grew ever more disturbing with each passing day. *What is the old bastard waiting for?*

However serious a concern Roi represented along its eastern boundary, their conversation this afternoon had so far focused on the opposite end of the empire, north of the Middle Sea in the province of Quistyn del Aurus. There, old, sickly King Dardan of Syrdis had been causing trouble. Word had reached Tier of a recent alliance between Syrdis and the Kylgahran clansmen of the west—a *defensive* alliance, although exactly what that meant remained open to interpretation. Apparently emboldened, Dardan had initiated a series of raids into Tieran lands east across the River Wyst.

"Jute's regiments are in place upon the Basyr?" Gaius asked.

"Confirmation arrived this morning," Nyus affirmed. Gaius had ordered General Leptavius Nervi Jute, and five veteran regiments of regulars redeployed to the province of Quistyn del Salia on the Basyr Peninsula. The move was intended to forestall any overt aggression on the part of the Kiosans to the north. Jute's command had originally been slated to join the Northern Expeditionary Force under Segus Gracci Versi.

"A move, however necessary, that young Segus will no doubt view as yet another excuse to loiter," Gaius surmised.

General Segus Gracci Versi had been dispatched to Quistyn del Aurus to deal with King Dardan or at least ward off any substantive aggression on the part of Syrdis. Since his arrival in Tyne, the capital of Quistyn del Aurus, three months prior, the Gracci had done next to nothing.

"Glabrio writes the additional time to train has been put to good use," Nyus said carefully. Given Jute's reassignment, Glabrio had become the Gracci's second-in-command.

"You know this Glabrio, do you not?" Gaius inquired, black eyes intent as ever.

"Quintus Glabrio Jens served under me for three years. He was an aide of mine for two." Nyus recalled, "A thoroughgoing professional that one, he pisses Tieran blue. Brave, of course, and competent." Nyus liked Jens; the man had not a political bone in his body.

"Ambitious, is he?" Gaius asked.

Nyus nodded. "Very. He intends to be a good soldier."

"A fool he is then," Gaius concluded, "bound to honor and all that."

"Aye, a fool who insists on being fair in a world that is not, but he is bloody useful in the field regardless," Nyus affirmed, thinking even the most gifted—Gaius was nothing if not gifted—gauged by but one standard: that of their own choosing. "The delay becomes onerous, but I do not see that any real harm has been done."

"I see no real good either," Gaius said flatly. "I am convinced *the Gracci*"—he placed a wry emphasis on the honorific—"needs some proper motivation."

"As do we all." Lydia Sylvus Gant had a most pleasing voice, even when vexed. The mere sound of Gaius's younger sister's cultured tone was one of the few things left in this world with the capacity to sooth the evermore mercurial temper of Tier's new emperor. Lydia glided through the open door of the study.

"Lydie." Gaius turned toward her, smiling. "Well met, little sister." He held out his hands.

As she walked toward her brother, Nyus could not deny the

swell of affection he held for his niece. Lydia stood in no measure a large woman, a couple of finger widths below medium height, small boned and slim hipped. At thirty years of age, her bosom, clearly outlined by the dark-blue silk gown she wore, appeared high and neat. Her hair, if worn loose, was long enough to reach her hips and showed a light brown streaked naturally blond in places. She had it coiled atop her head at the moment in a manner elaborate enough to suit the current fashion.

Nyus's wife, Oriel, assured him that gossips all over the court were determined to discover how Lydia managed to color her hair. Nyus knew the truth: Lydia's hair looked just like her mother's, and its coloring had nothing to do with dyes or cosmetics. Her eyes were a kinder version of her brother's, large, shimmering black, and every bit as intelligent. His niece's features were regular and not nearly as stark as the emperor's. She couldn't avoid her family heritage entirely, poor girl, and as a result was beautiful without ever quite being pretty. How she managed that, Nyus had no idea. *Perhaps*, he thought, *it is so because Lydia exudes a unique ability to be herself.*

Placing small white hands in her brother's much larger, sunburnt brown ones, she smiled sweetly up at him. "You really are a bastard, you know that."

The emperor released her hands. "Who told you?" he inquired softly. When Gaius Sylas Endryk spoke in that tone of voice, brave men shivered.

Ignoring him, Lydia turned to Nyus. "Uncle." The one-word greeting was accompanied by a smile that Nyus had no doubt was genuine.

He allowed himself to bask in its warmth for a moment. "It was I who told her, Primus," Nyus said evenly. "Primus" served as the official honorific for the emperor of Tier.

"Nyus, you?" Gaius registered surprise; his uncle was nothing if not discrete. "Why, for God's sake? You knew I intended to tell her myself."

"Lydia came upon me and my aide, Cretio, discussing our travel plans earlier this afternoon," Nyus replied with the smooth erudition of a well-practiced diplomat. "She was naturally inquisitive. As we are to be traveling companions, Lydia and I, it seemed disingenuous not to tell her."

"You are sending me to Tyne." Lydia waded without hesitation into a sudden silence. "And subsequently to…what was the name of the place, Uncle?"

"Henfyrd on the southwestern coast of the Chestyre Peninsula," Nyus supplied.

"Henfyrd. A lovely place it is, I'm sure," Lydia purred, "especially, no doubt, if one enjoys the piquant aroma of cow shit."

"Henfyrd is quite a large town, Lydie, served by a modern aqueduct," Gaius replied. "I understand the fountains there are remarkably lovely."

"I want to go home, brother." Lydia made no attempt to hide the longing and pain in her voice.

"You think I do not?" Gaius shot back, his voice still carefully controlled.

Lydia stepped into her brother's arms, reached up around his neck, and kissed him lightly on the lips and then on his left cheek. *She is the only person in the world who could get away with that,* Nyus thought. "I am become a stranger to my children, Gaius. My boys do not know me," Lydia entreated.

Gaius hugged his sister briefly, his face softening, and then he reached down to pat her affectionately on her bottom. *The poor man has no idea how much he needs her,* Nyus thought. Gaius's wife, who was a stunningly beautiful young woman with hips as sinuous as an eel and snake-cold eyes, had no such claim on the emperor's heart. The empress's father, however, reputedly stood the wealthiest man in Tier long before Gaius's meteoric rise.

"I'll send the boys to you this summer," Gaius promised. "You may coddle them as much as you like until your return."

Lydia relaxed in her brother's arms, her affection unfeigned and as natural as a sunrise. "I'm no soldier, Gaius. How can I possibly serve you in this?"

"Your head works remarkably well, Lydie, and Uncle Nyus will be at your side." Gaius's tone said he understood her objections but that his mind was made up. "I trust your judgment." The emperor allowed just enough of an edge to enter his voice to let her know he meant business. "You, for example, know when to keep your mouth shut." His eyes flicked to Nyus. The veteran general perceived no heat in the glance and felt himself relax a little.

"If you trusted my judgment, you would have put the Gracci to death quickly and quietly months ago." Lydia's quiet tone was devoid of any emotion whatever, as if announcing the sum of two plus two equaled four. She must have overheard their conversation on her way into the room, Nyus concluded.

Sighing, Gaius replied, "We need to bind wounds, Lydie."

"With the best will in the world, Gaius, some wounds will fester," Lydia responded without rancor. "Segus Gracci Versi will never see beyond his own ambition. I should know. I was married to a man just like him."

"Then our objective must be to see that his ambition serves the empire," Gaius told her, pausing for a moment to add a little extra weight to his conclusion. "Just as in the case of your late husband."

Lydia's husband, one Paulus Sylvus Gant, had ranked among the richest men in the Tieran Empire until he fell last spring at the pivotal Battle of Prysium. The Prysium fight had been a close-run thing, the only time Gaius had ever come near defeat in battle. By all accounts, Paulus had died well.

Nyus knew that the luster of her name had been Lydia's principal attraction in the eyes of Paulus Gant. How a man could be so shrewd in all manners pertaining to the accumulation of wealth and be such an utter fool otherwise escaped him. Paulus was nearly twenty years Lydia's senior. Perhaps that had something to do with it. Gant had been a notorious philanderer, apparently one with an affinity for buxom blondes. Lydia dutifully bore him two sons early in their twelve-year marriage. To say she had been a reluctant bride constituted a deep understatement. That had been Albys's doing, not Gaius's. Her period of mourning neared its end.

Lydia remained both young and attractive enough to embody an extremely valuable political asset. She was also intelligent enough to know it. Would Gaius barter her away a second time? Nyus had no doubt that he would. Lydia's soft thighs would again be spread in service of House Sylas. *God damn politics and politicians*, Nyus thought. *I'm getting too old for this.*

Brushing the back of his hand lightly across her cheek, Gaius released his sister and stalked across the room to stare out a window set into the far wall. He moved with the easy grace of a natural athlete. "I think we should expand your merry band of travelers to include the Gracci's wife."

"Julyah is a dear," Lydia remarked, "a sweet girl. You are so clever, brother, and so brave." Lydia's soft voice reached out, tender and compelling. "Must you be cruel?"

"I'm sending the man his wife," Gaius growled. "What is cruel in that?"

"It is not him I am thinking of, Gaius," Lydia said promptly.

"I will have but one chance, Lydie"—Gaius turned back toward her and spoke with a quiet intensity—"to restore the Tieran Empire. One opportunity to pull the poor battered thing out from the cesspit of civil war and regain some semblance of its former glory. One slim hope of ascribing real meaning to all the blood spilled and lives shattered. If I falter, I'm done. We're done and the empire with us." His voice turned to steel. "I will do what I must."

Lydia's delicate chin raised, black eyes flashing, ready to fight. She saw then the pain in her brother's eyes—pain he would allow her to see and no one else. Crossing the room, she took a seat on a couch placed under the window. Patting a spot beside her, she invited him to sit. Gaius hesitated a moment and then joined her on the couch. "Have you been sleeping at all?" Lydia asked.

"Like the dead," her brother replied bitterly.

Clasping his arm with one hand, she gently stroked his shoulder with the other. "How is your stomach?"

"Better," he replied automatically. At her arched eyebrow, Gaius continued. "Truly, I've been avoiding fried foods. I'm even developing a taste for vegetables. Nyus can attest to that."

Lydia looked to her uncle, who smiled. "The bugger tricked me into sharing a bowl of cauliflower with him yesterday. Bloody dreadful that stuff is."

Lydia laughed, and with it, all tension in the room seemed to fade. "I should like to have seen that."

"Your boys will remember you, Lydie," Gaius assured her. "For you are unforgettable."

"Flattery, brother?" Lydia's smile took on a playful cast. "Has it come to that between us?" He shook his head, conceding the point. Lydia's gentle voice became serious. "You are a man, Gaius. Blood flows through your veins, pushed by a heart that beats within your breast. You are not a thing of steel, absent feeling." She looked at him, black eyes soft and entreating. "Should you become such, even if you gain an empire in the doing it will avail you naught, for you will be devoid of life, lost to the Light."

"One man's life weighed against the good of the empire counts for less than nothing, Lydie," Gaius responded. "Mine least of all."

"Your life is precious to me, brother." Lydia's voice throbbed. "But it is your soul of which I speak."

"This conversation has drifted rather far afield, Little Duck." Gaius enfolded her hands in his. "Little Duck" was a childhood endearment. He had not called her that in years. "I will not sell my soul at any price; that I promise. And you," he paused slightly for emphasis, "shall travel north and west, listen and learn, and help me determine what best to do there." He paused again. "With any luck, we will all be together in time for the Winter Solstice: you, your boys, Amelyah and I, and our girls. Amelyah is breeding again, did you know?"

"She's with child?" Lydia brightened. "That is good news." Amelyah, her brother's wife, was reputed to be the most beautiful woman in Tier: long-legged, slender, and voluptuous with honey-blond hair and striking green eyes. Amelyah's beauty was matched only by her temper, which was equally legendary. "Be kind, brother," Lydia admonished.

Unfortunately, Gaius thought, *Amelyah tends to interpret any act of kindness as a form of weakness.* His sumptuously lovely young wife, exactly eight years his junior, was as ruthless as a spider. Theirs was, of course, an arranged marriage. Amelyah's father, Daryus Evander Kyle, had accumulated enormous wealth. His father-in-law's riches and his wife's shrewd counsel had been valuable assets early in his career. Amelyah had born him a son, their first child. The boy died of a sudden fever at age two. Since then, there had been two girls. They both looked like their mother. Good fortune that; if he were a girl, he would much rather look like Amelyah than him.

They'd grown apart over the years, him and Amelyah. The ever-present civil war ripped and tore; it was easy to blame, but he knew there were other things. Amelyah could never see past the immediate, her vision too limited. She had also advocated the Gracci's death. Instead of Lydia's carefully measured opposition to keeping Segus Gracci Versi among the living, Amelyah had shrieked at him, crying out for vengeance. She viewed the young head of House Gracci as a danger to her children and her legacy. House Gracci was finished, broken, no longer a threat for at least a generation, but no amount of reasoning would convince Amelyah of that. She stood blind to the greater need. Gaius's decision not to execute Segus was, to Amelyah, merely the latest in a string of betrayals.

The Syrdisians nipping at the empire's heels in the northwest, the Roi looming as ever in the east…Gaius winced, his stomach not quite as docile as he'd led Lydia to believe. For all that, Gaius knew money or, rather, the lack of it represented the real threat. The empire's coffers were stretched too thin. He was going to have to punish some of his more prosperous enemies and reward some of his allies. It was a delicate matter—one that, if mishandled, could lead to disaster.

House Galba, in particular, would require compensation. Despite his father-in-law's wealth, House Galba formed the most influential member of the Sylatic faction. Antonine Galba Rhys, head of House Galba, had fought a brilliant holding action against the Dyraii throughout the past summer and fall. Though outnumbered, Galba had managed to check the Dyraiis' every move, losing both an uncle and a cousin in the process. Antonine's youngest brother had fallen valiantly, fighting to secure Gaius's critical victory at Arym.

Antonine was a childhood friend, a schoolmate. Galba's wizardry in the northeast had enabled Gaius's victories in the south. Gaius understood this well, and more importantly, so did Galba. Antonine had a younger brother, Ayristes, but two years Lydia's junior and unwed. Considering the worth of the dowry she possessed the now, perhaps a marriage between Lydia and Antonine's brother might serve as a start.

Gaius awoke, startled to find his head resting in Lydie's soft lap, his body reclined on the couch. One of her hands lay lightly upon his shoulder, and with the other, she gently stroked his brow, crooning low something old and familiar—a lullaby, he thought. Sitting up, he turned back toward her.

"How long have I been asleep?" Gaius asked.

"It is now the second hour after sundown," she said by way of answer. Looking about, he realized that it stood full dark out. The study was bathed in lamp light.

"Where is Nyus?" His head felt stuffed, and his voice sounded oddly muted to him as if he had cotton in his ears.

"Off doing something soldierly, I think," Lydia replied. "He said he would see you at the morning briefing, whatever that is. If you need him sooner, his aide Cretio will know how to find him."

All of which Gaius reckoned most likely meant that Nyus was off plowing some woman this evening. Where the old bugger got the energy to do that ranged beyond him. Gaius gazed at Lydie. His sister looked lovely, vulnerable but without a hint of weakness. In her luminous, sable eyes, he saw an unshakable trust born of a childhood shared, whispered hopes and fears. He did not think Lydie would deny him anything he truly wanted. Gaius felt a dark hunger rising and quelled it harshly. The effort required left him shaken. He looked away and wondered if Lydie perceived the darkness roiling inside him.

"Are you hungry?" Gaius inquired politely.

"Famished," she responded. Lydia took his hand. "I'm thinking of something boiled, with no gravy and lots of vegetables." The emperor of Tier laughed, in full control of himself once more. He was going to have to marry her off and soon. Not immediately, though.

He could give her that and wait until sometime after this year's Winter Solstice festivities. In the meantime, she would serve him well as an emissary, and he would hang on as best he was able to whatever remained of his soul.

24

Changing the Game

Summer roared into Quistyn del Aurus with a fiery vengeance. In the three days since their arrival in Tyne, it seemed to Lydia she had done little but sweat. Seated the now at a table in the reception hall of the forum complex, the citadel that housed the imperial ministry in the provincial capital of Quistyn del Aurus, she let her eyes wander about the large ballroom and the crowd milling about. The sun was nearly down, but the heat remained fierce and unrelenting. Rows of large windows, set into the long walls opposing one another in the rectangular hall, stood open, but not a breath of air stirred.

Lydia found the heat stifling, nearly as oppressive as the bombast just delivered by their host, General Segus Gracci Versi. The man's demeanor reminded her of nothing so much as an overbearing house guest. The general's address had not been overly long, and he had said nothing stupid or even plainly offensive. Condescension fairly oozed out of the Gracci, however, much like the perspiration now clinging beneath her breasts. He managed to be elegantly off-putting. She doubted that, armed with such a personality, young Segus could get laid in a buttock shop. No, that last rang unfounded. His name alone would assure him plenty of willing quim.

Lydia reined herself in carefully. She had perhaps finished a second cup of wine too quickly. The wine was valerian, outrageously expensive, dark, and much too sweet for her taste. She blamed the heat. She'd been parched. A lame excuse but the best she had at her disposal or at least the best she would admit to under the circumstances.

Lydia and her uncle, General Nyus Sylas Cain, had accompanied the Gracci's young wife, Julyah Gracci Versi, to Tyne. Julyah was sweet-tempered with a lush, clean-limbed body and a wealth of medium blond hair. Julyah's light-colored eyes, Lydia thought, were often sad. Their journey required that Julyah leave her children, a pair of boisterous five-year-old twin boys and a delicate eighteen-month-old baby daughter, in the keeping of strangers handpicked by her brother Gaius for their loyalty to House Sylas. Her boys were robust little fellows, but her daughter's health had been fragile, and Julyah was reluctant to leave her side. While no doubt genuinely worried for her daughter's well-being, Lydia's intuition told her that Julyah's reluctance to travel had more to it than concern over her youngest child's health alone.

As was the case for most women of noble birth, Julyah's children were the focus of her life. She could love them with all her heart and be loved in return. The thought brought to mind Lydia's own children, two sons by her late husband, Paulus. Flavius, her eldest, was eleven, thirteen months older than her younger boy, Tristan. Both Lydia's sons resided in her husband's home, a villa in the most affluent section of Quinto, capital of the Tieran province of Quistyn del Orro, long the seat of power for the House of Sylas. Lydia had not seen her sons in months, and the pain of separation goaded her as mercilessly as the summer sun.

Lydia's dark eyes, black as a raven's wing, again swept the room, searching for her dinner companion. Earlier that afternoon, Nyus had formally introduced her to Quintus Glabrio Jens. Her designated escort for the evening, General Glabrio stood second-in-command of the Northern Expeditionary Force under Segus Gracci Versi. She saw no sign of him yet.

Lydia fidgeted, adjusting the folds of her cream-colored silk frock. The dress was sleeveless with a neckline that suddenly appeared to plunge a bit more daringly than when she had first donned the garment. She thought then that Uncle Nyus would be her dinner partner. She'd worn her nearly hip-length hair, brown, streaked here and there with blond, in a simple braid—not as fashionable as many women present but less likely to wilt in the heat. A widow and mother of two at age thirty, she would have thought the prospect of spending the next couple of hours conversing with a man, a fellow Tieran, would not be as intimidating a circumstance as she found it. She was the emperor's sister, for pity's sake, a princess. Lydia stood well aware that she held only a temporary claim to the title, valid only so long as her brother served as emperor. Still, a princess she was for nearly six years to come, more than enough, it seemed to her, for any sane person. If anyone was to be intimidated, it should be this Quintus fellow.

Burn her uncle for surprising her like this. Lydia felt comfortable enough in most social situations, but she found the prospect of talking with a man—one she did not know, essentially one on one—discomfiting. Glabrio was a professional soldier. He'd most likely want to spend the evening discussing logistics or, worse yet, say nothing at all. As a junior officer, he'd served under her Uncle Nyus years ago. During the Gracci's speech, Quintus had taken up a position on the rostrum just behind and to the right of his commander. Lydia noted he carried himself as she would expect a soldier to, moving easily with an erect posture.

Scanning the room once more, she saw him approaching. Of medium height, Glabrio appeared well built with broad shoulders and firmly muscled arms and legs. He'd dressed in a military-style cotton tunic, Tieran blue, of course, belted at the waist. Crafted of good material, she observed, though unadorned. He wore no armor, but she saw a sword strapped to the belt on his left side and a dagger in a sheath over his right hip. The sword was long bladed, a spada, the cavalryman's weapon, not the infantryman's Glavius.

Her brother, she knew, always bore a spada as well. Quintus had a cotton neck cloth loosely tied about his throat. The fiber showed a natural color about that of oatmeal. A pair of sturdy leather sandals adorned his feet. He was bareheaded.

The heat appeared not to bother Quintus Glabrio Jens in the least. He came to a halt, standing alongside the vacant chair to her right, and bowed.

"Good evening, General," she ventured. "How are you?"

"I'm fine, Your Highness," Quintus replied. He smiled at her. "Well rested, certainly."

Servants had lit the lamps within the hall already. The soft light of the setting sun still filled the room, spilling through the open windows. His eyes were not quite green, more of a hazel color, she thought. He had dark hair, close cropped as befitted a military man.

Was his comment a jab at his commander's continued reticence to move from his base at Tyne? The emperor had dispatched an additional two thousand soldiers, militia infantry, gathered from Quistyn del Orro as an escort for Uncle Nyus, Julyah, and herself. Upon their arrival in Tyne, the men joined the Northern Expeditionary Force.

According to Gaius, the correspondence she and Nyus also brought with them intended to make plain the emperor's desires. The Gracci needed to move and do so quickly. *Will he?* She wondered.

"Please be seated, General," Lydia invited. Nyus had said Quintus Glabrio Jens was intelligent. "My uncle speaks highly of you," she told him, watching his eyes.

They warmed at the mention of Nyus Sylas Cain, and his smile broadened. "I was his aide for two years, Highness. He could hardly claim otherwise without owning up to the mistake." Quintus sat, removing his sword belt and looping it over the back of his chair as he did so, and sipped from a cup of wine a servant placed before him.

Returning his smile, Lydia commented, "He said that you were both courageous and resourceful."

"My experience with General Cain, Your Highness, is that he is capable of saying just about anything." Quintus raised his hand in the direction of her uncle, who was deeply engrossed in conversation with a statuesque widow young enough to be his daughter. "It is what he does that makes him such a good man."

What cheek, Lydia thought, *and how true*. "It is too warm for honorifics, General. Please call me Lydia." At his nod, she observed, "I understand you were at Prysium."

A shadow flickered in those light-colored eyes of his at her remark. He was good-looking, Lydia decided, if not entirely handsome. "I was," he acknowledged. "A hard day to forget."

"My husband was killed at Prysium," Lydia informed him. Glancing down, she discovered her third cup of wine stood nearly empty.

"I did not know," he replied. "I am sorry to hear of it."

"I was not," she said tartly and then paused. "I suppose I am the now, a little." Looking into his eyes, she inquired, "Do I shock you, Quintus?"

"Honesty is always a little startling upon first encounter," Quintus responded.

"Is it true, Quintus, that you piss Tieran blue?" *Sweet light*, Lydia nearly panicked. *He'll think I'm a simpering idiot.*

"Not that I've noticed," Quintus replied wryly. "If I take on anymore of this stuff, who can say?" He indicated the cup of valerian in his hand.

"Valerian is a little cloying," Lydia allowed, "something of an acquired taste."

"It's nearly as hard to swallow as one of the Gracci's orations," Quintus observed.

Lydia laughed. "I see what you mean about honesty." Her countenance sobered, and Lydia found herself wondering what it would be like to kiss him. "Segus has all the personality of a lamppost, an arrogant one at that."

Quintus shook his head. "Do you disagree?" Lydia asked.

Quintus's smile returned. *He has a nice smile*, she determined, gentler than one would expect of a professional soldier. "No, I concur. I was just having some difficulty envisioning an overly proud lamppost, but I take your meaning. The Gracci is about as engaging as…" Quintus paused as if searching for an apt description.

"A haughty in-law, the sort of house guest one cannot be rid of," Lydia supplied, smiling down into her now-empty third cup of wine.

Quintus laughed. "That may be a little harsh, Lydia."

Lydia's black eyes glimmered. "Have you never heard that truth has hard edges, Quintus?"

"Yes," the dark-haired general acknowledged. "The first time, I was ten. I'd just announced to my father that I intended to join a circus. He had a few words to say about duty and the truth of my obligations."

"I've often thought of running away to join a circus." Lydia's smile became wistful. "I always wanted to be a flyer. In your case"— Lydia regarded him carefully—"a sad-faced clown, I think."

"How did you know?" Quintus sounded mildly astonished.

"You have very expressive eyes, Quintus," Lydia intoned, "well suited for a sad face."

Dinner was served. They ate in silence. A shared quiet, Lydia thought, not uncomfortable. By the conclusion of the meal, Lydia had nearly finished her fourth cup of valerian.

Daintily wiping her mouth, she fixed her ebony-eyed gaze on Quintus. "The Gracci," she asked bluntly in a whisper registered for his ears alone, "is he competent?"

"He's no dullard," Quintus replied just as quietly. "He does not lack determination, and he has courage."

Lydia's sable eyes narrowed slightly. "That is no answer, Quintus."

"Nyus said you were the smart one in the family," Quintus japed. He glanced into her eyes and paused for a moment before continuing. "He's young, Lydia, and has only just realized the full weight of the burden he carries. He has done nothing incompetent."

"Then his intransigence is calculated," Lydia concluded, resting her eyes once again on those of Quintus Glabrio Jens. Glabrio was an ancient House, older than her own by generations, its sigil that of a sunburst. "My brother says every commander leads in his own way," Lydia recollected. "He said further that, thus far, the Gracci's generalship compares most favorably to a peculiar form of statuary."

25
Maneuvers

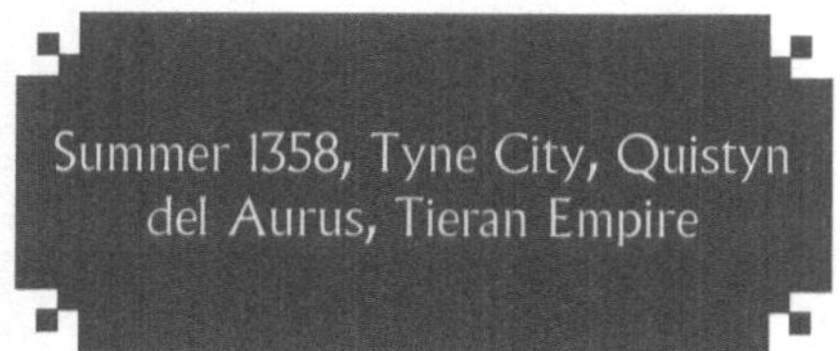

"Victory in the field most often devolves into achieving what is known as a localized superiority of force," Quintus said, unable to suppress a smile when, in response, Lydia regarded him as if he'd suddenly sprouted a third ear. "If you go too soon with too few, you get thumped," he expounded.

"And should there be no more to send," she inquired, "what then?" Lydia, he saw, had eyes as black as her brother's, radiating a keen intelligence. The similarity ended there, though. The emperor's eyes glinted with determination, ever shrewd and often forbidding. Lydia's eyes shone, softened by kindness, Quintus thought, or perhaps a sense of loss. Quintus found himself wondering what it would be like to kiss her.

"Then duty calls," Quintus admitted. "In this case, I suspect the Gracci and the emperor harbor differing views as to the best use of available resources."

"If you were he," Lydia queried, "what would you do?"

"Were I the emperor," Quintus replied, intentionally misinterpreting her question, "I would be devastated at the realization that the most attractive woman in the entire realm was my sister."

"You should not flirt, Quintus," Lydia admonished, almost, but not quite, able to suppress a satisfied smile. "You don't do it well." Quintus smiled openly in reply but said nothing.

"Segus Gracci Versi is an impeccably well-mannered brute, as was his father and so many others, characteristic of the breed," Lydia whispered softly, bitterly. She looked across the room, and Quintus noticed her gaze had settled on Julyah Gracci Versi.

"He knows what honor is." Quintus matched her tone. "I have some sympathy for the man."

"Then you are a fool," Lydia hissed sharply.

"There are worse things," Quintus shot back.

"Yes," Lydia countered in a fierce murmur, "like being married to an unfeeling lout who cares for nothing but his own ambitions and his precious name."

The pain in her voice and her eyes was evident and still raw. "I am a fool," he acknowledged gently.

"You are a man of the breed referenced." Lydia sighed. "A Tier-an nobleman." The emphasis she placed on the last two words was damning.

Quintus took refuge in silence. Some time passed with neither of them speaking. Finally, Lydia questioned, "Is it that I embarrass you, Quintus, or have I merely become boring?"

"You are incapable of being boring, Lydia," Quintus responded sincerely. He liked the sound of her name on his lips. "And any embarrassment I may feel is purely of my own doing." Sadness seemed to have taken root in her luminous dark eyes. "My silence was a tactical withdrawal," Quintus explained, smiling ruefully. "A maneuver designed to avoid being routed completely. I fear I may have initiated it too late."

"I am poorly versed in military matters, Quintus." She paused, looking none too pleased with him. "Nyus says you are competent but lack ambition."

Lydia's eyes sparked as she spoke. Quintus's smile warmed at the sight. Her irritation seemed to melt away. Emboldened, he re-marked, "In order to gauge a man's ambition, Lydia, you must first come to know what he wants."

The music had started. A Tieran military band played an old, slow tune. A few couples had already stepped onto the dance floor.

Lydia fixed her sable eyes upon him. They shone like twin pools of liquid midnight. "What do you want, Quintus?"

"To dance with you," he said promptly, "if you will allow it."

Rising, she extended her hand. "Is this what you call a counter-attack, General?"

In Quintus's opinion, Lydia was beautifully proportioned. Her legs were long for a woman of her height. Standing, she would fit nicely just under his chin. The gown she wore highlighted the pert rise of her bosom and the slender, supple curve of her hips.

"Yes, indeed," Quintus affirmed. Taking her hand, he climbed to his feet and led her onto the dance floor. "Watch your flanks, Highness." He smiled once more. "And rear."

26

A Compelling Message

From where he sat at the front of the hall, Segus Gracci Versi watched as Quintus squired the emperor's diminutive sister upon the ballroom floor. *Glabrio, dutiful as ever,* Segus thought. The fellow's reputation for calm, clear-eyed competence was well founded, the Gracci had learned. Despite this, Segus could not warm to the man, perhaps because he felt Glabrio had earned his reputation by becoming a little too good at killing Graccis.

This evening's festivities were ostensibly in honor of Her Highness Lydia Sylvus Gant. *I wonder what Quintus thinks of her.* A saucy little piece, if a bit too old for his personal taste, and too high-handed by half was the Gracci's opinion. Lydia had made no attempt to hide her disdain for him. Segus did not think it was personal; after all, he hardly knew the woman. It might be only that he hailed from House Gracci and she from that of Sylas. Some women of his acquaintance had opened play upon their first meeting by feigning indifference or even hostility toward him. Sometimes emotion of one type led to another much more satisfying form of passion. *Why has Gaius Sylas Endryk even sent her to Tyne?* It rated a mystery, that, especially with

Nyus Sylas Cain along to accompany her. The emperor was nothing if not efficient. The both of them together seemed redundant.

The presence of his wife, Julyah, formed yet another quandary. *What is the emperor trying to accomplish by allowing our reunion?* Julyah's greeting waxed as warm and submissive as ever. Six years younger and more lushly endowed than the emperor's skinny little sibling, Julyah proved as welcoming as Lydia had been aloof. More biddable and beddable as well, Segus had little doubt. Still, there remained something enticing about Lydia's black-eyed beauty. If things went well, he promised himself he'd have her one day, whether she wanted it or not.

By way of contrast, the message contained in the correspondence Nyus had delivered—directly, the old general said, from the emperor's hands—composed no mystery at all. The letter, brief and to the point, directed Segus to move the bulk of his forces to Henfyrd, a coastal town located on the Bay of Alum just to the east of the river Wyst. The Syrdisian city of Tensys occupied a portion of the opposite bank of the Wyst at the river's juncture with the bay. The Bay of Alum opened into the Middle Sea to the south. From Henfyrd, the Northern Army would be well positioned to directly counter any movement in force the Syrdisians made east across the Wyst into Quistyn del Aurus, and their presence in Henfyrd would pose a direct threat to Tensys itself.

An accompanying and even more compelling message passed on to him from the emperor through his emissary Nyus came in the form of a small, intricately carved wooden box. Inside the box were three dolls: children's toys with cloth bodies and brightly painted wooden heads. Two of the dolls were identical and clearly depicted dark-haired boys. The third, smaller doll represented a blond-haired baby girl. Segus's twin, black-haired boys were five the now and his fair-haired daughter a frail one and a half. The heads of one of the boy dolls and that of the baby girl had been neatly severed.

He found no note included in the box; the message conveyed required no embellishment. Should he disobey, the lives of two of his children would be forfeit, but an heir, his heir, would be carefully preserved forever in the custody of House Sylas. It was a cruel message but readily understood. The price one paid for losing a civil war was steep.

Fortunately, moving just the now fit nicely into his plans. He wondered if Nyus was aware of the particular content of the messages he'd placed in Segus's hands. The letter and the box had both been sealed, the wax tab bearing the emperor's mark, not merely that of House Sylas. Segus felt certain the old bastard had to have known. *What of Lydia? Does she know the specifics?* Somehow, he thought not.

Deciding to break with custom, Segus excused himself from his dinner partner, the plump, pretty spouse of one of Tyne's city councilmen, and made his way down the table to Julyah's side.

Touching her lightly on the arm, he asked, "Would you care to dance?"

Smiling up at her husband, Julyah Gracci Versi inquired of her dinner companion, the provincial governor of Quistyn del Aurus, one Tentius Sylas Dunn, "If you will excuse me, sir?"

"Gladly, my lady," the tall, fifty-eight-year-old nobleman, a distant cousin of the emperor, responded. "Your company will be sorely missed, but at my age, it's too hot for dancing, and music should not be wasted." Dunn smiled at her. "Especially when beauty such as yours is present."

Long-winded old fusspot, Segus thought and, taking Julyah's hand, led her onto the dance floor.

27

The Unthinkable

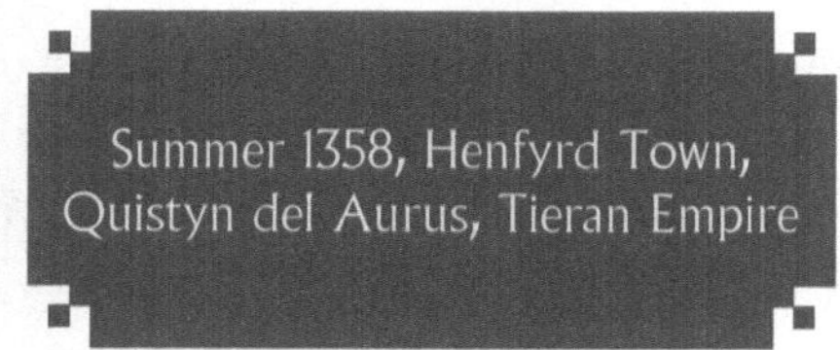

Two days later, the first contingent of the Tieran Northern Army boarded a ship bound for the port of Henfyrd. Available transport proved insufficient to carry all the Gracci's troops in one go. Two trips would be required to land the whole of the Northern Army at Henfyrd. A third would be necessary to deliver all their supplies and equipment. Quintus Glabrio Jens held command of the first contingent. Six regular-infantry regiments and virtually all of the auxiliary troops plus five hundred light militia cavalry made up the bulk of the forces Glabrio would lead ashore.

Quintus's orders were to establish a permanent camp in the low hills just outside of the seacoast town of Henfyrd, large enough to accommodate the whole of the Northern Army, reinforce the Henfyrd garrison, and reconnoiter to assess Syrdisian deployment in the area. The encampment, known as a compaglium, would require fortification, a large perimeter ditch and wooden palisade. Militia cavalry with help from the local population were intended to do the scouting.

Virtually all of Quintus's original command was incorporated into the first contingent of troops, and he wasted no time in sending Jon Tiberius Elder and his doughty band of scouts off to see what they could. He proceeded more cautiously with the militia cavalry, organizing a series of patrols focused mostly along the banks of the river Wyst. The people of Henfyrd were glad to see them. News from the north had not been good lately. Syrdisian raids were growing, it appeared, both in size and ferocity. Henfyrd itself had not been threatened, but the locals reported a steady stream of Syrdisian forces had been moving to and through the city of Tensys on the opposite bank of the Wyst for weeks.

Quintus reckoned it would be two to three weeks before the rest of the Gracci's command arrived, including the general himself. The Gracci's arrival was significant in Quintus's view for two reasons. For one thing, offensive operations on the part of the Northern Army would only be initiated after the commanding general disembarked. As to the second reason, Quintus was aware that Lydia Sylvus Gant would be traveling with General Gracci. Of late, Quintus's dreams and even quiet moments were haunted by Lydia's black-eyed visage.

Moths and flame. Quintus smiled, wryly. *Such didn't usually bode well for the poor bug.* The dark fire in the princess's eyes had stirred to life embers too long dormant in his heart to be ignored. Lydia was a widow. Assuming she maintained a suitable degree of discretion, Tieran custom allowed a widow, even one of noble birth, a free hand to associate with men of her choosing.

Still, her brother wore the imperial mantle. For someone like Quintus, a soldier of middling means, even a mild flirtation might be construed as reckless—and anything more substantive unthinkable. Quintus knew he should walk away. But the memory of how she felt in his arms as they danced and the subtle scent of her, sweet with a slightly citrus tang, argued otherwise. If the attraction proved mutual, well, he'd risked his neck for less. If it was only his imagination, then, until he knew for sure, it made for a pleasant sort of maundering.

28

An Expression of Trust

Summer 1358, Antium City,
Kingdom of Ayle

Jaryd Hume didn't like being nervous. The prospect of meeting Dyrileah's parents made him downright jittery. He often went to some considerable lengths to avoid situations that would cause him to feel so, but there would be no ducking this. He'd confessed as much to Uncle Spats. Spats responded by saying that there was usually one of two things wrong with young men: either they were too full of themselves or not full enough.

"You'd best take hold of life, son," Spats concluded, "or one day it will take hold of you."

"About half the time, Spats," Jaryd complained, "I don't have any idea what you're trying to say."

"Don't fret yourself, lad." Spats grinned. "About half the time, neither do I." Spats's well-worn countenance sobered after a moment, and he went on. "Be with them who you are with her, and you won't miss by enough to matter."

"That's worth a try, I suppose." Jaryd sighed, straightening his jacket, one Spats had loaned him, a buttery, brown leather design with cotton quilted lining.

The two of them were standing in the sitting room of Spats's cottage. The afternoon sunlight slanted gently through the window. Spats folded his arms across his chest and gazed out. "One of life's cruelest ironies is that all too often, you can only see the path you trod by looking back upon it." He turned to lay a hand on Jaryd's shoulder. "Sometimes with the best will in the world, understanding comes too late or not at all. On the bright side, every now and again, you just get lucky. Whatever else comes, winning the love of a girl like Dyrileah was a rare stroke of good fortune."

"I can't argue with you there." Jaryd smiled briefly. "I just wish…" He hesitated, balling his right hand into a fist. "Dyrileah is frightened of something, Spats, and she is not the type to scare easily. She's afraid of what it might do to us. The not knowing is starting to spook me."

"Give her time," Spats advised. His usually gruff tone softened. "When she tells you, boy, whatever it turns out to be, remember to listen with your heart as well as your head and without judging. Remember also when you get to my age, pride turns out to be cold comfort, not nearly as warm or welcoming as a pair of soft, sweet thighs."

"I would never have figured you for a romantic, Spats." Jaryd looked at the normally pragmatic chief gardener with just enough of a twinkle in his eyes to let Spats know he was teasing.

Meeting the younger man's gaze, Spats smiled ruefully. "I'm just old, Jaryd, with more than my fair share of regrets." He slipped his hand into his tunic pocket and withdrew a small black velvet bag. Extending his hand, he proffered the bag to Jaryd. "It's about time I got this back to you."

"Back to me?" Jaryd queried. Opening the bag, Jaryd saw a medal suspended from a silver chain. Examining the medal more closely, he saw a Fey rune symbol fused to a circular disk. Both the disk and the Fey rune appeared to have been forged of black iron. "What is this?"

"It is called a Fey amulet," Spats explained. "Your Fey carving was fused onto the disk."

"Fused how?" Jaryd asked. "The rune symbol is noticeably smaller than the one I carved, and it looks the now to be made of black iron."

"The fusing process shrinks the original resin of the carving onto the disk, and it mixes with the iron somehow. The disk itself was originally made of iron." Spats ran his finger over the rune symbol as it lay in Jaryd's palm. "The result is something the Elves call pellinwahr. It looks like black iron, but it isn't. As to how it's done"—Spats winked—"a bit of old magic. I couldn't say exactly without betraying a confidence."

Hefting the medallion in his hand, Jaryd said, "Thanks. What am I supposed to do with it?"

"The Fey amulet you hold is a powerful talisman," Spats informed him, the gardener's low, rich voice suddenly taking on a purposeful tone. "The ward that enables it is ancient but formidable. Worn about your neck, the Fey talisman will protect you against adverse magic of any known form."

"Adverse magic being what exactly?" Jaryd inquired.

"Adverse magic is that intended to do you harm," Spats expounded. "The Fey amulet is sophisticated enough not to interfere with beneficial magic, a healing flow, for example. It wards only against that which is designed to do the wearer injury."

"Who are you, Spats," Jaryd asked, raising his eyes to those of the old gardener, "and what are you?"

"I'm your friend, young Jaryd," Spats said sincerely, returning Jaryd's intent look. "You believe that, don't you?"

Jaryd held the old man's steady gaze. "I do," he replied simply, "just as I am yours."

Spats nodded, shuffling his feet. "Aye, well, then you know all you need to know for the now." He glanced again out the window, gauging the time. "You'd better get moving."

Jaryd slid the Fey amulet's chain over his head and down around his neck. The medal felt warm against his skin. "I don't suppose this Fey amulet is any good at charming Elsacian parents, is it?"

Spats shook his head. "I'm afraid not."

Jaryd extended his hand. "Here's hoping my luck holds then."

Spats took his hand, giving it a brief, firm shake. Jaryd grabbed his cap, pulled open the cottage door, and stepped through into the softening summer sun.

Having had ample practice, Jaryd could time the walk from the gardeners' cottages on the Hall campus to the front steps of the Antium Library to within a moment or two. He'd been waiting only a short while when he caught sight of Dyrileah walking toward him. The young Elsacian girl had a lightweight woolen wrap, dark green in color, wound about her head and shoulders. She was wearing a light-green cotton frock.

Green was Dyrileah's favorite color. Jaryd thought it went well with her large, slightly tilted brown eyes. Dyrileah's eyes were the color of fresh maple syrup, a rich golden brown. Jaryd spied a few curls of honey blond hair peeking out from beneath the wrap. Pretty by any standard, when Dyrileah smiled and those marvelous eyes of hers lit from within, she took his breath away.

"You're right on time." Jaryd launched a smile of his own in greeting. "Something must have gone terribly wrong."

"So far, so good actually." Dyrileah returned his smile, and Jaryd felt his heart thump. Her eyes took on a mischievous glint. "Of course, it is early yet."

"You look lovely," Jaryd observed quietly, taking her hand.

"You look like a young fellow who has taken hold of a wolf by the ears." Dyrileah's eyes glowed. "Don't let go, farm boy."

"Of you," Jaryd vowed, "not ever." Offering her his left arm, Jaryd squared his shoulders. "Shall we go?"

Jaryd had often walked Dyrileah from the library to the Porter's Gate, a main entry point to the Elsacian Quarter of the city. At her insistence, he had never ventured further. The shortest path to the Porter's Gate led through a series of narrow side streets east of the library grounds. As it was First Day afternoon, very few people were out and about. They had just stepped into the mouth of an alleyway, when Jaryd sensed motion to his right.

Turning, he saw two men moving quickly toward them. Neither matched Jaryd's height, but both looked to be sturdily built. Bareheaded, they were each clad in workman's garb, rough woolen shirts and trousers. The men separated as they approached, one moving to his left, the other to his right. Without a word, the one to Jaryd's left whipped a wooden truncheon out from behind his back and swung it overhand at Jaryd's head. Stepping closer to the man, Jaryd instinctively raised his left arm to ward off the blow. The truncheon struck. Despite the padding offered by the lined leather jacket, Jaryd felt a sharp pain run down his arm. Jaryd rushed the man, pressing close. The fellow grabbed Jaryd's collar with his left hand, raising the truncheon to strike again. Driving his right hand upward, using the strength of his shoulder and hips to lend power to the blow, Jaryd slammed the base of his palm into the man's chin.

Spats had taught him that he could hit harder with the heel of his palm than ever he would be able to with his fist, but that he had to be close to his opponent to do so. The man's head snapped back, his jaw clacking shut as Jaryd struck him. Jaryd felt him stagger and hit him again, as hard as he could, smashing the butt of his palm into the base of his adversary's jaw on the left side of his face.

Jaryd grappled with the man using his left hand. Even with the urgent heat of fear and anger coursing through his blood, Jaryd could feel pain and weakness. He feared his arm was broken. The man brought his truncheon down. Jaryd ducked his head, and the blow largely dissipated along his back and shoulder. Raising his right fist like a club, Jaryd chopped the edge of his hand down atop the bridge of his attacker's nose.

With savage pleasure, Jaryd felt the cartilage crunch under his hand; blood spurted, sticky warm to the touch. Pivoting, Jaryd rammed his right knee into the man's groin and then shoved using his right forearm and shoulder. His foe toppled backward, sprawling on the cobblestoned street, truncheon clattering as he dropped it. Whirling about, Jaryd yanked his Hawken from its sheath with his right hand to confront the second assailant.

The man stood at Dyrileah's back, his left arm about her throat. The girl was standing stock still, not struggling at all. With his right hand, the man reached behind him and drew a long-bladed knife. The blade shape formed a wicked curve, ideal for slashing. The man's face appeared ordinary-looking. He had closely shorn brown hair and brown eyes. He didn't even look excited.

"Drop the knife, boyo," the stranger grated, "or I'll cut her."

"No," Dyrileah said calmly, her eyes fixed upon Jaryd's. Reaching up, she laid the fingers of her right hand gently on the back of her attacker's left. After a moment, the man blanched, stiffening with pain. The long-bladed carving knife dropped from suddenly nerveless fingers to clang on the stone-covered street. Eyes rolling back in his head, the man collapsed and lay thrashing and gasping upon the ground, looking to Jaryd's eyes like a fish out of water.

Extending her hand toward Jaryd, Dyrileah spoke softly but urgently. "Jaryd, come. We must be away from here."

Jaryd glanced at the man he'd downed. The fellow had rolled onto his belly and had placed both hands under his chest to lever his head and shoulders off the ground. He was groggily shaking his head, blood dripping from a badly broken nose. Sheathing his knife, Jaryd stepped up to Dyrileah and grasped the Elsacian girl's left hand with his right. Together, they rushed down the street. At the next intersection, they turned to their right, passing quickly through the Porter's Gate into the Elsacian Quarter of Antium. Dyrileah led him rapidly to the end of the first block and turned right once more, walking briskly but no longer running. They traveled another block before turning left. A short way down on their right was an open space, a park, Jaryd thought. Stepping onto the lawn, Dyrileah guided him to a bench on the far side of the green space. They sat, breathing deeply.

"Are you all right?" Dyrileah inquired anxiously. Jaryd's left arm hurt. The pain throbbed to match his pulse, deep and steady, radiating along the full length of his arm.

"I think my left arm is broken," he replied, a little surprised at how normal his voice sounded in his own ears. "What did you do to that fellow with the knife?"

"Something forbidden," Dyrileah responded matter-of-factly. "I was afraid he might hurt you," she appended, as if doing so would explain everything. "You will need to take off your jacket. Gently the now. Let me help you."

Together, they pulled the leather jacket off Jaryd's right side, working the garment around his back and finally slipping his injured left arm free of the sleeve. Rolling his shirtsleeve back with infinite care, Dyrileah examined his arm. A bruise had already formed about midway down his forearm, and some swelling was evident. Dyrileah turned, looking carefully about them. They were alone in the small park. Taking his left hand in her right, Dyrileah placed the fingers of her left hand on his forearm just above the bruise. Her touch was feather light. Still, he expected it to hurt. Jaryd was startled to discover that it did not.

"This also is forbidden." Dyrileah raised her eyes, a gentle golden brown, to his. "May I?"

Not really understanding, Jaryd nodded. At this, Dyrileah closed her eyes. Jaryd felt a warm tingle radiating, it seemed, from deep within his left arm. The feeling spread, running the length of his arm and up into his chest. A moment passed, and the tingling grew more intense, like a hand or a foot gone asleep did when circulation was first restored. Her left hand gripped his elbow. Dyrileah pulled firmly on his wrist with her right. The tingling sensation peaked as she tugged, just at the edge of pain, and then receded.

Dyrileah opened her eyes. "I'm afraid that is the best I can do. Healing bone is complex, especially in its final stages. If I go further, I may do more harm than good."

Jaryd flexed his fingers in amazement. "My arm feels fine." He felt no pain whatsoever, perhaps a bit of stiffness, but nothing like the deep ache of a few moments before.

"I assure you it is not yet fine," Dyrileah said crisply. "We will need to bind the arm, and you must promise to treat it gently for a couple of weeks at least until your body has a chance to mend it fully." She paused a moment and then inquired, "What is it that you wear about your neck?"

"Spats gave it to me." Jaryd slid a finger under the chain and lifted the Fey medallion free of his shirt so that Dyrileah could see it. "It's called a Fey amulet. It is supposed to ward against adverse magic."

"It does more than that," Dyrileah told him, a note of wonder in her voice. "As soon as I touched you with the healing flow, I could feel it pulling at me, amplifying the power of the weave. I've never felt anything like it."

"Thank you, Healer," Jaryd said quietly, slipping the amulet back into his shirt.

Tears filled Dyrileah's eyes, spilling quickly onto her cheeks. She dropped her gaze and slipped her hands free of his grasp to lay them in her lap. "I am, as my people say, of the Wycken." Her voice faltered, and she would not look at him. "What your people would call a witch."

"Aye, well," Jaryd said wryly, "that explains a few things."

"You think it is funny?" Dyrileah flared, raising tear-drenched eyes to his. "I am, according to what your people would say, a spawn of evil."

"My *people*," Jaryd parroted, "say all kinds of things." He extended his hand to tenderly brush a tear from her cheek. "For example, I've heard witches can't cry."

"Errant nonsense." Dyrileah sniffed.

"Apparently," Jaryd acknowledged. "I have it on good authority, however, that witches serve up stolen infants and small children, roasted in raspberry sauce, as the main course at their Winter Solstice feast." He raised an eyebrow expectantly.

"Blatant falsehood," Dyrileah whispered fiercely.

"Most significant from my personal perspective," Jaryd continued, lowering his voice to a near whisper, "I've also heard it said that witches have a habit of transforming wayward young men into various barnyard animals: hogs, goats, that sort of thing."

"Now, that, we do." Dyrileah smiled at him through her tears. "Regularly. Especially farmers' sons who think they are possessed of a sly wit."

Jaryd took firm hold of her hand, so small and soft. "I love you, Dyrileah Quirow," he said with gentle intensity. "I love you with all my heart. You will have an easier time convincing me that the moons are about to tumble from the sky than you will getting me to believe there is anything evil about you."

"Oh, Jaryd." Dyrileah flung her arms about his neck, hugging him tightly. "I was so afraid you would not understand."

"Understanding is one thing, and loving is another," Jaryd replied, returning her embrace, favoring his left arm. "I'm very sure I don't understand much of anything, but I trust you." Dyrileah was sobbing the now. Jaryd held her close, gently running his hand down her back, easing the tears out of her. She quieted after a bit, and Jaryd asked, "Those two from the alley, did you recognize either of them?"

"No," Dyrileah responded. "I never saw either one of them before."

"That's good." Jaryd sighed with relief. "Neither did I. It is unlikely they know us then either. If the one you hexed or whatever carries a tale to the authorities, he won't be able to identify you or me."

"Wycken don't hex," Dyrileah replied automatically. "Do you think a criminal would be..." She paused. "What was it you said? Carrying tales to the authorities?"

"I don't know," Jaryd surmised. "Maybe if he thought he could get something out of it. I suspect he would leave out the part about accosting us first. In any case, I don't think you should venture out of the Elsacian Quarter for a few days, at least not through the Porter's Gate." Unknotting his neckerchief, Jaryd handed it to Dyrileah. "Come on the now; let's get going. I'm perishin' hungry all of a sudden." Winding the neckerchief tightly about his left wrist and arm, Dyrileah tied it in place. She then helped Jaryd back into his jacket, and they resumed their journey to her parents' home.

What remained of the walk passed uneventfully. Jaryd had never ventured into the Elsacian portion of the city. The Elsacian Quarter was one of the older parts of the modern City of Antium. The streets were narrower than in the newer sections but looked much the same, perhaps a little cleaner than the usual. The smells were different, not unpleasant but a bit unusual. The Elsacians were known for the spices with which they prepared their food. Perhaps that was it.

Jaryd's left arm felt funny. The limb didn't hurt but instead felt hollow somehow. After binding Jaryd's left wrist and forearm using his neckerchief, Dyrileah told him not to flex his wrist for a while.

Beneath his jacket, the wrapping hardly showed. Dyrileah stepped round to his right side, not his left. Compared to the start of their walk, he couldn't help but think that to outward appearance, nothing of consequence had changed. *Appearances*, he found himself thinking, *can indeed be deceiving.*

29

A Basket of Apples

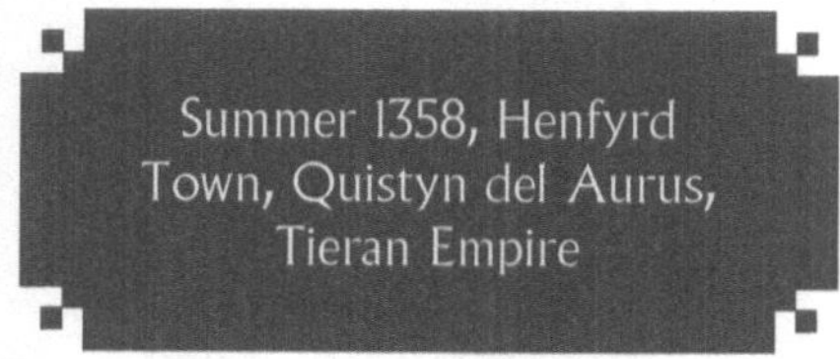

Mat Bayrd was tired of digging. They'd had a bellyfull of it since their arrival in Henfyrd. First came the ditch lining the perimeter of the fortified camp, called a compaglium. Earth removed from the ditch was piled and tamped into the foundation for the palisade wall erected just inside the trench line.

Most of the palisade was constructed of wooden stakes milled from the pine forest mantling the low hills north and east of Henfyrd. Each stake measured eight span long, sharpened at both ends and driven at a forty-five-degree angle into the formed earthen rampart. Reinforced wooden gates, positioned at the midpoint of all four walls, were also incorporated into the compaglium's design. A retractable wooden bridge over the trench, known as a portus, fronted each of the four gates.

Segus Gracci Versi, the general in charge of the Northern Army, who refused to refer to his command by its official name, the Northern Expeditionary Force, had landed one week prior. Mat couldn't fault the general for his preference in nomenclature. Northern Expeditionary Force sounded like something some clerk would utter. Northern Army, in Mat's opinion, seemed much more soldierly.

The Gracci stayed in Henfyrd only long enough to disembark the full weight of his forces. General Segus Gracci Versi then marched north, headed upstream along the eastern bank of the river Wyst with the bulk of the Northern Army. The Gracci's field strength totaled some twenty-seven thousand men, anchored by eight full regiments of Tieran heavy infantry; a like number of light infantry, militia spearmen mostly; five regiments of Tieran lancers and one of missile-armed light cavalry; and a mixed contingent of about five thousand auxiliaries, slingers, archers, and crossbowmen.

General Quintus Glabrio Jens now held charge over the troops left to garrison Henfyrd. Glabrio's command included all 1,194 militia archers of the 133rd Auxiliary Regiment.

For the first time in weeks, Mat stood encumbered by neither mattock nor shovel. Better yet, he had the entire day off, with a signed leave to prove it. Mat and two companions—long, lanky Danel Owen and stocky, broad-chested Davyd Lee, also in possession of day passes—had decided to break their fast in Henfyrd and then see the sights.

At twenty-four years of age, Danel Owen was the oldest and the tallest trooper of Third Company, 133rd Auxiliary Regiment. A full half -span taller than Mat, Danel had brown hair and blue eyes. Long-limbed and lean, he didn't look particularly strong until you tried to throw him. Danel could outwrestle the lot of them, Mat included—well, some of the time anyway.

A farmer's son, blond-haired with keen hazel eyes, the square-shouldered Davyd Lee stood the best archer among them, especially since Byan Hume had been promoted to regent and was no longer, strictly speaking, part of Company Three.

After breakfast, Danel suggested they take a walk down toward the river. The better taverns were supposed to be located there, or so he'd heard. Danel wanted a taste of the Kylgahran liquor called wysoi. Davyd Lee had a few pennies left and was determined to try his hand at a game of dice. Mat didn't have a better idea, so off they went. They weren't sure of the best route and generally just headed west. A short while later, the trio found themselves wandering through the market district.

The three militiamen were approaching the edge of a building, the front of which was occupied by a row of stalls with vendors hawking everything from spices to religious icons, when a young girl raced around the corner. Fleeing like a frightened deer, peering back over her shoulder, she ran headlong into Danel Owen. Staggered by the collision, Danel instinctively took hold of her, laying a big, long-fingered hand on each shoulder.

"Whoa, there," Danel exclaimed. "Are you all right?"

"Lemme go," the girl cried. Mat saw she was a little bit of a thing, fourteen or fifteen maybe, with a tousled mass of walnut-brown hair. Clad in a simple cotton frock belted at the waist, the girl tried to twist out of Danel's grasp. Sleeveless, the dress was typical of what many women wore in the summer months around the shores of the Middle Sea. The garment had once been blue but was so faded by the sun and countless washings so as to appear pearly gray the now. The girl wore no socks and had what appeared to be a pair of home-made leather sandals on her feet.

"Easy," Danel said. "I ent going to hurt you."

"I said lemme go," the girl hollered. Rearing back against Danel's grip on her shoulders, she kicked him hard at the side of his knee. Her homemade sandals were sturdily put together, and Danel swore as she gave him a good lick, loosening his hold. Wrenching free, the girl spun about and collided next with Mat.

To avoid sharing Danel's fate, Mat simply tucked the little mort under his left arm, pinning both of hers against his side.

The youngster bucked and heaved in a desperate attempt to break free, crying, "Turn me loose, ya great lummox."

Davyd Lee sidled up with a grin on his face. He had a pug nose, a smattering of freckles across it, and a dimple in his chin. Not even his momma thought him handsome, but he had a winning smile.

"There's not much point in wrigglin', lass," Davyd Lee informed the girl. "Mat Bayrd's what got a hold of you. Old Mat is a black-smith. I reckon he could tote a tiny little thing like you around all day long and not even break a sweat."

The girl stopped struggling, but Mat could feel the tension in her slim young body, like a fawn ready to bolt at the sight of a wolf.

"Please let me go," she implored. "I gotta get on right the now."

Just then, two men barreled around the corner. Both were of medium height, dark-haired and brown-eyed. They wore loose-fitting white cotton shirts over billowing tan cotton trousers that fell to mid-calf. The men had silk sashes about their waists in lieu of leather belts. Each bore a long, curved knife in a leather sheath thrust into the sash at his middle. The first around the corner appeared to be the older of the pair, about forty, Mat judged. He had a wooden truncheon in his hand. Close behind, the second fellow, at least ten years younger, carried a large wooden mallet.

"Yah," the older one shouted, "you've got the little minx. Well done, soldier. The slippery bitch is a thief."

"Who are you?" Mat inquired. The young girl under his arm twisted hard once more in a vain attempt to free herself and then, uttering a soft, anguished cry, went still to hang, trembling, over his left hip.

"I am Julyan Vorros," the older man replied. His Aylitic was flavored by an accent Mat couldn't place. "And this," he jerked a thumb at the young man standing just off his shoulder, "is my nephew Leonys. We are merchants, grocers, in the next street over." Vorros was balding. He had a widow's peak and wore his hair oiled in long ringlets over his ears. A gold earring bobbled in his left ear, and his smile looked to Mat to be even greasier than his hair.

"You say she stole something from you?" Davyd Lee queried.

Looking from one militiaman to the other, it was Leonys Vorros who answered, "The dinky cunt nearly emptied our coin box." His accent sounded even more pronounced than his uncle's.

Mat decided he didn't much like Julyan Vorros or his nephew Leonys either. "She's a little young for you to be calling her that." Mat did not speak loudly, but both Danel and Davyd, who knew him well, heard the edge in his tone.

"No one's going to hurt you," Mat told the girl. "I'll put you down the now. If you haul off and kick me the way you did Danel over there, you're in for a good talking to, understand?" The wriggly little waif under his arm made a soft huffing sound that Mat chose to interpret as acknowledgment. He gingerly lowered her to her feet. Keeping one big hand firmly wrapped about a slender wrist, he stepped back. The girl raised her face to his, and Mat felt his breath catch. The lass looked so much like Bode at age fifteen that Mat could not believe his eyes. Her hair was the same lustrous medium brown, her eyes a smoky gray, the color of an autumn thunderhead, accentuated by a slightly heart-shaped face.

"Hoi," Davyd Lee clamored. "Mat, lookee. If she ent the spittin' image of…"

"Pure trouble," Mat interrupted. "I know the look." Focusing his attention on her tempestuous gray eyes, Mat asked, "What's your name, lass?"

"Emilyn Harris," she replied, peeking up at him from under improbably long eyelashes, burnished a warm golden brown. A bruise, yellowing the now, mantled Emilyn's cheek just above her left jaw. The supple curve of her lower lip was marred by a split that, though nearly healed, remained evident still.

"Hullo, Em," Mat offered quietly, still struck by her resemblance to Bode. "My name is Mat Bayrd. The tall fellow over there," Mat pointed at Danel, "with the limp is Danel Owen." Mat next indicated the stocky archer to his left. "The towhead with the hole in his chin is Davyd Lee. We're Tieran militia out of Greystock in the Three Rivers."

"Well…" Em looked from one of them to the other in turn. "Don't reckon I'll hold it agin ya. If you let me loose, that is."

"Did you steal from that fella?" Mat inquired, looking her carefully in the eye.

Em squared her shoulders and raised her chin. "I did," she allowed, speaking softly but clearly. "I know it were wrong, but he didn't have no right to treat me the way he done neither." Mat still clasped her left wrist. Emilyn pointed to Julyan Vorros with her free hand.

"She's admitted to the theft, soldier," Julyan asserted. "Hand her over to us, and we'll see justice is done."

"What is it that he did, Em?" Mat questioned.

"He's a grocer," Em explained. "We been sellin' him apples. He agreed to pay six pennies for a full basket. Ol' Lige sent me along with one this mornin' an' said if I was ta come back home with anythin' less than half a dozen coppers, he'd thump me good." Once she cut loose, Em commenced to talking louder and faster as she went along. "When I toted em' in this morning, the basket of apples that is, he"—she jammed a damning finger in the general direction of Julyan Vorros—"said some of the fruit was goin' and the basket was only worth four pennies. There ent nothin' wrong with none of them apples, I swear," Em noted furiously. "He said"—she indicated the grocer once more—"that if I was to help him clean the back of his shop, he'd pay me the difference: two pennies." She paused just long enough to gulp a breath. "Soon as we got there to the back of his shop, him and me, he grabs aholt of me and stuffs one hand down the front of my dress while trying to lift my skirt with the other."

"She lies," Julyan Vorros objected.

"You'll get your turn," Mat told him. "Go on, Em. What happened then?"

"I whacked him in the nose with my elbow and fetched a knee up twixt his legs," Em responded without hesitation. "He let go, all bent over like, and I thumped him on the head with a skillet. I reckon it was wrong to do it, but I grabbed his coin purse; it were a-lyin' on a table there, and I lit out. I reckon I didn't hit him hard enough with the skillet 'cause I no more got to the head of the alley than he come through the door hollerin', 'Stop, thief.'" She glared at Mat. "I was nearly clear of them when I run smack into you three."

"Do you have his coin purse?" Mat asked. At her nod, Mat extended his hand, palm up. Eyes hot with unshed tears, Em angrily stuffed her right hand down the front of her dress and extracted a small, washed leather bag. She thrust it toward him. Mat accepted the bag, saying, "Don't you run off." With that, he released his grip on her left wrist. Hefting the bag in his hand, he looked to Vorros, whose nose appeared red and swollen. "What do you say?"

"She stole my purse," Julyan growled. "The rest of what she says is a lie."

Mat returned his gaze to Emilyn Harris. The girl tugged down the loose-fitting neckline of her frock to reveal the upper contours of her left breast. Mat saw three vivid, parallel scratch marks, fresh and angry red in appearance. "Go on," Em fairly hissed at him, "take a good look."

Mat looked at Vorros's fingers, coiled round the truncheon in his hand. He saw the long, lacquered nails. "Master Vorros," Mat directed, "lead the way back to your shop." Vorros hesitated and then nodded briefly and turned away.

"Why, exactly," Danel Owen wanted to know as they started off, "are we goin' back to the grocer's?"

"I want to get a look at Em's basket of apples," Mat informed the bunch of them.

The return walk to the Vorros grocer shop did not take long. The front was covered by a large striped canvas awning. On display in various boxes and baskets under the shade of the awning lay a variety of fruits and vegetables. The front door of the shop hung open, and a dark-haired, dark-eyed young girl about Em's age lounged, standing in the doorway. A wicker basket of apples rested on the stoop. They were golden apples called Yellow Boys, usually the first variety to ripen in and around the lands of the Middle Sea. "Davyd Lee, you'd know best. Do you think that basket of Yellow Boys is worth six pennies?"

Davyd sauntered over and took a close look, fingering a couple of the apples as he did so. "I reckon so, Mat; they look nice and ripe anyway."

Reaching into his wallet, Mat counted out six pennies. "Here you go, Em. Me and the boys will buy your apples." He handed the coins to a suddenly wide-eyed Emilyn Harris. Tugging at the throat of the grocer's washed leather bag, Mat examined the contents and extracted a silver talent. He handed that to the Harris girl as well. Em hesitated a moment and then also accepted the silver piece. Pulling taut the cloth strings to close the bag, Mat tossed the purse back to Julyan Vorros. "I reckon she told us the truth. The talent is for the fright you caused her and the hurt."

"You believe the little bitch because she is of your blood," Julyan Vorros accused, "and you rob me as surely as she."

Mat fought to hold on to his temper. He didn't know what blood Vorros was referring to, but any man who would force himself on a young girl stood a bastard in Mat's book, whatever vintage flowed in his veins.

Mat's jaw clenched. "I'm all through talking with you, Vorros."

Danel Owen stepped quickly between Mat and the grocer. "When Mat goes all clench-jawed, mister, he's gettin' mad. The last fella Mat got mad at was half again your size, and after, well, he couldn't see straight fer a week. I don't reckon the little gal scratched herself that-a-way. Let's just call it even and save ourselves a tussle."

Vorros spat but said nothing as he turned and shouldered his way past the girl in the door to reenter his shop. Davyd Lee grabbed the basket of apples, and the three militiamen escorted Emilyn Harris out into the street.

"Burn me, Em," Davyd Lee remarked, "this basket's heavy. You mean to say you toted it all the way from your farm into town by yourself?"

"I used my daddy's wheelbarrow right up to the town gate," Em explained. "I left the barrow with the watch there. One of the watchmen, he carried the basket to the head of the street." She pointed a slim finger at the nearest intersection. "Only cost me one apple fer his help; said he was goin' this direction anyhow." Em paused, glanced down at the coins clutched in her other hand, and then looked up at the three archers, her eyes wide and gray and so like Bode's that Mat's heart ached at the sight. "I want to thank you boys fer what you done."

"That's all right, Em," Davyd Lee hastened. "That grocer was a damn stingy gut; anybody could see that."

"Good apples are hard to come by," Danel Owen put in. Mat remained silent.

Em sniffed. "I won't forget, is all."

"You boys take those apples back to camp," Mat ordered. "I'll walk Em home."

"How come we got to haul fruit while you walk a pretty gal home?" Davyd Lee groused.

Mat merely pointed to the three stripes on the left breast of his tunic. "You'd best save me an apple or two if you know what's good for you."

"Right you are, Sajar." Danel tossed Mat a mock salute. A pair of rope handles was affixed to the top of the basket. Grasping one, Danel squinted at Davyd Lee. "Come on, recruit." Davyd took hold of the other handle, and the two of them started up the street back toward the compaglium, the basket of apples suspended between them.

"You don't have to walk me home, you know," Em said, giving Mat a slantwise look.

"I reckon not," Mat agreed, "but I'm going to anyhow. You want to argue?"

Em shook her head. "Don't seem to be much point in arguin' with a fella what can tuck you under one arm without so much as breaking a sweat." Em headed down the street, and Mat stepped up alongside her. "What are them stripes fer anyways?" she asked.

Mat indicated the bottommost stripe on his tunic. "That one is for stubbornness." He shifted his finger upward to the second. "This one is for being ornery, and"—he paused for emphasis—"they gave me this last because I'm so good-looking."

Em smiled, gray eyes twinkling. "I believe two out of three anyways." Her eyes swept downward. "I heard old Danel call you Sajar. That there is some kind of boss soldier, ent it?"

Mat thumbed his watch cap further back atop his head. "If officers own the farm and soldiers are the working hands, I guess a sajar is something like a foreman."

"Do you like being a soldier?" Em queried.

"I'm a blacksmith," Mat said firmly. "Soldiering is only temporary. I don't like it much."

"You ent no older than them other two," Em observed. "You must be pretty good at it, bein' a sajar and all."

Determined to change the subject, Mat inquired, "Are you hungry?"

Em grinned like an imp, a very pretty one, Mat thought. "I know a place that sells spicy strips of beef on a stick. Want some?" Em brandished her silver talent. "I'll buy."

Two streets over, Mat's nose caught the savory scent of meat cooking long before Em guided him up to a shop with a large roasting pit in front of it. A tall man wearing a leather apron toiled over the pit, basting a plate of beef steaks with a tangy-scented red sauce.

"Hullo, Jaspyr," Em piped in greeting.

At the sound of her voice, Jaspyr raised his eyes from the task before him. He was a man of middle years with thinning brown hair and lively brown eyes that lit when they settled upon young Em.

"Emilyn Harris." The lanky shopkeeper smiled. "How are you and that pretty mother of yours?"

"Middlin' fair, Jaspyr." Em returned the tall fellow's smile. "Middlin' fair. Jaspyr Tate, I'd like you to meet Mat Bayrd." Em indicated Mat with a wave of her hand.

Tate glanced at Mat and nodded. "What are you doing wandering around with a soldier, Emilyn?" Mat watched Tate carefully examining Em's face. The older man's eyes tightened, and he fixed Mat with a hard look.

Em's smile stretched to a grin. "Don't worry, Jaspyr. Ol' Mat's all right, despite his ornery stripe." She walked up and gave Jaspyr Tate a hug. "We'd like three spicy beef skewers, one fer me and two fer him, and somethin' cold to drink." Em held aloft her silver talent. "You can put the rest of this agin' what me an' Momma owe you."

"That isn't necessary, Emilyn," Jaspyr said automatically.

"You been real good to us, Jaspyr," Em said fondly, "so it's extra necessary. Take it the now, you hear?"

Without further comment, Jaspyr accepted the coin and slipped it into his pocket. "Three skewers of beef and two mugs of apple cider coming right up. Why don't you step around back and have a seat?"

Em led Mat down an alley between Jaspyr's shop and an apothecary's next door to a fenced open space filled with an array of wooden tables and chairs. She walked to a small round table in a far corner and sat down. Mat joined her, and shortly after, Jaspyr brought them their food and drink. The spicy beef was as good as Em said it would be and the cider too.

"Why didn't you sell your apples to Jaspyr?" Mat wondered.

"Jaspyr grows his own—that is, him and his brothers do," Em replied. "Besides, Ol' Lige don't want us sellin' fruit to Jaspyr Tate."

"Is Lige your father?" Mat asked quietly.

"No, he ent," Em flared, speaking in low, fierce tones. "He's just the sorry cuss what married my momma after Daddy died. Lige Cotton is his name."

"Do you have any other family hereabouts?" Mat inquired.

"No," Em responded, "just me and Momma and Lige and Rupert. Lige was a widower when he married up with Momma. Rupert is Lige's son from before." Em frowned. "There's a baby on the way the now. Momma's with child."

Mat swirled the cider left in his mug. "How did you get that bruise on your cheek, Em," he asked carefully, "and the cut on your lip?"

"Pig wrestlin'," Em answered, taking a long swallow from her mug of cider.

"Is that so?" Mat scratched his ear. "Who won?"

"I guess it was mostly a draw," Em replied, looking at him over the rim of her fired clay mug. "But since the worldly remains of that particular pig wound up in a pot or hangin' in the smokehouse, I reckon I came out on top after all."

"Pigs have a reputation for being rough customers," Mat acknowledged. "I've heard the same thing about pig farmers, some of 'em anyways." Em did not rise to the bait, and they finished what remained of their meal in silence.

They retrieved Em's wheelbarrow from the guard station at the town gate. Mat hefted the barrow and rolled it experimentally back and forth. "This is well made."

Em smiled in remembrance. "Daddy was good with his hands. He made us some fine things."

"Do you want a ride?" Mat offered.

Em put her hands on her hips and glared at him. "I ent a little girl no more, Mat Bayrd."

"Well," Mat observed, "you are definitely a girl, and you aren't very big, which as far as I can see makes you little, but I take your point. How old are you exactly?"

"I'm nigh on to sixteen," Em declared indignantly. Taking note of the dubious expression on Mat's face, she amended, "Well, fifteen and a half, nearly."

The dirt track leading away from Henfyrd's northern gate toward the Cotton farm was called the Northridge Road. Outside Henfyrd to the north, the countryside stretched lush and green into a series of low treelined hills and grass-filled meadows, at least wherever local farmers hadn't put in crops. It appeared to Mat to be good farmland.

Em nattered pretty much continuously as they trudged along. Mat nodded and shook his head on occasion, slipping in a word or two here and there. Finally, Em peeked up at him and observed, "You don't talk much, do ya?"

Mat smiled. "That makes us a good pair."

"How's that?" Em queried, cocking her head to one side.

"You talk enough for any two people," Mat responded matter-of-factly. "Together, the both of us balance out just about right."

Em's gray eyes darkened like thunderheads for a moment, and then she laughed. "I reckon that's right." The walk from Henfyrd to the once-Harris, now-Cotton farm did not take long. Topping a low rise, Mat caught sight of a wood frame farmhouse with a thatched roof and beside it a barn of similar construction. There were a couple of smaller outbuildings too, likely one of which was the smokehouse Em mentioned. A vegetable garden was sprouting just to the side of the barn. A stone-lined water well with a wood roof cover stood just in front of the farmhouse. Mat noticed an apple orchard spread out behind it. The buildings looked neat and reminded him of his own family's place just outside of Greystock back in the Three Rivers.

Em pointed. "There it is, home."

Mat nodded. "Fine-lookin' farm it is." He reckoned he was about out of time. Setting down the wheelbarrow, he took a breath. "Nobody has the right to hit you, Em—nobody."

"Mat Bayrd, I done tol' you—" Em insisted.

"I'm just saying," Mat overrode her gently, "you don't have to stand for that."

Em raised her eyes to his for a moment and then shook her head. "What world do you live in, Mat Bayrd? Not this 'un, that's fer sure."

"The world isn't just as you find it, Em," Mat argued softly but intently. "It's what you make of it. Friends can help sometimes."

"And sometimes they cain't," Em replied just as softly. Her wide-set eyes, so like Bode's, looked sadder and more knowing than any fifteen-year-old girl's should.

"My name is Mathias Bayrd," Mat said evenly, "Fourth Squad sajar with the Third Company, One-Hundred-Thirty-Third Auxiliary Regiment. Repeat that so I know you got it right." Em parroted his words correctly, and Mat continued. "We have an officer with us, a regent named Byan Hume. He is a good man." He paused, waiting, and Em dutifully repeated Byan's name and rank. "If it gets bad, Em, and you don't know where to turn, come see us. You know where the fortified camp is, right?" The girl nodded. "Go there and ask for me or Byan Hume. We'll work something out. We'll find some way to keep you safe. Do you understand?"

"I'll be fine." Em took a hesitant step toward him. "Don't worry none about me."

"If you say so, good and all." Mat reached out to take one of Em's small, work-roughened hands in his own. "Just promise me you won't forget."

"You know when you sent Danel and Davyd Lee back to camp with them apples," Em gazed up at him, dove-gray eyes glinting, "I half figured you'd wind up draggin' me off into some bushes afore we got near the way home."

"I reckon that's no way to treat a lady," Mat said.

"I ent no lady, Mat Bayrd," Em insisted.

"A friend then." Mat smiled.

Em's eyes softened as she returned his smile. Mat bent down to kiss her lightly on the mouth. Her lips were soft and sweet, shy but willing too. Mat broke off the kiss, knowing he had no right. Em had closed her eyes. Her fingers clutched his tightly.

"Take care of yourself," he admonished quietly.

"I will," Em promised. Her eyes slid open, and she released his hand. "You too."

Mat could think of nothing more to say. Reluctant, he turned and strode away. Afraid of what he might see and feel, Mat did not look back.

30

Mistress Cotton's Choosing

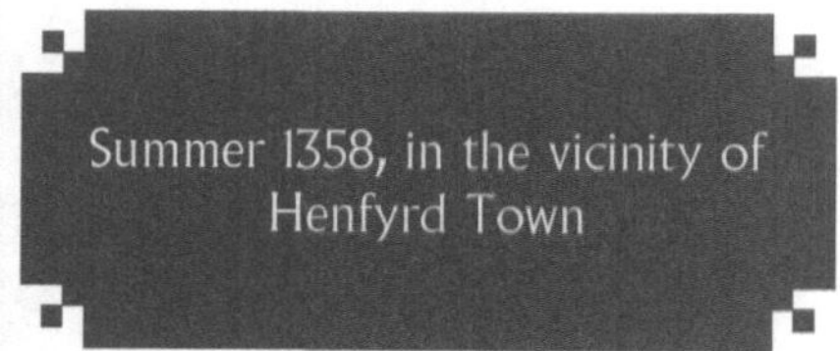

A week and a day after meeting Emilyn Harris, Sajar Mat Bayrd and
the nineteen other men of Fourth Squad were assigned to repair a
washed-out section of the Northridge Road near Dover's Creek, a
couple of kylos outside of Henfyrd. Fourth Squad was, in turn, divided into two files of ten men apiece. As sajar, Mat counted as the
tenth man in the first file. He'd put Danel Owen in charge of the
second. They brought a mule with them loaded down with trench-
ing tools, shovels, and mattocks mostly. Damage to the road wasn't
severe, and they'd pretty much finished clearing the brush and de-
bris and repacking the earthen roadbed when Mat heard a familiar
voice calling, "Hey, soldier, want to buy some apples?"

Mat drove the head of the mattock he'd been toiling with into
the dirt at his feet and turned to see Emilyn Harris approaching
astride a dark-gray mule. A set of wicker panniers rested across the
shoulders of the mule. Mat spotted Yellow Boy apples in one and
what looked like plums in the other. Em was wearing a green cotton
frock nearly as faded and wash worn as the blue one she'd had on
when first he'd met her. Sleeveless, the dress belted at the waist. De-

236

spite the summer heat, Em had a light woolen shawl, gray in color, wrapped about her upper arms. Her long, light-brown hair bound into a simple ponytail, she sat astride the mule. Consequently, a goodly portion of slender leg and thigh were showing.

"Maybe," Mat hollered back, "if the price is right."

"I was gonna take this lot into town," Em announced, reining the mule to a stop nearby. "Thought maybe I'd dicker with you in-stead."

"Hullo, Em," Davyd Lee greeted her, leaning on his shovel. "How do you fare?"

"Davyd Lee," Em cried, smiling in response. "Tired of apples yet?"

He grinned. "Depends on who's sellin' 'em."

Looking about, Em singled out Danel Owen. "Hoi, Danel," she shouted, "how's the knee?"

"Pretty fair, Em," Danel replied, grounding his mattock as well. "Creaks when it rains the now, though."

Reaching into the pannier on the right side of the mule, Em selected a large purple-skinned plum. "Here, I'll save you a Tankered plum fer your pains, no charge."

The sight of a pretty young girl riding a mule loaded down with fruit and talking as sassily as she was hadn't done much for Fourth Squad's work ethic. Taking note, Mat shook his head. "Fourth Squad," he hollered, "stand easy. We'll break for a midday meal."

Walking over so he could lay a hand on the mule's withers, Mat looked up at Em. "What have you got there?"

"Fresh apples—Yellow Boys, they are. Tankered plums…" Em smiled down at him. "Some dried apricots and jerked beef."

"How much for the lot?" Mat inquired.

"For you"—Em's smile broadened—"just one score of coppers."

"Twenty pennies," Mat groused. "Girl, you have turned to thiev-ery."

"The jerked beef is mighty good, Sajar," Em cajoled, gray eyes flashing bright. "Fresh and spicy. Everybody says my momma's dried apricots is the best there is."

"All I have is twelve," Mat admitted.

"Here, Sajar," Davyd Lee said, strolling over with Danel Owen at his side. "We'll make up the difference."

"That's mighty big of you, Davyd Lee," Mat grumbled. "I still say we're being robbed."

"Aye, well," Danel opined, stepping up. "I've never seen a prettier bandit." The lanky archer inquired, "May I help you down, Em?"

Her smile brightening even further, Em said, "Why thankee, Danel, thankee kindly." Extending his hands, Danel took gentle hold of Em, gripping her about the waist. Em leaned into Danel's grasp, wincing a little as she did so. Danel eased her to the ground, and Em rewarded him with a brief hug and then proffered the plum she'd promised. Grinning, Danel held the fruit aloft in salute to her and then took a bite.

"Hoi," Danel commented juicily, "this is good."

Mat lifted the panniers from the mule and carried them into the shade of a nearby elm. Em took a seat, a bit gingerly Mat thought, just behind the panniers and began handing out fruit and strips of jerked beef to the soldiers of Fourth Squad as they gathered around. Mat took a knee nearby just in case, but he needn't have worried. The boys were well behaved. Em chattered away like a little gray-eyed magpie, teasing the now and again. The archers, many of them only a few years her senior and lonely far from home, ate it up, smiling shyly, most of them, and teasing back a little, the bolder ones anyway.

Nevyl Dowtry, one of Mat's oldest friends, gaped as he drew near. "Mat," he exclaimed, "she looks just like Bode. Burn me if she don't."

Em looked to Mat as Nevyl spoke. Mat smiled. "Prettiest girl in two counties," he allowed. His observation earned him a pleased but puzzled smile from young Em, and she turned to say a few friendly words to Nevyl.

Em's victuals were rapidly distributed. Happy and flushed a little at so much attention, she finally turned to Mat. "Here," she said, holding out a strip of dark-colored beef, dried and spiced. "You best get some of this afore it's all gone." As she extended her arm, her shawl fell away some, and Matt saw the smooth, lightly tanned flesh mottled by fresh bruises, an angry mix of purple, brown, and yellow.

Taking a seat beside her, Mat gently tugged the shawl down off her shoulders. The flesh of both her upper arms was similarly marred, mantled with partly healed bruises.

"God dammit, Em," Mat grated through clenched teeth.

"You shouldn't take the Lord's name when you cuss, Mat Bayrd," Em chided him softly. "It ent right."

"Danel, Davyd Lee, get over here," Mat barked. The two archers trotted up. Mat pointed at Em and said flatly, "Take a look at her arms."

"Oh, Em," Davyd Lee breathed.

"Haven't you boys ever heard it ent polite to stare?" Em gathered her shawl back up around her shoulders.

"Why'd you wince so when I handed you down, Em?" Danel asked.

"You've got big ol' hands, Danel Owen," Em declared, glaring at each of them in turn, "mostly as strong as Mat's, and you nearly squeezed the life out of me." Her voice trailed away to silence, and she dropped her eyes.

"How badly are you hurt, Em?" Mat inquired gently.

"Not so bad the now." Em raised her eyes to Mat. He saw tears welling. "I'd have come to you like you said, honest, except fer the first two days I could scarcely walk, and then…and then I…" Em swallowed hard, tears spilling over onto her cheeks. "Don't be mad at me, Mat. Please don't be mad."

Taking one of her hands in his, Mat assured her, "I'm not mad at you, Em. Look at me," he commanded softly. When she complied, tear-washed eyes wide with worry, he continued. "This has got to stop, Em. It's gonna stop right the now."

Climbing to his feet, Mat called, "Nate!" A gangly, towheaded archer, youngest in the squad, looked to him in response. "You've been transferred to second file for the rest of the afternoon." That brought a series of hoots and catcalls directed Nate's way by the rest of his first-file mates. "Nevyl, take second file back to camp. Have them loose a sheath's worth on the range, and then you can knock off for the day. If anybody at camp asks you any questions, have them see me."

"Aye, Sajar," stocky, dark-haired Nevyl Dowtry replied. "Will do."

"First file, on me," Mat ordered. "Danel, you're coming with us." Turning back to Dowtry, Mat went on. "Nevyl, leave us the mule, unloaded. Second file can carry the tools back." That brought a chorus of groans. "Small compensation," Mat reminded them forcefully, "for the fresh victuals and the short afternoon."

With second file headed back to camp, Danel helped Em back aboard her mule, and first file strung out singly behind Mat. The militiamen of Fourth Squad had left their body armor in their tents. Each archer, however, was armed with both pole axe and longbow with a full quiver of arrows slung across his back. The last man in line, red-headed Evram Dade, led the unloaded army mule. Davyd Lee walked alongside Em's mount.

Danel Owen joined Mat at the front of their short column. "Where are we headed?"

"To the Cotton farm," Mat replied, "where Em lives. It's her stepfather's place."

"What do you intend to do when we get there?" Danel inquired mildly.

"Get her away from them," Mat said shortly.

"What if they don't want her to go?" Danel pressed. "What if Em doesn't want to go?"

Mat's big shoulders hunched, but he said nothing. "Mat," Danel prodded, "are you sure you got the right?"

Mat's green eyes were normally mild, warmed by golden flakes set deep within them. The look he turned on his friend Danel was pure green and jade-hard. "What I'm sure of, Danel, is that nobody has the right to beat her like that." Mat took a breath. "You don't have to come along if you don't want to. None of the boys do."

"I'll stick," Danel committed. "Me and Davyd Lee both. The rest might as well tag along; less likely to be trouble that-a-way." Danel doffed his watch cap for a moment to wipe his brow with a stringy, hard-muscled forearm. Slipping his cap back atop his head, Danel squinted at Mat. "Once you get Em away from that there farm, what do you plan on doing with her?"

Mat had put some thought into that over the past week or so. "Put her on a packet boat and send her off to Greystock. The Maywells, Logan and Ellah, can look after her. Ellah's got three boys. She always said she wanted a girl. The Maywells will do right by Em, and I reckon she'll be good for them too."

"Not a bad idea," Danel allowed. "What if Em don't like it?"

"She'll come round," Mat stated firmly.

"Packet fare ent cheap," Danel spat into the dust at their feet. "What are we going to use for money?"

"We've got plenty of back pay coming." Mat shrugged. "It's bound to show up sometime soon. Byan Hume might be able to help us, or if the packet boat captain knows Logan Maywell, maybe he'll take her aboard on credit. We'll work something out."

Mat called them to a halt about three hundred paces short of the Cotton farmhouse. "Davyd Lee, Ben, and Eddard," he called, "limber your bows. Don't you loose on anybody unless I tell you. Got that?" Ben Davys and Eddard Malleus Holt were both fine archers, nearly as good as Davyd Lee.

The three archers chorused, "Aye, Sajar." Slinging pole axes across their shoulders, they fitted an arrow apiece to their bows.

Mat walked up beside Em's mule. "We're going to take you away from here, Em. We'll get you someplace safe, somewhere folks will treat you decent. I promise."

"Mat, you cain't." Em shook her head.

"Do you trust me, Em?" Mat asked quietly.

Em's large gray eyes, soft and sad, rested upon his. "You know I do."

"Look me in the eye, Em," Mat's low-pitched voice rang with intensity, "and tell me you want to stay here."

Em shook her head. "I cain't leave my momma now that she's pregnant."

"Do they beat her too?" Mat questioned. Em shook her head again. "Is it Lige who has been at you?" he inquired. Em shook her head a third time. "This fella Rupert then…he's the one," Mat concluded.

"He's mean when he gets riled, Mat," Em warned. "Quick he is and plenty strong."

With his pole axe in one hand and his bow in the other, Mat led the way up to the barnyard. A tall, dark-haired fellow in farmer's garb stepped out of the vegetable patch near the barn and walked toward them carrying a hoe in his hands. Mat signaled first file to stop. Driving the spiked butt end of his pole axe into the ground, he leaned his bow against the haft of the pole arm and stepped forward. The farmer was about Matt's age, a hand span or so taller, and leanly muscled. He had a battered straw hat on his head, a faded red neck cloth tied loosely about his throat, and wore a sweat-stained gray cotton shirt and woolen trousers. A pair of rough, homemade sandals covered his feet. A two-day stubble of black whiskers mantled his chin and jaw. His eyes were brown and wary.

"Em," he called, "what are you doin' with this lot?"

"Is your name Rupert?" Mat asked.

Rupert's brown eyes flicked to the broad-shouldered soldier at the front of the group Em rode amidst. "It is, but I don't see that's any business of yours, mister."

"You're the one who has been beating her," Mat said evenly.

"I don't know what you're talkin' about, soldier," Rupert declared.

"You are a lying piece of filth," Mat growled, advancing upon him.

Rupert slid back a step, hefting the hoe as a man might a quarterstaff. "Come any closer, soldier, and I'll lay you out."

"You're welcome to try," Mat grated and continued his advance.

"Bastard, I warned you." Rupert spat and swung the blade end of the hoe at Mat's head. Mat had anticipated the blow. As soon as he saw Rupert shift his weight to lend power to the strike, Mat darted forward. Stepping inside the arc of the farmer's swing, he warded the hoe strike with his left forearm, catching the wooden haft of the tool well below the sharpened metal head. Swinging a vicious body blow with his right hand under the wooden shaft of the hoe, Mat struck the tall farmer hard, squarely in his solar plexus. The punch drove the wind from Rupert's lungs, and he hunched forward, gasping.

Grabbing hold of the hoe with both hands, Mat slipped his left foot behind Rupert's right and shoved. The farmer toppled backward, and Mat wrested the hoe away from him. Tossing the farm tool aside, Mat closed on his adversary as Rupert rolled to his feet. He landed a short, hard left to Rupert's jaw that staggered him. Crowding forward, Mat grasped a double handful of the tall farmer's shirt front and bull-rushed Rupert backward, smashing him against the side of the barn. Releasing him long enough to land both a solid right and left to Rupert's midsection, Mat again took hold of the farmer's shirt front and slammed him up against the barn again and then once more. Each time, the back of Rupert's head crashed into the thick wood siding. Grim-faced, Mat stepped back, both hands balled into fists. Rupert slumped to his knees in front of him.

The door of the farmhouse banged open, and a man dressed in farm clothes rushed out, armed with a charged crossbow.

"Hoi, mister," Davyd Lee called out, "drop the crotch knocker right the now, or we'll loose into you." "Crotch knocker" was the derisive term long bowmen used to describe the powerful, deadly, and much-despised crossbow so often deployed against them.

Davyd Lee and the two archers flanking him pressed their bows. The farmer looked to be an older version of Rupert. Similar features and coloring he had, except his face was lined and his hair thinner and flecked with gray.

"Get away from my boy," Lige Cotton cried. He held the crossbow in front of him but did not aim at anyone.

Stepping further back away from Rupert, Mat turned to face the older man. "We're done with him." He indicated the crossbow. "You'd best put that down."

"Be damned if I will," Lige sputtered.

"Be dead if you don't," Davyd Lee promised.

A woman stepped through the door of the house. She was small and slender but heavy with child. Her hair and face looked just like Em's. The woman's eyes, though, were a deep blue. She wore a loose-fitting cotton frock the color of oatmeal. Her feet were bare.

"I reckon that soldier means business, Lige," she said calmly, nodding her head at Davyd Lee. "They's a few too many of them ta argue with by any road."

Slowly, reluctantly, Lige Cotton laid the crossbow at his feet. Davyd Lee and his two compatriots eased off their bows but stood poised warily, arrows at the ready.

"What do you mean comin' here like this, beatin' on my boy?" Lige asked.

"Have you seen what your boy"—Mat placed a scornful emphasis on the last word—"has done to Emilyn?"

"Emilyn's right sassy," Lige stated, raising his hands. "She's got a sharp tongue sometimes and speaks out of turn."

"As if that were any kind of justification." Mat took a step forward, big hands knotting once again into fists.

Emilyn's mother stepped between Lige Cotton and Mat Bayrd. "Why have you come here, soldier?"

Mat stopped. Looking Mistress Cotton in the eye, he said, "Em's coming with us."

"No, she ent," Rupert Cotton protested as he struggled to his feet, leaning against the wall of the barn. "Emilyn will be a whore by sundown if she does, Mistress; you know that."

"Danel," Mat ordered, "if he opens his mouth again, you shut it for him."

"Right, Sajar," Danel Owen replied, hefting his pole axe.

Speaking gently, Mat directed his words to Emilyn's pregnant mother. "We're militia from the village of Greystock in the Three Rivers." He raised a hand to indicate the file of archers ranged behind him. "My name is Mat Bayrd. There are some folk, good people, the Maywells in Greystock. We'll send Emilyn to them. They'll keep her safe and look after her. They'll treat her decently, ma'am, my word on it."

"How would you get her there?" Mistress Cotton inquired.

"By packet boat," Mat replied. "They run regularly. It may take a while to arrange passage. We'll look after her until then."

Mistress Cotton's vivid blue eyes locked onto Mat's. "My Emilyn is a good girl. She's got a good heart. I wouldn't want to see her used."

"We'll keep her safe, ma'am," Mat vowed. "I promise."

"Promise," Lige scoffed. "Bea, we all know what a soldier's promise is worth when it comes to safeguarding a sweet little piece like Emilyn."

Bea Cotton looked to her daughter. "Do you trust this soldier, Emilyn?"

"Mat Bayrd ent the kind what lies, Momma," Em spoke without hesitation.

"If you like, Mistress Cotton," Mat offered, "we'll take you along too."

"Bloody be damned if you will, boy," Lige yelled. "That's my wife yer talkin' about."

"I wasn't speaking to you, Cotton," Mat growled at Lige. "You've got no say in this."

Bea Cotton shook her head. "This is my place. It was my daddy's before and my first husband's too." She pointed over her shoulder. "They're buried on a little hill back there a ways, as I will be someday." She looked again to Mat Bayrd. "You swear to me you'll take proper care of my girl?"

"I swear," Mat said evenly.

"Me too," Davyd Lee called.

"And I," Danel Owen vowed.

"We'll all swear, ma'am," said Eddard Malleus Holt. Eddard's declaration was echoed by the rest of the first-file archers.

Bea Cotton nodded. "Wait," she directed. Turning on her heel, she stepped back into the house. A short time later, she returned, bearing a blanket-wrapped bundle in her arms. Bea walked up beside her daughter, and Em slipped down off the mule. "I put some things in here for you. A couple of spare dresses, my momma's comb, your daddy's prayer book, a few small things to remember us by. I wish it could be more."

"Momma," Em sobbed, stepping into her mother's arms.

"I'm sorry, baby." Dropping her bundle, Bea Cotton wrapped

her arms about Emilyn and told her, "I'm so sorry. I ent done right by you, an' I know that, but it don't mean I don't love you 'cause I do. Think kindly of me now and again, will you?"

"Momma, I love you," Em cried.

"That's what matters in the end, ent it?" Bea Cotton kissed her daughter once just above each of her eyes. "You go on the now an' be a good girl. Do the best ya can. That's all a body can do."

Bea swung round to face Mat Bayrd once more. As she did so, Mat asked, "Are you sure, Mistress, that you don't want to come along?"

"Just you keep your word, Mat Bayrd." Bea's blue-eyed gaze latched a final time on to Mat's. "Do you that, an' I'll bless ya forever." Without a further word, she walked back to the house. She paused by Lige's side. "Supper will be ready in half an hour. Best get Rupert cleaned up." She disappeared into the farmhouse. Lige stood blinking as if he couldn't quite grasp what had just happened.

Picking up Em's bundle, Mat escorted her to the army mule and helped her aboard. Pressing the bundle into her hands, he called, "All right, let's go."

First file made its way quickly away from the Cotton farm. Davyd Lee, Ben, and Eddard brought up the rear, bows still at the ready. Em wiped her tears and sat very straight. Mat noticed she did not look back.

Civilians, especially young women, weren't allowed within the confines of the military camp just north of Henfyrd, where the 133rd was stationed. They hadn't the funds to put Em up in town. Mat wouldn't have been comfortable leaving her alone in an inn anyway. Byan Hume was away from camp, off with Elder, the scout. At least until the regent got back, they'd have to smuggle Em into the camp and hide her there.

Calling first file to a halt in a copse of trees a quarter kylo or so outside the camp boundary, Mat sent Danel and Eddard to fetch a hand-drawn, two-wheeled cart often used to carry firewood. He set the rest of the boys to gathering wood. The cart had a canvas cover. Mat figured they could hide Em in the cart until they were through the gate. The guards wouldn't look twice at a load of firewood, especially one escorted by a file of archers.

Handing Em down off the mule, Mat hunkered on his haunches beside her as she sat hugging her bundle. "Are you all right?"

"Why shouldn't I be?" Em's gray eyes sought his. "I'm among friends, ent I?"

"You are that," Mat assured her.

Em's eyes grew still and watchful. "Who is Bode?"

"Bode is my intended," Mat answered, speaking gravely.

"I look like her, do I?" Em inquired. "Is that why you been helpin' me?"

"Bode is nearly nineteen the now," Mat informed her. "You look so much like her at fifteen that the sight of you makes my heart ache." Extending his arm, Mat gently enfolded Em's hand in his own. "Who you look like caught our attention, Em, that's all." Mat paused, seeking the right words. "I'd like to think we're helping you because it is the right thing to do and because your presence brings a kind of warmth. You're full of light, Em, somehow. I don't have the words. But being with you is like coming home." Mat squeezed her hand, small and calloused. "You're not anybody else, Em. Something special there is about you, something all your own. It is very important you believe that."

Em smiled slowly, bringing dimples to her cheeks. "I'll believe it if you say so, Mat." He sighed with relief. Em lowered her eyes, her smile fading. "Mat, there's somethin' you should know about me." Em fell silent, unable to say more.

"Rupert did more than beat you, didn't he?" Mat said softly.

Em nodded. "Him and Lige both have been at me one time or another, fer months the now."

Mat tightened his grip on her hand. "Not your fault, Em, not a bit of it, you hear me?"

"However you get dirtied up, Mat," Em's voice quavered slightly, "it ent so easy ta get clean, not never again."

"Bad things happen sometimes, Em." Mat spoke urgently. "Life is like that. I don't know why. I do know what happened to you won't matter, not to a man worth cooking a meal for, let alone giving your heart to. If he loves you, it won't make any difference. If he doesn't, then he doesn't deserve you in the first place."

"I suppose you believe that too?" Em asked.

"I do," Mat affirmed.

"Well, then, so will I. Leastways I'll try." Em smiled. "Your intended…she's waitin' on you back in Greystock?"

"No," Mat replied, "she's in Antium City, studying at the Hall there."

"She must be real smart then," Em observed. "You'll be marrying her when she's done with her studies?"

"I don't know." Mat felt his heart turn over at the truth of his words.

"Do you love her?" Em wondered.

"Since my thirteenth birthday, I reckon." Mat smiled in remembrance.

"An' she loves you, don't she?" Em pressed quietly.

"Yes," Mat said, thinking of the last evening he and Bode had spent together. "I think she does."

"Well, then," Em started, sounding puzzled, "if you love her an' she loves you, why don't you know about gettin' married?"

"Bode wants something of life, Em, something I can't give her." Mat had never put the thought into words before, not exactly. "She might want it more than she wants me. If she can't have it and me too…" Mat's voice trailed away for a moment. He released Em's hand and wiped his palms on his thighs. "There's more to marriage than love alone."

"I've never heard nothin' as foolish as that, Mat Bayrd," Em declared, storm-cloud eyes flashing. "Momma says love is the only thing that lasts between a man and a woman. Comes to bein' married, love is all that really matters. Even I know that."

"Seems to me your momma didn't pay much attention to her own advice," Mat offered. "Not so far as this last time round is concerned."

"People make mistakes all the time, Mat." Em reached out to reclaim Mat's hand. "Because they're scairt or lonely or just worn out. Married folk can get by with no love between 'em, I reckon, but that's all they'll ever do without it: get by. That don't make it right."

Em's work-roughened fingers felt small and girl-soft in Mat's hand. He gently firmed his grip. "Aside from Bode, I have two friends in the world, Em, who I know I can count on no matter what. One's a farmer's son from back home; Jaryd Hume is his name. He's Byan Hume's eldest. I've known him all my life." Mat looked into Em's wide, dove-gray eyes. "The other is you."

Mat could not have explained how he knew, but he did.

Em smiled slowly, a radiant smile, the first he'd seen from her truly free of worry or doubt. "Daddy used to say one good friend is all you really need."

31

A Measure of Faith

Bardus and Ester Quirow lived with their five children in what Antium City dwellers referred to as a townhome, a two-story, wood-framed, brick-walled building with a slate roof. Many of the townhomes in the Elsacian Quarter were centuries old. Dyrileah informed Jaryd that the house she had grown up in was relatively new, constructed, or actually rebuilt, after a fire about ninety years before.

Dyrileah was the oldest of the Quirow children. She had two younger sisters and a pair of younger brothers. Everyone still lived at home, and she warned Jaryd that the place would be crowded and a little noisy, especially around dinnertime on First Day.

Jaryd's stomach growled as he approached the Quirow home. The aroma of fresh bread and roasting meat wafted from within, almost cruelly tantalizing. Nervous as he was, he hadn't had much of an appetite when he left the Hall. Jaryd certainly felt hungry the now. Dyrileah walked up the front steps. Neither nerves nor hunger prevented Jaryd from appreciating the subtle sway of her slim hips as he followed. Without bothering to knock, Dyrileah pulled the latch down and swung the door open. She beckoned him through. Tugging off his watch cap, Jaryd stepped across the threshold into a hallway filled with cheery voices and laughter.

A girl about twelve, looking like a younger version of Dyrileah with the same honey-blond hair and enormous brown eyes, peeked around a corner into the entryway and called back over her shoulder, "Maman, Patua, they're here."

Darting down the hallway, she stopped in front of Jaryd and bobbed a curtsey. "Hullo," she piped in greeting. "My name is Tamyra." Eying him for a moment, she observed, "You are very tall."

Jaryd stood above average height but thought it likely he'd only be considered very tall if gauged by Elsacian standards. In comparison with most folk who hailed from Ayle, the Elsacians tended to be both relatively short and slight. Dyrileah, who stood no taller than Bode, was considered willowy for an Elsacian.

"I'm only tall on one end," Jaryd assured Tamyra with a smile. "I'm very glad to meet you, Tamyra."

Tamyra returned his smile. He did not think she would ever quite match Dyrileah's beauty, but there was something immediately engaging about her smile.

"Did you just say something clever?" she asked, looking up at him expectantly.

Jaryd shook his head. "Silly is more like it." He appended in a confidential tone of voice, "I'm a little nervous." Dyrileah hung her wrap on a wall-mounted rack near the door.

Tamyra's smile broadened. "Don't worry; we hardly ever bite, except for Caryleah. You will need to watch out for her."

Helping Jaryd out of his jacket, Dyrileah placed it beside her wrap and then stepped across the hall to slip an arm around her younger sister. "Let's go in. You can be charming later."

The three of them stepped into the kitchen. Dyrileah's mother stood at the table in the center of the room. Ester Quirow had the same shade of hair as her eldest daughter and shared Dyrileah's facial features, except her eyes showed green, not brown. She wore a pale-blue keppi, the style of dress favored by the Elsacians, with its characteristically snug-fitting bodice. About forty, Jaryd guessed, her mother remained nearly as slender as Dyrileah and had a white cotton apron draped about her waist.

Bardus Quirow had been seated at the kitchen table with a girl child on his lap when Jaryd stepped into the kitchen. The child must be Caryleah, the Quirows' youngest, aged ten, according to Dyrileah. Bardus had a full head of blond hair of a slightly lighter shade than his wife and two elder daughters. Jaryd figured he must be about the same age as his wife, maybe a year or two older. His eyes were brown. Bardus climbed to his feet, sliding Caryleah off his lap. The Elsacian stood behind his youngest daughter with both hands resting lightly on her shoulders. Bardus was about half a head taller than his wife, spare of flesh but well-muscled. Dyrileah had told Jaryd that her father worked as a silversmith.

Little Caryleah had her mother's green eyes and her father's light-blond hair. Her features were delicately formed, and Jaryd harbored no doubt young Caryleah was destined to become a great beauty.

"Maman," Dyrileah said, giving her mother a quick hug. "Pat-ua," Dyrileah added, nodding to her father. "May I present Jaryd Hume?"

"Dyrileah," Ester Quirow chided her daughter, sounding mildly scandalized, "you should have taken him to the sitting room. What will he think being ushered into the kitchen like this?"

"My mother says the kitchen is the heart of any home." Jaryd smiled. "I haven't smelled anything so good since leaving hers."

"Welcome to our home, Jaryd Hume." Ester smiled back at him. Releasing her daughter, she curtsied.

"Welcome to our home, Jaryd Hume." Bardus repeated his wife's greeting.

"Thank you, Master Quirow." Jaryd nodded to Bardus and then turned to Ester. "And thank you, Mistress. I am glad to be here."

Caryleah stepped forward, wide green eyes examining him intently. "You do not have any hay in your hair," she announced, looking pointedly at Dyrileah.

"Cary," Ester Quirow exclaimed, genuinely scandalized the now, "what a thing to say. You must forgive her, Master Hume."

"I'd be honored if you'd call me Jaryd, ma'am," he replied, dropping to one knee so he could look young Cary in the eye. "Dyrileah gave me a good scrubbing on the way here," he told the girl. Glancing up at Ester, Jaryd continued. "It tends to grow back in pretty fast. If you look closely, I suspect you'll see some before the evening is over."

Cary cocked her head, considering. Her green eyes widened. "You've hurt your arm."

Holding up his neckerchief-wrapped left wrist, Jaryd nodded. "Yes, a little; your sister fixed me up."

Cary very gently laid her hand on Jaryd's makeshift bandage. Her eyes widened further. Casting her gaze upward to her eldest sister, she asked, "Dyrileah, what have you done?"

Dyrileah looked to each of her parents in turn. "Maman, Patua, we need to speak, in private, I think, right away."

Ester took a breath. "The boys are not yet back from Mistress Poinwyr's. We can't go into supper until they return. Tamyra, please take Cary with you to the sitting room. Wait for us there."

"Yes, Maman," Tamyra replied, taking her little sister by the hand. "Come on, you troublemaker." The two girls left the kitchen and headed across the hall to the sitting room, closing the door behind them.

Ester indicated the chairs standing round the kitchen table. "Please sit, Jaryd. Would you like some tea?"

"Yes, ma'am, thank you." Jaryd took a seat. Bardus did as well, sitting on the other side of the table.

"Please slice him some bread and cheese, Maman, as well," Dyrileah requested. "He is going to be terribly hungry soon. Healing does that."

Without comment, Ester first served him a steaming mug of tea. She then carved a large chunk of bread from a fresh loaf and cut two thick slices from a block of whitish-looking cheese on the cupboard. Putting the food on a plain white ceramic plate, she placed it in front of Jaryd.

No one said anything. The silence stretched a moment, and Jaryd heard himself saying, "Feeding me has a number of advantages, Mistress Quirow." He met Dyrileah's mother's steady green-eyed gaze. "Chief among them is that my manners are just good enough not to talk with my mouth full." He took a healthy bite of the bread. He'd never tasted anything so good.

Bardus smiled slightly. Ester turned her gaze toward her daughter. Dyrileah stepped up behind Jaryd to lay both her hands on his shoulders. "He has an unfortunate sense of humor, Maman. I love him despite that," she said steadily. "More than my life, which he saved this afternoon. He will not betray us."

Dyrileah went on to explain in detail not only what had transpired on their walk from the Antium Library earlier that day but the whole of their relationship, starting from the moment they met. Dyrileah's frank description of him and his actions made him blush. *She knows me too well*, Jaryd thought. The look in Ester's eyes as Dyrileah completed her story proved stark enough to still even his raging appetite, and he sat saying nothing. "When he asked me for the third time to marry him," Dyrileah concluded softly, "I could only say yes."

Ester's green eyes heated. "You chose to say yes, daughter, knowing what it would mean?"

"Yes," Dyrileah shot back, "and I would do so again. Would you have chosen to walk away from Patua?"

"Your patua is of our blood, Dyrileah; this young man is not." Ester did not raise her voice, but at the sound of it, Dyrileah's fingers tightened on Jaryd's shoulders. "Your choices have placed our family in danger."

"The danger we face is unchanged, Maman," Dyrileah argued. "I trust Jaryd, and you can also."

"Is that cool reason speaking, daughter," Ester challenged, the edge in her voice more pronounced than ever, "or the heat in your loins at his touch?"

"My loins stir at his touch, Maman." Dyrileah wasn't budging as much as a finger's width. "How could I love him if that were not so? I know his heart. He is a good man."

"He is a boy, Dyrileah." Ester folded her arms beneath her breasts. "And a foolish one at that."

Jaryd glanced at Bardus, saying quietly, "I hear that a lot. I'm beginning to think there may be something to it." Bardus smiled briefly but maintained his silence.

"You have revealed your true nature to an outsider, Dyrileah, an infidel. That is forbidden." Ester spat out the last word as if she could not stand the taste of it in her mouth. As Jaryd understood it, "infidels," those not of the true faith, served as the term Elsacians reserved for Penitents. "You could be banished for this."

Jaryd craned his neck around so he could look at Dyrileah. She raised her chin. "If the Wycken so judge, I shall accept banishment as long as no harm comes to Jaryd."

"Wait." Jaryd stood to his feet, turning to Dyrileah. He could feel his pulse pounding. "Banishment to where?"

"It does not matter, dear one." Dyrileah lifted her eyes to his. He perceived a surface calm and naked fear roiling in the golden-brown depths beneath. "You cannot follow."

"You are not going anywhere except with me." The look in Jaryd's gray eyes as he spoke the words was enough to make Dyrileah's heart swell. "We could go to the Three Rivers, far enough away so that secrets will be easy to keep hidden. I could return to the plow. My folks will help. We'll make out."

The fear in Dyrileah's eyes burned like an icy dagger in his belly. Despite her fear, Dyrileah smiled. "Return to a farm, Jaryd Hume, to the shearing of sheep? I understood you could not bear it."

"The only thing I cannot bear is the thought of being parted from you," Jaryd said quietly.

"It is a beautiful dream, Jaryd, but I cannot." The fear was banished all of a sudden from Dyrileah's eyes, replaced by determination and something behind that, something powerful and serene. "I am of the Wycken, dear heart. I have a duty to serve my people and to protect them. I cannot walk away from that obligation, not even for you." She stepped into his arms, pressing her face against his chest. "Forgive me, please forgive me."

Jaryd wrapped his arms about Dyrileah and cast his gaze toward her parents. "What do you want?" Ester and Bardus exchanged glances but said nothing. Jaryd pressed, "'Could' and 'if' sound to me like a bargain is to be made. Am I wrong?"

Dyrileah had never heard Jaryd talk so. His voice rang cold and hard. She stirred in his arms. His grip tightened, and she relented, taking refuge in his embrace.

"He thinks like a lawyer," Bardus observed calmly. "You are studying law, are you not, Jaryd?"

Jaryd fixed his eyes on Dyrileah's father. "What if I were to go away—alone?"

"Would you be willing to do so?" Bardus asked.

"Yes," Jaryd replied, "for a price."

"What price?" There was an edge the now to Bardus's voice as well.

"Proof that Dyrileah has not been banished for placing her trust in me," Jaryd said evenly.

"Proof in what form?" Bardus queried.

"Dyrileah knows the head gardener at Antium Hall." Jaryd responded. "He is a mutual friend. If she is allowed to continue to visit him after I go, he will inform me. That will suffice. Dyrileah and I will have no direct contact. I'll give you my word on that."

"That," Bardus spoke slowly as if still mulling over Jaryd's offer, "sounds reasonable."

"No." Dyrileah reared back in Jaryd's arms so she could look him in the face. "Jaryd, you mustn't—"

"You made your choice," Jaryd cut her off, his voice tightly controlled. "You have no say in this the now."

"No say?" Dyrileah pushed her way free of Jaryd's arms. "No say? Do you think I will let you throw away your life, all you've worked for?"

"I'll be going home, Dyrileah, to a place where people love me," Jaryd said, unrelenting. "Banished, where will you go?" In her eyes, he saw the weight of that blow land. "Do you think I could do that to you and live with myself?" His voice strained at the last, barely more than a whisper.

Dyrileah's face crumbled, tears welling, and she turned toward the wall, her shoulders shaking. Stepping up close behind but without touching her, Jaryd pleaded, "Please, Dyrileah, don't turn away from me."

She whirled and flung herself once again into his arms. With his right hand, he gently touched her hair. Soft as honey-colored silk it was beneath his fingers. He saw that she'd dressed it in an elaborate braid. "I like your hair like that."

"Took you long enough to notice," Dyrileah murmured, holding him closer.

"Do we have a bargain?" Jaryd raised his voice and directed his eyes to Bardus.

Still seated at the table, Bardus rapped his knuckles softly against the oaken surface. "No, I don't think so." He uttered the words quietly and shifted his gaze from Jaryd to his wife.

Ester's wide, slightly tilted green eyes locked on to Jaryd's. "I trust him," she announced firmly.

"As do I," Bardus agreed, rising from his seat.

Dyrileah's eyes were drawn irresistibly to her mother's. "Maman?" Dyrileah asked tentatively.

Ester opened her arms; a pair of great, fat tears trickled down her cheeks. "My little one."

Brushing her lips lightly against Jaryd's, Dyrileah rushed into her mother's embrace. Striding across the kitchen floor, Bardus briefly laid a gentle hand on Dyrileah's shoulder and then walked to where Jaryd stood.

Gazing steadily into the younger man's eyes, Bardus said, "I am sorry, children, to be so harsh. We had not planned this, not this evening, but after what Dyrileah told us, we had little choice." Looking from Jaryd to his wife and daughter, he waited until Dyrileah raised her tear-rimmed eyes to his. "We had to be certain that both of you understood the gravity of your situation. Peoples' lives, dear to us, hang in the balance."

"This was some sort of test?" Jaryd's voice was cold no longer. Dyrileah heard rage in it, simmering just below the surface. Looking up, she saw it in his eyes, dark and dangerous.

"If God is kind, your marriage will be blessed with children," Bardus said, unflinching. "Among Dyrileah's children, very likely there will be at least one who is of the Wycken. If so, upon a time, Jaryd Hume, you will face a day such as the one I've just spent." He paused, and then his voice lowered. "Judge me then. In the meantime, you are welcome to join our family." He extended his hand. Jaryd hesitated, taking a breath, and then slowly clasped Bardus's hand.

"Does this mean you approve?" Dyrileah inquired, her voice hushed with pent-up emotion.

"No," Ester and Bardus said emphatically in unison and then smiled at one another. "It is clear how much you mean to one another. So long as you both recognize the danger and the obligations you will incur and are prepared to face up to them," Ester spoke for her and her husband, "we will not stand in your way."

"What of the other Wycken? Will they allow it?" Trepidation again threaded through Dyrileah's soft tone.

"They will not deny us," Bardus said confidently. "Come, sit," he enjoined Jaryd, pointing to the kitchen table. "I want to see what my daughter has done to your poor arm." Feeling a little lightheaded, Jaryd returned to his place at the table. "If I may?" Bardus sought permission. Jaryd nodded, and the Elsacian took gentle hold of his left hand. Bardus's brown eyes narrowed in concentration, and Jaryd felt a warm tingle run up his arm. The feeling was distinct but not as intense as Dyrileah's healing. "Good enough," Bardus pronounced after a moment or two. "Knitting bone is tricksome. This will need proper binding."

"You're the witch?" Jaryd asked somewhat incredulously. "I thought…" His voice trailed away, and he could not help casting a glance at Ester and Dyrileah.

"You never know," Bardus commented. "Dyrileah and I are of the Wycken, as is young Cary. Ester is not. We don't know yet about Tamyra. At least the boys are free of it."

Jaryd heard clearly the wistful tone in his voice. Penitents referred to the ability to invoke the Yir, the Gyft, as the great calling. Some desired it mightily; others dreaded the possibility. He supposed the same must be true of manifesting whatever power drove the capacity for witchcraft. Jaryd's father had told him a time or two that wanted or not, responsibility came along with capability and authority. Responsibility weighed heavily. Jaryd thought he could see the mark of it in Bardus's eyes.

"That is quite a bauble you are wearing; may I see it?" Bardus requested.

Jaryd lifted the Fey amulet from his shirt for Bardus to examine. "I have heard of the Fey talismans," Bardus remarked. "They are said to be of ancient origin. This one is not." His eyes found Jaryd's. "How did you come by it?"

"It was a gift from a friend," Jaryd answered. Bardus raised an eyebrow, and Jaryd smiled. "I can't say more without betraying a confidence."

"It would appear you are to be a man of many secrets, Jaryd Hume," Bardus commented.

"Looks like I'll have to keep a few," Jaryd acknowledged. "I suppose that is true of most everyone sooner or later."

Without further comment, Bardus opened a cupboard and removed a leather satchel. Placing it upon the table, he opened the case and extracted some wooden splints, bandages, and a large pair of scissors. Using the shears, he cut a pair of splints to size. After wrapping Jaryd's left wrist and arm with a thin layer of bandage, Bardus fitted the splints. He secured them in place with a double wrapping. "You will need to be careful with this arm for two full weeks. Lift nothing heavier with it than a cup of water and do not flex your wrist."

Putting away his scissors and the unused portion of the bandage roll, Bardus looked to his wife and daughter, who now stood side by side with one arm each around the other. "My tea is cold," Bardus observed, "and our guest is hungry." As if to emphasize his point, Jaryd's stomach growled vigorously. Ester and Dyrileah busied themselves pouring fresh tea and slicing more bread and cheese.

Dyrileah's two brothers, Tate and Soryn, aged sixteen and fourteen, respectively, returned a moment later from Mistress Poinwyr's bakery bearing a large layer cake flavored with honey and cinnamon and covered with a buttercream frosting. After the strain of the kitchen conversation, supper proved to be a somewhat subdued affair but pleasant. The meal began with a serving of fresh roasted vegetables, yellow squash with carrots and onions.

Between the vegetables and the main dish, roast lamb, Tamyra suddenly bubbled at Jaryd, "You are only tall on one end." She laughed triumphantly. "I get it."

The lamb was followed by generous helpings of bread, cheese, salted almonds, and green olives. Mistress Poinwyr's cake was served for dessert. During the meal, the children peppered Jaryd with a constant flow of questions. They wanted to know about life in the Three Rivers and were especially enthralled by tales of the fearsome Indiquoi. Both the boys fair-hankered for a look at Jaryd's Hawken knife. After obtaining permission from Bardus, Jaryd passed the blade along.

By the time the meal finished, full dark had settled. Ester invited Jaryd to spend the night, saying they would set up a pallet for him in the front parlor.

As they rose from the dinner table, Tamyra said to Dyrileah, "He's not as handsome as Rysah but much nicer, I think."

Jaryd felt tired. He didn't know if it stemmed from the healing of his arm or the fear and tumult of the physical encounter in the alleyway or the emotional highs and lows of the evening that followed. By any road, he was glad enough to accept Ester's invitation. He told everyone he would need to be off by first light the next morning. He had an early lecture to attend and some chores to take care of beforehand.

Dyrileah brought him a pillow and some extra blankets. "Who is Rysah?" Jaryd asked.

Dyrileah hesitated, a moment only, before replying, "He was a young man, an Elsacian, one of the Wycken. We were betrothed two years ago. He undertook a mission, one that led him from the city. His ship was lost at sea. No one survived."

"I'm sorry," Jaryd said automatically. "Did you love him?" As soon as the question slipped free of his mouth, he wished he'd not asked.

"I don't know," Dyrileah answered him softly. "We were to be wed upon his return. I felt drawn to him. I hoped for love. We had so little time together." Dyrileah's eyes, wide and soft in the candle-light, sought his. "I know I love you."

Jaryd smiled and pulled her gently into his arms. They had time only for a brief hug and a kiss before Ester and Bardus joined them to say goodnight.

Despite the swirl of events of the preceding day, sleep came readily enough. To Jaryd, it seemed as if he'd just settled in, wrapped snugly in Dyrileah's blankets, when he felt a gentle hand on his shoulder.

He awoke to find Dyrileah kneeling beside his pallet. "Good morning," she greeted him with an engaging smile. The young Elsacian girl had an oil lamp in her hand. She set it carefully down upon the floor.

"It feels more like the middle of the night," Jaryd groused. Dyrileah wore only a blue woolen wrap over a sleeveless white cotton shift. She was barefoot, and the shift fell to just below her knees. Her hair flowed unbound, tumbling about her shoulders in a honey-blond cascade.

"You did say first light," Dyrileah reminded him cheerfully. "I wouldn't want you to be late and claim we were a bad influence upon you."

Looking about the room, Jaryd observed that they were alone. "Why don't you climb in here," he invited, "and let me be a bad influence on you?"

Dyrileah's eyes warmed to match her smile. She leaned forward to kiss him gently on the mouth. Jaryd started to slip his arms about her. She pulled away, shaking her head. "My parents are both awake. They are in the kitchen, awaiting our arrival. So is Tamyra. She seems quite taken with you." Her expression became serious, but the warm light in her eyes appeared to grow brighter. "As am I."

32

A Secret for a Secret

By the time Jaryd Hume reached the gardeners' cottages on the grounds of Antium Hall, the sun shone, full up. His left arm felt funny. It didn't really hurt but emitted a deep, dull throb that became more noticeable the longer he walked. Spats answered his knock almost immediately.

"Out all night, were you?" Spats greeted him. "That's either got to be real good or real bad."

Jaryd could not keep the grin off his face. "I'm betrothed officially the now. We haven't set a date yet, maybe as soon as this fall if Bode and I don't head back to Greystock this summer." With the militia deployed and opposing armies potentially on the move during the summer months, travel plans were suddenly up in the air.

Spats grinned in return. "She's game, that Dyrileah." He winked at Jaryd. "Her judgment may be none too sound, but she's game as all get out."

Jaryd slipped out of the leather jacket Spats had loaned him, intending to return it. "You might as well keep it, lad. I've become

"

too scrawny in my dotage to wear the bloody thing." Spats's eyes narrowed, and then he asked, "What happened to your arm?"

"We tussled with a couple of street toughs on the way from the library to the Porter's Gate," Jaryd explained. "Wouldn't you know the one time I really needed your walking stick, I was without it."

"Here. Sit down," Spats invited. "Mind if I take a look at it?"

"Dyrileah's folks bound it up for me," Jaryd said, extending his arm to the white-haired gardener. Spats sat down beside him and took hold of Jaryd's left hand with his right. The gardener laid his left hand on Jaryd's arm just above the binding. In a moment, Jaryd felt a slight tingling, similar to the sensation that he'd experienced when Bardus examined him. "This arm's been broken," Spats observed. His rich voice rumbled speculatively. "And healed, at least most of the way."

Spats leaned back in his chair so that he could look Jaryd in the eye. "Was the healing Dyrileah's doing or her folks?"

"How do you know my arm was healed?" Jaryd countered.

"Magic, in whatever form, leaves a residue, an aura of sorts, that can be detected by any mage," Spats replied quietly. "This is Dyrileah's work, I think." He paused. "I've sensed her aura once before, here in the cottage, my bedroom, to be exact, on the night of your father's visit. I couldn't be sure then."

"You are still guessing." Jaryd stalled. He trusted Spats implicitly, but he'd promised Dyrileah and her parents to tell no one of her or her family's abilities. Confirming Spats's suspicions would be tantamount to breaking his promise.

"She is not a sorcerer," Spats went on, ignoring Jaryd's comment. "If she had been, I would have sensed that immediately. Like is attuned to like. While sorcerers and witches can detect the aftereffects of one another's magic, they can't sense each other's presence directly." Spats's voice drifted slightly, as if into thought or remembrance. "I've always found that inconvenient." The old man's tone firmed. "An Elsacian, not a sorcerer, who can heal—a witch, in other words. She must be one of the Wycken."

Jaryd sat silent, staring at the floor. Spats patted him on the shoulder.

"I swore never to reveal her secret," Jaryd said in disgust, "and the first person I speak to knows all."

"The first person you spoke to has an unfair advantage," Spats commiserated. "Do you mind if I finish what young Dyrileah started?" Jaryd raised his eyes to Spats. The old man's blue-eyed gaze was warm and steady.

"Go ahead," Jaryd assented.

Taking hold of his arm once again, Spats remarked, "Healing is a funny thing. Great, gaping wounds that you'd think would strain a healer's capacity are for the most part pretty straightforward. On the other hand, knitting bone, even a simple fracture, requires a fine touch." Jaryd could feel the tingle begin again running up and down his arm. "You are fortunate in the location of the break, right at about mid bone. If the fracture was in or near a joint, I'd leave it be. As it is, I think..." He paused a moment. "There, done and done."

Jaryd flexed the fingers of his left hand and then his wrist. His arm felt whole and strong as if the injury had never been. "That feels fine, thanks." Jaryd looked again into Spats's eyes. "Are you going to tell me who you are the now?"

"A secret for a secret, eh?" Spats smiled, "Well, fair is fair, after all. My name is Sebastyn Card."

"And I'm Uncle Time," Jaryd retorted without thinking and then took note of the serious cast to the old man's lean features. "Spats, that's impossible."

"Damned unlikely, I'll grant you that," Spats allowed sardonically.

"Card lived more than a century ago," Jaryd spoke incredulously. "If he were alive today, he'd have to be at least two hundred years old."

"Two hundred thirty-eight next autumn," Spats affirmed. "I'm not the man I was. This past century or so has taken quite a toll."

"How is that possible?" Jaryd still couldn't bring himself to believe what Spats had just told him. "I thought the lifespan of a sorcerer was no longer than that of the average person."

"That is correct; as a rule, sorcerers live no longer than anyone else." Spats shrugged. "If you are looking to me for an answer, lad,

I have none for you." He stuffed his hands in his tunic pockets. "I suspect that I and a few others were exposed to the Yir in an unusual way in our youth, an experiment gone wrong, if you will. A couple died instantly, but the rest…well, those not killed since by some means fair or foul are still kicking. I don't know why."

"Are the stories true?" Jaryd wondered. "The exploits of Sebastyn Card and all that, is there any truth to the tales?"

"I imagine there is some truth to every tale." Spats smiled. "While what folks call history is mostly a pack of lies. A goodly portion of what is true is cause for regret, I'll say that much."

"Did you really battle Lylith Caddow the White Witch and travel to Dar Shan with Hexus Rygg?" Jaryd knew he was gushing like a schoolboy but couldn't help himself.

"Lylith and I spent the better part of a lifetime trying to kill one another," Spats affirmed. "Hexus and I covered a lot of ground together. We parted friends."

"Did Lylith really try to destroy time itself?" Jaryd queried. That particular Sebastyn Card adventure had always been his favorite.

"Lylith doesn't believe in time." Spats's smile broadened in recollection. "That squabble was actually over a magic talisman, a making charm of considerable potency. The little minx fooled me in the end and made off with the thing, for all the good it did her." Spats sounded sad at the last.

"They say you killed the White Witch by sealing her in a mountain of ice," Jaryd recalled. "Is that true?"

"There was an avalanche that trapped her in a cavern of ice. My doing it was." Spats's eyes were far away. "I had no choice. I went back when I could to look for her. I never found her." He fell silent.

"She is dead then?" Jaryd prompted.

"I hope not," Spats replied. "She was quite a girl."

"Did you love her?" Jaryd inquired, wondering if he'd interpreted the expression in the old gardener's eyes correctly.

Spats blinked. "Don't be daft, boy. If she is alive and our paths crossed, she'd have my liver on a plate quick as dammit."

"Be that as it may," Jaryd contended, "I notice you didn't answer the question."

"Did I not?" Spats growled evasively.

"It is a pleasure to meet you, Sebastyn." Jaryd extended his hand. "And an honor."

Sebastyn Card grasped Jaryd's hand firmly, and they shook briefly. "I feel the same, lad. It has been a while since I made a friend."

"Who knows who you really are?" Jaryd asked next.

"Not many. A few here at the Hall know. Regys the mathematician for one; he doesn't believe in time either, you know."

"What are you doing here, Sebastyn?" Jaryd fixed his eyes intently on Card's.

"Besides gardening, you mean?" Sebastyn smiled. "I'm waiting, Jaryd—waiting and watching."

"Waiting and watching for what?" Jaryd pressed.

"Knowing that is liable to do you more harm than good," Sebastyn said evenly. He turned to look out the window. "I'll tell you if and when it becomes necessary for you to know but only then. Should others—enemies or competitors, shall we say—learn what I'm about, the time I've spent here and the harm done to those I care about as a result are likely to come to naught." He turned back to once again look Jaryd in the eye. "We need to trust one another, lad, and while doing so, honor the secrets each of us must preserve. Can you do that?"

"Aye, I reckon I can," Jaryd promised. "My word on it."

33

Accord

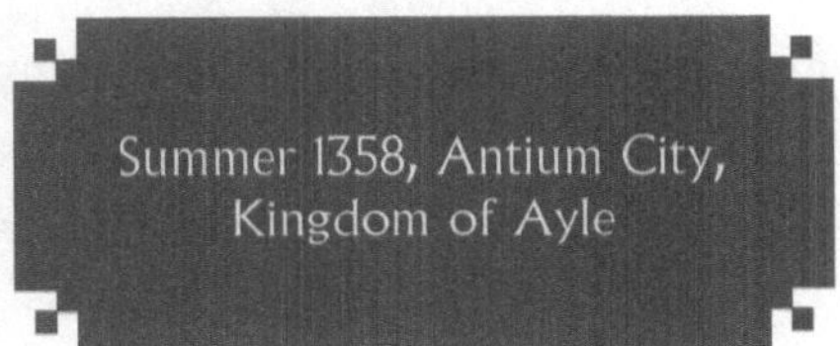

In keeping with their usual practice, Dyrileah and Jaryd met on the front steps of Antium Library. Midmorning it was, and the dawn cool had not yet fully succumbed to the mounting summer heat. Jaryd had been standing at the head of the steps for some time when he spotted her.

Clad in a sleeveless cotton dress, pearl gray in color and bound at the waist by a kyrobi, Dyrileah strode toward him. The hem of her garment fell to mid-calf, accentuating her long legs as she moved with an easy, almost feline grace.

Dyrileah was wearing a regular frock, Jaryd noted, not the more characteristic Elsacian keppi. The more ubiquitous frock, styled after dresses typically worn by the women of Antium and the Middle Sea region in general, would draw less attention outside the Elsacian Quarter.

Invisibility, Dyrileah had told him once, was sometimes the last, best refuge for a minority scorned. Though there had been no outright violence yet, nothing beyond the occasional act of vandalism, tension between the Elsacians and the Penitent Ayle majority in Antium had been on the rise in recent months. Dyrileah was at a loss as to why.

Jaryd loved the girl and so admitted to some bias in the matter, but he reckoned invisibility wouldn't work insofar as Dyrileah was concerned. Any man with one good eye and a pulse would likely notice her.

She smiled at him, a special, private smile, and Jaryd felt his heart lift. "Early again, was I?" he greeted her, plucking his watch cap from his head.

"I was daydreaming," Dyrileah explained softly, "about a farmer's son with hay in his hair. I can't think why." Stepping close, she reached up to lightly run her fingers through his hair, just above his left ear.

"I thought we were in a hurry," Jaryd replied, returning her smile.

"No longer." She expounded, "Maman was called away at the last moment." Dyrileah's mother was a person of some authority within the Elsacian community, "elder" being her official title. She was often called away to address some concern or another. "I told Aunt Sorileah, who stopped by the house just after breakfast, that I wasn't feeling particularly well, and since Maman couldn't be there, I added that perhaps we should go shopping for my nuptial linens some other time." She shrugged her shapely shoulders. "It seems we have the whole day to ourselves."

Jaryd had no idea what nuptial linens were and decided he'd just as soon not find out. "Aye, well, *that* being the case," he observed wryly, "at least we won't be late."

Dyrileah stuck her tongue out at him.

"Funny," Jaryd continued, squinting at her, "you don't look sick."

Dyrileah ducked her head. "I never said I was sick, not exactly."

"I see," Jaryd surmised. "It would appear that time is, for the present, on our side. Just how, my lady, would you care to spend our newfound bounty?"

Dyrileah lowered her chin before shyly suggesting, "I thought perhaps we should inspect your rooms."

"My rooms," Jaryd repeated incredulously, "in the gardeners' quarters?"

"Have you any other lodgings?" Dyrileah asked a little tartly.

"You've seen my rooms half a dozen times," he pointed out, reasonably.

"Casual visits only," Dyrileah responded immediately. "I think a more complete examination is warranted. Maman says you can tell a lot about a man by the way he keeps house."

Slipping his cap back on, Jaryd turned in the direction of the Hall and offered her his left arm. "Any room in particular strike your fancy? I have only two, you know."

Taking his arm, Dyrileah drew her golden eyebrows down as if in careful thought. "The bedroom, I think, to begin with; it should provide a more personal perspective."

Jaryd shook his head sadly. "Fibbing," he accused her, "to your dear auntie so that you can spend an entire day doing who knows what with some boy. Dyrileah Quirow, what has come over you?"

Laughing softly, Dyrileah hugged his arm. "You are indeed a bad influence."

Subtly increasing his pace, Jaryd enthused, "Let's get a move on then. With a little luck maybe, I can go from bad to worse."

Though tiny, Jaryd's lodging was neat and snug with white plastered brick walls, a rock-lined chimney, thatched roof, and door and windowsills painted bright green. Jaryd unlocked the door to his cottage and followed Dyrileah inside. Closing the door, he removed his watch cap and set it atop a peg in a rack affixed to the back of the portal. His heart pounded, and his mouth felt suddenly dry as he led her into his bedroom. Waving his hand in a vague gesture encompassing the room, Jaryd became acutely aware of a pair of socks lying on the floor in front of a straight-backed chair with a soiled and sweat-stained gardener's tunic draped over it. Thank God he'd made the bed.

"Well, what do you think?" he inquired. "Of my husbanding prospects, that is."

Dyrileah gazed up at him, her eyes as wide and soft as any doe's. "I love you more than I thought I could love anyone. As long as you are with me, I would be happy living in a hole in the ground."

"Doesn't sound very sanitary," Jaryd commented, stepping forward to slip his arms about her. Dyrileah returned his embrace. His nervousness fled, banished by sheer delight in her presence.

Dyrileah kissed him, a sweet, lingering touching of lips, her mouth soft beneath his. Breaking off the kiss, she pressed her face into the crook of his neck. "A hovel then, aboveground, with a leaky roof."

"Won't wash, girl," Jaryd growled. Bending his head down, he nuzzled the silken-soft tresses of her hair. "All that damp and draft, you'd be grumpy as all get out in a fortnight."

Holding him tight, Dyrileah sighed. "I suppose there is no help for it. You'll just have to take proper care of me."

"We'll take care of each other," Jaryd vowed.

Nodding, Dyrileah gently pushed him away and stepped back. Turning around she reached behind her. With a few deft movements Dyrileah removed the kyrobi at her waist and undid the buttons lining the back of her dress and slipped free of it. Lifting a hand she tugged the shift beneath down off one shoulder and then the other, allowing the garment to fall. Stepping gracefully aside Dyrileah stood apart from the small heap of clothing at her feet. Jaryd saw how her slender torso tapered to her waist before flaring again into the supple curve of her hips.

Slowly Dyrileah turned toward him, crossing her arms as she did so to cover the swell of her bosom. Fair and creamy smooth, her skin seemed to glow. Her eyes sought his. Removing his shirt Jaryd closed the distance between them and put his arms around her. Dyrileah embraced him in return, and he felt the firm press of her breasts against his upper abdomen. He marveled at the silken warmth of her body.

"There is no hurry," Jaryd said. "I'll love you more tomorrow than I do today."

Dyrileah raised the fingers of her right hand, placing them gently over his mouth. "No more waiting. I am for you, Jaryd Hume." She kissed him then with unrestrained passion, her slender form molded ardently to his.

Divesting himself quickly of his loincloth, Jaryd lowered her down onto the bed. She moaned quietly as he mouthed her breast, running his tongue lightly over the taut bud at its crest.

"Jaryd," she gasped, her voice low and urgent, "let it be the now."

He placed his hand between Dyrileah's slender thighs, curving his palm over the down-covered mound he found there. She stirred beneath his hand, the gentle probing of his fingers. Her back arched, and her legs slid apart. The trust she placed in him, the joy evident at his touch, warmed his heart just as the sight and feel of her sleek, supple body fired his loins. Jaryd covered her gently, pressing his length slowly into her moist, yielding flesh.

Dyrileah cried out softly as he mounted her. Jaryd's experience with women was limited. He'd only been with a couple of girls, both a little older and much more knowledgeable than he. Those encounters had seemed more like play than anything else, promising nothing more than a brief exchange of pleasure. Dyrileah gave of herself, a gift precious to him because of what it meant to her. He began to move atop her slowly, trying not to hurt her. Dyrileah shivered, clinging to him. He withdrew partially and then thrust deeper. She uttered a slight, mewling sound even as her hips rose to meet him. Conscious thought fled, and he lost himself in her, consumed by a longing sharper and sweeter than any he'd known.

After, she lay quiet in his arms. "How do you fare?" Jaryd asked.

Dyrileah pressed closer against him. "Thank you," she murmured.

"I think you've got that the wrong way round," Jaryd said lightly. "Shouldn't I be thanking you?"

"You'll not make a joke of this, Jaryd Hume," she told him firmly. "The first time for a girl, for a woman," Dyrileah corrected herself, "should be special. Thank you for making it so for me."

Jaryd smiled. "If there is anything else I can do for you, you'll let me know?"

"Of all the men in the world," Dyrileah remonstrated, rolling her eyes, "I had to fall in love with a fool of a..." She paused as if searching for the right word. "*Farm boy.*"

"You think that's bad?" Jaryd asked rhetorically. "Before too much longer, you'll find yourself married to a *lawyer*."

"Whatever and whoever you become," Dyrileah responded quietly, "so long as you remain *you* in the doing, I shall love and be glad of it."

34

Welcome, Little Sister

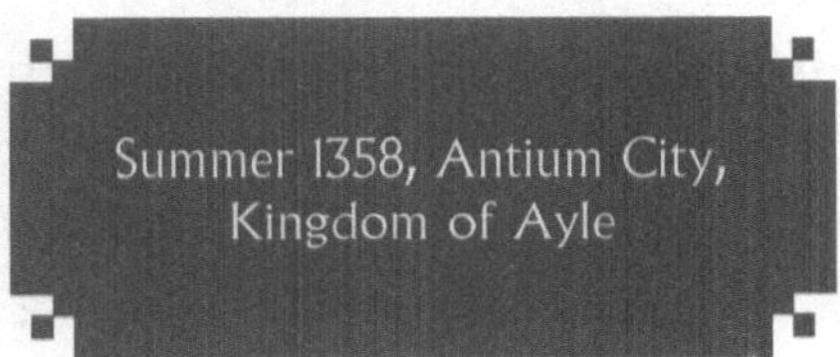

Fright gripped Bodewhin Ware. She did not understand what was happening to her. For months, she had been experiencing a vague unease, but the past few weeks, after the joy of seeing Mat again had begun to fade, unease had turned into something more palpable and terrifying. A fortnight after Mat left, Dehlia had filled a large vase in Bode's room with fresh red roses, the first cuttings of the summer bloom.

The flowers were beautiful, and that night Bode experienced a vivid dream about them. At least she thought she was dreaming. She awoke the next morning with a piercing headache and noticed each of the petals had been plucked cleanly from the flowers and arranged in a heart-shaped pattern on the carpet beside her bed. Bode had no recollection of leaving her bed during the night. She had never walked in her sleep. She had no explanation for what had transpired.

A week later, she returned to the house after an evening at the theater with Ned Bly. Ned was his usual charming and solicitous self, but despite this, she'd managed to grow cross with him, and they had argued. Feeling out of sorts and averse to explaining anything to anyone, Bode had gone directly to her room. She closed the door but did not bolt it. She heard footsteps in the hall, her aunt's undoubtedly. Not wanting to speak with her, Bode cast a frantic look at her bedchamber door, and the latch slammed shut, apparently of its own accord. Perhaps her aunt heard the bolt being shot; for whatever reason, she turned away and never came to the door. Bode sank to her knees, unable to credit what her eyes had just witnessed.

Sitting alone in her room last evening just before sundown, Bode found herself staring intently at a set of candles on her writing table. She had not been eating well; her stomach roiled at the very thought of food these days. It growled at her as she sat, and still she had no appetite. A notion occurred that on the surface seemed crazy, but her mind seized upon it. Time passed, the moments dripped away, and the gloom deepened.

Try as she might, she was unable to stir the candles to light by will alone. With the room darkening, Bode turned from the candle holder in disgust, glaring at the fireplace. Suddenly, a whirling ball of flame engulfed the fire pit, threatening to burst forth into the room itself. Bode screamed in terror as consciousness fled. An hour or so later, Dehlia found her, lying dead to the world upon the carpet. Bode had not slept since. She had to speak with someone. She knew she could trust Jaryd with her life, and Spats, who seemed to know so much, perhaps could help her.

The next morning, Bode hurried to the gardeners' cottages on the grounds of the Hall, oblivious to the bright blue sky overhead and the trees and flowers blooming all around. She wore a light-blue cotton frock that fell to mid-calf; sleeveless, the dress belted at the waist with a silk sash of dark blue. In a hurry, she'd combed and bound her long brown hair into a ponytail. Bode knocked upon the brightly painted green door of the cottage. A moment later, it swung open, and before her stood Dyrileah Quirow. Jaryd's intended had been baking; she had a flour-dusted apron wound about her waist. She was wearing a light-green keppi.

"Bode," Dyrileah exclaimed, "what a joyful surprise. Good morning."

"Is Jaryd here," Bode inquired anxiously, "or Spats? I need to speak with them."

"They are both out early today. In summer, the gardeners' work is never done." Dyrileah's large, slightly tilted brown eyes widened at the sight of Bode's haggard, hollow-cheeked appearance. "Are you well, Bode?"

"I don't know, Dyrileah," Bode replied weakly, fighting to control her emotions.

Removing her apron, Dyrileah tossed it aside and pulled Bode into the sitting room of the cottage, closing the door behind them. She laid her hand alongside Bode's temple, and her golden-brown eyes darkened with concern. "Poor darling, you are deep in transition with no one to guide you." Bode felt a warm tingle gently envelope her body. Her sense of panic began to ease. "You must not fear me, Bode," Dyrileah urged, her voice calm and steady. "Never will I harm you."

Stepping back, Dyrileah held her hands out in front of her breasts, palms perpendicular to the floor. She closed her eyes for a moment, and a perfect sphere of softly pulsing green light appeared between them. "Place your hands on mine, Bode," Dyrileah commanded gently. Bode complied, and Dyrileah lowered her hands. To Bode's amazement, the glowing sphere remained hovering between her outstretched fingers. "That is enough for the now," Dyrileah directed. "Release the ward, Bode." Without thinking, Bode reacted instinctively, and the light winked out.

Bode could only stare at Dyrileah in disbelief. "You are what my people would call an inborn, Bode," she explained, clasping both of Bode's hands. "The Power of the One stirs deeply within you, determined to become manifest. This is rare and marvelous, a sign of great potential." Dyrileah looked unflinchingly into her eyes. Bode saw neither fear nor censure in her warm umber gaze, only strength and compassion. "You are of the Wycken. I bid you welcome, little sister."

Sweet light. Bode's mind skittered like a bead of water on a hot skillet. *She's a bloody witch, and so am I.*

Bode stepped back, alarmed. Dyrileah smiled. "You look as if I've sprouted a pair of horns."

"I'm sorry. It's just…" Bode stammered. Shamed by the pleading tone that crept into her voice, she decried, "This can't be. I don't want it."

Dyrileah's expression sobered. "The One chooses, Bode. Among my people, its presence is usually hard-won, attainable only after being ardently sought. You are the exception. The Power has embraced you, Bode. You cannot turn away."

"I can," Bode insisted, "and I will."

"I know you were taken unawares," Dyrileah soothed. "Believe me when I tell you this is a blessing, not a curse."

"My people burn witches, Dyrileah." Bode felt her cheeks flame as she blurted the words but could not call them back.

"Not so much these days." There was no mistaking the wry twist to Dyrileah's answering smile. "Flogging has become the more usual practice."

"I meant no insult," Bode hastened. "But this goes against everything that I have been taught."

Dyrileah grasped Bode's hand and squeezed gently. "Not everything, Bode. Only one thing," she argued. "Ignorance and prejudice are human characteristics; they exist everywhere and among everyone, plaguing all cultures and all faiths."

"I have been taught that witchcraft is inherently evil," Bode maintained.

"Evil is a choice," Dyrileah stated flatly. She looked Bode full in the eye and inquired sharply, "Have you sought out the Dark Powers?"

"No," Bode cried, horrified.

Dyrileah released Bode's hand. "I'd say that amounts to one theory disproved, wouldn't you?"

Taken aback, Bode dropped her eyes. "Perhaps unintentionally, I—"

"No one stumbles across the Dark Powers," Dyrileah interrupted firmly. "They can be accessed but only through the use of consummate skill and explicit purpose. No novice, not even one with the strength I sense in you, could summon them by accident."

"I don't know, Dyrileah," Bode said hesitantly. "There is so much I do not understand."

"Sweet lamb." Dyrileah hugged her. "How could you? You have much to learn before attaining any hope of understanding." Kissing Bode lightly on her cheek, Dyrileah walked to the window and looked out upon a fine summer day. "Do you see evil in me, Bode? Do you think I would bring hurt or harm to you or to Jaryd?"

"Of course not," Bode exclaimed and realized, even as she spoke the words, that she meant them. "Does Jaryd know…about you, I mean?"

Dyrileah turned back toward Bode and smiled. "He expressed some concern about being transformed into a barnyard animal. Aside from that, he's been remarkably accepting."

Despite everything, Bode could not help but smile back. "I don't suppose we could actually do such a thing."

"No," Dyrileah affirmed crisply. She tossed her head. "More is the pity."

"You've known all along, haven't you?" Bode queried softly.

"From the moment we met," Dyrileah affirmed. "You must have felt it too—that sense of familiarity you mentioned, remember?"

"Yes," Bode recalled.

"The One is vast, as natural as a sunburst, free of malice or greed or envy. It exists to serve. But once summoned, the Power of the One cannot be denied." Dyrileah focused her eyes once more upon Bode's, her gaze compelling, unrelenting. Transfixed, Bode could not look away. "You must accept this, Bode, or be consumed. In your heart, you know I speak the truth."

Slowly, reluctantly, Bode nodded.

"Acceptance is the first step and, often, the most difficult." Dyrileah's eyes softened. "So I say, again, welcome, little sister."

She held out her arms. Bode hesitated only a moment before stepping into them.

35

Allegation

Having spent some time commanding a line company, Altyrn Wyllem Varus Quin had decided he preferred serving as a staff officer. Wyll amended his assessment to allow for a dependency upon whose staff he joined. He liked being a member of Quintus Glabrio Jens's staff better than running a line company. He was allowed greater range of assignments and remained generally free from the often mundane and sometimes complex set of responsibilities that inevitably stemmed from dealing with large numbers of subordinates.

People, he'd found, were complicated creatures, and groups of them flung together even more so, firm and fair old Thadius Bourne had counseled. The sajar first was right—good advice that—but it made the business no less onerous. Making decisions that directly impacted the lives of others was not easy. Even acting in their best interests did not ensure those affected would like the choices you made.

Stocky, of medium height, with light-brown hair and gray eyes, Wyll, at twenty-three, had been in the army long enough to enjoy the good assignments while they lasted. The army being the army,

Wyll knew the worm would eventually turn. Even the best jobs occasionally rankled. He sighed, today being a prime example.

One of his duties as a staff officer entailed hearing complaints generally couched by magistrates or lawyers representing the local citizenry of Henfyrd determined to address wrongs allegedly committed by some member of Quintus Glabrio Jens's garrison force. Henfyrd was large enough for the local populace to interact substantially with the troops stationed there and at the same time remained sufficiently rustic to be affronted by said interaction on a regular basis. Wyll had become accustomed to smoothing ruffled feathers. This morning's exchange, however, surfaced a potentially serious charge, one that involved the alleged kidnapping of a young girl by a group of auxiliaries.

Of course this would happen on the same day the general intended to escort Her Highness Lydia Sylvus Gant on a tour of the military installations in and around Henfyrd. Wyll was supposed to join the entourage. He had been responsible for planning the tour. If something went awry and he wasn't there, well, maybe having a good excuse to be elsewhere would turn out to be a blessing after all. A moment's further reflection caused Wyll to doubt it; for all his calm demeanor, Jens was a stickler for detail, unlikely to forget who stood responsible for what.

Quintus had established his headquarters in a building known as the Old Granary. It had been a two-story grain exchange overlooking the bluffs leading down to the eastern bank of the river Wyst. A new and significantly larger grain exchange had recently opened in the northeastern quarter of the town. Since then, until being taken over by the elements of the Northern Army under Jens, the Old Granary had been used primarily as a warehouse. The first floor was spacious with a series of stalls lining the interior walls. The second floor housed a number of individual rooms that had been converted into officers' quarters.

Two men, civilians both, stood before Wyll and the young optius or company clerk, assigned to him for this morning's session, just inside one of the first floor stalls. The optius, quill in hand, sat at one small folding writing desk, while Wyll leaned against a sturdy but battered table, a remnant of the Old Granary's better days. Though bareheaded, both Wyll and the optius were in uniform and fighting kit, chain mail armor worn over jaltryns and military tunics with short swords and daggers belted at their waists.

One of the civilians was a tall, leanly built farmer by the look of his clothes. He was a bit bleary-eyed in appearance, and Wyll could smell the wine on him. The man had dark hair, thinning and streaked with gray. He looked decidedly uncomfortable.

The tall man had just given his name as Lige Cotton and confirmed that he was indeed a local farmer. His daughter, Emilyn, had been identified as the victim of the supposed abduction. The second man Wyll knew, a local magistrate, a lawyer named Hertius Grover. Grover was short, tubby, and pugnacious. Wyll had encountered him on more than one previous occasion. The lawyer dressed as usual in a pale cotton tunic and, despite the summer heat, a somewhat tattered, brown silk waistcoat, ink stained on both cuffs. Gray-haired with smallish, dark-brown eyes, Grover appeared equal parts harried and irritated. Cotton had apparently come into town the night before, stopped at a local tavern for a cup of wine or two, and in the process began complaining to those present that his daughter, a fifteen-year-old, had been carried off by a rapacious collection of Tieran militia, archers stationed in Henfyrd.

By pure chance, Grover had been taking a meal at the tavern and overheard Cotton's outraged discourse. Determined to see justice done, he had insisted that Cotton stay over so the two of them could pursue the matter in the morning. Cotton, who at that point had evidently consumed considerably more than two cups of wine, consented. If the allegations proved true, Grover had informed Wyll that he intended to file charges against both the men responsible and the army that spawned them. Local courts were not sympathetic when it came to the sometimes boisterous antics of the troops flooding Henfyrd the now, and Grover had already won a couple of small settlements.

"Do you know who the alleged perpetrators are?" Wyll inquired.

"The sajar in charge is named Mat Bayrd," Grover replied. "He is among a group of militia archers called up from the Three Rivers."

The optius, named Tilius Barum Kline, remarked, "That would put them in the 133rd Auxiliary, sir." Tilius set aside his quill. "The 133rd is stationed here at the compaglium just north of the town. Shall I check the muster scroll, sir?" Wyll nodded, and Tilius rose from his seat and walked briskly toward a larger stall located near the corner of the building.

"Exactly when was this supposed to have happened?" Wyll asked next.

"The abduction took place three days ago," Grover answered again, speaking for his client.

Wyll looked directly at Lige Cotton. "Why did you wait three days before registering a complaint?" Lige shifted his feet but said nothing.

"Altyrn," Grover responded once more, "Lige Cotton is a poor farmer, an illiterate man who knows only that he was beaten and his child forcibly removed from his home by marauding auxiliaries from this command. At first he did not know where to turn."

"Beaten, you say." Wyll looked carefully at Lige Cotton's face. "He appears more hungover than anything."

"The miscreants struck him in the body, sir," Grover expounded indignantly. "Their leader, this sajar, is a very powerfully built man, a rogue, and a bully. Great harm has been done, sir, and justice demands recompense."

"Recompense," Wyll said mildly. "I would have thought his daughter's safety would be Master Cotton's first concern and yours as his representative."

"Of course, of course," Grover hastened. "But surely, sir, you must see that by now the poor girl has undoubtedly been ruined; no decent sort will have her in marriage. Her safe recovery is but the first step in seeing justice done."

The optius returned to report, "There is a Sajar Mathias Bayrd assigned to Third Company, 133rd Auxiliary Regiment, section D, tent twelve, sir."

"Please convey my apologies to the general," Wyll directed the optius. "You know where he is supposed to be?" When Tilius nodded, Wyll continued. "Apprise him of this matter and tell him I will join him as soon as I have attended to it."

"Yes, sir." Tilius saluted and then strode away.

Wyll was relieved to find that a man he knew well, Thadius Bourne, stood assigned as sajar of the guard that morning. He and a file of 3rd Regulus spearmen accompanied Wyll and the two civilians to the fortified camp. Upon their arrival, a guard informed them that the archers had already been called out to assemble for inspection by the general and his party. *Something I should have remembered,* Wyll thought, adjusting the chinstrap of his Tieran Army standard, open-faced helmet. Nodding, he decided to have tent number twelve in Section D searched anyhow.

"You don't think they'd be stupid enough to stash the girl in their bloody tent, do you, sir?" Sajar First Thadius Bourne asked softly of his onetime company commander.

"No," Wyll admitted in a similar tone, "but it is a place to start and one less thing to do later. Who knows? We might find something."

"This lawyer is an oily critter, sir," the tall, broad-shouldered sajar opined in a bass rumble intended for Wyll's ears alone, "and the farmer is a turd if ever I saw one."

Wyll smiled at Bourne in the rueful manner junior officers do when they agree with their sajars but can't admit to it openly. "Take four men and give tent twelve, section D, a quick search. Catch up to us in the assembly area. I'll take the civilians with me and see if we can locate this Sajar Bayrd."

"As you say, sir." Bourne saluted and called the first four troopers in the accompanying file to follow him. With the four of them on his heels, Bourne headed off in the direction of the tent ground.

The assembly area was located just inside the eastern gate of the fortified camp. It also served as the parade ground. The bulk of the 133rd Auxiliary Regiment, archers all, and elements of the light-missile-armed militia cavalry, filling the roster of the 122nd Auxiliary Regiment, had been drawn up for inspection by General Quintus Glabrio Jens and Her Highness Lydia Sylvus Gant. The troops were arrayed in company formation, standing at ease. Apparently, the general and the princess had yet to arrive.

The archers were decked out in full kit, their long bows slung over their shoulders along with a quiver of arrows. They held their pole axes in their right hands with the butt end of the weapon resting upon the ground. The bowmen wore boiled leather cuirasses over blue cotton tunics with gray neck cloths looped about their throats. Atop their heads, they were clad in Three-Rivers-style watch caps, not helmets. Strictly speaking, Wyll supposed this put them out of uniform, but he knew the watch caps had become an emblem of pride for the auxiliaries and was certain their state of dress was in keeping with their commander's wishes.

Locating Third Company, Wyll introduced himself to the commanding officer, a provincial who gave his name as Sedgwyck Ward. Altyrn Ward was a big man with a shock of pale blond hair and dark brown eyes. Wyll explained the two civilians accompanying him had sworn out a complaint against one of Ward's sajars, a man called Mathias Bayrd.

"Bayrd?" Ward exclaimed. "Are you certain?" At Wyll's nod, Ward explained, "Bayrd is as steady as a rock. I would never have figured him for a troublemaker."

"Accusations are one thing," Wyll allowed. "Proof of any wrongdoing is often quite another. Given the complaint, I still need to speak with Sajar Bayrd."

"Do you want to speak with him before or after the inspection, sir?" Ward inquired. Though both were altyrns, Wyll was senior by a few months and therefore entitled to the honorific.

"Let's do so the now, quietly off to the side of the formation," Wyll suggested.

Third Company, Fourth Squad happened to be located at the far-right end of the regimental grouping near the front. Ward signaled the sajar first, a hard-bitten veteran if ever Wyll saw one, and a young, wide-shouldered junior sajar to join him, Altyrn Ward, the two civilians, and the five regulars standing with them just to the side of the troop formation. The pair walked over and saluted crisply. The sajar first introduced himself as Nathyn Biddle, and the burly junior sajar gave his name as Mat Bayrd.

"Is this the man?" Wyll asked Lige Cotton.

"Yup," Lige Cotton replied shortly.

"Do you know this man, Sajar?" Wyll asked of Mat Bayrd.

"Yes, sir," Mat answered. "His name is Lige Cotton. He's a farmer hereabouts."

"He has accused you, Sajar," Wyll informed Bayrd, "of kidnapping his daughter, Emilyn Cotton."

"Emilyn prefers to go by the name of Harris, sir," Mat replied evenly. "This man, Cotton, is her stepfather. We kidnapped no one, sir."

Before he was able to question the young sajar further, Wyll noticed Thadius Bourne approaching from around the rear of the formation, half dragging and half carrying a furious young girl. The four troopers sent with Bourne to search the archers' tent trudged along behind.

"Let loose of me, dammit," the girl cried as they approached.

"Easy the now, darlin'." Thadius tried to calm her. "We're almost there. See? Your daddy's waiting."

"My daddy's dead, you lunkhead," the girl spat at Bourne. "Let me go." She couldn't have been more than fifteen, Wyll reckoned, small boned and slim hipped with a glorious mass of medium-brown hair falling loosely about her shoulders, trailing nearly to her hips, and flashing gray eyes. A very pretty little thing she was and madder than a wet cat.

With some difficulty, Bourne held onto her. "Altyrn Quin, may I present Emilyn Cotton?"

"Emilyn Harris," the girl insisted, glaring back over her shoulder at Bourne. "I done tol' you that, you big stupid."

"Hush the now," Bourne grumbled. "There's officers present." He tightened his grip on the indignant young woman, causing her to yelp slightly.

"Don't hurt her," Mat Bayrd growled, the menace in his voice clear to all. Bayrd and Bourne locked eyes. Thadius was taller and just as wide across the shoulders, but Bayrd was younger, deeper through the chest, and more heavily muscled.

Wyll took a breath, ready to draw the two of them to attention, when Emilyn Harris called out to the young sajar, "He ent hurt me none, Mat." She raised wide, gray eyes to the big archer. "He keeps sayin' he's gonna hand me over to Lige Cotton." The girl sounded frantic the now, fearful as opposed to angry.

"That isn't going to happen, Em," Mat Bayrd said steadily. "Everything is going to be all right."

"Stand to attention, Sajar Bayrd," Wyll commanded. Mat stood to, looking directly to his front.

"Good morning, gentlemen," Quintus Glabrio Jens announced, swinging down from his horse, a placid brown mare of unremarkable proportions. "What seems to be the problem?"

36

A Tale Retold

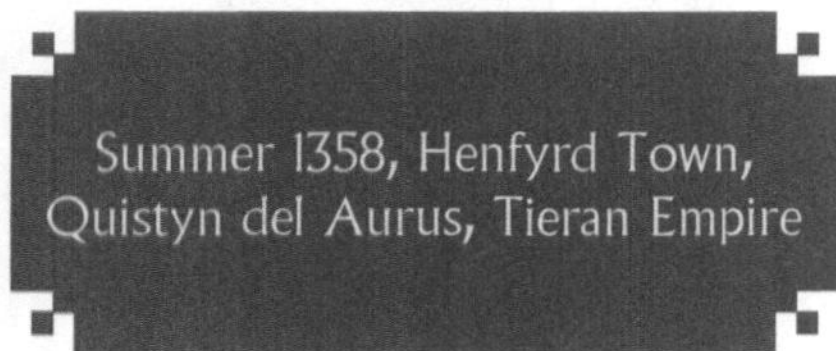

Looking in the direction of Jens's voice, Wyll caught sight of Her Highness Lydia Sylvus Gant sitting smartly astride a spirited filly with clean, supple Enduyi lines. In an instant, Wyll realized he'd managed to disrupt a regimental review in the presence not only of his commanding general but her bloody highness, the emperor's sister, as well. Just behind the princess, Wyll caught sight of an already dismounted, somewhat worried-looking kernyl who he recognized as Sagitus Turo Salt, officer in command of the 133rd. Apparently, the young optius Wyll had sent hadn't succeeded in catching up with the general.

Glabrio will have me supervising latrine maintenance for the next year for this, Wyll thought. He said, "Good morning, sir. Sorry for the disruption. We are investigating an alleged kidnapping."

Stepping to her side, Glabrio reached up to hand the princess down. Without hesitation, Lydia leaned into his grasp and alighted gracefully in a swirl of divided, gray silk skirts from her riding dress. Belted at the waist by a broad kyrobi fashioned from brocaded linen, the princess's dress was long-sleeved with a conservatively high neckline. The gray silk still managed to cling enticingly to her slim form.

The general was clad in a Tieran blue uniform tunic. He wore no armor but bore both sword and dagger affixed to a sturdy leather belt wound about his middle. In deference to the looming summer heat, the general also wore a strictly nonmilitary broad-brimmed leather hat. The princess had a straw hat dyed jet-black, set at a jaunty angle atop her head pinned to her hip-length brown hair, dressed today in a thick single braid. Here and there, Wyll saw streaks of blond threaded as if by magic through the plait.

"Had to do that just the now, did you?" Quintus inquired, looking to Wyll like a farmhouse cat might to a cornered mouse.

"The matter seemed to be of some urgency, sir," Wyll offered. "The situation has turned out to be something other than what I expected."

"Situations tend to do that, Altyrn," the general remarked, "when one acts precipitously."

"Yes, sir," Wyll replied.

"Who was allegedly kidnapped?" Quintus asked.

"The young lady there, sir." Wyll indicated Em with a wave of his hand. "Her name is Emilyn Harris."

"Do we know who the alleged kidnapper is, Altyrn?" Quintus inquired.

"Sajar Mathias Bayrd," Wyll said, pointing at Mat, "Fourth Squad, Third Company, 133rd Auxiliary Regiment of archers, is the alleged ringleader, sir. Apparently an entire file of archers was involved with the supposed abduction."

"Who made the complaint?" Quintus next inquired.

"The girl's stepfather." Wyll nodded toward the wary-looking farmer. "His name is Lige Cotton."

"The fellow standing next to Master Cotton," the princess spoke in a smoothly cultured tone, "is, I surmise, a lawyer?"

"He is, Your Highness," Wyll responded, "one Hertius Grover." Grover bowed as deeply as his rotund form would allow.

Lydia exchanged a brief, knowing look with Quintus and smiled slightly. "Fascinating."

Turning to the young girl, the general said, "My name is Quintus Glabrio Jens. I am the general in command of these miscreants." He indicated the assembled troops with a nod of his head. "This," he continued, acknowledging the emperor's sister with a sweep of his hand, "is Her Highness, Princess Lydia Sylvus Gant."

Gray eyes wide as saucers, Em bobbed a curtsey. "Hullo, Your Honor," she said to Quintus and then smiled shyly at Lydia. "Your Highness."

Lydia nodded graciously, returning Em's smile. Quintus asked, "Were you kidnapped, Emilyn?"

"No, sir," Em replied emphatically.

"Why would your stepfather say otherwise?" Quintus questioned further.

"Ol' Lige lies pretty regular, Your Honor," Em answered promptly, "especially if he's been drinkin'."

"I see." Quintus fought to suppress a smile. "But you have been staying here, inside the camp, I mean?"

"Yes, sir, goin' on four days the now." Em's smile brightened. "Inside the tent with Fourth Squad, Third Company. I'm sort of honorary, Eddard Malleus Holt says."

"Eddard Malleus Holt? Who is he?" Quintus wondered.

Em pointed to a barrel-chested young bowman standing among a nearby company of archers. "He's the stocky one, third file in from the right."

Quintus looked. "Altyrn Quin," he ordered, "turn out Fourth Squad, Third Company so we can get a look at them."

Wyll nodded to Sedgwyck Ward. "Third Company," Altyrn Ward cried, "Fourth Squad, right face."

The nineteen archers remaining in Fourth Squad complied with the order and stood facing the general. He surveyed the group for a few moments, saying nothing. He seemed nice enough, the general, but there was something about his face and eyes that scared Em a little. He appeared to have the same effect on the boys as well.

"You've been staying in their tent the entire time?" Quintus asked finally.

"With the first file," Em responded. "Mat or a couple of the boys generally take me out fer a while after sundown wearing a cloak so's I can get a little air."

"Where have you been sleeping, Emilyn?" the princess wanted to know.

"In Mat's cot." Em grinned. "Mat's been a-sleepin' on the floor alongside. They's plenty of room on the bed. I keep tellin' him it's a powerful waste of mattress." Em lowered her voice a little, speaking more confidentially. "Mat's a little muley about some things."

Lydia responded in kind, "Most men are, dear. Have you had enough to eat?"

"Yes, Mum," Em enthused. "The boys are always bringing me somethin'. If this keeps up much longer, I'll be fatter than him." She pointed to lawyer Grover. A couple of the archers laughed outright. Matching glares from Thadius Bourne and Nathyn Biddle silenced them immediately. The princess smiled. The general cleared his throat, and the princess smiled more broadly.

"How did you come to be here, Emilyn?" Quintus inquired, shooting the princess a look that bordered on the insubordinate.

"I was hidin' in the locker," Em explained. "The boys strung a sheet of canvas across one corner of the tent fer me to hide behind an' put a camp stool in it. I was darnin' socks." The young girl looked to Mat Bayrd. "I know you tol' me to stay hid out, Mat, but I had to make water something fierce. That one," she pointed an accusatory finger at Sajar First Thadius Bourne, "busted into the tent so fast he nearly caught me a-squattin' over the bucket. I couldn't get away from him no how. He's near as strong as you are. He hauled me over here. I'm real sorry, Mat."

"It's all right, Em," Mat said reassuringly.

"You are at attention, Sajar," Wyll snapped. Mat brought his eyes back to the front and squared his shoulders.

"Is it because of me you've got Mat all stood up straight like that?" Em's large gray eyes sought the general's, and she implored, "Please, Your Honor, it don't seem natural."

"I think we've made our point, Altyrn," Quintus relented.

"Stand at ease, Sajar," Wyll ordered.

Mat stood at ease and, in the process, winked at Em. Em grinned and then turned a grateful smile on the general. Quintus felt the power of that smile. "What I meant to ask, Emilyn," he said patiently, "was how you came to the fortified camp in the first place. Start from the beginning and take your time."

"A couple of weeks back," Em began and proceeded to recount her travail at the hands of the grocer. Her gaze swept from the general to the princess and back again as she finished. "I know it weren't right, takin' his purse like that, but he ought not to have done me that a-way neither. The grocer and one of his relations took out after me. I came tearin' round a corner and run smack into Danel Owen." She aimed a slim finger at a lanky archer in the front row. "Danel is that tall fella in front there." Em smiled and waved at Danel Owen, who smiled back and briefly raised his pole axe in salute. "Danel grabbed hold of me. I didn't know Danel then, an' I was mighty scairt, so I fetched him a kick in the knee. It's mostly healed the now. Danel says it creaks when rain is coming, but I reckon he's just teasin'. Anyway, Danel let go, but the next thing I know, I run into ol' Mat. He tucked me under one arm like I was a sack of flour or somethin'.

"Davyd Lee, he's the towhead over yonder"—Emilyn indicated a blond archer, who flashed a ready smile—"said that Mat's a blacksmith what could tote me around all day long without breakin' a sweat. I bucked some, but it weren't no use. The grocer come up and called me some names, saying I was a thief. Mat started askin' questions like you been doin', Your Honor." Emilyn nodded at Quintus. "Except Mat's questions was pretty short an' sharp. He don't talk much, ya see, not at all like a general."

"I understand, Emilyn," Quintus said gravely. "Please continue."

Em resumed her tale, describing Davyd Lee's inspection of the fruit. "Mat determined to buy my apples fer his squad. He pays me the six pennies out of his own pocket. You know, Your Honor, that's about all the money he had. Mat and the boys ent been paid in three months. Sorry, Your Honor, but that don't seem right. Soldierin' ent sa easy as folks make out what with all the marchin' around and diggin' out roadbeds an' such."

The general turned to the princess. "We're working on it. Pay for militia units has been abominably slow." Lydia nodded.

"Mat made me give the grocer back his purse," Emilyn went on, "but not before he took a silver talent out from it. Mat said to the grocer that the coin was fer scarin' me an' all. The grocer didn't like it none, but about then, Mat was startin' ta get mad. He gets all clench-jawed when he does, ya know. Ol' Danel tells the grocer the last fella Mat got mad at still walks kindly wobbly an' all or some such, and that grocer, well, he finally seen the light an' didn't say no more. Mat walked me home that day an' he saw I had a bruise above my jaw and a split lip. He asked me how I come by 'em. I lied, but he didn't believe me any. Mat said nobody's got a right to hit me. He told me that if things went bad and I was scairt, I should go to him at the army camp, and he'd see me safe somehow. I didn't rightly believe him."

Em turned and looked toward Mat Bayrd for a moment. "That night, Rupert—he's Lige's son—wanted to know what I been doin' with a soldier. I guess he saw Mat walkin' me back. Sassed him some, I reckon, 'cause he sure lit into me. Couldn't hardly walk the next mornin'. My own fault it was, a little anyway." She raised her eyes to the princess. Her Highness's eyes were dark and kind, and Em decided to tell the rest, speaking directly to her. "You see, I don't like Rupert touchin' me the way he does, and I won't pretend otherwise. Riles him somethin' fierce; if I made out that I wanted him even a little, he'd be gentle enough, but I won't, so sometimes after, he gets mean." Em smiled briefly. "One thing about ol' Lige, he didn't care one way or the other; he'd just bang away like an ol' billy goat." At her words, a number of the soldiers present cast hard looks at Lige Cotton. The long-shanked farmer shifted his feet but said nothing.

Em recalled next meeting up with Mat and his squad, smiling fondly in remembrance. "Mat an' them bought my victuals all right. I got a good price fer 'em too." Her smile brightened. "Mat don't dicker worth a durn. Danel helped me down off the mule, an' I was sittin' by my panniers, talkin' with the boys and teasin' 'em some. I was having a good time, an' I reckon I got careless 'cause the shawl

I was wearin' slipped down enough fer Mat to see the bruises on my arms. He asked me what happened, and I couldn't lie to him like before. Mat got all the way mad then. He sent half the boys back to camp and brung the rest of them to the farm with me up on the mule."

Em directed her gaze back to the general. "It's gettin' to be a long story, Your Honor," she said apologetically.

"Take all the time you need, Emilyn," the general encouraged her.

"When we got to the farm," Emilyn went on, "Rupert, he takes a swing at Mat with a hoe. Mat flattened him quick as got ya. Mat sure is somethin' when he gets riled." Em tossed a meaning-ful glance back over her shoulder at Thadius Bourne, who merely smiled. "Lige come barrelin' out the door of the farmhouse with a crossbow in his hands. Davyd Lee hollers at him to put the crotch knocker down. 'Be damned if I will,' Lige yells out. 'Be dead if you don't,' Davyd Lee shouts right back. Momma comes out the door about then. She's heavy with child. She talked some sense into Lige, and he finally put aside the crossbow. Momma asked Mat what he was up to, and he tells her they—the boys an' him—are gonna take me off and send me back to their village—Greystock, it's called, in the Three Rivers—to stay with the Maywells. They're good people, Mat says. Momma took a long look at him and asks me do I trust him."

Em looked Mat's way again, gray eyes warming at the sight of him. "'Of course I do,' I told her. Mat ent the type what lies. Mat asked my momma if she wanted ta come along. She wouldn't hear of it. Stubborn sometimes, my Momma is." Em turned back to the princess to finish her story. "Mat swears he'll take proper care of me, an' then so does Davyd Lee, and Danel, he swears too, an' before I know it, all the boys is swearin' to look after me."

"And have they kept their word, Emilyn?" Lydia inquired, her black-eyed gaze lit with concern. "Have you been cared for properly?"

"Oh, yes, mum," Em affirmed readily.

"What is your secret, Em?" Lydia wondered. "How have you managed to win the hearts of these men so thoroughly?"

"Tain't no secret, mum," Em responded, wide-eyed. "They's good boys. Comes to men, you got to start with a good 'un right from the jump. There ent no redeemin' a bad 'un."

"Emilyn, did Sajar Bayrd explain to you just how he intended to get you to Greystock in the Three Rivers?" Quintus Glabrio Jens queried.

"Mat said they was gonna put me aboard a packet boat as soon as they could swing the fare," Em replied. "They ent been able to on account of not being paid, and ol' Mat, he was startin' to fret. I reckon that's all there is to tell, General, except I wish you wouldn't get mad at Mat and the boys; they was just tryin' to help me."

The general clasped his hands behind his back. "I understand. Thank you, Emilyn. That was very informative." Quintus cast an appraising glance at Mat Bayrd. "A packet boat, at her age, alone…is that wise?"

"We know many of the captains, sir," Mat answered. "Most of them are good men. We wouldn't let her go with anyone we didn't trust."

"I see." Quintus nodded and then addressed Emilyn Harris. "Emilyn, Sajar Bayrd was correct in that your stepfather and stepbrother have not the right to treat you as you say they did. Do you wish to press charges against them?"

Em looked at Lige Cotton. "I don't reckon there's anything to be gained by that, Your Honor."

"Master Cotton," Quintus said evenly, "unless you wish to dispute what Emilyn has told us, you are free to go. What say you?" Without a word or a backward glance, Lige Cotton turned away and took to his heels.

"General," Hertius Grover said urgently, "surely you must realize I was misled."

"If I were you, Grover," the general advised, "I would leave just the now." Grover blinked, nodded as if to himself, and departed. Watching him go, Quintus assayed a slightly self-satisfied smile in the direction of Princess Lydia. "Any morning that sees one of his ilk scuttle off is not entirely wasted."

Lydia returned his smile fondly as she might to a favored child.

"General, if I may," the princess requested, "I have a proposal to make that might resolve this situation."

"By all means, Your Highness." The general bowed. "What do you suggest?"

Lydia walked up to Em, stopping just in front of the young girl. "I am in need of a maid, someone who will work hard and cheerfully and, most importantly, someone worthy of both my affection and my trust. Emilyn, I think you will do very nicely. Would you be willing to enter my service?"

"Would we be stayin' round here, mum?" Em questioned. "And would I be able ta see the boys occasional?"

"That's important to you, is it, Em?" Lydia asked.

"Yes, mum," Em replied sincerely, lowering her voice. "They're good boys, mum, but fresh off the farm. Mostly, they don't know nothin'. Somebody's got to look after them."

Lydia smiled. Em thought, up close, the princess looked even more beautiful. "I think that can be arranged, only on occasion, mind you. Should it become necessary for me to depart, it will be your choice whether or not to accompany me. If you choose not to continue in my service, I will arrange passage for you to Greystock. Agreed?"

"Yes, mum." Em nodded and curtseyed. "Thank you ever so much."

Lydia shifted her black-eyed gaze to Mat Bayrd. "Does this arrangement meet with your approval, young man?"

"God bless you, mum," Mat Bayrd declared in a tightly controlled voice.

"Kernyl," Lydia called to Sagitus Turo Salt, "though I believe it was with the noblest of intentions, I suspect the young sajar here has violated a number of military regulations."

"That is true, Your Highness," Sagitus Turo Salt responded a little warily.

"Are these violations serious enough to cost him his stripes?" Lydia inquired.

"Yes, Your Highness," Salt answered, "without a doubt."

"I see." Lydia pursed her lips for a moment. "I suppose there is no alternative, the demands of discipline and all that. You must take his stripes away then immediately." She paused a second time to look directly at Sagitus. "I do not wish to meddle in military affairs, Kernyl, but can you think of any reason why he couldn't get them back by, say, dawn tomorrow?"

In her official capacity as an imperial emissary, Lydia Sylvus Gant had no direct authority over Tieran military personnel. It was widely known, however, that she also stood the beloved sister of the emperor, who most certainly did.

Sagitus Turo Salt was not a fool. "No, Your Highness, I am aware of nothing that would prevent that."

"Very well, Kernyl Salt." Lydia smiled. "You will let me know should any difficulty arise?"

"Of course, Your Highness," Kernyl Sagitus Turo Salt promised.

Stepping to Mat's side, Lydia announced, "You will need to bend down a little, Trooper Bayrd."

Mat did so. Her Royal Highness Lydia Sylvus Gant rose on her tiptoes and very carefully, so as not to foul her bonnet, kissed him on the cheek. "God shall bless you, Mat Bayrd, of that I have no doubt," she whispered. Blushing furiously, Mat straightened and found himself speechless.

"With your kernyl's permission, of course," Lydia ordered Mat, "Trooper Bayrd, you will escort Emilyn to my quarters—Altyrn Quin can direct you—by sundown this evening. Be certain she has her personal belongings with her."

"Yes, mum," Mat replied.

Turning on her heel, Lydia walked back to General Quintus Glabrio Jens's side. "This has been most intriguing, General. What is next, pray tell?"

"The artillery park, Your Highness," Quintus informed her. "We thought you might enjoy smashing something."

"By all means, General," the princess enthused, "let us smash away."

Returning to their horses, Quintus handed her up. As she mounted, a cry arose among the archers nearest them, "Hoorah, the princess." Ragged at first, the cry spread rapidly, and soon the entire regiment was cheering. Quintus swung into the saddle beside her, and together they sat astride, nearly stirrup to stirrup. The princess maintained her seat with a poised graceful posture, while the general sat his horse like a sack of potatoes. Peering out into the sea of mostly young faces before them, Lydia raised her hand and waved. This only fanned the flame, and the cheer became a roar.

"You are good for morale, Highness," Quintus observed.

"Get me out of here, Quintus," the princess implored, "before I make a fool of myself."

"Steady, old sock." Quintus pitched his voice low so that only she could hear. "You're doing just fine." Nodding to the young officer in charge of their cavalry escort, they began to move. "Find yourself a mount, Altyrn," Quintus ordered Wyll Quin, "and catch up to us."

Lydia clung to her composure as they rode away, touched beyond words, the cheers of those boys ringing in her ears.

37
Secrets Shared

As had become their custom, Dyrileah and Bode met just after first light at the gardener's cottage on the grounds of Antium Hall. They'd been laboring for hours the now, grappling with the mystery embodied by the Power of the One. However reluctant she may have been at first to answer the call of the One, Bode's acumen had proved astonishing.

Bode seemed destined to become the most powerful Wycken that Dyrileah had ever encountered. Not plagued by false modesty, Dyrileah well knew her own strength placed her among the more potent of witches. But even the most gifted usually had to seek the One. The Way had to be learned. Bode stood an exception. The power awoke within her unbidden; she seemed instinctively capable of wielding incredible amounts of it with uncanny precision.

Though her progress was remarkable in many ways, rather than learning the Wycken's craft, Bode seemed to be reacting or, even more eerily, remembering something she already knew. That, of course, was impossible, which left Dyrileah at a loss. The usual drills had so far proven to be largely a waste of time. Dyrileah did not favor wasting time.

Three small orbs of softly pulsing green light hovered in front of Bode about chest high. Bode's task was to align them in a triangular pattern, so far without success. The orbs kept wobbling about, almost but not quite settling into a stable triangular formation. With a growl of frustration, Bode waved her right hand, and a fourth green orb appeared. She set two of them rotating in a tight circle while orbiting the second pair around them in the opposite direction.

"That is quite enough of that," Dyrileah spoke in firmly patient tones. Bode released the ward, and the four orbs winked out.

"I'm sorry," Bode said contritely, "it is just that..." She paused for a moment, folding her arms tightly beneath her bosom. "All of this is so vexing."

With some effort, Dyrileah managed to control her amazement. Given years of diligent practice, one Wycken in five might be able to accomplish the feat Bode had just exhibited in a fit of pique without thinking, as effortlessly as if she were drawing breath. Dyrileah sighed. "You cannot simply grasp the One by the scruff of the neck and bully it about. You must learn to embrace it and submit. By submitting, you become a channel through which the power flows. Only then can you guide the flow ever so gently."

"*I know,*" Bode protested softly. "I am trying."

That's true enough, Dyrileah thought. Bode was nothing if not determined. She pushed herself dangerously hard. She had accomplished more in weeks than Dyrileah thought possible even in her wildest imaginings. *She needs a more experienced mentor.* "You must learn to try less and do more."

"Now you sound like Uncle Spats." Bode pouted.

"Pouting will avail you nothing," Dyrileah chided, trying not to smile. Taking a deep, calming breath, she went on. "You would benefit from a more experienced mentor. I will arrange it."

"No," Bode exclaimed. "I will do better, Dyrileah, I swear it. Please, I trust only you."

Bode looked near to tears. Dyrileah had never met anyone with so little guile. Knowing full well she should not be dissuaded, Dyrileah finally tossed her head and stepped forward to embrace Bode.

"All right, little sister," Dyrileah whispered, "for a while longer anyway."

In response, Bode hugged her fiercely. "I'll try again."

"No, you won't, at least not today," Dyrileah said crisply. "You've been at it for hours. You are tired and impatient. You need to rest and eat and think of other things…broad-shouldered blacksmiths, for example. Have you heard from him lately?" Dyrileah knew she had. Jaryd told her earlier that morning that Bode had just received a letter from Mat.

"Yes, yesterday." Bode smiled, her vexation melting away. "Mat's well. He writes to say he's mightily tired of digging." Reading the expression on Bode's face, Dyrileah proffered, "Mat seems a remarkably sturdy fellow. I'll keep him in my prayers." She hesitated a moment and then stipulated, "So long, that is, if you do not think he would mind an Elsacian prayer."

Bode's smile returned. "Mat Bayrd could give mules lessons on how to be properly stubborn, but he's not a complete fool. Your prayers would be most welcome and much appreciated."

Dyrileah smiled back. "Stubbornness seems to be in ample supply among Three Rivers' folk. Is it the water, do you think, or mayhap mother's milk what does it?"

Before Bode could conjure a suitable reply, the front door swung open, and Jaryd Hume stepped across the threshold.

"Hoi," Bode called out, "have you not heard of knocking?"

Jaryd turned toward them. Two musk melons were balanced on his left arm, while a basket of fresh tomatoes occupied his right hand. His clothes were rumpled, and the bareheaded young farmer's son was covered with sweat.

"It was all I could do to swing down the latch without dumping my plunder. I chose safeguarding victuals over manners." Jaryd grinned. Even Bode had to admit it was a winning expression. Twenty years of age the now, Jaryd remained, in her estimation, still three parts in five all boy.

Bode had known Jaryd her whole life. Aside from Mat, there

was no one she trusted more, not even Dyrileah. Jaryd and Dyrileah were betrothed. Jaryd knew Dyrileah was a witch. Bode had not yet told him that she was.

Jaryd walked across the room and deposited the fruit on the table. "Did you remember the parsley?" Dyrileah inquired.

Jaryd was clad in the green cotton tunic that was standard kit for the Hall gardeners. A pair of sturdy sandals covered his feet, and a wide leather belt encircled his waist. Depositing the basket of tomatoes on the floor, Jaryd reached into his tunic and produced, with a mild flourish, a fistful of the grass-green herb.

"It might be a little salty," he warned, handing the parsley to Dyrileah.

Jaryd leaned forward with the intent of kissing his intended. Dyrileah stopped him by placing a firm hand on his chest. "You," she declared, "smell like a horse." Dyrileah wrinkled her nose. "Outside right the now," she directed. "There are soap and water and a clean towel on the front porch."

Jaryd straightened a pained expression on his face. "Aye, well, glad I am to see you too, beloved."

"Scoot," Dyrileah demanded, pointing imperiously at the door.

Jaryd retraced his steps. Before crossing back over the threshold, he cocked his head over his shoulder. "Looks to me like the sweetling time is over before it ever began." The sweetling time referred to the period just after a wedding, while the newlyweds were settling in together, each, in theory, determined to be sweeter to the other than common sense and familiarity would soon allow.

"You are pretty when you sulk," Dyrileah tossed back at him unrepentantly.

After Jaryd closed the door, Bode commented, "If you wait for him to grow up, you'll not wed before you are thirty."

Dyrileah smiled. Her eyes warmed, lit from within. "A risk I'm willing to take. Truth to tell, I hope he never grows up, at least not all the way."

Jaryd returned shortly, freshly scrubbed, and Dyrileah rewarded him with a lingering kiss. Bode looked away. Time spent alone with either Jaryd or Dyrileah never failed to lift her spirits. Their friendship meant more to her than she could put into words. Still, the sight of them together, their obvious delight in one another's company, was sometimes hard for Bode to bear. She missed Mat terribly and never more so than when she witnessed firsthand the love Jaryd and Dyrileah shared so easily. What she would not give to feel the touch of Mat's hand or to see the light in his eyes of green, colored as they were by flecks of gold. Though it shamed her to admit it, she could not help but begrudge Jaryd and Dyrileah their happiness. It was all so unfair.

Spats entered the cottage less than an hour later. He'd evidently spotted the wash bucket and soap sitting on the front porch as he was still toweling himself down when he stepped through the door.

Striding into the room, Spats sniffed the air. "Peach pie, is it?" he asked with a smile.

"We thought we'd try the cobbler," Dyrileah informed him, referring to the dish cooling atop the kitchen counter. She stepped into the old gardener's embrace, hugging him briefly.

Spats grinned at Bode over the slender Elsacian girl's shoulder. "Can't wait for a taste. Why don't you two lasses sit a while, and me and the shyster will see to frying up some potatoes and bacon." In Spats's opinion, the terms "lawyer" and "shyster" were synonymous.

"I heard that," Jaryd called from the kitchen. "You can peel the rest of these potatoes all by your lonesome."

Spats waited until they'd finished eating and then took a breath. "The time has come, I think, for the four of us to share a few secrets."

He extended a sun-browned hand, palm up. A bright, translucent sphere of shimmering blue light formed. Spats's blue eyes narrowed slightly, and the orb expanded in size, growing to that of a watermelon before dividing into six pulsing globes each about as large as a peach. The globes formed into a circle and began to whirl slowly about, gradually moving faster and faster.

Spats snapped his fingers, and the half-dozen balls of light winked out, leaving behind only a faint afterglow. "A pointless bit of magic that," he observed quietly, "but it does help to clear the mind."

Sebastyn peered about the table. Jaryd was smiling. Both the young women looked as if you could knock them over with a breath of air. Very satisfactory, all things considered.

"My given name," he continued quietly, "is Sebastyn Card. Next month marks my two-hundred-and-thirty-eighth year." Both young women gaped, saying nothing. Sebastyn smiled. "You two look like the goodwife who awoke one day to find a timber wolf in her front parlor."

"If even half the stories about Sebastyn Card are true," Dyrileah said evenly, "you are far more dangerous than some poor wolf."

"Sebastyn Card," Bode fairly squeaked. "How is that possible?"

"I wish I knew, lass." Reaching out, Sebastyn gently took her hand in his own. Swinging his gaze from Bode to Dyrileah and back again, he continued. "I mean you no harm. You've my word on that."

"Why would you say that?" Dyrileah inquired.

"I've had some difficulty dealing with Wycken in the past." Sebastyn smiled. "One in particular comes to mind. She was nearly as pretty as the two of you."

"How long have you known?" Dyrileah breathed, fixing her eyes on Sebastyn.

"I became fairly certain of you the night Jaryd's father and young Mat Bayrd visited," Sebastyn answered, steadily meeting Dyrileah's brown-eyed gaze. "My suspicions were further confirmed the morning after Jaryd here returned from visiting your parents' home for the first time sporting a partially healed broken arm."

"Was it you who fully mended Jaryd's arm?" Dyrileah's tone made her question sound more like an accusation.

"A few final touches only," Sebastyn confirmed.

Dyrileah turned to Jaryd. "You said only that the healer was a friend of one of your teachers."

Jaryd met her gaze. "I promised Sebastyn I'd say nothing about his identity." Jaryd saw something change in Dyrileah's eyes, a withdrawal that bespoke broken trust.

Before Jaryd could say anything further, Sebastyn spoke in

gently emphatic tones. "I would have thought an Elsacian Wycken would understand the burden such a promise entails." Dyrileah lowered her eyes.

"I was not sure about Bode until more recently," Sebastyn expounded. Noting Bode's perplexed expression, Sebastyn explained, "The use of magic in any form leaves behind a sort of residue, like footsteps in the sand along the seashore. With time, the residue fades as if washed away by a following tide. Each practitioner's mark is unique." Sebastyn smiled. "My nose tells me you are both formidable, especially you, Bode."

Jaryd tore his eyes from Dyrileah and exclaimed, "Bode's a witch?" Bode, too, lowered her gaze and sat very still, her hands folded in her lap. "You little bugger," Jaryd declared, "you might have said something."

"I haven't known all that long." Bode's voice was scarcely more than a whisper. "I was afraid you might not understand."

"More likely," Jaryd countered, "you were waiting until Dyrileah taught you how to turn me into a goat or something so you could demonstrate your newfound abilities properly."

"I can't turn you into a goat. No Wycken can," Bode flared. She took note of the gleam in his eyes. "More is the pity indeed," she added crossly, launching a quick, meaningful glance Dyrileah's way.

"Uh-huh," Jaryd said skeptically.

"I did not seek to become a witch." Bode's normally self-assured tone sounded anything but. "I've never tried to call upon the Dark Powers, nor will I. Upon my soul, I swear it."

"Bode," Jaryd chided, astonished. "Have you taken the notion that ever I would think that?"

Bode raised her eyes to his. Jaryd slipped off his chair to kneel at her feet. "Bodewhin Ware"—the Three Rivers lad sounded angry—"I ought to tan your bottom. You are as stubborn as the day is long, with a temper worse than a gray bear in spring, and you can be a touch high-handed." Bode's stormy gray eyes flashed, and her jaw firmed. "But I've never met anyone so full of light." Jaryd's eyes swung briefly to Dyrileah. "Well, practically no one. I've known you most all my life. I've also known that if ever I was in trouble, bad trouble, I could count on you. Nothing is going to change that. Not even your turning me into a goat." Jaryd paused for a moment. "So long as you turn me back, that is."

Tears spilled onto Bode's cheeks. Jaryd put his arms around her. "You little knucklehead," Jaryd growled gently. "No one who loves you is going to think less of you, Bode."

Bode's arms stole up around his back, and she clung tightly. "I am *not* high-handed. You take that back, Jaryd Hume."

Gathering Bode close, Jaryd let his gaze settle on Sebastyn Card. "I may have overstated," Jaryd allowed, "just slightly, mind." He winked.

Sebastyn smiled. "One of these days, I should like to see this Three Rivers of yours. It must be quite a place." Jaryd released Bode and reclaimed his seat.

"Why reveal yourself to us the now?" Dyrileah asked abruptly, standing.

A shadow flickered across Sebastyn's well-weathered face. "Something is going to happen," he replied calmly. "I can't say exactly what or when, but I think the time has come for us to determine if we can trust one another."

Dyrileah returned his gaze steadily but still wary. "I must tell the Wycken of this."

Sebastyn Card shook his head. "You are *supposed* to tell the Wycken of this. You must do nothing of the kind."

"Why not?" Dyrileah challenged softly.

Rising to his feet, Sebastyn turned away from Dyrileah and walked slowly to the fireplace. He stood in front of the hearth and stared for a moment into the fire pit. "If the Elsacian Wycken here learn who I am and where I am, others will as well. That would be dangerous for you, for the Wycken, for those you care about." He pivoted back around to face them. "I must ask you to trust me as I have decided to trust in you. Be patient a while and tell no one. Before the time comes to act, we will speak again. This I promise."

Dyrileah shook her head slowly, resolutely. "You are asking me to lie to those I love, to those who have placed their faith and trust in me."

Jaryd rose to his feet. "He has known for weeks, Dyrileah. He has not betrayed you, nor will he."

"He speaks of secrets, beloved." Dyrileah's eyes reached out to Jaryd's. "All secrets conceal—some to protect, others to deceive or beguile. I will make no promises until I know more."

"You remind me of a girl I knew once, the Wycken I spoke of earlier." Sebastyn smiled with genuine pleasure. "I met her for the first time when I was about Jaryd's age and she yours. A pretty little thing with hair nearly your color, Dyrileah, and eyes"—the old sorcerer's gaze settled upon Bode—"just like yours, Bode, gray as a goshawk's wing." Sebastyn chuckled. "She turned out to be a lot of trouble." He regarded Dyrileah once more. "Knowledge always bears a price. Anything further I say will cost you."

Dyrileah swallowed once and then nodded. Jaryd stepped to her side and slid his arm around her. She looked up at him. Their eyes touched for a moment, and she leaned into him.

"What do you know of the Nuestyrn?" Sebastyn's voice deepened as he spoke, filling the room with dread, or so it seemed to Jaryd.

Jaryd could feel Dyrileah stiffen. Her chin came up, and his intended replied firmly, "We do not speak of them."

"How very enlightened of you." Sebastyn's voice, normally rich and warm, cut like a knife.

"They are vanquished," Dyrileah declared, "shunned. What vestige remains will wither and die."

"They are dispersed," Sebastyn retorted. His voice took on no emotion whatever; the sound of it was remorseless, unrelenting. "Like choke weed scattered throughout a vineyard. Ignored, left alone. In time, it will not be the weed that withers, but the hapless vines."

"We are far from hapless," Dyrileah shot back.

"And more vulnerable than you know," Sebastyn decreed. The white-haired sorcerer and the blond witch locked eyes.

"Who were the Nuestyrn?" Jaryd prompted to break the sudden silence.

Dyrileah turned to face him, laying gentle fingers alongside his cheek. "Beloved, no. This is not a thing of which we should speak."

"I did warn you," Sebastyn observed and then without pausing said, "Centuries ago, many of those with the ability to invoke the Yir or call upon the One died suddenly. No one knows why. It was no plague; laymen were not affected. Most suppose something must have gone terribly awry with the source or sources of magic, but no explanation that could be proved has ever been found. Mages call it the great dying. Some believe virtually every mage, be they witch or sorcerer, then living perished. Evidence exists that contradicts this, but many were lost."

Sebastyn returned to his seat at the table. "Slowly, a period of recovery followed, and with it, a radical belief arose among some of the Wycken that only those called by the One were the true descendants of the Creator. These radicals called themselves the Nuestyrn. The Nuestyrn were said to have adopted a new and virulent form of witchcraft."

Dyrileah stirred, raising her head as if she was about to say something and then thought better of it. Sebastyn smiled once more. "The Elsacians believe the Power of the One is as old as creation itself. To the followers of Almyr, what they call the One is an ancient and unchanged form of magic. And like the Yir, the One can be put to good or nefarious use as a matter of choice."

Sebastyn placed both hands palm down on the tabletop. "The truth may be one thing or the other or a mix of the two."

"I've read," Jaryd interjected, "some scholars believe no real difference exists between sorcery and witchcraft."

"They are much alike," Sebastyn allowed, "but for every compelling similarity, there appears to be an equally stark difference. On the surface, Skeg whales and spotted sharks are similar creatures. Both swim in the sea, both often hunt the same prey, both give live birth to their young. Look closer, though, and you find two very different animals. The whales breathe air; the sharks cannot. Sharks are solitary creatures; the whales roam in packs. The two are separate species and natural enemies."

Sebastyn's blue eyes twinkled. "Unlike whales and sharks, witches and sorcerers, and laymen too, are first and foremost human beings. Our common humanity binds us in powerful and subtle ways."

His eyes darkening, Sebastyn continued. "The Nuestyrn denied this. Their belief was that all things change with time and that all living things evolve. This evolution takes life down many pathways. Some flourish; others fall away. If enough time passes and sufficient change transpires, what once may have been the same can become something altogether different."

The old sorcerer's flattened palms balled into fists. "The Nuestyrn concluded that the ability to work magic was a result of evolution. Those with the ability are intended by the will of the Creator to rise, to dominate all lesser species. The Nuestyrn consider laymen to be among them—the lesser species, that is."

"I protest," Jaryd stated with a smile.

"Understandably." Sebastyn nodded Jaryd's way with a wry smile of his own. "The Nuestyrn credo was that laymen are unstable, inherently violent, and because of their sheer numbers, dangerous. With inspired leadership, firm discipline, and, where necessary, some culling, the Nuestyrn believed laymen could be appropriately managed for the betterment of all. Sorcerers, on the other hand, qualified as enlightened beings."

"Whatever their differences, both the Yir and the One represent some form of magic. As they were enlightened, and relatively few in number, sorcerers and, of course, any witch who did not subscribe to the tenets of the Nuestyrn doctrine were to be given a brutally simple choice: convert or die."

"Though always a minority," Sebastyn continued, placing both hands in his lap, "the Nuestyrn sect gained a substantial following during the time of recovery, including many laymen devoted to their enlightened masters and a number of sorcerers, converted or perhaps seduced, by the promise of arcane knowledge and commensurate strength."

Shadows in the room lengthened. As unobtrusively as he could, Jaryd stepped away from Dyrileah's side to light a taper using a candle already burning on the hearth and, in turn, set alight an oil lamp. The subtle golden glow of the lamp did little to soften Sebastyn's grim discourse.

"A war began, waged without boundaries, battle lines, or safe havens. The struggle raged for nearly a century between the Nuestyrn and those arrayed against them, sorcerers and witches who refused to subscribe or submit. Laymen, too, were involved, ranging from peasants to warriors and kings, supporting one side or the other, sometimes unwittingly."

Sebastyn's blue eyes again settled upon Dyrileah. "Elsacian Wyc-ken stood always in the forefront, opposed to the Nuestyrn extremists. A proud tradition, one that has sadly been forgotten or, perhaps more accurately, conveniently ignored by we infidels in more recent times."

Dyrileah sniffed, folding her arms beneath her breasts, but remained silent.

"The fighting never spilled over into open warfare between nations." Sebastyn sighed. "Something to be grateful for, I suppose. There were no great battles, only a seemingly endless cycle of small, vicious, deadly encounters. Cruelty and atrocity abounded on both sides. Outnumbered, the Nuestyrn were slowly overwhelmed. Toward the end, many witches were falsely accused. In some cases, entire Wyckens, the full population of witches in a region or town, were wiped out. A deep rift grew into being between sorcerers and witches. In some areas where one form of magic dominated, the minority were killed or driven out altogether."

His shoulders slumping, Sebastyn concluded. "The strife we see today between sorcerers and witches can be traced principally to the chaos sown by the Nuestyrn radicals. When first I became a sorcerer, the Nuestyrn insurrection was in its final throes. One of my early assignments was to track down a handful of remaining radicals. I joined a society of warriors, scholars, sorcerers, and witches devoted to that grim task. Most believed that we, in conjunction with other similar groups throughout the lands of the Middle Sea, succeeded. The violence slowly faded away. As Dyrileah says, there are many who believe the Nuestyrn were vanquished, diminished to the point that they no longer represent a credible threat. Those few of us closest to the task of eradicating them never subscribed to that belief. Battered and bloodied, yes, but vanquished—never. Their beliefs were too strong."

"You speak of a time centuries gone." Dyrileah finally broke her silence.

"That is true all right enough," Sebastyn acknowledged.

"Time would appear to have proven you wrong," Dyrileah pronounced.

"Appearances can be deceptive." Sebastyn's smile took on a sly aspect. "Again, a concept I would think an Elsacian Wycken would appreciate."

"This quest of yours, this determination to wipe out a dangerous group of radicals, has warped over time into prejudice." Dyrileah's fine, wideset eyes heated. "Fueled, no doubt, by those like you who refused to see its end."

"I have my reasons, Dyrileah." Sebastyn met her angry gaze. "I cannot deny that you and yours have been deeply wronged but not by me. Either you believe that, or you don't."

"If I don't, then what?" Dyrileah challenged.

"Dyrileah," Jaryd protested, his shock evident.

Sebastyn raised his right hand as if to hold Jaryd still for a moment. "A fair question." Without pause, he continued. "If you cannot accept my word, if you cannot believe that my quest, as you describe it, continues out of need and must do so in secret, then the elders at Antium Hall will have to find a new chief gardener. The time will have come for Sebastyn Card to disappear."

"You proffer no threats?" Dyrileah sounded surprised.

"Dyrileah, that's enough," Jaryd insisted.

Ignoring the young man's outburst, Sebastyn merely shrugged. "You do not know enough yet to do any real harm. This would not be the first time Sebastyn Card has had to vanish."

"We are friends here," Jaryd pleaded, looking first to Dyrileah and then Sebastyn. "There is no need for this."

"We were friends here, Jaryd," Sebastyn said. "It is for Dyrileah to decide if we still are."

"You seek to find a Nuestyrn cell in Antium?" Dyrileah asked.

"I watch and wait for the truth to be revealed," Sebastyn replied. "I do so for what I believe are good and sufficient reasons. If I am wrong, well, it will not be for the first time. I will accuse no one falsely."

"What you are asking goes against all that I have been taught," Dyrileah protested.

"No, child." Sebastyn shook his head. "What first you were taught was to serve and protect. To do so requires courage, strength, and wisdom. The time has come for you to choose."

"You've told me nothing," Dyrileah cried.

"I have told you all that I can," Sebastyn replied. "That was my choice. Now you must make yours."

Dyrileah gazed intently into Sebastyn's eyes. A long moment passed. The room was completely silent. Finally, the young Elsacian witch nodded her head, slowly but decisively. "I will say nothing of what we have discussed here this evening to anyone without first apprising you. You have my word."

Sebastyn returned her nod. "I am sorry. I wish there was another way. I must ask your word as well, Jaryd, and yours, Bode," he added, looking to the two Three Rivers folk.

"You have my word," Jaryd said simply.

Bode nodded. "You have mine as well."

"All right enough." Sebastyn appeared more weary than relieved. "I can promise no answers, but do any of you have any further questions of me the now?"

Bode ended the brief silence that ensued by gushing, "Did Lylith Caddow, the White Witch, really try to destroy time itself, and is it true you sealed her into a mountain of ice?"

38
Gifts of Regard

It was Bode and Dyrileah's turn at the dishes. They'd nearly finished drying the last of them when Dyrileah asked softly, "Did you really think Jaryd would turn away from you?"

Bode shook her head. "He is betrothed to you, after all. Jaryd is a little muley but not so wool-headed as that." She continued to work the dish towel in her hands, absently wiping the surface of a perfectly dry ceramic plate. "Others dear to me may not be so open-minded."

"You mean Mathias Bayrd," Dyrileah prompted. "Surely you cannot think his love so flimsy a thing as that?"

"Mat won't stop loving me." Bode spoke the words with a soft smile. "He might decide that I should do the right thing."

"What do you mean?"

"The Penitent faith does not shun those who can call upon the One," Bode answered. "We were taught that should a witch recant, publicly confess, foreswear any subsequent use of the Power, and seek forgiveness, it shall be granted."

"How generous," Dyrileah murmured wryly.

"From the Penitent perspective, it is," Bode observed. "Of course, my own point of view has shifted recently. I've come to know myself so much better. It is as if a great burden has been lifted." Bode looked to her mentor. "I have you to thank for that." Dyrileah said nothing but reached out to gently squeeze her arm.

"Jaryd has never been particularly religious," Bode explained. "His is a facile, inquisitive mind. Jaryd tends to see life, good and bad things, in shades of gray. Mat, on the other end, is deeply religious, as direct and pragmatic as a hammer blow. He lives in a world of right and wrong, black and white. I will not foreswear the calling. Doing so would be to deny who I am."

Bode carefully placed the dinner plate down atop the counter. Her fists knotted in the towel. "If I have to choose between the calling and his love"—she paused to draw a ragged breath—"I don't know what I'll do." *That's a lie,* Bode chided herself amid the silence that followed her declaration. *Mat will have me as I am or not at all.* Whatever the cost, Bode had made her decision. Mat would have to make his.

Later that evening, Jaryd walked the two girls home. Bode's Uncle Haryld's house was the first stop. Jaryd carried Sebastyn's walking stick and his grandfather's Hawken, sheathed at his waist. Since being accosted by two men the day he first met Dyrileah's parents, Jaryd never left the Hall grounds without both stave and heavy bladed knife.

The three of them strolled most of the way in silence. As they approached her uncle's residence, Bode said quietly, "I should have told you. I didn't know how."

Jaryd smiled very gently. "No harm done, and somehow it all makes sense." His smile stretched into a familiar grin. "You always have been a contrary little critter."

"You're just lucky you are wearing that *thing* around your neck," Bode sallied, in reference to the Fey amulet Jaryd wore suspended from a chain about his throat.

"Bloody useful it is from time to time." Still smiling, Jaryd winked at Dyrileah. The Elsacian girl tossed her golden-haired head as if vexed, but Bode could see the corners of her mouth quirk upward in an answering smile.

"Thank you for being my friend," Bode said sincerely.

Jaryd hugged her briefly. "Always," he murmured. Bode and Dyrileah exchanged a quick, parting embrace as well. Bode then hurried up the stairs to the front door of the two-storied house.

Jaryd and Dyrileah continued on their way. The sun had set by the time they parted company with Bode. He normally escorted her only to the Porter's Gate. This summer evening, however, Jaryd kept walking at Dyrileah's side.

"You will have a long walk back," she warned.

"A fair stretch of the legs," Jaryd acknowledged. He reached out to take Dyrileah's hand. "Good company, though, half the way."

"Are you angry with me?" Jaryd thought he heard a slight tremor in Dyrileah's voice as she posed the question.

"Angry? No," Jaryd replied thoughtfully. "Bode chose to confide in you. I can understand the why of that. What passed between you and Spats this afternoon, that's harder to comprehend."

"However charming and well-spoken, he is a dangerous man, Jaryd," Dyrileah insisted softly, "more so than you can imagine."

"He is also a friend," Jaryd retorted, more strongly than he intended.

"You trust too easily," Dyrileah contended.

"Fully, not easily," Jaryd countered. "If you cannot see the difference, I'm going to have to give you a good talking to." His voice trailed away into silence for a moment. "Are you angry with me?"

Dyrileah arched one golden eyebrow. "If I were angry with you, farm boy," she purred, "you would not doubt it."

"I made you a promise the day I first met your parents," Jaryd recounted, ignoring her jest. "When I returned to the cottage on the Hall grounds the next morning, I walked through the door. He took one look at my arm, and he knew."

"You broke no promise, Jaryd," Dyrileah assured him promptly. "You had no way of preventing him from learning what he did by examining you."

"I could have told you about it," Jaryd responded. "It was as he said; I promised him I would not. Sebastyn told me then who he was. We made a bargain, a secret for a secret."

Dyrileah stopped and peered anxiously up into Jaryd's face. "Secrecy coils, beloved; it trips and entangles." Stepping into his arms, Dyrileah pressed her face against his chest. He could feel the warmth of her and smell her scent, subtle and sweet like a freshly crushed rose petal. "He is a creature of legend, a man cloaked in secrets. He spins and threads them together with the skill of a spider."

"Aye." Jaryd made no argument. "He's had a fair bit of practice, I reckon. I'm not saying there is no danger." His voice lowered a notch, becoming fully serious. "Who knows what he'll find or what it might entail? For all that, I see no harm in *him*, Dyrileah, only a deeply bedded desire to do what is right."

"What *he* thinks is right, you mean," Dyrileah asserted.

Jaryd sighed. Dyrileah raised her mouth to his and kissed him. Savoring the sweet warmth of her lips upon his, Jaryd returned her kiss. After a time, Dyrileah pulled her head away. Ducking beneath Jaryd's chin, she held him close. "No more secrets between us, no matter what. Promise me."

Jaryd briefly tightened his embrace. "No more secrets, my word on it."

A short time later they approached the Quirow house in the Elsacian quarter of the city.

Dyrileah preceded him through the front door of her home. The small entryway, lit by an oil lamp set atop a standing table against the wall to the right of the door, offered access to two hallways. A short one immediately to the left went to the kitchen. A longer hall directly ahead led to the sitting room, with its large, brick-lined fireplace. Just beyond the left-hand hallway were the stairs to the second floor, where the bedrooms were located. To the right was the front parlor, as the Quirows called it. Jaryd had slept there on more than one occasion.

No sooner had he and Dyrileah stepped into the entryway than Tamyra rushed down the hall from the sitting room. "Dyrileah," the young girl cried. Tamyra's was usually a buoyant spirit, full of smiles and laughter. In the lamp light, her face seemed pale; her eyes, so like Dyrileah's, were wide as saucers.

"Tamyra"—Dyrileah's soft voice registered immediate concern—"what is wrong? You look as if you have seen a ghost."

Tamyra was clad in a dark-blue keppi. "No ghost, Dyrileah," she responded, "but rather the nearest thing." Dyrileah's sister took a breath as if steeling herself. "Rysah Kudreau has returned. He is in the sitting room the now with Maman and Patua."

Standing at her side, Jaryd heard Dyrileah's breath catch. "How is that possible?" Her voice sounded hushed, incredulous.

"A shipwreck, Rysah says," Tamyra related. "He was taken by the Relwyn. His return was long and arduous, to hear him tell of it." Tamyra's voice was laced with doubt, hinging upon scorn. *This isn't like Tamyra at all*, Jaryd thought.

Dyrileah turned to face Jaryd. "Remember I told you about Rysah Kudreau? We spoke of him only once before, beloved. He and I were betrothed, long before I met you. These past two years, we thought him dead, lost at sea." Dyrileah's normally crisp, self-assured manner suddenly dissolved. She spoke absently, as if distracted.

This isn't like Dyrileah either. A tingle of dread wormed its way up Jaryd's spine.

"I've been sent to fetch you," Tamyra announced.

Dyrileah briefly squeezed Jaryd's hand and, without another word, led the way down the hall in the direction of the sitting room.

Upon entering, Jaryd saw the remainder of the Quirow family—Dyrileah's parents, her two brothers, and youngest sister, Caryleah—and a stranger who could only be Rysah Kudreau. The man was a few years Jaryd's senior, mid-twenties at least. Tall for an Elsacian, he lacked Jaryd's height by only a couple of finger widths. He was well built, leanly muscular, with dark-gray eyes featuring the distinctive Elsacian cast. His hair was dark and wavy, unusual as most Elsacians were blond. His features were strikingly handsome, with a strong jaw and a wide, full-lipped mouth.

Rysah, who stood in front of the hearth, was clad in a long-sleeved, white cotton shirt with fine, decorative stitching about the collar and close-fitting, dove-gray, woolen trousers. Expensive-looking half boots covered his feet, and a long, curved dagger with a bone handle in a red leather sheath was suspended from a narrow belt about his waist. From what little Dyrileah had said of him, Jaryd recalled Rysah was also of the Wycken, a witch of considerable strength.

Rysah smiled broadly at the sight of Dyrileah, flashing even, white teeth. "Leah," he exclaimed, his eyes warming. He bowed formally in the odd Elsacian manner, his left leg extended before him. "How I have longed for the sight of you. You are even more beautiful than when last I saw you."

Leah, is it? Jaryd fought to keep his expression neutral. *They were once betrothed, after all. But she's mine the now, you bugger.* Jaryd was suddenly glad of the Fey amulet worn about his neck. A potent shield against adverse magic, the talisman would even the odds between him and Rysah if it came to that. *Easy the now; the man hasn't even said hullo to you.* Still, Jaryd could not quell the queasy feeling that gripped his belly. A memory leapt unbidden into his mind, that of his father, Byan, describing a similar sensation the first time he caught sight of an Indiquoi war band.

Dyrileah responded with a curtsy, sweeping her left leg gracefully in front of her as she dipped. Jaryd had seen her curtsy in that manner only once before, when first she met Spats, responding then as the now to a bow such as the one Rysah had just executed. Dyrileah's large, slightly tilted brown eyes seemed to devour the dark-haired Elsacian standing before her. A blush mantled her cheeks. "It is good to see you as well, Rysah. How are you?"

Rysah's expression brightened even further. "Better, now that I have seen you once again." His gray eyes shifted Jaryd's way, steadily regarding the taller Three Rivers youth. "My name is Rysah Kudreau. I do not believe we have met."

"My apologies," Dyrileah stammered, sounding somewhat flustered. Jaryd had heard Dyrileah speak when happy, sad, vexed, worried, frightened, and impassioned. He'd never heard his intended flustered before. *Shit,* Jaryd thought. Recovering quickly, Dyrileah said, "Rysah Kudreau, may I present my betrothed, Jaryd Hume of the Three Rivers, a student of law at the Hall in Antium."

"A pleasure," Jaryd said, proffering a plain, no-nonsense Three Rivers bow.

Rysah nodded perfunctorily to Jaryd with a slight bow of his own. His eyes settled quickly and intently again upon Dyrileah. "After all this time, I thought to find you married."

"What happened to you?" Dyrileah inquired, still speaking a little breathily. "We heard your ship was lost along with all aboard."

"Our vessel did indeed sink, claimed by a freak storm," Rysah explained. "A few of us managed to survive, clinging to the ruin of one of the small boats. We washed ashore on the coast of Relwyn. We were taken by the Tryars and cast into slavery." The Tryars were one of the more powerful Relwyn tribes, perhaps second only to the mighty Megyars. "However savage, the Relwyn respect those who are empowered to answer the Mother's call." Rysah's dark-gray eyes fixed on Jaryd Hume's, and he paused for a moment as if to allow the weight of the words he'd just uttered to settle. "I was able to win my freedom and those of my companions. The way back was long and difficult."

"Evidently without pen and ink," Tamyra observed wryly. She'd taken up station in a corner of the room, about as far from Rysah as she could get. The two boys were seated upon a settle on one side of the fireplace. Ester Quirow occupied an overstuffed chair placed near the opposite end, while her husband, Bardus, stood at her side.

"Tamyra," Ester exclaimed. Jaryd caught himself smiling. *At least Tamy is on my side.*

"There was little in the way of reliable post," Rysah responded dryly, dismissing Tamyra's comment as if it were of no concern. "If you will allow," the dark-haired Elsacian directed his comments to Dyrileah's father, "I have with me a couple of small regard gifts. May I present them?"

Bardus smiled. He was an easygoing, affable man. Jaryd couldn't help thinking, though, that his large, slightly tilted brown eyes missed nothing. "Your offering is most welcome."

Rysah reached into a brown leather satchel resting upon a side table and extracted a pair of paper-wrapped objects. He handed the larger of the two to Ester Quirow and then passed the second along to Dyrileah. Mother and daughter exchanged smiles.

"I shall claim the honor of going first," Ester Quirow announced.

Ester opened her package, careful not to tear the paper wrapping. Inside was a figurine carved from a dark-green stone, depicting a potbellied pig reclining on a wheelbarrow with a silly grin on his porcine face.

Ester laughed, delighted. "Oh, Rysah, this is lovely, a warming token to watch over our kitchen. Is this jade?"

"Yes." Rysah smiled. "I am glad you like it."

Green jade was a rare item in the lands of the Middle Sea. The carving in Ester's hands was the size of a small conch shell. Jaryd had no idea what a warming token was or why one would watch over a kitchen, but he knew it would have been expensive, certainly more so than ivory. He reckoned aside from precious metals or jewels, only white jade, even more rare, would have been costlier. Ester passed the token about. Bardus gazed at the object appreciatively and walked it over to the boys, who, in turn, handed it to Dyrileah. She directed a smile at Rysah before proffering the jade carving to Jaryd. The thing felt smooth and solid in his hand, cool to the touch. Jaryd turned toward Tamyra, who briefly but decisively shook her head. He returned the regard gift to Ester.

Dyrileah opened the second package to reveal another carving, this time of a potbellied rabbit seated precariously upon a log with a grin on his face silly enough to make the pig look scholarly. The thing was a bit smaller than the first token and was hewn from white jade.

"For you," Rysah intoned.

"Thank you," Dyrileah murmured, her blush returning.

Apparently taking note of the puzzled expression on Jaryd's face, Rysah explained, "Another warming token, one, it is said, that promotes fertility."

"Thoughtful," Jaryd said shortly, looking Rysah directly in the eye.

The dark-haired Wycken smiled. "When is the wedding?"

"We have not set a date yet," Dyrileah answered before Jaryd could respond. "Sometime in the new year."

"Early winter then." Rysah raised one dark, curved eyebrow. "But how could you have displayed the notices without setting a date?"

"We have not placed notices." Dyrileah seemed incapable of looking at anything but her shoe tops.

"Sweet Mother," Tamyra gasped. "Dyrileah, you mean you've never canceled your betrothal to Rysah?"

"That's enough, young lady." Ester Quirow spoke to Tamyra in a tone only a genuinely vexed mother could produce.

"There seemed to be no need." Dyrileah raised pleading eyes to Jaryd. Uncertain how to respond, he merely took her hand, the one without the bloody bunny in it.

"A formality only," Rysah soothed, "especially under the circumstances. A matter of little consequence."

"What circumstances would that be?" Jaryd inquired.

Rysah only smiled. "You are an infidel," Tamyra said evenly in answer to Jaryd's question. "A notice is required only if you intend to wed within the temple."

Jaryd understood that as he did not share Dyrileah's Diadym faith, they could not be wed inside a temple of Almyr. An Almyran priestess would officiate, however, making the marriage binding in Elsacian eyes. Once a certificate of marriage was filed with the authorities in Antium, their wedding would also be legal insofar as the government of Ayle was concerned.

"Some advantage it would appear, then, after all," Jaryd said quietly, "to religious diversity."

He kept his eyes on Dyrileah's. Her pleading look vanished in a trice, and trouble flashed back at him quick as summer lightning. He smiled. His intended didn't return Jaryd's expression fully, but hers softened, and the corners of her shapely mouth quirked as she squeezed his hand tightly for a moment.

Bardus walked up to Rysah from behind to lay a hand on the younger man's shoulder. "You cannot imagine how pleased we were to learn of your safe return. Thank you for your visit and the exquisite nature of the regard gifts you so generously proffered. We shall treasure them. Know that our door is open to you and that you will be equally welcome in all circles as you stand once again among your brethren here in Antium City. We shall look forward to your next visit." Bardus looked to his wife. "My love, would you be so good as to see our guest to the door?" Ester nodded and rose smoothly to her feet.

Left with very few options, Rysah bowed graciously, recovered his satchel, and bade all present a good night. Bardus waited for a few moments after Ester and Rysah had left the room before saying, "Goodnight, boys. Caryleah, it is time for bed."

The three children offered quick goodnights to Jaryd and then exited quietly. Tamyra started to follow but came to a halt near the door when Bardus directed her to remain. Bardus did not sound angry, but with him, it was difficult to tell.

Ester stepped back into the sitting room a few moments later. The ire she directed toward her middle daughter was as clear as a thunderclap. "Tamyra, your behavior was inexcusable. You are no longer a child, and Rysah Kudreau was a guest in our home."

Tamyra's chin rose. "He killed Bosco."

"Tamyra," Ester intoned, shocked. "That was years ago when you *were* but a child. You have no proof whatsoever that Rysah did any such thing."

"I know he did it," Tamyra flared, "and I hate him." Tears sprang into her eyes. "Why won't you believe me?" Without waiting for an answer, she whirled about and rushed to the door, fleeing down the hall.

Ester started to follow but paused when Bardus called out to her, "Let her be for the now, beloved. I need to speak with you and Dyrileah." He spoke calmly, his voice as mild as ever, but there was no mistaking the underlying tone of command. Bardus glanced at Jaryd, his meaning clear; this discussion was not for the younger man's ears.

"Perhaps I could speak with her," Jaryd requested.

Bardus nodded, and Dyrileah said, "She's likely to be wedged into the window of the front parlor. Bosco was a cat, a family pet, her particular favorite. He died soon after Rysah and I were betrothed. For some reason, Tamyra has always blamed him. I don't know why." Dyrileah's eyes sought and found Jaryd's for a moment only, but to Jaryd, her gaze felt like a caress. They shared a brief smile, and he left the room.

Dyrileah's prediction turned out to be accurate. Tamyra was

huddled in the corner of the front parlor window frame. Her knees were pressed to her chest. The base of the window was wide enough for the twelve-year-old to tuck her feet onto the sill such that her shoulders were at a right angle with the windowpane. The parlor was lit by a single oil lamp. Tamyra was not large for her age, even by Elsacian standards. She looked tiny in the soft light. She wasn't sobbing, but Jaryd could clearly see the tracks of her tears lining the subtle curve of her cheeks.

Without a word, Jaryd sat close beside her, his back toward the window, both feet resting upon the floor. Slipping a hand into the pocket of his tunic, he extracted a small paper bag filled with licorice candy. He silently offered the bag to Tamyra.

The young girl sniffed in response. "I'm no longer a child, Jaryd Hume, to be mollified with a bite of candy."

"You are not a little girl anymore; that's true enough," Jaryd allowed. "My experience is, however, that a bit of licorice never hurts." So saying, he popped one of the licorice chunks into his mouth and chewed appreciatively.

Eyeing him slantwise, Tamyra hesitated a moment longer and then reached into the bag to take a piece for herself. "No one ever pays any attention to what I say," she proclaimed, speaking a little juicily around her licorice portion.

"I don't know about that," Jaryd opined. "You usually have plenty to say. Keeping up is quite a chore. Every now and again, something is liable to slip by even with the best will in the world."

Tamyra wrinkled her nose at him but said nothing, chewing industriously on her bit of licorice instead.

"Tell me about Bosco," Jaryd prompted gently.

"Bosco was a kitty, a tabby, and my particular friend," Tamyra recollected fondly. "He could purr louder than any cat in the neighborhood, and he liked for me to tug on his ears. He used to sleep at the foot of my bed, and he always watched over me." Tamyra scrubbed a tear from her cheek with the back of her hand. "When Rysah would come around, Bosco would hiss a warning and place himself between me and"—she paused for a moment—"*that person.*"

She twisted about slightly so she could look directly into Jaryd's eyes. "Rysah never liked Bosco; I could tell. One day, I found Bosco lying dead on the back porch. Bosco was a young cat. He was never sick. Rysah poisoned him. I know it."

"Can you prove it?" Jaryd inquired.

Tamyra stared intently into Jaryd's eyes. "No, I cannot," she admitted reluctantly.

Jaryd sighed. "Knowing is one thing, proving another." Stretching out a hand, he gently squeezed her shoulder. "If it helps any, I don't much like the slick bastard either."

At his language, Tamyra laughed briefly, covering her mouth with one hand. Her eyes shone above it, sorrow banished or at least receding. "I would not worry," she told him confidently. "You are much nicer than Rysah, and Dyrileah is not a complete fool."

"That's good to know," Jaryd replied with a grin. "Even better, it's good to learn you're on my side."

Tamyra swung her legs back over the base of the window frame to sit at his left. Jaryd proffered her a second piece of licorice. She accepted without a moment's hesitation. Tamyra chewed quietly for a little while. "Do you think I'm pretty?" she asked suddenly in a hushed tone of voice.

"I do," Jaryd assured her.

"Just not as pretty as my sisters," Tamyra surmised.

"There are all kinds of pretty," Jaryd explained. "You're different from them is all." He paused a moment, considering. "Something special there is about the way you smile and the light in your eyes when you do. Any boy who can't see that is an idiot."

Tamyra regarded him very seriously. "You wouldn't fib just to be kind?"

Jaryd put his arm around her. "Fibbing about something like that would not be kind. I told you the simple truth, just the way I see it."

Tamyra pressed close to his side. "Thank you."

"You're welcome," Jaryd said.

"Tell me about the Three Rivers," Tamyra entreated.

"I could talk all night about the Three Rivers," Jaryd noted. "Is there anything in particular you would like to know?"

"Tell me about your family," Tamyra requested. "Do you have any brothers?"

"I'm fair loaded down with brothers," Jaryd recounted. "Three of them there are. I'm the oldest, followed by Micah; he's eighteen the now and lucky, considering that he's the one what looks like my mother. Next there's Branyck, who is going on seventeen. His hair is as red as mine, but his eyes are like Mum's, green as emeralds. Finally, there be Oryn, still fourteen, with red hair and gray eyes. Oryn looks something like me, poor bugger, except that if he grows into his hands and feet, he'll wind up some bigger. Good lads all, if I do say so myself. Farmers to their toenails. All us Hume boys are fair hands with a bow. My da is the best archer I've ever seen. Oryn, he's got the touch just like Da."

"Oryn," Tamyra breathed, settling more comfortably against him. "I should like to visit the Three Rivers someday."

"A high-toned city girl like you," Jaryd chided gently. "You'd probably be bored out of your skull in two shakes."

"I don't know about that," Tamyra ruminated sleepily. "The change might be good for me."

Jaryd couldn't keep the smile from his face. If little Tamyra ever got within striking range, poor Oryn would likely find himself surrounded. He kept talking softly of the home he loved so well. *Funny,* Jaryd thought, *how sometimes you must walk off away from something for a spell to see it clearly.*

Jaryd knew he wanted to go home—that is, back to the Three Rivers—when he'd finished his schooling. Just exactly how a freshly minted lawyer would earn a living there was a bit of a puzzler. Dour old Titus Wilkes had done all right; maybe he could as well. *What if Dyrileah doesn't want to leave Antium?* When first he met her, such a consideration didn't seem to matter much. If it came to a choice, well, there was none really; he would stay at her side, come what may.

The parlor door swung silently open, and Dyrileah stepped into the room. Glancing a little anxiously at her sister, she whispered, "Is Tamyra all right?"

Jaryd smiled at his intended. "Aye, nothing a sympathetic ear and a couple of pieces of licorice wouldn't cure."

"She is asleep?" Dyrileah asked.

Jaryd nodded fondly. "I've always wanted a little sister. Do you think I might borrow yours?"

Dyrileah responded with an answering smile. "I don't think Tamyra would have it any other way." She tossed her golden-haired head. "She is so grown up the now so much of the time. I can't understand her behavior tonight. She has never cared for Rysah, no matter how hard he tries to please her."

"She has her reasons." Jaryd's smile vanished. He could hear his voice tightening. "Can't say that I blame her."

Dyrileah cocked her head slightly to one side, and her smile took on a mischievous cast. "Jaryd Hume, are you jealous?"

"I never considered that," Jaryd replied mildly. "Mostly it is just that I've never seen you flummoxed before."

"I was not," Dyrileah declared. Jaryd's smile broadened knowingly. "Rysah has always been just that much older, so accomplished and self-confident," she acknowledged and then sighed. "I must have looked a right fool."

"Not foolish so much as smitten," Jaryd observed.

Dyrileah's countenance sobered, her teasing look replaced by one of genuine concern. She stepped quickly to his side. "Jaryd," she protested softly, "you can't think—"

"Can I not?" Jaryd cut Dyrileah off and then reached out to take her hand.

"Silly farm boy," Dyrileah scolded throatily. "I ought to box your ears." Instead, she ran her fingers of her free hand lightly through his hair.

"Still looking for hay, are you?" Jaryd queried.

"Not just the now." The smoky timbre of her voice cheered him considerably. "For someone who prides himself on trusting fully, your faith in me seems easily shaken."

"Not surprising," Jaryd retorted, "considering the fellow you are officially betrothed to is not me."

"You really are jealous, aren't you?" Dyrileah exclaimed.

"Fiercely," Jaryd acknowledged.

Dyrileah's eyes shone in the lamp light. "Good." Their eyes met and clung for a moment.

"Did Bardus have anything interesting to say?" Jaryd inquired.

A guarded look swept across Dyrileah's delicate features. "Not really."

"It was a foolish vow, wasn't it?" Jaryd intoned. "No secrets between us." He didn't seem angry, only sad. The tone of his voice, rimmed with sorrow, tore at her heart.

"Beloved," she began.

Jaryd tossed his head, a negligent gesture, forestalling any further comment from her. "Let us promise instead to look out for one another always and to let no lie stand between us."

Dyrileah nodded. Her eyes warmed with unshed tears. Leaning forward, she kissed him tenderly. "I shall always love you, Jaryd Hume."

"I'm counting on it." Jaryd's smile returned, and his voice brightened. He tilted his head toward Tamyra, still slumbering peacefully at his side. "I'll carry her up if you'll tuck her into bed."

"She'll be mortified in the morning," Dyrileah prophesied.

"Not if we don't twit her over it," Jaryd countered. "Let her be a little girl this night. She doesn't have many such left."

Tamyra hardly stirred as Jaryd lifted her into his arms. After depositing Tamyra on her bed, he waited in the hall outside her second-floor bedroom until Dyrileah rejoined him. "She's out liked a snuffed candle," Dyrileah commented as she stepped into the hallway, carefully closing the bedroom door behind her.

A single oil lamp suspended from a stanchion set high in the wall about halfway down the hall burned low. Dyrileah laid a hand gently on Jaryd's arm. "Are you all right?"

The light in the hall was too dim for Jaryd to discern the color of her eyes, but still they reached out to him, as compelling as ever. "Are we all right?" he asked.

She kissed him more ardently than in the front parlor—a long, lingering kiss that sought and found, questioned and answered.

Dyrileah broke off the kiss, pressing the length of her body close to his. "What do you think?"

Holding her gently, Jaryd could only shake his head. "I think that for me there will never be another you."

"Just you remember, farm boy," Dyrileah's voice sounded soft and sultry, "mine you are, the now and forever."

39

Kindred Spirits

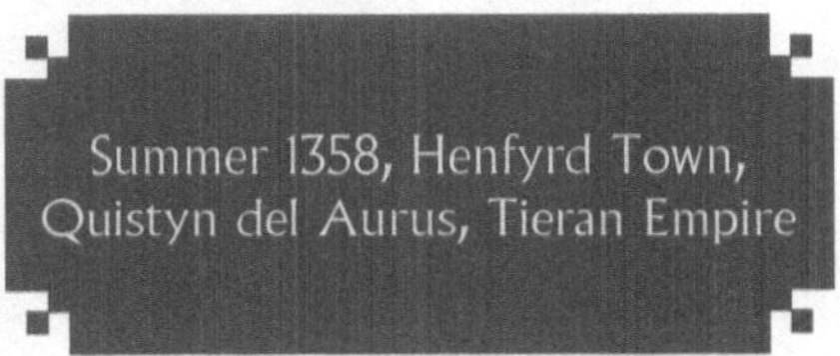

The inspection tour ended well ahead of schedule. A fierce midafternoon sun beat down as Quintus Glabrio Jens accompanied Princess Lydia Sylvus Gant back to her quarters. While in Henfyrd, Lydia had rented a private residence. The house was a large, two-story design made of stone with a red tile roof that stood upon a bluff near the western edge of town overlooking the river Wyst.

Upon returning to the walled courtyard that fronted the home, Quintus dismissed the light cavalry escort, including a somewhat subdued Wyll Quin of House Varus. Quin was a fine young staff officer. Most fine young staff officers had a tendency to think a little too highly of themselves. While less afflicted than the majority of his peers, Quin was not immune to the malady. This day's lesson in the nature of the unexpected would do him some good. Still, watching Wyllem ride off, Quintus determined he would have to say something suitably avuncular to the young altyrn and soon.

"Please come in, General," Lydia invited as she dismounted, passing the reins of her horse to a sturdy-looking marine guard. "Let us get out of this heat."

Swinging down, Quintus handed the reins of his mount over to the same guard and followed the princess toward the door of the house, acutely aware of the subtle sway of her hips as she preceded him.

"Did you enjoy the inspection tour, Your Highness?" Quintus inquired politely as they stepped through the portico.

Lydia smiled at him over her shoulder, black eyes flashing. "Bolt throwers are intriguing devices, General." She clasped her hands to a pert bosom, sighing dramatically. "And all those berms and trenches, absolutely enthralling."

"I noticed, Highness," Quintus said dryly, "the struggle evident when it came to containing your enthusiasm."

"Show me again, General," Lydia's smoky gaze darkened slightly, "in the cool of the fall, and my reaction will be positively giddy, I assure you."

"Should thirty thousand Syrdisians attempt to roll over us, Lydia," Quintus chided just a little, "you may discover a newfound appreciation for the camp's defenses. They are, in fact, more secure than the town walls."

"Are thirty thousand Syrdisians likely to make such an attempt, Quintus?" Lydia inquired.

As they were standing alone together in the downstairs parlor, Quintus granted himself the luxury of allowing his vexation to show. "They are out there somewhere, Lydia. Elder is due back tomorrow. I hope he'll bring me something definitive. As a matter of general principle, I wish you would move closer to the camp."

"Shall I join you in your granary?" Lydia teased.

"I'm sure we can find suitable accommodations, Your Highness," Quintus countered.

"When you've located said Syrdisians, should they be anywhere in our vicinity, I will proceed with all the haste decorum affords to the protection of your camp," Lydia promised. "In the meantime, I think the company of marines you have surrounding this place will suffice insofar as security is concerned while providing me the opportunity to enjoy the occasional cooling breeze from off the river."

"If the Syrdisians turn up in force anywhere nearby, I would prefer to see you aboard a warship bound for Tyne," Quintus grated.

"Ah, but you see, General, I am not under your command." Lydia smiled again, enjoying herself. "Besides, I suspect Admiral Barr has other uses in mind for his warships."

"You are a nuisance, Your Highness," Quintus complained, "a very lovely one, to be sure, but pure trouble all the same."

"As an imperial emissary," Lydia pointed out reasonably, "I believe I am supposed to be exactly that—a nuisance, I mean." She paused a moment, raven-colored eyes suddenly inscrutable. "I thought you said earlier today that I was good for morale."

"And so you are, Highness," Quintus allowed, smiling. "You've certainly done wonders for mine."

Lydia's maid Edelle, a sprightly, gray-haired woman no larger than the princess herself, entered the room to inquire if either of them needed anything. "Something cool to drink, Edelle, on the veranda please," Lydia replied. Extending her hand to Quintus, she bade, "This way, General."

Marveling at the feel of her small white hand in his, Quintus was happy to be guided across the parlor floor through a wide double door and out onto the veranda. Located on the western side of the house, the first-floor veranda was a wide porch offering shade throughout even a midsummer afternoon.

The veranda ran the full length of the building and was accessible via a number of rooms. He knew Lydia used a spacious first-floor corner suite, the door of which he could see standing open at the northwestern end of the porch, as her bedroom, the downstairs rooms being noticeably cooler in summer than those upstairs. He could not fault her choice for comfort but would have preferred a second-floor apartment from a security perspective.

They stood together in silence for a few moments until Edelle brought them a pitcher of lemon water and a pair of large drinking glasses on a varnished wooden tray. Carefully placing the tray on a side table, Edelle straightened and turned to await her mistress's pleasure.

"This evening at sundown," the princess informed Edelle, "one of Quintus's soldiers, a young man with a very impressive pair of shoulders named Mat Bayrd, will escort an even younger girl called Emilyn Harris to this residence. Emilyn is going to enter service for me. She will be a great help to you."

Lydia paused, casting a level look at her maid. Edelle nodded. "About bloody time. I'm fair wore out." The woman had been looking after Lydia literally all of the princess's life and had long since become much more than merely a servant. An even sixty years of age, Edelle had very bright, very blue eyes that narrowed suddenly. "Light, girl, you haven't been out gathering strays again, have you?"

"She's fifteen, Edelle, a country girl, sweet and lovely, and she's had a hard time." Lydia's crisply accented voice lowered slightly. "The hardest kind for a girl that age. You will be gentle with her, promise me."

"Oh, aye, if you say so, lass," Edelle grumbled, glaring at Quintus. "Men," she snorted. "Darlings you are from swaddling on until you get the itch, and then blighters you become, half of ye."

Lydia smiled at Edelle with genuine affection. "That will be all, Edelle, thank you. Please inform the sajar of marines outside that the general will be staying for dinner." She cast a questioning glance in Quintus's direction, seeking confirmation, and smiled at his nod. "We are not to be disturbed," the princess directed, "unless at least twenty thousand Syrdisians are seen storming the walls."

"I'll paraphrase that last if you don't mind, my lady," Edelle replied and grinned when Lydia made shooing motions at her with both hands. The maid sauntered off, not hurrying in the least.

Unpinning her hat, Lydia removed it, placing the bonnet on a second side table. She surprised Quintus then by undoing the broad brocaded belt about her waist. With a sigh of relief, she set the ky-robi down on the table as well. Pouring lemon water into each of the glasses, she proffered one to Quintus. The afternoon heat was oppressive, and they both quickly quaffed the cool, citrus-flavored water. Lydia returned her glass to the tray and looked again out over the river.

"Your soldiers, Quintus," she remarked, a wistful tone threaded softly through her voice. "Those archers in particular, Em's country boys, the ones what mostly don't know nothin'," she continued, perfectly mimicking Emilyn Harris's West Country drawl. "They're awfully young, aren't they?"

"Indeed they are, Highness," Quintus affirmed. "That is the way of things."

"Yours is a vile business, General." Lydia raised her soft, sable eyes to meet his.

"While politics, on the other hand," Quintus said evenly, "is so noble an undertaking."

"Oh, shut up, do." Lydia sniffed. She liked the man standing beside her in the private, shaded recesses of the veranda; she liked him immensely. Quintus was not particularly large, but he was strong, with a soldier's hardy build and pragmatic turn of mind. He was also clever, easy to talk with, a little reserved, almost shy, except in private, and startlingly kind. He was fair. His men, she knew, thought well of him in part because he was courageous and had a reputation for being lucky in battle but mostly for the simple reason that he left them their dignity, treating them always with respect. She'd begun to think of him as her general—a reckless thing to do and potentially dangerous for him. She should never have invited him to dinner.

"Do you know something, Princess?" Quintus deposited his glass beside hers on the tray and stepped forward to place a hand on either side of her waist. At his touch Lydia inhaled sharply. He saw her breasts rise beneath the thin fold of her silk riding dress. "You are a bit of all right."

Lydia very lightly touched his right cheek with the fingers of her left hand. "Em is correct about one thing at least." Her eyes, black as night, warmed, devouring his. "When it comes to men, if a woman is to have any hope of happiness, she must choose a good 'un right from the jump."

Quintus bent forward and kissed her. Lydia's lips were soft and warm and clung to his. He raised his head, intending to gauge the expression in her eyes, only to find them closed. Lydia swayed slightly, and he enfolded her in his arms to steady her. His heart pounding, Quintus kissed her a second time, the way a man kisses a woman when he wants her.

Lydia's response was immediate. Sliding her hands upward, she twined her arms about his neck, pressing her mouth and her hips firmly against his. Lifting her easily, Quintus strode purposefully toward the cool, beckoning dark of her bedchamber.

Despite the thick stone walls of the house and the shade afforded by the deeply recessed veranda, the warmth of the afternoon sun and the heat of their bodies combined to leave both Lydia and Quintus slicked with sweat after furiously coupling atop the wide bed in the princess's sleeping quarters. At thirty years of age, Lydia's slender form embodied all Quintus longed for in a woman and more: lithe as a girl with high, taut breasts adorned by large nipples the color of molasses cream.

Lydia was a widow and a mother of two. He expected to find her a woman well-schooled or at least well-practiced. She surprised him, however. Lydia made love like a willing maid, sweet but shy, also passionate and enchantingly uncertain.

He lay back into the overstuffed feather pillows that abutted the heavy mahogany headboard of her abominably too-soft bed and slipped one arm about her. Quintus felt a relentless, tearing affection for the slim little woman at his side, wanting at that moment more than anything else in life to keep her always from hurt or harm. She wriggled up on top of him to gaze into his eyes.

"You are awfully quiet, Quintus," Lydia murmured. "What are you thinking, exactly?"

"You want to know exactly what I am thinking?" he echoed. "Just the now, you mean?"

"Yes," she said tentatively, certain he would express some regret for the rash behavior they'd indulged in a little while ago.

"You are certain," he pressed, "that you want to know exactly?" Lydia nodded insistently. "'Nice pair of lungs on this lovely, Quintus, you lucky old son,'" he offered. "My thoughts just the now, exactly."

"Ooh," Lydia exclaimed, startled. She thumped him on the chest with a diminutive fist. "I begin to suspect your intentions, General."

"Ow," Quintus grunted in response. "A bit late for that the now it is, Your Highness."

"I think you are a bounder, Quintus Jens," Lydia huffed, "preying upon the affections of lonely widows."

"A bounder, am I?" Quintus shook his head. "And a blighter, too, I reckon. Lydia, you and Edelle really ought to get out more often. Real people don't talk like that any longer."

"Are you suggesting I am not a real person?" Lydia's stygian eyes glowed dangerously.

"A little sheltered is all," Quintus said carefully. He extended a hand to brush a strand of light-brown hair off Lydia's forehead, guiding it backward over her ear. "There is a dreamlike quality to the events of this afternoon. That, I'll allow. This conversation has certainly taken a turn toward the surreal."

"Hmm," Lydia growled softly, only partly mollified, running her fingers lightly over the firm muscle of his chest. "I still think I've been tumbled into bed by a reaver and a rogue."

"Reaver the first go and rogue the next." Quintus smiled a satisfied smile. "Something to look forward to."

Lydia laughed briefly and snuggled close in spite of the heat. "My husband," she spoke very quietly, "said that I was an adequate lover."

"He was a fool," Quintus asserted.

"No," Lydia interrupted, "just a man bound up in a marriage not of his choosing to a mere chit of a girl he did not love. I could have forgiven him that if only he'd shown a little kindness later." She fell silent.

Quintus craned his neck forward to kiss the top of her head. "I love you, Lydia Sylvus Gant," he declared gently but firmly. "And I shall love you more with every beat of my heart from this day forward. You have my word on that." He lay back and closed his eyes.

Lydia reared up and prodded him on the shoulder with a slender forefinger. "Quintus." He did not respond, and she poked him more vigorously, calling his name again.

Quintus opened one eye. "Formidable though your arsenal is, Highness," he ground out, "at the moment, any attempt to entice me further would be a waste of weaponry."

"Quintus," Lydia insisted plaintively, "you can't say what you just said to a woman, to me, so sweetly and with such tender regard and then just lay back and go to sleep."

Closing both eyes, Quintus said shortly, "Watch me."

"I'm going to cling to you, Quintus Jens of House Glabrio, like a limpet," Lydia threatened. "And in this heat, you will sleep abysmally." She flopped down and held him close. A moment of silence passed and then another. "Quintus?" she inquired softly.

Quintus sighed, eyes still determinedly shut. "What?"

"Would it be all right, do you think," Lydia asked demurely, "were I to love you in return?"

His eyes snapped open, and Quintus nodded. "Suit yourself," he told her matter-of-factly.

"Thank you. I shall, then. I'll leave you to sleep comfortably," Lydia whispered and started to rise.

"No, lass," Quintus pled urgently, the lean muscles of his torso coiling as he sat up partway. "Please stay." He reached for her, and Lydia allowed herself to be gathered again into his arms. Quintus kissed her tenderly and stretched out, lying back down.

Pleased as much by his plea as by his pledge, Lydia settled against him in a sort of sweaty bliss. Madness this was, Lydia knew, harebrained and hopeless and perfect. She pressed her ear to his chest, her general, and lay still, so still she could hear the beat of his heart, echoing his promise of love.

40

A Change in Fortune

At the sound of the knock on her bedroom door, Bodewhin Ware rose from the chair beside her writing table. "Come in," she called.

The door opened, and Dehlia, her aunt and uncle's principal maid, stepped quickly and quietly into the room. Without a word, she handed Bode a thick sheet of vellum folded and sealed. A quick look proved enough for Bode to recognize the hand that wrote it. Upon first glance, she felt glad to receive the letter from Mat, despite the bleak expression on Dehlia's face as she passed it along. She and Mat had corresponded regularly since his departure last spring, after their one magical evening together.

In some strange way, Bode was glad their time had been so brief. She could remember every word, every moment. Like a small, perfectly crafted piece of jewelry, she could tuck the memory of that precious little while away in her heart and keep it safe and warm until she saw him once more.

According to his most recent letters, Mat had been in battle, at a place called Tensys. Mat claimed his participation had not amounted to much. Following the battle he'd been assigned to escort a group of civilians. He warned that while their route would take them nowhere near a battle zone, they would be traveling through rough country, and it might be some considerable time before he could write again.

Several weeks had slipped by since Mat's last missive, and despite his appraisal, she had begun to worry. Oddly, the letter passed on to her bore no date. Mat was particular about things like that. Then she saw the words, written just below her address in his neat, square hand: "To be posted only in event of my death." A Last Letter it was. Tieran military custom was for soldiers to write a Last Letter home before going into battle, to be sent to loved ones should they fall. Her heart froze. All of a sudden, it seemed as if some invisible hand had ripped all the air out of her bedroom. Bode found herself on her knees, Dehlia's arm about her. With trembling fingers, she broke the seal on the letter, opened it, and read:

Bode,

If you are reading this, I have broken the promise I made you. I am sorry.

Since last I held you in my arms, I have looked upon the face of war. I understand better the now something my grandfather once told me. He said those who think any good will come of going to war have never been.

I cannot know the manner of my death, but I can tell you the why of it. I did not die for a flag or even a country and certainly not for glory. I died for those standing at my side, fighting to earn the right to return home to you. I hope someday you will be able to forgive me.

The shadows have lengthened here, where I am the now, and the western sky is a burnished blend of gold and red. Before beginning, I thought I would have a lot to write. My intention was to pour a lifetime's worth of hopes and shared dreams and loving you into these lines. Sunset feels like the right time to be writing this. Still, the words won't come.

They would be futile anyway. Nothing I could conjure will make memories of lost tomorrows.

What I need most to say is pretty simple. I want you to be happy. I pray you will live the life your heart yearns to live. I hope you meet a man worthy of you and that you will love him as fiercely and tenderly as you have loved me. From time to time, perhaps of a quiet evening, with the sun just going, you will think of me.

I ask only that you remember this: I will have loved you with all my heart for so long as there was breath in my body and shall love you with all my soul thereafter, forever.

One day we shall meet again, my dear one, in a better place.

Godspeed, beloved, until then.

Mat

A second letter arrived the next day, marked with an official-looking military stamp. The note was brief, signed by an altyrn named Sedgwyck Ward. Bode remembered the name from one of Mat's earlier writings. Mat died, Ward's letter said, while on detached service, lost in an avalanche while attempting to rescue another member of his company.

At least he didn't die in battle. The vision in her mind's eye of wide-shouldered, gentle Mat fighting and killing had hurt her. The pain she'd felt at the thought was nothing compared to this, to the loss of him. *Oh my God*, her heart wailed, *Mat's dead.*

Three weeks and a day passed. Morning came. Bode awoke; soft light filtered through her bedroom window. For one delicious moment, just as she had every day for the past five days running, she thought all was right with the world, and then she remembered. Grief laid its callous hand upon her then, rending her heart once more with a remorseless, searing pain. She'd never known anything like it. When her brother, Ayden, died, well, he'd been so hurt and so changed, so diminished by his injury, that his death, while unexpected, brought with it a sort of relief.

Death had released her brother, brought an end to his suffering, but not so with Mat. Mat brimmed with life. He should have had years and years. She felt the sob rise within her. Turning, she pressed her face into her pillow. She didn't want to cry anymore. By the time she went down to breakfast, her eyes would be puffy, bag-laden wrecks. Still, wracked by sorrow, she wept.

Bode ate sparingly and excused herself as quickly as she could, slipping away into the garden. Exhausted by grief too heavy to bear and impossible to set aside, she sought solace in solitude. Over the past weeks, her friends and family tried to help. She could barely tolerate them any longer. Only Jaryd and Dyrileah brought her any real comfort. Jaryd because he shared her pain; he offered no platitudes, made no attempt to make her feel better. He simply lent her his strength, allowing her room to grieve. Dyrileah because, in her presence, she was able to concentrate on something else. Bode was determined to master the Power of the One. For months, she'd been pushing herself hard, even more so since Mat's death.

"Bode," Dyrileah had chided her just yesterday, "the Power of the One is vast and untamed. Once you learn to understand its nature and so long as you respect it, the One will serve you, but it will not be cowed, not by you, not by anyone. People have died attempting to wield only a fraction of the Power you are capable of summoning. You must take heed and curb your impatience. It is either that or perish. You will accomplish nothing by throwing your life away."

Dyrileah's angry outburst had reached Bode in a way quiet counseling had not. Wasting her life was foolish and selfish. Mat would not have wanted that.

Bode remained in the garden at the back of her uncle's house later that morning when she heard Michaela call out to her. Turning, Bode saw her slim-hipped young cousin walking toward her on the arm of Lord Eddard Bly. Tall, dark-haired, and blue-eyed, Ned Bly looked every bit of him the nobleman he was. Clad in the dark-green military waistcoat and gray trousers worn by the soldiers of Ayle, Ned smiled a greeting.

"I thought you'd been posted to the frontier," Bode found herself saying. The last person she expected to see this day was Ned Bly.

"So I was," he said offhandedly. "The army in its wisdom reassigned me as an aide to General Pots. The general was in turn reassigned to the capital, and here I am. Better to be lucky than good, eh?"

Better to have a father with deep pockets and a bucketfull of influence, Bode reckoned but said nothing. His handsome features sobering, Ned went on. "My condolences, Bode."

"Thank you, Ned," she replied.

To Ned's eyes, Bode looked a little pale, wan, and careworn, and more beautiful than ever. Her long brown hair was dressed in a shimmering, walnut-colored braid that fell to the small of her back. Her striking, dove-gray eyes were rimmed with sorrow. Though the day showed fine, she wore a gray cloak of winnowed wool to guard against the coming chill of a late autumn afternoon.

"I'll leave you two to catch up," Michaela announced amid a swirl of silk skirts as she spun about and walked away. *Poor Michaela,* Ned thought. *Bright as a penny she is, but next to Bode, she'll never be more than almost pretty.*

Stepping close, he asked seriously, "How do you fare?"

"Well enough," Bode answered, as if it didn't matter. He saw the haunted cast to her wideset eyes.

They talked for a while about small things—that is, he talked; Bode made brief, noncommittal responses as if every utterance were a chore. "It is a beautiful day, Bode," Ned said finally. "Why don't we go for a walk?"

"Thank you, Ned, but no," she answered in a subdued tone. "I wouldn't be much company."

"That's for me to decide, isn't it?" Ned asked rhetorically. Taking a breath, he squared his shoulders. "Your blacksmith is dead, Bode," Ned said firmly, "and you are not." She stared at him as if he'd slapped her. "You are going to have to accept that or be destroyed by it. You're too strong to let that happen."

"You have no right," Bode flared, tears welling.

"I have every right," Ned retorted. "Mat wasn't the only person in your life to care for you. Shutting out the rest of the world and those who care about you won't help you heal, Bode. I know." Ned paused, his jaw tightening. "My best friend was killed. He was a good man, a better soldier than I'll ever be, brave and honest and kind-hearted, and still he died in my arms, choking on his own blood, slain in some meaningless border skirmish that accomplished exactly nothing."

Ned sighed, running long fingers through his thick, black hair. "Life can be incredibly cruel, but it's the only merchant at the fair. Those of us who survive go on because giving in to despair is worse than dying." He could see some color in her cheeks; whether it was due to anger or shame mattered but little to him. "You are going to walk with me this fine day, Bodewhin Ware. You don't have to like it, but you're coming even if I have to drag you along." He offered her his arm.

Bode glared at him. "I never figured you for a bully, Ned Bly."

Ned smiled his usual, easy smile. "Hidden virtues." Bode took his arm.

41
Complications

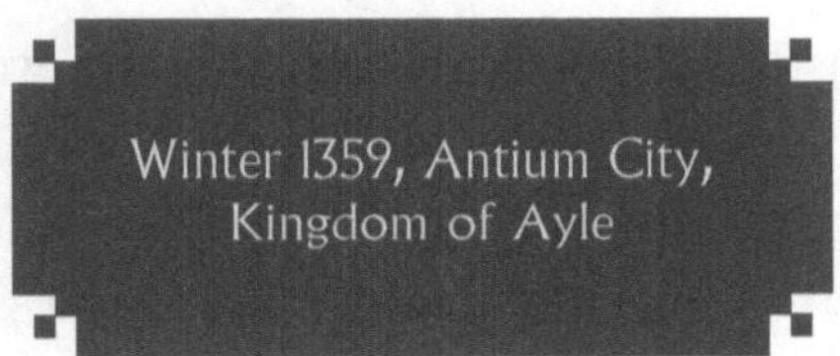

As he hurried through the narrow streets of the Elsacian Quarter, Jaryd Hume was glad the rain had stopped. Slick, wet cobblestones glistened in the waning light of a cloud-laden winter afternoon. Jaryd had a sack full of regard gifts slung over one shoulder, a small, special present for Dyrileah stuffed into the pocket of his tunic, and another little something for Tamyra tucked away inside his cloak.

Jaryd wore his boots instead of sandals—better he reckoned, for keeping his feet dry on such a day. His cloak was fashioned of winnowed wool dyed gray in color, as was the Tieran-style cotton tunic he had on beneath. A good Three Rivers watch cap slanted at what he hoped was an appropriately jaunty angle across his brow. His Hawken, sheathed, was stuffed into the wide leather belt at the small of his back.

"Mat's dead." The memory of how he'd blurted the words to Dyrileah some weeks back still burned.

The smile of greeting on Dyrileah's lips faded, and a look of concern flooded the umber depths of her eyes. "Oh, Jaryd, I am so sorry." She clasped his hands. "How? When? Do you know?"

"Not exactly," Jaryd managed. "An accident of some kind looks like. It's official, though; Bode has a letter from the army."

Dyrileah put her arms around him. She'd worn her hair down that day. Jaryd remembered burying his face into the silken mass, holding her close. "I've known him all my life. He was always so strong and steady, like an oak. I can't believe he's gone."

He cried then like a baby. Jaryd supposed he should have felt ashamed by that. He didn't, though, only grateful for her warmth and understanding.

Poor Bode, usually so self-assured…in the weeks since Mat's death notice had arrived, the gray-eyed beauty looked and acted like nothing so much as a whipped pup. *Time,* Jaryd thought hopefully. *Bode needs time.*

Jaryd shifted his grip on Sebastyn Card's heavy walking stick, held in his left hand. More often than not, Jaryd still thought of the sorcerer as Uncle Spats, head gardener at Antium Hall. Strictly speaking, Jaryd supposed, Sebastyn was both things. A little hard it was to come round to the notion that his friend, wise, irascible old Spats, stood, in truth, as one of the most revered sorcerers ever to have lived—a man whose life remained steeped in secrecy.

Dyrileah hated secrets, viewing them as a necessary evil. She felt Sebastyn reveled in them. Why would a sorcerer out of legend be-friend a penniless farm boy with a lopsided sense of humor? Blunt, his little witch could be when she put her mind to it. It didn't seem likely, Jaryd readily acknowledged, nearly as improbable as her fall-ing in love with him. That had hauled her up short, at least for a while.

Jaryd had come to care greatly for Sebastyn. He respected him. Sebastyn was a fountain of knowledge, and he spoke the truth. While there was much Sebastyn did not say, Jaryd had never caught him in a lie of any kind. When he did speak, Sebastyn's words were braced by a wry sort of wisdom that was hard-won, born most times of bitter experience.

Sebastyn did not try to minimize his mistakes. "Better it is," he said, "to learn from them instead."

Night had fallen by the time Jaryd mounted the steps to the

Quirow townhouse. Tamyra answered the door with a bright, welcoming smile. "Neither Patua nor Dyrileah is home yet," she informed him, "another one of their *meetings*. They missed supper again. Maman is quite put out."

"Aye, well, let's see if we can't cheer her up some then," Jaryd suggested. Tamyra offered to take his cloak, but he demurred. "I'll keep it on awhile."

Jaryd found the lot of them still seated round the kitchen table. Ester sat at one end of the table, her two sons, Tate and Soryn, along one side, and little Caryleah squirmed determinedly in her chair on the other.

"Jaryd," Ester greeted him with a smile, "we weren't expecting you."

"I wasn't sure I could get away," Jaryd explained. "I understand I've been tardy in providing you all with regard gifts. If you'll allow, I hope to make amends this evening."

"Regard gifts are an indulgence, Jaryd," Ester said gently. She well knew his means were limited. "You are under no obligation."

"In future, when it comes to interpreting Elsacian customs, I'll be sure to speak with you first," Jaryd promised. "As things stand," he slung the sack from his shoulder, holding it up in front of him, "it is too late for that this time round."

"Neither Bardus nor Dyrileah is here," Ester protested.

"That will teach them not to miss supper." Jaryd grinned and began passing out the gifts. The first went to Ester. "This is for you and Bardus to share anyway, Mistress." Jaryd still had a hard time calling Ester Quirow by her given name. The paper wrapping contained a book of Elsacian poems. Sebastyn had given it to Jaryd, who had only a few words of Elsacian and could neither read nor write in Dyrileah's native tongue. The volume was handsomely bound; he could say that much for it. Ester seemed pleased.

Jaryd was confident the boys would like their gifts; each received a matching belt knife with a blade length of about half a span, forged of good, honest steel, with a sturdy bone-handled grip. Caryleah's present was a doll—a baby girl it was, featuring a painted porcelain face and a cloth-stuffed body. Little Cary's green eyes lit at the sight, and she began mothering her new baby immediately. The bag was empty by the time he worked his way round to Tamyra. Shrugging his shoulders, Jaryd tugged at an ear. "I could have sworn there was a present here for you somewhere."

Shrewd beyond her years, Tamyra folded her arms beneath her breasts and squinted up at him. "You're teasing me."

"Maybe," Jaryd allowed, "just a little." Reaching into his cloak, he pulled free the kitten, a male tabby, yellow-eyed, with a coat of alternating red and gold stripes.

Tamyra's eyes widened with delight. "He's beautiful!" Jaryd watched as Tamyra cradled the sleepy kitten against her chest. The little fellow began to purr.

"His name," Jaryd told her, "is Fredward."

"Look at the size of his feet," Tamyra exclaimed softly. "He's going to be enormous!" She raised her eyes to his. Jaryd could see tears glimmering. "Fredward is a silly name for a cat."

Jaryd extended his hand, scratching the kitten between his ears. "You can change it if you like. Just don't call him Dancer or Prancer or some damn fool name like that."

"Jaryd Hume," Ester Quirow chided him in a tone used by mothers everywhere. "Really."

"Sorry, Mistress." Jaryd stood his ground. "But how would you like to go through life being called Fluffy?"

Tamyra was still laughing at that when Dyrileah, closely followed by Rysah Kudreau, stepped into the kitchen. "Jaryd..." Dyrileah's smile always began in her eyes. "What are you doing here?"

"I heard a fella could get a meal," he replied.

Dyrileah stepped into his arms, hugging him close. "Jaryd has been distributing regard gifts," Ester Quirow informed her eldest daughter.

"Beloved," Dyrileah reproached him gently. "You didn't have to do that."

"If I *had* to do it," Jaryd said, smiling, "it wouldn't have been any fun." Out of the corner of his eye, Jaryd noticed that Tamyra had stepped surreptitiously behind him, turning her shoulder to shield little Fredward from Kudreau's line of sight.

"Good evening, all," Rysah said graciously. The dark-haired Wycken was dressed simply in a well-tailored cotton shirt and trousers of dark gray, over which he wore a stylish black woolen waistcoat. A long, curve-bladed dagger was suspended from the narrow black leather belt fastened about his lean middle, encased in a lacquered red leather sheath. "I do not wish to intrude on such an occasion." His dark gray eyes rested upon Dyrileah. "I will see you tomorrow."

Dyrileah slipped free of Jaryd's embrace. "I'll walk you to the door."

"No need." Rysah waved his hand with a smile. "I'll show myself out."

"Are you really hungry?" Ester asked Jaryd once Rysah had left the room. "I thought you had already eaten?"

"You've never heard of second supper?" Jaryd responded, a look of pure astonishment on his face. "I thought that was the one Tieran custom everyone knew about."

Dyrileah and her mother exchanged glances. Tamyra giggled. "Nobody eats a second supper, not even you insufferable Tierans."

"I'm a Territorial," Jaryd declared staunchly. "We're only partly insufferable, and the roast chicken smells delicious."

"There is fresh bread too," Ester assured him. "Dyrileah, would you like something?"

"No, thank you, Maman. I've eaten. Father said he won't be much longer."

Ester sighed. "That man." She looked at Jaryd and pointed a slim finger at the empty chair occupying the head of the table, where Bardus usually sat. Jaryd took the proffered seat, feeling a little out of place. "All right, children, thank Jaryd for the gifts he's given and then wash for bed."

The children chorused their thanks and filed out.

Tamyra paused near the door, still cradling her kitty in her arms, and rushed back to plant a kiss on Jaryd's cheek. "Thank you. Fredward and I shall become great friends. I know it." She dashed off.

Dyrileah sat to Jaryd's immediate left. Arching one golden eyebrow, she inquired, "Fredward?"

"A good name for a cat," Jaryd pronounced.

Dyrileah shook her head but said nothing. His betrothed wore a keppi with a close-fitting, scoop-necked bodice that Jaryd couldn't help thinking went just fine with her firm young bosom. The dress was green, Dyrileah's favorite color, and her hair was done in an elaborate double braid.

"You look nice," Jaryd observed.

"Thank you," Dyrileah intoned with a small, pleased smile.

Ester served Jaryd his food and stepped back. "I'll leave you two the privacy of the kitchen. Take your time, Jaryd. There is plenty more if you'd like a third go at supper this evening." Ester shifted her gaze to Dyrileah. "When your father gets home, tell him he can fend for himself. He can also do the dishes. Tell him for me that he'd better if he knows what's good for him. This is the third night this week." With that, Ester draped her apron over the back of the chair she'd been sitting in and walked out of the room, carrying in both hands the book Jaryd had given her.

"Marriage seems…complicated all of a sudden," Jaryd heard himself saying.

"Getting nervous, are you, farm boy?" Dyrileah tore a small chunk of bread from the half loaf Ester had placed in front of him and popped it into her mouth.

"Will you?" Jaryd asked.

"Will I what?"

"See him tomorrow," Jaryd supplied. There was no need for him to specify who the "he" in question was.

"We are a small community, Jaryd," Dyrileah answered as if speaking to a recalcitrant child. "We of the Wycken are smaller still. I could hardly avoid Rysah even if I wanted to do so." She laid a hand on his arm, adding, "Jealousy is attractive, beloved, only for a little while."

"After we are married," he proposed lightly, "perhaps we could move away and put some distance between you and this particular entanglement."

"Jaryd," Dyrileah responded seriously, "I thought we'd settled this. Antium will offer you ample opportunity to practice law. The Elsacian community will benefit from and pay handsomely for the services of a well-respected young lawyer who also happens to be a Penitent in good standing and a Tieran citizen." She shifted in her seat. "I've also told you I can't simply walk away from my obligations here. I thought you understood that."

"I understand only that I love you very much," Jaryd told her. "I'll wager a truly talented member of the Wycken could find new and equally worthwhile obligations wherever it is that she settles."

"Perhaps." Dyrileah's eyes dropped to her shoe tops. "But that won't be necessary in our case, will it?"

Slipping his hand into his tunic pocket, Jaryd drew forth the small package containing Dyrileah's gift. "This is for you."

"Silly," Dyrileah chided him, brown eyes shining coyly. "You don't give your betrothed a regard gift."

"A Three Rivers custom," Jaryd informed her. "You're going to have to make a few concessions, you know."

Dyrileah hastily tore away the paper wrapping. "Oh, Jaryd," she breathed, "it's beautiful." She held aloft the pendant and chain he'd given her. The chain was of silver and the pendant fashioned from white gold with a small but perfectly formed sapphire at its center.

"It belonged to my grandmother," Jaryd said quietly. The necklace had been the last thing he'd packed before leaving home. Then, Jaryd could not have said why he'd done so, but he was glad of it the now.

Before Dyrileah could respond, the kitchen door swung open, and Bardus Quirow stepped through. Glancing furtively about the room, he settled his gaze upon the two young people seated at table. Somewhat apprehensively, he asked, "Is it safe to come in?"

42

Accused

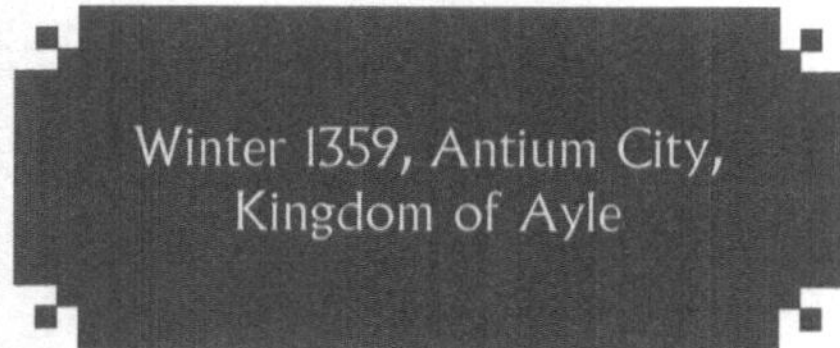

For the first time since he'd met her, Jaryd Hume had reason to question his relationship with Dyrileah Quirow. They were to meet that evening at the fountain in White Garden, a small park at the edge of the Elsacian Quarter of the city. Jaryd arrived early. He was a little anxious. Dyrileah and he had been quarreling some the past few days. As was true with most couples, Jaryd suspected, they argued over small things because they either could not or would not speak of what was really wrong.

Their wedding had been delayed the now until the first week of spring. Dyrileah had insisted but remained studiously vague as to her reasoning, saying only that it was for the best. Jaryd wanted a wife, someone who could put their marriage first in her life.

He'd come to realize Dyrileah would forever be first and foremost of the Wycken. She could love and marry, have children, and make a home for him and them, but always her first concern would be to serve, to bear the burden of the Blessed, as the Elsacians referred to the Wycken among them. She'd tried to tell him that from the outset. At first, he'd been too enamored to care. As time went on, Jaryd had come to understand, a little, just how heavy a load Dyrileah's duties represented. That understanding was part of it.

In part also was Jaryd's growing desire to go home, to return to the Three Rivers. He could not explain it. He'd felt no such want a year ago. Perhaps it was the burgeoning war with Syrdis, or what had happened to Mat, or maybe it was nothing more than the dawning realization that he couldn't, not if he wanted Dyrileah in his life. She was bound to Antium and her people there by a yoke far too heavy for him to lift.

And then there was Rysah Kudreau. A member of the Wycken also, Rysah understood and was able to share a part of Dyrileah's life, the portion that most defined her, in a way Jaryd never could. Jaryd's jealousy shamed him, but he seemed unable to set it aside. The young Elsacian had given no offense. He was never overly familiar with Dyrileah. It was just that Rysah was always around, more than happy to walk Dyrileah to or from some meeting or another that Jaryd could not attend. Handsome and charming, Rysah always and ever appeared impeccably gracious and well-mannered. He never so much as put a foot wrong. Jaryd couldn't stand the bugger.

Jaryd straightened the collar of his waistcoat. The garment was new, purchased with his earnings from work as a gardener at the Hall. He felt a little guilty about that. He still owed Sebastyn Card for the regard gifts he'd purchased for the Quirow family. Sebastyn had waved him off. From the outset, the wily old sorcerer had tried to talk Jaryd into accepting the loan as a gift. Still, Jaryd remained determined to pay him back.

Jaryd had taken up station at the base of a stately elm. From his vantage point, he had a clear view of the fountain as it burbled away in the center of the small park. Jaryd and Dyrileah met often at White Garden, a place where they could walk and talk and be alone together.

He saw them, Rysah and Dyrileah, stepping through an opening in the trees on the far side of the fountain. Dyrileah was holding onto Rysah Kudreau's arm. They appeared to be deep in conversation. The sun had not yet set. Dyrileah was a little ahead of time—practically unheard of as the girl was perpetually late. The couple stopped and stood, holding hands and gazing into one another's eyes. A handsome pair they were, the lean, dark-haired Rysah and the slender, fair-haired Dyrileah.

They kissed. Jaryd's heart leapt into his throat. This was no chaste exchange between old friends but rather a lingering, passionate embrace. Dyrileah broke off the kiss, but instead of pushing Rysah away, she clung to him as if she lacked the strength to stand on her own. Jaryd's shock turned to outrage. Fascination bound him, though, and he continued to look on, unmoving.

Dyrileah said something to Rysah and turned away. Approaching from behind her, Rysah laid a gentle hand on her shoulder as he responded. He stepped back after a moment and strode off in the direction from which they'd come. Jaryd waited until Rysah was lost to sight among the trees of the park.

Jaryd walked toward her. She stood at the base of the fountain, wearing a light-blue keppi, the hem of which reached to about mid-calf. She'd wound her hair into a simple single braid. Dyrileah looked lovely. Her eyes were closed, and she was biting her lower lip. Jaryd found himself saying, "You're early, and they say miracles never happen."

She turned toward him, and her wideset eyes sought his. "Jaryd," she cried. Taking two quick steps, Dyrileah flung herself into his arms.

After what he'd just witnessed, Jaryd didn't know how she would react to his arrival, but he had not expected this. Holding her close, he said, "Aye, well, glad I am to see you too." She said nothing, but her arms tightened about him. "What is the matter?"

"Nothing," Dyrileah replied. "I am just being foolish. I am glad to see you, awfully glad."

"Have you been waiting long?" Jaryd asked.

"No, not long," she answered.

"Did you come alone?" Jaryd inquired next, his heart pounding.

Dyrileah pressed her face into his chest. "Yes." A lie—he and Dyrileah had vowed to let no such thing stand between them. *Where one lie is uncovered, a clutch lies buried.* He'd heard that somewhere.

"Won't you tell me what is wrong?" Jaryd asked.

Dyrileah shook her head. "I feel as if the world is trying to come between us. I never thought to find you. I don't want to lose you." *Then what were you doing kissing Rysah Kudreau as if he were the last man in the world?* Jaryd intended to ask her. He meant to but somehow found he could not. They walked for a time. Dyrileah clung to his arm as if she feared he would float away. She appeared so careworn that he didn't have the heart to confront her. At least they didn't argue.

As the couple approached the Quirow townhouse, Jaryd said, "I will see you tomorrow."

"Yes," Dyrileah affirmed. "Bode and I will be studying at the cottage." The cottage in question was the head gardener's quarters on the campus of Antium Hall, where the sorcerer Sebastyn Card lived in the guise of Spats, the chief groundskeeper. Studying, Jaryd knew, meant Bode would be attending witch practice under Dyrileah's careful tutelage. Considering the animosity that existed between the two groups of magic wielders, it seemed ironic to Jaryd that the two young witches felt safest honing their craft in the home of one of the most revered or notorious—with Sebastyn, one could pretty much take one's pick—sorcerers ever to have lived.

While Jaryd stood upon the curb, Dyrileah mounted the first step leading up to the front door of her parents' home. Given the difference in height between them, this placed them eye to eye as they embraced. Jaryd took a quick look up and down the street and saw it was void of traffic for the moment. Dyrileah's sweetly curved little bottom was suddenly much too handy for him to ignore. Reaching around, he squeezed her bum gently. Empty street or no, this was too public a venue for Dyrileah to let him get away with that. Expecting a good talking to or at least a firm look, Jaryd was surprised when all she did was slip her arms about his neck, making no protest whatever.

Sliding his hands upward to a more respectable location, Jaryd whispered, "You are not going to lose me, beloved. I won't let you."

"Tomorrow," she said. Jaryd could see the tears glistening in her eyes as he released her. *Tomorrow,* Jaryd vowed to himself, *we are going to have this out.*

Early the next morning, Jaryd immediately answered Dyrileah's knock on Sebastyn's cottage door. She smiled at him in surprise. "I thought you would be working the grounds by now."

"I appealed to the curmudgeon's sense of humanity," Jaryd replied with an answering smile, jerking a thumb over his shoulder.

"When that didn't work," Sebastyn called from within the sitting room of the cottage, "he bribed me with the promise of a game of stones this evening." Sebastyn never tired of the strategy game. Jaryd doubted he'd ever take a match against the wily sorcerer. He couldn't have been much competition for Sebastyn, but that didn't seem to dampen the old fellow's enthusiasm for a game one whit. "We have some fresh biscuits," Sebastyn offered, "and strawberry jam."

"Your biscuits are hard on my waistline," Dyrileah proclaimed and then sighed. "I don't suppose one would hurt but no jam," she added firmly. Entering the cottage, Dyrileah removed her woolen wrap of dark-forest green. Beneath, Jaryd saw she was wearing a high-waisted, light-green cotton frock with a scooped neckline, the latest in Antium fashion, according to Bode, and nothing like an Elsacian keppi.

Dyrileah took a brief look about. "Bode isn't here yet?"

Jaryd shook his head. That was a little unusual. Bode was never late for witch school.

The three of them had just sat down at the table when an authoritative knock sounded at the front door. "Open up in the name of the King," a man's voice called from without.

"Hold your horses," Sebastyn hollered irritably in reply. "I'm an old man." Steady blue eyes fixed upon Jaryd. "Take Dyrileah into the bedroom," he whispered. "The two of you wait there. Stay calm."

Jaryd and Dyrileah crossed quickly into Sebastyn's bedroom. Once inside, Jaryd left the door open slightly to better hear what was said in the sitting room. The front door creaked softly as Sebastyn opened it.

"You are the one called Spats, the chief gardener?" a young man's voice inquired.

"That I am," Sebastyn affirmed. "And who might you be?"

"My name is Gordyn Rhow, a captain of the City Watch," the same voice answered. "We are looking for Jaryd Hume. He is to be served with a summons to appear. Is he here?" A summons to appear was a notice to render testimony at a trial. Once called, failure to appear as a witness constituted a serious crime.

"Hoi, Jaryd!" Sebastyn looked in the direction of the bedroom, raising his voice so as to be heard clearly even through a closed door. "An officer of the watch is here with a witness notice fer ye."

At the sound of his name, Dyrileah clutched Jaryd's arm tightly. He gently pried her fingers loose and guided her deeper into the room, well clear of the door. Gripping her hand briefly, reassuringly, Jaryd snatched up a towel and stepped through the portal, wiping his hands upon it.

"What?" Jaryd exclaimed. "I don't understand. The most interesting thing I've witnessed lately is some striped rutabaga."

"Are you Jaryd Hume?" Judging from his perfunctory tone, the captain of the watch apparently had no regard for vegetables whatever. The officer stood just inside Sebastyn's sitting room. Lacking Jaryd's height by a couple of finger widths, he was perhaps a few years older, well-muscled, with dark hair and penetrating blue eyes. The uniform of the Antium City Watch featured a black leather jerkin bound at the waist by a wide leather belt of the same color. The captain's insignia, a winged hawk, done in bronze, was pinned to his left breast. Over his left hip swung a straight sword in a well-oiled leather scabbard. Two others in the black livery of the City Watch had taken up station in the doorway. Big men both, they stood silently, their postures alert. A short-billed black woolen cap was tucked into the captain's left armpit. In his right, he carried a sheaf of papers.

"I am," Jaryd stated.

The captain of the watch presented Jaryd with the papers. "This is a notice to appear as a witness at the trial of Bodewhin Ware, who stands accused of the crime of witchcraft. A form of affidavit is attached." The captain's blue-eyed gaze was rock hard. "You are a known associate of Ware's, are you not?"

"Bode and I grew up together," Jaryd confirmed.

"Witches are not solitary creatures. Among her friends and acquaintances will be others who have embraced the Dark Powers." Rhow paused for a moment. *To make me sweat*, Jaryd reckoned. "You are not a suspect. All that we require from you is a list of her friends and associates. Fill out the affidavit, list the names and whereabouts of those you know, sign the form, and return it to the judiciary office in the courthouse complex on State Street by noon tomorrow. You must attend the first hearing scheduled for the second hour after noon. A listing of trials pending and the courtrooms housing them will be posted in the main entry hall of the courthouse. Should you be called and are not present, a warrant for your arrest will be issued. Refusal to appear is a serious offense, especially damaging to one who aspires to a career in law."

"You appear to know a good deal about me," Jaryd remarked.

"Good day to you." Gordyn Rhow made no response to Jaryd's observation. Instead, his vivid blue eyes scanned the room briefly but thoroughly. Turning smartly about, the captain waved his two men on, and the three of them departed.

Sebastyn followed the captain to the door. After closing it behind the watchmen, he peered out an adjacent window. "They've gone," the sorcerer said firmly enough for Dyrileah to hear. She stepped out of the bedroom and walked to Jaryd's side to lay a hand on his arm.

"I'll bet he's nothing but fun come Solstice Eve," Jaryd remarked, staring at the door.

Sebastyn turned toward the young couple. "I'm afraid this is a rather serious matter."

"Bode?" Jaryd sounded incredulous. "Taken for a witch. I know she is one, but, still, that just doesn't seem possible. Bodewhin Ware is not the type of person who gets arrested."

"The *law*," Dyrileah's soft voice fairly dripped scorn, "requires three accusers. In reality, all it takes is one with a little influence or a bit of coin. Witnesses are easily bought. This has been happening to us for generations."

"What will happen to her?" Jaryd directed his question to Sebastyn.

"A trio of judges will oversee a first hearing. The charges will be reviewed. Witnesses may be called to testify by the prosecutor, evidence presented. The judges will determine if sufficient cause exists to warrant a trial."

"I know that," Jaryd said a little impatiently. "What I mean is what will happen to her in the meanwhile? Where will she be held? Will we be allowed to see her?"

"The watch is a secular authority," Sebastyn explained. "She will be bound over to the city prison. No visitors will be permitted prior to first hearing, nor will counsel be allowed to represent her. Her fate is in the hands of the judges. If she is remanded for trial, the tribunal will determine the terms of her confinement." Jaryd knew the term "tribunal" referenced the three judges who would oversee the proceeding.

"At a minimum," Sebastyn went on, "the services of a solicitor will be allowed then. If the accused is unable or unwilling to name a lawyer within three days, the court will appoint one. From the time of her arrest until judgment at first hearing has been rendered, the authorities are not allowed to put Bode to the question. The captain did not say when she was arrested—yesterday, probably. She has likely spent last night and will no doubt spend this one in a cold, dark place, but she won't be harmed, at least not physically. No watchman, no matter how zealous, would risk incurring the wrath of a tribunal. Next to the King himself, the last person in Antium you want angry with you is a high court judge." An accusation of witchcraft was serious enough as to fall directly within the purview of the high court.

"What will you do?" Dyrileah asked of Jaryd.

"I guess I'll attend first hearing," he replied. "I would have even without a formal invitation." He held aloft the summons and affidavit in his hand. "I'll fill in my name and those of her aunt and uncle, along with some speakers whose courses I know she attends." Jaryd shrugged. "I don't really know many of her other friends." He looked Dyrileah in the eye. "I won't list you or any member of your family."

Dyrileah's expressive, brown eyes widened. "Jaryd, I never meant to imply—"

"You needn't worry." Jaryd cut her off, unable to keep the anger out of his tone.

"If the prosecutor decides your affidavit response is less than satisfactory," Sebastyn put in, "you will be called to testify."

"I cannot be compelled to give evidence," Jaryd stated.

"No," Sebastyn affirmed, "but if your response is insufficiently forthcoming, you could be accused of impairing justice or, worse, of being an accomplice. If that happens, should the judges find in favor of the prosecutor's appeal, you could be arrested on the spot."

Jaryd merely shrugged. "A chance I'll have to take."

"My father must hear of this and the Wycken," Dyrileah said. She took Jaryd's hand. "Could we meet this evening beside the fountain in White Garden at the bottom of the hour past sundown?"

"Do you want me to walk you back?" Jaryd inquired.

"No," Dyrileah replied. "It is probably best if I go alone. I will see you tonight." She kissed him. "You must be strong, beloved."

"Give me a moment to make certain no one is watching," Sebastyn said. "If I whistle, you'll know the way is clear." Dyrileah donned her wrap, and the young couple waited in silence until Sebastyn's whistle sounded. Exchanging a final, brief glance with Jaryd, Dyrileah departed.

"You have an alternative," Sebastyn said as he stepped back into the cottage.

"What do you mean?" Jaryd asked.

"Every witness called has the right to challenge the proceedings," Sebastyn responded. "You don't have to submit an affidavit or respond to questioning on the part of a prosecutor until the challenge is resolved."

"Are you talking about a trial by combat?" Jaryd queried. "Offering myself as Bode's champion? I thought that right was reserved for the nobles of Ayle only."

"The statute is little used these days," Sebastyn acknowledged, "but is available to all commons subject to the King's law in Ayle."

"I am not a citizen of Ayle," Jaryd pointed out.

"You are, however, a student entered upon the rolls of the Hall in Antium," Sebastyn countered, "all that is required in this case."

"I am to don armor and square off against some champion of the court?" Jaryd was aghast. "If I don't perish of pure embarrassment on the spot, any bugger they name will likely chop me into sausage bits in two shakes."

"When called to witness at first hearing, respond by giving your name and then say in lieu of testimony, you offer challenge to the proceedings. The court will inquire as to what manner. You answer by naming the Yeoman's Challenge." Sebastyn continued patiently, ignoring Jaryd's outburst. "The Yeoman's Challenge comes in multiple forms." He paused, blue eyes twinkling. "The Archer's Form is, I think, the one best suited to your martial capabilities, and," he added sagely, "the choice least likely to produce a truly competent opponent. You have a right to demand the court name a champion from among those present at first hearing."

"Just exactly what is the Archer's Form of the Yeoman's Challenge?" Jaryd inquired. Sebastyn's description was both specific and detailed. Jaryd's throat felt as dry as toast by the time the sorcerer had finished. An alternative it was—one that, if he succeeded, would see Bode freed without the need either for a trial or for him to give testimony. If he failed, Bode would be condemned and, subject to the high court's discretion, Jaryd himself might be charged as an accomplice.

"I won't try to diminish the risk, Jaryd," Sebastyn concluded. "You are a fine hand with a bow; I've seen that myself. I think you stand an excellent chance of prevailing. Bode would not have been arrested unless someone powerful wished it so. I don't know the why of it, not yet, but there is only one outcome to a witch trial. The only uncertainty is the severity of punishment. If charges against her are not dismissed at the outset of the first hearing, you are her best chance."

"I'd better see to Dark Hope then," Jaryd acceded, referring to the long bow Sebastyn had given him from the weapons archive of the Hall. That was the same day the sorcerer had passed along the styaxe also in Jaryd's possession the now. "I'll want to select my three best arrows too."

Sebastyn insisted upon accompanying Jaryd that evening when

the younger man went to meet with Dyrileah. "I thought you had an old friend to visit?" Jaryd remarked as they made their way across the Hall campus. Before Dyrileah's arrival that morning, Sebastyn had been ebullient with news of an old friend's arrival in Antium just the day before.

"I'll have ample time to see him later," Sebastyn replied. "Besides, the bugger went and became a Penitent priest in his dotage, don't you know? He'll likely want me to mend my sinful ways. I'm in no hurry to do that."

Twilight found the two of them making their way down the narrow lane that ran past the Temple of Almyr on Elm Street. Jaryd was not sure what the lane was called. As far as he knew, it represented the most direct route to White Garden from the Hall grounds. It was the path Dyrileah had taken the first time they had made the walk from the campus to the park. The western sky clung to a rosy glow as the sun dipped below the horizon. The coming night would be steeped in winter chill.

Clad in a sturdy tunic woven of gray wool beneath his lined leather jacket, Jaryd also wore his watch cap, a battered remnant of his youth in the Three Rivers. The cap had been new then, a Solstice gift it was, from Bode and Mat. Jaryd's jaw tightened. His Hawken, sheathed, was stuffed into the belt about his waist at the small of his back. He carried his styaxe in his right hand. He'd felt a little silly going about armed so, but Sebastyn would not take no for an answer.

Sebastyn had equipped himself with a long-bladed dagger, worn over his left hip, and his heavy walking stick. "I can't very well go trooping about with a sorcerer's stave," he'd muttered while shrugging into an old-fashioned, fleece-lined cloak worn over his usual gardener's tunic. Sebastyn was bareheaded but carried a woolen scarf stuffed into the pocket of his cloak. "For the walk home, just in case."

Two crossbowmen stepped out of the shadows without warning, no more than a dozen paces away. The weapons they carried were half the size of a military-class crossbow. Assassins' tools they were, intended for closeup work. One of them shouted something. Jaryd's

Elsacian was pretty sketchy. All he caught was Dyrileah's name. The pair leveled their crossbows. Sebastyn quickly stepped in front of Jaryd.

The bowmen shot. Sebastyn had raised his hands as he crossed to Jaryd's front. One of the bolts seemed to bounce off something just in front of the sorcerer and went clanging off the brick wall of the building—a shoe works, Jaryd thought it was—to their right. The second quill slammed into Sebastyn's chest, taking him high, just under the collar bone. The white-haired sorcerer collapsed in a heap at Jaryd's feet.

Jaryd had no recollection of crossing the distance separating him from their two assailants. He must have, for the next moment he was slashing at the bugger on the right. The man fended off Jaryd's first cut using his crossbow as a shield. He was reaching for the knife in his belt when Jaryd's reverse stroke caught him squarely in the throat. Blood erupted; the man toppled wordlessly, his body heaving and twitching on the cobblestone street. The second man fled, racing around a corner, down an alley in which the two had apparently been hiding. Jaryd gave chase. The alley lay deep in shadow. Jaryd caught a glimpse of the man as he scrambled over a chest-high wooden fence at the rear of it. He rushed back to kneel at Sebastyn's side. The sorcerer was conscious. He was holding his scarf, wadded around the crossbow shaft protruding from his chest. The sorcerer's fingers and the scarf itself were already stained with blood.

"Are you all right?" Jaryd asked.

"A fine time this is," Sebastyn growled in response, "for you to indulge in stupid questions."

"Dyrileah is a healer," Jaryd suggested. "We are only a short distance from the park."

"Best not chance it," Sebastyn rasped through gritted teeth. "My friend is a healer too. He'll be staying at the Penitent Sanctuary on Owl Street." He nodded his head in a northerly direction. "It's just off that way, about the same distance as the park."

"What do you mean 'best not chance it'?" Jaryd pressed.

Sebastyn's blue eyes hardened. "Did you understand what that fellow said?" Jaryd shook his head. "Dyrileah sends her regards." Sebastyn spoke the words as if they pained him more than the wound in his chest. "His words exactly."

Jaryd shook his head again, this time in denial.

"Help me up," Sebastyn grated. "We'll figure this out once I'm not bloody bleeding all over the place."

The sanctuary wasn't far. "Ask for Hexus," Sebastyn muttered to Jaryd somewhere along the way. The building was a residence maintained by Penitent monks, called brothers by the faithful, used in part to accommodate priests and other church officials while they traveled from place to place. Sanctuaries in rural communities usually had farms attached. In cities such as Antium, there was often a candle works, or a leather shop, or some other commercial venture the monks used to maintain themselves. Jaryd had never been inside a sanctuary before.

A monk with shoulders to rival that of Mat Bayrd met them at the front gate, a sturdy, wrought-iron affair set into a stone wall at least eight span in height. As soon as the monk saw that Sebastyn was injured, he unlocked the gate and allowed the pair of them inside. Sebastyn kept slipping in and out of consciousness. Jaryd had been forced to carry him most of the way. The old man wasn't all that heavy, but Jaryd was nearly exhausted; he stumbled into the courtyard of the sanctuary.

The big monk closed and locked the gate. "I'll take him," he offered. "My name is Brother Mycious."

Jaryd gave his name. "I was told to ask for Hexus."

"Were you the now?" Brother Mycious rumbled as he lifted an unconscious Sebastyn easily into his massive arms. The man had a deep voice, well-suited it seemed considering the size of his chest. In the torchlight illuminating the gate, Jaryd could not quite make out the color of the monk's eyes—brown, he thought. The big fellow's head was shaved. "By him?" Mycious thrust his chin at Sebastyn.

"Aye," Jaryd acknowledged. "He said there was a healer here."

"Indeed there is," Brother Mycious stated. "Follow me." He strode quickly away, carrying Sebastyn's limp form as if it were no burden at all. Mycious led Jaryd up a short flight of stairs into a large, well-lit chamber filled with stuffed bookshelves and an array of reading tables surrounded by a gaggle of simple, straight-backed wooden chairs. Walking briskly across the entry hall, library, or whatever the book-filled room was properly called, Mycious passed under an arched, brick-lined doorway into a second, smaller chamber and then through an open wooden door at the back to a third. The third room was apparently a sleeping quarters. Though sparsely furnished, it looked clean, and there was a bed. Depositing Sebastyn gently down upon it, Mycious slipped past Jaryd back into the hall outside, saying, "Wait here; the healer will be with you in a moment."

Jaryd knelt by Sebastyn's bedside and felt for a pulse. The sorcerer's heartbeat was slow but steady. Sebastyn's scarf and tunic front were drenched with blood, and his face was nearly as white as the bedsheet. Jaryd sensed movement out of the corner of his eye. He was turning his head as a familiar voice said, "Jaryd, I'm sorry to see you carrying that."

Jaryd blinked. Before him, clad in the simple robes of a Penitent priest with a small leather satchel slung over one shoulder, stood Axton Vars Nebus Bayu—Father Vars, as he was known in Greystock village back in the Three Rivers. Axton was his official title, that of senior priest. Of medium height and spare of flesh, Father Vars was largely bald, the fringe of hair remaining to him about his temples and ears and the back of his head a stately gray. His eyes were dark blue. Jaryd noticed the priest's gaze rested with marked disapproval on the styaxe he held in his left hand, its wickedly curved blade still splattered with gore.

"Father Vars." Jaryd gulped, disbelieving. "What are you doing here?"

"I am going to try to save this scoundrel's life." He pointed at Sebastyn. "Why don't you put that thing away before you cut yourself? Have you been injured as well?"

"No," Jaryd replied, "I don't think so." He rose to his feet and started to lean the styaxe against the wall in the corner of the room.

"Wipe the damn blade down first, boy," Father Vars barked at him. "I doubt the good brothers here will appreciate having blood smeared on their walls." Even as he spoke, Father Vars knelt and clasped Sebastyn's wrist, muttering, "Will you never learn, you old fool?"

Brother Mycious entered the room a moment later carrying a wicker basket full of rolled bandages and neatly folded, sparkling white towels. A second monk followed at his heels bearing a large copper kettle of steaming hot water. "Wait outside please, Jaryd," Father Vars instructed. "This will take some time."

Jaryd sat on a wooden bench in the anteroom outside. Brother Mycious brought him a platter filled with bread and cheese and a mug of tea. Hours passed. Sebastyn's words, "Dyrileah sends her regards," kept ringing in Jaryd's ears, a noisome echo that would not fade, drowning out all other thoughts.

Jaryd reckoned it was about midnight when Father Vars walked up to him. "The healing technique we use is ancient. It works more slowly than the sorcerer's way but, I think, more surely. The old bugger will live; I am convinced of that. He's awake and insists upon seeing you. A brief visit will be easier on the lot of us than trying to argue him out of it."

"Thank you, healer," Jaryd offered sincerely. "Are you the old friend he spoke of?"

Father Vars smiled. "I've been friends with Sebastyn Card for," the priest squinted in recollection, "two hundred and twenty-four years, give or take. When first he and I met, I was known by a different name, Hexus Rygg."

Hexus Rygg was yet another sorcerer out of legend. "I'll be damned," Jaryd exclaimed.

"Watch your bloody language, boy," Hexus Rygg growled. "You're standing in the middle of a ruddy sanctuary."

Jaryd's attempt at a smile faltered. "It is awfully good to see you, Father."

Hexus laid a gentle hand on Jaryd's shoulder. "I'm glad to see you too, son. Don't be too long; the old fool really does need to rest whether he realizes it or not."

"How do you fare?" Sebastyn inquired as Jaryd took a seat on the stool placed next to the sorcerer's bed.

"So asks the fellow with a hole in his chest," Jaryd observed, settling himself upon the stool.

"You had to take a life tonight—your first, I believe," Sebastyn pointed out.

"He had it coming," Jaryd said evenly.

"That he did. See you remember it," Sebastyn advised. "You'll sleep better for it, maybe."

"Thank you," Jaryd said, "for saving my life."

"You're welcome," the sorcerer responded shortly. Sebastyn paused for a moment and then went on. "Did anyone besides Dyrileah know the two of you planned to meet at White Garden this evening?" Jaryd shook his head. "Do you think she would have told her father?"

"That's likely," Jaryd opined. "Her mother, too, probably. I can't believe Dyrileah or her parents would have had anything to do with an attempt on my life."

"Those two buzzards with the baby crossbows didn't show up by accident," Sebastyn stated firmly. "Dyrileah must have confided in someone who wants you dead." He winced. "Old Hexus never has learned how to heal properly." Shifting his head slightly, Sebastyn continued. "My guess as to the why of it is that either someone doesn't appreciate your relationship with Dyrileah, or they fear what you might say when called to give testimony tomorrow."

"I can think of no one who has taken exception to our betrothal," Jaryd replied. "As for my giving testimony, I really don't know much."

"What little knowledge you do have could be very damaging to the Elsacian Wycken here in Antium," Sebastyn insisted. "You know Bode and Dyrileah are powerful witches. You also know Dyrileah's father is as well and a member of some standing in the Wycken hierarchy. Should Dyrileah or her father be put to the question, who knows what secrets might be revealed? The Wycken may well have determined silencing you was their best option regardless of how Dyrileah feels about it."

"Secrets." Jaryd's jaw tightened. "I begin to see just how noxious they are."

"We'll debate that someday, lad, you and I," Sebastyn replied. "Something else is bothering me. I was unable to ward against that second quill because it carried a heartstone tip. Hexus remarked on it when he dug the bugger out of me."

Gray colored and glassy in appearance, heartstone, could be knapped like flint into spear points and arrowheads. Capable of holding a fine edge, heartstone possessed the unusual property that no mage no matter how powerful could ward against it as a weapon.

"Makes sense if you are shooting at a sorcerer," Jaryd said without thinking.

Sebastyn shook his head. "Even if Dyrileah has been carrying tales, no one knew I would be accompanying you, all of which is beside the point. That attack was aimed at you, son, not me. The question that pertains is why would anyone be trying to kill you with a heartstone-tipped weapon?"

43

First Hearing

Seated alone in a darkened cell, Bodewhin Ware thought something must be wrong with her. She should have been terrified. Instead, she felt numb. The room was small, scarcely larger than the clothes closet in her bedroom at Uncle Haryld and Aunt Rayleen's house on Copper Street. The only light was that which trickled in under the door from a lantern, she supposed, in the corridor somewhere outside. Dank, the tiny prison cell smelled, for some reason, like a root cellar. They'd allowed her to keep her cloak. She wasn't cold, really. She wished it wasn't so dark. By Bode's reckoning, tomorrow would mark the third day of her confinement.

Bode was very aware of the wrought-iron chain studded with lodestones fastened around her neck. The iron felt coarse to the touch; the links weighed heavily. She could not summon the Power of the One while being collared so. At first, she'd wanted to try, desperately. Now it seemed impossible to even think of it. Her strength had fled. Nothing seemed real. If she wore the collar long enough, Bode knew she would sicken and eventually die. That would take weeks, though. Her ordeal would end long before then. Justice acted swiftly and surely in Antium City. They still burned unrepentant witches in Ayle, although Bode understood hanging was more common these days.

"*Rope and collar wound without*
Watch 'em dangle and dance about."

She'd forgotten the rest. Just as well. She never cared for that particular verse.

They'd arrested her there, at her aunt and uncle's house. The four of them—Bode, Uncle Haryld, Aunt Rayleen, and her cousin Michaela—had just returned from service. Bode still wore her First Day dress, a conservatively cut, gray cotton frock. Being taken for witchery on First Day, her prayer book still in her hands, seemed ironic somehow. Michaela had fled, weeping, as the watch captain announced the charges against Bode. Her uncle looked stunned. Two burly watchmen, one bearing the collar chain, the other a pair of manacles, stepped purposely toward her. A third stood watching warily nearby with what appeared to be a toy crossbow in his hand, a small feathered dart set to the string.

Aunt Rayleen leapt between her and the watchmen, crying, "Don't you touch her."

The one with the manacles pushed her aunt aside. "Haryld," Aunt Rayleen shouted, "do something."

Her uncle demanded to see the warrant. The watch captain, a young, dark-haired man with intense blue eyes, had identified himself as Gordyn Rhow. He handed over the thick vellum script, placing it in her uncle's hands without saying a word. Uncle Haryld read the warrant. His face paled. "A sealed warrant, authorized by a full tribunal." He spoke the words as if pronouncing his own death sentence. "There is nothing we can do, Rayleen."

If she lived a hundred years, Bode knew she would never forget the cold, rough feel of the iron chain as it was locked into place about her throat. The manacles, though heavy and uncomfortable, seemed somehow less awful. As they led her away, Aunt Rayleen called out to her, "This is a mistake, darling. We will never abandon you. Be strong."

They would not speak to her. The four watchmen said nothing to her at all. Aside from a few terse orders the captain issued to his trio of watchmen and their even briefer responses, the entire journey through the streets of Antium to the prison everyone called the Old Mill was made in silence. Four young men—the captain, at least, was even attractive in an austere sort of way—and they wouldn't as much as look at her. This was not the reaction her presence usually engendered in males, especially those about her age. She found it unsettling, even more so than the stares of passersby.

Bode had quickly come to realize that the worst part of being accused was that she could no longer deny her guilt, at least not to herself. A witch she was. Bode had willingly summoned the Power of the One. Dyrileah had told her repeatedly she had no choice in the matter. The One had called to her. Bode could accept the calling and embrace the One or be consumed by it. No other choice remained.

Was that true or merely expedient from a Wycken's point of view? Bode had never felt so isolated. She made no attempt to wipe away the tears trickling down her cheeks. Alone, in the dark, what did they matter?

By the time they came for her, Bode had lost all track of time. Two City Watchmen clad in their distinctive black leather jerkins opened the door to her cell and stepped inside. One was short and stocky, the other tall and thin. The tall, skinny one carried a lantern, and the short, stocky one placed a bucket of water and a reasonably clean towel on the floor beside her.

"First hearing," Short and Stocky said. Those were the first words anyone had spoken to her in some time. They earned Short and Stocky a baleful glare from Tall and Thin. Bode washed her face and hands as best she could. She had neither comb nor mirror. She knew she must look a fright. Still, to be let out, even for a little while, seemed a blessing.

The sunlight dazzled her as she was led outside. Midday it must have been or nearly so. The Old Mill prison occupied one side of a large quadrangle known as Judgment Square. The courthouse building stood opposite to it on the far side of the courtyard. The walk did not take long. Her guards escorted her up a flight of wide, marble-clad stairs to a second-floor courtroom marked with the numeral three.

As she entered, Bode saw the room was packed with dozens of people. Strangers all, or so it appeared; there wasn't a familiar face in sight. *Witch trials must be popular attractions.* Tall and Thin directed her to the station of the accused, a small, raised, rectangular platform surrounded by a highly polished wooden railing located near the front of the courtroom. Just ahead, at the very end of the chamber, the trio of chairs behind the judges' podium stood empty. The tribunal that would hear the charges against her had not yet entered. The prosecutor sat at a table behind her and to the left.

He was a tall, rail-thin man she'd never seen before. She knew he was the prosecutor only because the robes of office he wore, a deep gray in color, were unmistakable. The advocate's table stood bare. As this was a first hearing only, not a formal trial, no lawyer would serve in her defense.

The head bailiff, a large man, his black leather jerkin adorned with a thick, braided collar of white rope about his neck, took up his station at one end of the judges' platform and called, "Attend, all ye present. The High Court of Antium is in session the now. Judges of the Third Tribunal presiding." The buzz of conversation filling the room died as three old men in long black robes seated themselves at the judges' podium. Bode faced them. Tall and Skinny had curtly warned her to do so until they directed her to turn and look toward the gallery.

The first judge, furthest to her left, was of medium height and build and carried himself with a very erect posture despite his years. He had a stern yet learned face. The judge in the middle was apple-cheeked and portly and appeared years younger than his colleagues. Judge number three, seated to her right, was a thin-faced man with a very full head of very white hair and an impatient air about him.

"The matter before this court," the first judge spoke into the silence, his voice pitched to carry clearly to the back of the courtroom, "authorities of the King accuse one Bodewhin Ware of the crime of witchcraft. This proceeding will serve as first hearing. Is the accused present?"

"She is, milord," the prosecutor responded.

The first judge looked Bode in the eye. "You are Bodewhin Ware?"

"I am, sir," Bode replied.

"Speak up, girl," the impatient one chastened.

"I am she, sir," Bode said firmly.

"Who stands for the prosecution?" the first judge asked.

"Ferris Hardwick, milord," the prosecutor answered.

"Are you ready to proceed, Master Hardwick?" the same judge inquired.

"The prosecution stands ready, milord," Hardwick stated confidently.

A moment of silence ensued. "State the charges, man," the third judge growled. The prosecutor did so, naming Bode a witch, a willful practitioner of the Dark Arts. The judges listened impassively; not a one of them so much as blinked an eye.

When the prosecutor had finished, the middle judge spoke for the first time in a rich mellow tone. "The accused will turn and face the gallery."

As directed, Bode turned her back to the tribunal. She scanned the sea of faces before her. The first she recognized was that of Dehlia, Aunt Rayleen's principal maid. Her aunt sat next to Dehlia. Bode saw her Uncle Haryld was present also and her cousin Michaela as well. Michaela was seated between her parents, her eyes fixed upon the floor in front of her.

"The bailiff will now read the roll of witnesses," the impatient judge announced. "Master Prosecutor, do you have any changes to make to the list submitted prior to the start of this hearing?"

"No, milord," Ferris Hardwick replied.

"Very well." The third judge continued, speaking to the gallery. "When the bailiff calls your name, stand, repeat your name for the benefit of the court, and remain standing until further directed. Bailiff, you may begin."

The first name read by the head bailiff was that of Michaela

Tucker. Ashen-faced, Michaela stood, unable even to look in Bode's direction. She mumbled her name. The third judge barked at her. Swallowing hard, Michaela tried again. Her voice wasn't much louder, but the third judge said nothing, apparently deciding that to do so was a waste of time. *Michaela, what have you done?* The thought seared through Bode's mind like a hot iron. Bode had said nothing to her cousin or her aunt and uncle about the time she spent with Dyrileah. She could not explain to them what she didn't really understand herself. *What does Michaela know?*

Dehlia was called next. She stood, spoke her name clearly, and looked Bode in the eye. Dehlia's gaze was steady and determined. The list went on: two speakers from the Hall, both of whom she knew well, and two poorly dressed men she knew not at all. A couple of her classmates were summoned also and Ned Bly. She had not seen Ned in the courtroom. He looked handsome in his uniform. After giving his name, he smiled at her. The last name called was that of Jaryd Hume. Standing to his feet, Jaryd looked as if he'd just come in from the fields; the gray woolen tunic he wore appeared as rumpled as if he'd slept in the poor thing. He held a battered Three Rivers watch cap in his hands. He gave his name.

"That completes the roster of witnesses, milord," the bailiff informed the tribunal.

"Very well." Bode recognized the voice of the judge with the learned face.

Before the judge could continue, Jaryd Hume called out, "If it pleases the court, I challenge this proceeding." *Oh, Jaryd,* Bode's mind raced, *what are you playing at?*

"What manner of challenge?" judge number three inquired sharply.

"I offer the Yeoman's Challenge," Jaryd stipulated. His voice cracked slightly, and the gallery tittered.

"You have the sound of the west country about you, young man," the apple-cheeked judge observed. "Are you a citizen of Ayle?"

"I am a student, enrolled at Antium Hall," Jaryd replied.

"The Yeoman's Challenge has become a bit arcane," the first

judge stated. "Jaryd Hume, is it? Do you understand the nature of the challenge?"

Jaryd nodded. "Answer the questions, boy," the no-nonsense judge directed.

"Jaryd Hume is my name, milord," Jaryd replied; his voice sounded steady the now, and Bode realized he was speaking to her. "I understand the nature of the challenge and request the Archer's Form."

"Do you stand for yourself alone or for the accused as well?" the third judge queried.

"For myself and the accused, milord," Jaryd answered firmly, looking Bode directly in the eye as he spoke.

"The accused will turn and face the tribunal." This was from the middle judge.

Bode complied, raising her eyes to the three men in their stately black robes. The first judge addressed her. "Called as a witness, Jaryd Hume has challenged this proceeding. He has that right. He has offered to serve as your champion in what is known as the Archer's Form. This is an archery contest in which he will be pitted against a champion of the court. Should you accept Jaryd Hume as your champion, your fates will be conjoined. If he prevails, your champion will be released from summons in this matter and you will be freed, all charges against you overwhelmed by his challenge. Should he be bested, you will be found guilty; all that will remain for this tribunal to decide is your sentencing, and your champion will be subject to arrest as an accomplice at the discretion of this tribunal. Do you understand?"

Bode raised her chin. "Is the Archer's Form a contest of skill or actual combat, milord?"

"It is a test of skill," the judge replied, "a difficult one."

"I understand, milord," Bode responded.

"Should you deny him as your champion," the same judge went on, "and presuming his challenge stands, he will duel for himself alone. This proceeding will continue upon completion of the challenge regardless of outcome. The charges against you will stand. Do you understand?"

"I do, milord," Bode answered.

"Do you accept Jaryd Hume as your champion?" the first judge asked.

"May I speak with him, milord?" Bode inquired.

"You may not," the third judge snapped.

"That does not seem fair, milord," Bode protested softly.

"It is, however, the law," the third judge said in as kindly a tone as she'd heard him use. "You must decide and do so the now."

Jaryd was her friend. She did not think it right that he put his freedom and potentially his life in jeopardy for her sake. He had, though, and Bode knew him well enough to know he would never withdraw his challenge. Lighthearted as he was most of the time, Jaryd could be as muley as any lad in the Three Rivers when he put his mind to it. Bode squared her shoulders. "I accept Jaryd Hume as my champion."

The tribunal put their heads together. After a brief discussion, the middle judge announced, "An Archer's Form is to be staged on the grounds of Gladstone Park adjacent to the courthouse at noon tomorrow. This proceeding stands adjourned until the challenge is resolved."

"If it pleases the court," Jaryd called out a second time, "I believe I have the right to demand the court name its champion from among those present."

The judges conferred a second time. The first judge spoke in response. "You have that right. Bailiff, are there any archers among your company?"

"Ezra Collins is a fair hand with a crossbow, milord," the head bailiff offered.

The third judged looked to the prosecutor. "Does the prosecutor have a champion on hand to recommend?"

The prosecutor looked across the room. Following his eyes, Bode saw he was looking at the young watch captain who had arrested her, Gordyn Rhow. The captain shook his head. "No, milord," the prosecutor said.

"Is Ezra Collins present?" the middle judge asked of the bailiff.

"I'll have him fetched, milord," the bailiff reported.

"If it pleases the court," Jaryd stated, "that won't be necessary, Ezra Collins and his crossbow it is."

"Very well," the middle judge tried a second time. "If there are no further questions, this proceeding is adjourned until the challenge presented is resolved." Taking up a sturdy brass bell resting atop the desk in front of him, the apple-cheeked judge rang it once, sharply. "Bailiff, return the accused to custody."

As she was led away, Bode cast a last quick glance at Jaryd. He flashed her a smile. For the first time since her arrest, Bode felt a stirring of hope. She wasn't alone; she never had been.

Soon after the hearing disbanded Jaryd was sitting on a bench beside a bare-branched oak at the edge of Gladstone Park next to the courthouse when he heard a soft voice inquire, "Do you have any idea what you are doing?"

Turning his head, he saw Dyrileah, flanked by her father and Rysah Kudreau. The young Elsacian girl wore a gray woolen cloak over a decidedly ordinary blue cotton frock. She'd wound her nearly hip-length hair of gold into a thick single braid, the end of which was looped over her right shoulder. Her tone and the look in her distinctly tilted brown eyes reflected an aura of concern.

The Elsacian men accompanying her were cloaked as well and wore nearly identical, flat-crowned, broad-brimmed black felt hats. The folds of both men's cloaks were thrown back, and Jaryd could see that each was armed with a brace of long-bladed daggers. The men's expressions were as guarded as their postures. Jaryd sat with Sebastyn's heavy walking stick across his knees. His Hawken rested in its sheath over his left hip. He rose to his feet.

"I imagine Bode is asking herself that same question just the now," Jaryd replied with a wry smile. "If I can't best some City Watchman armed with naught but a crossbow, my da will disown me."

"Where were you last night?" Dyrileah asked anxiously. "I waited and waited."

"Did you tell anyone of our meeting?" Jaryd met her question with one of his own.

"Only my father. Why?" Dyrileah queried.

"Spats insisted on accompanying me," Jared recounted. "On the way to White Garden, we were attacked by a pair of Elsacian men wielding half-crossbows. They made a muck of it. I killed one. The other got away. Spats was hurt pretty badly."

"Oh, Jaryd, how terrible." Dyrileah took a step toward the young farmer's son, her hand lifted as if to touch him. The look in his eyes froze her in place, her arm only half raised. "Is Spats all right?" she managed. Dyrileah would never have imagined Jaryd could look at anyone so coldly, her least of all.

"He'll live," Jaryd declared shortly.

"Were you near the park?" Dyrileah asked next. Upon seeing his nod, she continued. "Why didn't you bring him to me?"

"One of our attackers shouted something as he shot. My Elsacian is pretty bad," Jaryd replied. "About all I could really make out was your name. Spats told me after what the man said was 'Dyrileah sends her regards.'"

Dyrileah's brown eyes, so beautiful, so often full of light, widened with shock. "Jaryd, you can't think—"

"You said you told no one but your father." Jaryd did not raise his voice, but still it rang, hard as steel. He locked eyes with those of Bardus Quirow.

Bardus's eyes were very like those of his daughter: wideset, tilted in the Elsacian manner, and a rich, walnut brown in color. "I know nothing of the attempt on your life, Jaryd."

"With respect, Bardus, that's a little hard to swallow," Jaryd said evenly. "Did you tell anyone about the meeting Dyrileah and I had planned?"

"I did not," Bardus answered without so much as blinking.

"My father does not lie." Anger laced Dyrileah's quietly spoken words. "There must be some other explanation."

"I'd like to hear it," Jaryd said flatly.

"Jaryd," Dyrileah pled as if she could not comprehend what he'd just said. "Surely you cannot think I would lie to you?"

Jaryd's jaw clenched. "It wouldn't be the first time."

Dyrileah's eyes flashed. "What do you mean?"

"I saw you," Jaryd grated, "and him." He thrust his chin at Rysah Kudreau. "By the fountain at White Garden the other night. I saw what passed between you. You told me you came alone."

"I was afraid you would not understand." Dyrileah's voice sounded barely a whisper the now.

"You were right," Jaryd ground out. "I remember a story you told me once, under a wintry sky in the moons' light, a beautiful story about the mere pressing of flesh. That wasn't true either, was it?"

Dyrileah shook her head, not in denial but in a plea for understanding. She extended her hands toward him. "I thought that part of my life was over. I meant what I said to you."

"The first time we lay together, you told me you were unknown to man," Jaryd said in hard, cutting tones. "Was that a lie too?" He regretted the words even before he'd finished speaking them but could not stop himself.

Dyrileah recoiled as if he'd spat on her. "You've twisted everything. You're choked with jealousy and spite. What we shared…How could you?" She flung the question at him as if it were a stone. From about her neck, she jerked his grandmother's necklace free, breaking the finely wrought chain. Extending her arm to full length, she dropped the keepsake into the dirt at his feet. Turning on her heel, she fled. Rysah Kudreau followed quickly after.

"When first we met, Jaryd Hume, I thought you a fool," Bardus Quirow remarked sadly. "I'd begun to hope I was wrong."

"Why are you here?" Jaryd asked harshly. "Did you attend the hearing?"

"Doing so was deemed too dangerous," Quirow responded. "An associate of ours was present, however; he relayed the happenings."

"Why did he do so?" Jaryd pressed.

"We were concerned about what might be revealed here today," Bardus told him.

"Concerned enough to have me silenced?" Jaryd queried, looking steadily into Bardus's eyes.

"I've already told you I know nothing of the attempt on your life." Bardus met Jaryd's gaze without flinching. "I will inquire. We will speak again once I've learned what there is to know." His voice hardened. "Until then, stay away from me and my family."

44

The Yeoman's Challenge

"Remove her manacles," Captain Gordyn Rhow directed Tall and Skinny while standing in the middle of a larger cell in the Old Mill prison. The chamber was stone-walled and windowless. Bode found herself longing for her original accommodations, however tiny and damp.

Tall and Skinny complied. For a moment, Bode was relieved to have the heavy steel things gone from about her wrists. "Hold her," Rhow ordered. Standing behind her, Short and Stocky clasped Bode's left arm just above the elbow. Taking hold of her right wrist, the watchman bent her arm painfully behind her back, lifting and twisting expertly just enough to make her cry out.

"Confess," Gordyn Rhow entreated, his voice soft and intense. "Confess, and there will be no need for any of this. A public flogging, that's all, a dozen lashes and it will be over. A healer will see that only a single stripe remains as a reminder of your penance."

"You can't do this," Bode gasped.

"You thought you were being clever, didn't you?" Rhow speculated. "Having your henchman offer to stand as champion. Clever indeed that was, but it will avail you naught. Tomorrow is a long way off, Mistress Ware, and you are mine until that time. Confess, and let us put an end to this."

"No." Bode wept, ashamed beyond words at her tears.

"Gag her," Rhow ordered. Tall and Skinny did so, tying a greasy cotton rag tightly across her mouth. "Remove her clothes." His eyes glinting nearly black in the harsh yellow light of the torch set into a wrought-iron stanchion in the wall of her cell, Rhow watched intently as Tall and Skinny reached for the laces at the front of Bode's dress. She screamed into the rag, heaving and bucking futilely in Short and Stocky's powerful grip, while Tall and Skinny methodically stripped her.

Naked, she was dragged to the rear of the cell, where her arms were lashed to a rugged wooden crossbeam. Square cut, about half a span on a side, the beam was fixed to ropes and pulleys. Hauling on the rope, Short and Stocky lifted Bode free of the ground, just far enough so the tips of her toes would reach the stone floor of the cell if she stretched her leg to its fullest extent. Rhow held the torch close to her face. She could feel the heat of it nearly singeing her flesh.

"Already the red wheals form," Rhow observed. He briefly fingered the crude links of the black iron chain about her throat. "Proof for any with eyes to see that a witch you are. I should run my dagger through your black heart and be done with it. But with justice, there is also mercy. Confess, witch, and you shall know mercy. Refuse, and you shall have none."

Bode shook her head; the gag tasted foul. She was terrified Rhow would burn her face with the torch. Instead, he lowered the burning brand. "The night is long, witch, and we have only just begun."

They left her there, dangling from the crossbeam in the dark of her cell. At first, the worst of it was the gag in her mouth. Bode wanted to wretch. She was able to ward off the dreadful urge by breathing slowly and deeply through her nose. After only a little while, though, breathing became increasingly difficult. Her arms and shoulders burned, and Bode soon found she could no longer take a full breath. Extending her right leg, she pressed her toes against the floor. That offered some relief, taking weight off her arms; her diaphragm expanded slightly. The air filling her lungs felt good, calming.

Very shortly, her right thigh began to tremble with the strain. She switched to her left leg but couldn't quite achieve the purchase she needed. Having no other choice, she changed back. Bode's right calf cramped; a powerful spasm rippled through her leg. The pain was intense. Her body sagged, her full weight pulling at her arms. She couldn't breathe, and panic took hold. Thrashing helplessly against the lashings securing her to the beam, she gasped and choked. Consciousness teetered.

The next she was aware, Short and Stocky held her by one arm, while Tall and Skinny grasped the other. Rhow stood before her under the harsh glare of the torch once more. They had removed her gag. Reaching out, the watch captain coiled her braid in his fingers, twisting her head back so he could peer into her eyes. "You are weak, witch. Others of your kind have withstood the beam for much longer. Confess."

Bode's throat convulsed, she could not form the word. She tossed head in the negative as best she could with him holding tight to her hair. Rhow smiled a hard, grim smile, void of mirth. "I say again witch, the night is long, and we have only just begun." His eyes flicked to Tall and Skinny. "Pin her, face down, over the table."

They must have brought it with them. The writing table, unvarnished, battered, and scarred, had certainly not been in the chamber before. The two guards held her, face down, across the table. The writing surface was tall enough so that her feet could not reach the floor. "You have known pain, witch, and a little fear," Rhow told her conversationally. "Next, you will experience humiliation. And then we shall begin in earnest." Rhow thrust his hand between her legs from behind and pushed his finger inside her. Bode cried out. "Confess, witch," Rhow rasped breathily, his voice thick and hot. "Confess, and we will spare you this." He worked his finger deeper into her most intimate flesh.

The knock that sounded on the cell door sounded firm and perfunctory. "I understand an interrogation is in progress, the subject of which pertains to witchcraft," a familiar voice announced. "As an axton of the church, I believe I have the right to be present."

"Tomorrow, Axton," Watch Captain Rhow said firmly. "Tomorrow you may interrogate the witch to your heart's content. Tonight, you must leave us to our work."

"That won't do, Captain." The Axton's rich voice sounded equal parts amused and scandalized. "We all have superiors, you know. Mine would never tolerate such a breach of duty. Either you will open this door, or to avoid difficulty with my superior, I shall have Father Laurence here fetch yours. Which shall it be?"

Rhow removed his hand. The two watchmen pulled Bode off the table and held her between them. Rhow opened the cell door, and Father Vars Nebus Bayu stepped through. The priest was clad in the robes of his office, simple woolen garments of gray wool. Bode was suddenly, achingly aware of her nakedness. Mortified, she began to sob.

"I see your methods are rather crude, Captain," Father Vars observed. "Has she confessed?"

"Not yet." Rhow bit off the words; his eyes glittered dangerously.

Apparently oblivious, Father Vars went on. "Your zeal is commendable, Captain, however ineptly applied. While I hesitate to beleaguer the point, I believe that in matters of this sort, officials of the church have first call when it comes to interrogating the accused. Is that not correct?"

"It is, Axton," Rhow grated.

"She appears to be rather stubborn," Father Vars mused, scratching his chin. "Most Tieran Territorials are, you know. This is liable to take some time. Father Laurence will attend to my needs, gentlemen." Bayu nodded toward a tall, wide-shouldered young priest standing in the doorway. "I assure you we won't misplace your prisoner while we are about it. You are welcome to stay, of course, in the spirit of cooperation between the church and, ah, the secular authority you represent."

Rhow looked to his two watchmen. "Stand guard outside. Keep a close watch." He turned and left, brushing past the muscular young priest. Short and Stocky and Tall and Skinny followed.

"If I need any assistance, Father, I shall call to you," Father Vars said to the younger priest. Father Laurence stepped out. The door closed; Bode and Father Vars stood alone in the cell. The flickering light of the torch, so harsh a moment before, seemed to have softened.

Bode fell to her knees. "Father Vars, I meant no harm..."

"Hush, child." Father Vars dropped to his knees beside her. Removing his cloak, he draped it about Bode's shoulders. "Silence is your best weapon the now—that and the keen eye of a certain young archer, eh?" He put his arm around her. "Be at ease. Come, let us sit down. These stones are hard on an old man's knees."

They sat in the corner of the cell; his arm felt warm, firm, and reassuring. "How have they hurt you, my dear?" he asked gently.

"I am not badly hurt, Father, only frightened and ashamed," Bode murmured.

"Here, then." Father Vars handed her a silk handkerchief. "Wipe your tears. You are made of sturdy stuff, Bode Ware. I've known that since you were ten years old."

"Oh, Father..." Bode began to weep.

"All right then." Father Vars put both arms around her. "That's all right." The priest held her close while she cried. When she quieted, Father Vars released her, saying, "I'll turn my back so you can dress."

Bode did so. It took her a while. Her whole body ached, and Bode's fingers felt stiff and clumsy for some reason.

When she finished, Father Vars turned to her. "It is nearly dawn. I got here as soon as I could. They...well, I had some difficulty. You have great courage, my dear, and great strength, more than you know. Let us pray, and then I think you should try to sleep a bit."

"I don't think I can, Father," Bode said. "Pray, that is. I'm not sure I believe anymore."

"My child..." Father Vars smiled. "When our faith is tested, when we are sore of heart and vexed by doubt, that is the best time to pray."

"I have prayed, Father, and prayed," Bode cried, her voice ragged with emotion. "He has taken Mat from me and then my freedom and my dignity. What has He left me? Why should I believe?"

"People choose, Bode, and we all bear the consequences," Father Vars said patiently. "That is our doing, not His." Bode shook her head. "Pray, child," Father Vars urged. "He will not abandon you. His love is greater than your doubt, your grief, and your rage. He will bear their weight and lift you up. Seek, and you shall yet find His purpose in your life. You see, Bode. The All Father does not exist because we choose to believe in him. The truth is we exist because, for some reason beyond all human understanding, He has chosen to believe in us."

Father Vars bent to his knees, his old man's knees, on the hard stone floor of the cell and clasped his hands before him. In a moment, Bode joined him, and together they prayed.

Jaryd arrived in Gladstone Park in the hour before noon. A beautiful winter day it was, chilly but bright. The sun shone overhead, while only a few wisps of feathery white clouds danced beneath the deep-blue dome of the sky above. He was surprised by the crowd. Hundreds of people lined the walkways of the park. He could see vendors hawking strips of braised beef on a stick and corn fritters. Air in the park smelled like that of a carnival. *Popular as a bloody hanging.* The thought raised a knot in his stomach.

Just ahead, he saw a small pavilion awning had been erected. Three large, intricately carved wooden chairs, placed atop a raised platform, sat empty in the shade of it. Reckoning the pavilion had to be for the benefit of the tribunal, Jaryd turned his steps toward it. In addition to the City Watch, whose officers were readily identifiable by their black leather jerkins, what looked to be a full company of soldiers, clad in the livery of the King's Guard, had also been turned out to keep order. Win or lose, Jaryd figured he would have just about worn out his welcome in Antium after this afternoon's contest. Probably just as well that twas. He never really wanted to be a lawyer in the first place.

A pair of targets had been placed at the far end of a treelined yard. Constructed of whitewashed boards, cut and nailed into a square about a pace to a side, the targets stood glistening in the midday sun. Affixed to the center of each board was an iron ring exactly, according to Sebastyn's Book of Common Laws, two-thirds span in diameter. The targets would be located seventy-five paces from a shooter's mark. The champion of the accused would shoot first. Three arrows would be loosed. If none struck inside the ring, the accused person's champion would automatically lose the challenge.

If one or more of the first contestant's shots landed within the ring, the court's champion would be required to better the marks achieved in order to prevail. In other words, from the accused champion's perspective, there were two ways to lose. Placing an arrow inside a two-thirds-span circle from seventy-five paces was a difficult but not impossible shot. Jaryd had done as well at archery contests back home and dozens of times while shooting with his father. Of course, his life and Bode's had never before hung in the balance. Jaryd was nervous and more than a little scared. He wished with all his heart his father were there to do the shooting. Byan Hume would not miss when it counted.

In his left hand, Jaryd carried Dark Hope, a powerful, doubly curved long bow fashioned mostly of golden yew. Dark Hope was a named weapon, as fine an example of the bowyer's art as Jaryd had ever seen, worthy of a hero's hand. Hefting the bow, Jaryd thought, *It's me you're stuck with the now, my beauty.*

Jaryd was clad in farmers' clothes from back home, a butternut brown woolen shirt that fell to a couple of finger widths above his knees fastened at his waist by a wide leather belt. He wore his favorite pair of boots, sturdy, well-worn, and comfortable, and a Three Rivers watch cap atop his head. In a sheath over his left hip he carried his grandfather's heavy-bladed Hawken knife, a full span of razor-sharp, layered steel; the weight of it at his belt lent him confidence. Across his back was slung a full quiver of arrows fletched with gray goose feathers.

A mix of broad-head and pile arrows they were. The pile or flight arrowhead was pyramidal in shape with long, shallow sloped sides that narrowed at the tip to form a needlelike point. Flight arrows were used for long-distance shooting and were ideal for punching through even the finest chain mail. Jaryd had selected three perfectly balanced flight arrows for the day's contest.

He saw Bode being walked out, flanked by a pair of black-clad watchmen, one tall and skinny, the other short and stocky. They made her climb onto the back of a small wooden cart, a condition designed both to publicly display and demean. Bode stood erect, her slim shoulders back. Her wrists manacled, a black iron chain about her throat, she looked straight ahead, ignoring the jibes and jeers directed at her by some in the crowd. Only a few, Jaryd noted. Most in the throng were silent and watchful.

The tribunal arrived next, the same trio of judges that presided at first hearing the day before. Dressed in the black robes of their office with small, round-topped, black silk caps atop their heads, the judges walked quickly to the chairs provided for them in the shade of the pavilion.

The head bailiff, also a veteran of yesterday's proceedings, took up his stance in front of the pavilion. "Attend, all ye present. The High Court of Antium is in session the now. Judges of the Third Tribunal presiding."

"Our purpose today is to witness a Yeoman's Challenge, to be conducted in the Archer's Form," the portly middle judge called in a firm, clear voice. "The outcome of said challenge is to determine the guilt of one Bodewhin Ware, who stands accused of the crime of witchcraft. Is the champion of the accused present?"

"I am, milord," Jaryd stated, trying to match the tone of the judge's voice.

"Is the court's champion present?" the same judge asked next.

"I am, milord," a stocky member of the City Watch, judging by the black leather jerkin he wore, replied. Collins, Jaryd thought the man's name was. His competitor was half a head shorter but noticeably wider across the chest and shoulders, with hair as red as his own. The crossbow in Collins's hands looked to Jaryd's eyes like all such weapons: squat, ugly, and dangerous.

"Are you ready to begin?" the third judge, a skinny fellow with an impatient air about him and a thick crown of very white hair, inquired.

Jaryd and the watchman Collins indicated they were. "Then let's be about it," the third judge directed. "The champion of the accused shall shoot first. To qualify, you must place at least one arrow inside the target ring."

As challenger, Jaryd had the choice of target. His heart hammering, he stepped to the shooter's mark on the left. Gazing downrange, he saw a flag on a pole rising above the courthouse, dancing to and fro in a swirl of wind. The target suddenly seemed impossibly far away. He felt panic welling in his breast. The breeze itself was no great impediment, but Jaryd knew with grim certainty if he shot the now, he'd never place an arrow anywhere near the ring.

Looking across the yard, his eyes latched upon Bode standing as if hewn from marble atop her little cart. Desperate, Jaryd turned toward a tall cavalryman standing guard a few paces away. Walking to him, Jaryd held Dark Hope out to the big, mail-clad soldier.

"What's this?" the soldier asked. Jaryd realized the soldier was about his own age, no more than a year or two older anyhow.

"Would you mind this for me a moment?" Jaryd requested. "There's something I need to do first."

"You should have piddled before stepping out here," the soldier guessed.

"That's not it." Jaryd found himself smiling.

The soldier took Jaryd's bow. "Best be quick, whatever it is," he warned.

Nodding, Jaryd turned and walked across the yard to stand before Bode's cart. "Get away from here," the tall and skinny watchman growled.

Ignoring him, Jaryd looked up at Bode. "How do you fare?"

Bode gazed down at him, her wide gray eyes calm and still. "Do you have any idea what you're doing?"

"The wind is swirling," Jaryd told her.

"Oh." Bode nodded. "Thank you, Jaryd."

"You might want to wait a bit until I've done something worth the thanking." Jaryd's self-deprecating smile was as familiar to Bode as the warm aroma of her mother's kitchen on First Day morning and as welcome.

"You've done more than you know already," Bode told him sincerely.

Raising his right hand to chest height, Jaryd clenched his fist. "Three Rivers," he called out.

Burdened as she was by the manacles she wore, Bode emulated Jaryd's gesture as best she could. "Three Rivers," she cried in reply.

The sight of her small fist, thrust through the cruel steel shackle, and the flesh of her slender wrist, torn and bruised, sent a wave of cold rage coursing through Jaryd's veins. *What right had they to treat her like that?* His step firmed with each stride as he walked back to the soldier's side.

"Thanks," Jaryd said as he took hold once again of Dark Hope.

"Do you have any idea what you're doing?" the soldier wondered.

"I wish people would stop asking me that," Jaryd muttered as he moved once more to the shooter's mark. Taking his stance, he looked again at the flag atop the courthouse. The banner hung blessedly still. Jaryd gazed intently downrange, focusing on the target. It was as if he could feel his father's hand upon his shoulder. Jaryd set the first arrow to his bow. Raising Dark Hope, he pressed and loosed. The heavy bow thrummed as the arrow leapt away.

Ned Bly stood at the edge of the crowd, only a few steps distant. A few of his troopers had been among those selected to provide security for the day's trial. As far as Ned could tell, the young archer in his rough farmers' clothes aimed not at all. Three times he shot—three long, fluid movements, unhurried but startlingly fast. Three times, gray fletched arrows streaked across the yard, tracing flat, wicked arcs in the bright noonday sun to stand quivering one after the other in the heart of the iron ring at the center of the left-hand target.

The crowd lining the pathways of the park stood in absolute silence. "Three Rivers," Bode's voice rang, pure as a bell. "Three Rivers," she shouted again, raising her manacled wrists above her head. Looking her way, Jaryd tipped the bill of his watch cap.

Ned watched as Jaryd walked over to stand at the big trooper's side. "Looks like you knew what you were about all along," the cavalryman, whose name was Dolan, commented.

"Not over yet," Jaryd replied.

Ezra Collins stepped up to the shooter's mark on the right. Leveling his heavy crossbow, Collins aimed and pressed the trigger. Ned heard the clang as the quill struck the iron circlet, slamming into the target a hair's breadth outside the ring. Collins lowered his weapon and turned away. No point there was in him shooting again. The match was done. Jaryd Hume had won.

45

Disparate Ends

"Champions, attend," the bailiff shouted, pointing to a spot just in front of the tribunal's pavilion.

Moments later, Jaryd stood beside Collins the City Watchman, gazing up at the trio of judges in their tall chairs. The apple-cheeked middle judge pitched his voice to carry all throughout the crowded park space. "The challenger has prevailed. This proceeding is closed. Release the prisoner."

Her two guards pulled Bode none too gently down from the small cart upon which she'd been standing. They removed her manacles but left the ugly, black iron collar chained about her neck. Jaryd walked toward her. The crowd began to mill. People suddenly drifted between them. For an instant, Jaryd lost sight of her.

"Jaryd," Bode cried. For the first time that day, he heard fear in her voice. Slipping by a portly fellow in a velvet waistcoat, Jaryd managed to close the distance between them. "Oh, Jaryd," Bode cried again, softly, as she stepped into his arms.

Holding her close, Jaryd felt his throat tighten. Bode had been a constant companion in his youth, a friend, a confidant, sometimes his nemesis. She usually gave as good as she got; he'd say that much for her. Her slender form felt small and soft and hurt in his arms. "It's all right the now, Bode," he told her. "It's all right the now."

No sooner were the words out of his mouth than Jaryd had cause to wonder. Glancing up, he saw three tough-looking men in shabby work clothes with heavy wooden truncheons in their hands working their way toward them. Aside from his bow, Jaryd was armed only with his Hawken. Lethal as she was at a distance, Dark Hope would be of but little use at close quarters.

Jaryd started to shift Bode behind him when a friendly voice called out, "Would you mind if we walked along with you?"

A tall young man wearing the uniform of the King's Guard stood confidently a few paces away; ranged behind him were an even dozen cavalrymen—among them, Jaryd noticed the big fellow with whom he'd left Dark Hope just before beginning the archery duel.

"Ned," Bode spoke from within the comforting circle of Jaryd's arms, "what are you doing here?"

Ned Bly smiled, blue eyes crinkling. "It's a nice day for an archery contest. A couple of the boys had the duty." He jerked a thumb at the tall soldier Jaryd had spoken with. "The rest of us thought we'd have ourselves a look, eat some braised beef on a skewer, and take a bit of a walk after. Couldn't decide where, so we thought we might tag along with the two of you." He glanced casually in the direction of the three toughs, his hand brushing the hilt of the long sword at his belt.

Eying the soldiers balefully, the trio melted back into the crowd without a word.

"I guess I'm not very popular," Bode said softly, watching them go. "Being seen with me might not be such a good idea."

"A little scandal will do wonders for my reputation." Ned scoffed. "As for this lot"—he indicated his men with a wave of his hand—"they're nothing but rogues end scoundrels to begin with." He lowered his voice. "As we are rather small in numbers, however, I suggest we get moving. Can you walk?"

"I'll bloody well run if I have to," Bode asserted.

Quiet laughter rippled through the cavalrymen at Ned Bly's

side. Two or three of them smiled openly at Bode. *Of course they would*, Jaryd figured. Accused of witchery or no, Bode was likely the prettiest girl any of them had ever seen and somehow, after all she'd been through, still full of sauce to boot.

Jaryd led them back to the sanctuary. As they approached, he could see Sebastyn and Father Vars—try as he might, he would never be able to think of Hexus Rygg as anyone other than the kindly prelate he'd known growing up—standing together at the top of the steps leading to the front door of the building.

Ned Bly called his men to a halt at the base of the stairs. "I don't suppose we'll be seeing much of one another after this," he said to Bode.

"It doesn't seem likely," she concurred.

"That's a damn shame." Ned smiled his easy, charming smile. "Probably just as well. You always were too good for the likes of me." Raising his voice, Ned called to his troopers, "C'mon, lads, time for you to collect the mug or three I promised." Sketching a brief but elegantly formal bow to Bode, the tall, young nobleman strode away at the head of his soldiers.

Bode nearly fainted when Sebastyn cut through the black iron chain and removed it from her throat. Ugly red sores had formed wherever the iron touched her skin.

Bode clung weakly to Jaryd and vowed, "I'll never be collared again. They'll have to kill me first."

"Let me heal you," Sebastyn requested gently.

Reaching out, Bode clasped his hand and nodded. The three of them were standing in a small sitting room overlooking the street below. Though not large, the room was comfortably accoutered with a quartet of overstuffed brown leather chairs and a thickly cushioned settee. A round writing table flanked by a pair of simple, straight-backed wooden chairs occupied the center of the chamber. Sebastyn placed one hand on either side of Bode's temple. Jaryd kept one arm firmly about her shoulders to steady her. Sebastyn's vivid blue eyes narrowed, and Bode shuddered. A few moments later, he stepped back. Jaryd saw that the welts on Bode's neck had vanished as if they never were. Her color was better, but her fine gray eyes, usually so lively, looked hollow still.

"Some things will take time," Sebastyn said in a soft, reassuring tone.

The door of the sitting room opened, and Father Vars stepped inside. He smiled warmly at Bode. "How are you, young lady?"

"I am alive and well and *free*," Bode replied with quiet dignity, "thanks to the three of you." Tears welled then. Sebastyn pulled a handkerchief from his tunic pocket and passed it on to Bode.

The three men spent the next few moments looking uncomfortably at one another, the books lining the shelves built cleverly into the walls, the dust motes dancing in the sunlight as it filtered through the window, and generally anything except the young woman standing in their midst, silently wiping her eyes.

Finally, Father Vars cleared his throat. "Some news, I'm afraid," he told them. "I am reliably informed that the authorities are planning a series of raids in the Elsacian Quarter with the objective of rounding up so-called known witches and their accomplices, beginning at dusk tomorrow. My source was unsure as to who exactly would be targeted, but the raids are said to be extensive. Soldiers will be called to support the action in addition to the City Watch. Even a handful of sorcerers from the Ryll are supposed to be participating."

"That tears it." Sebastyn sighed as he stalked to the window. "I think it is time for me to be going."

"Don't be too hasty," Father Vars urged. "I do not think anyone knows who you are or what your purpose is here. This will undoubtedly cause a disruption, but it will pass."

"That may be, Hexus," Sebastyn countered, "but I'm tired of waiting and accomplishing not enough. Perhaps if I spoke with Ellyendre?"

"That is not likely to end well," Father Vars said in reply.

"She's helped us before," Sebastyn pointed out. "If you're right and my purpose here remains hidden to our foes, then the attempt will cost us nothing but a bit of time."

"Time may be running short," Father Vars warned.

"Which is why I feel compelled to do *something* while this city descends into chaos," Sebastyn retorted.

"I'm surprised you've stuck it out this long," Father Vars relented. "You and your itchy feet."

"I'm going to do some traveling," Sebastyn announced, looking Bode's way. "Going cap in hand, as a matter of fact, to beg a favor from a witch nearly as charming as you are, my dear. I could use your help. Would you be willing to come along?"

Jaryd saw the hollow expression in Bode's tear-washed eyes fade just a trifle. "If you think I could be of help, of course I will."

"What about you, son?" Sebastyn's blue-eyed gaze settled on Jaryd. "It's liable to be a good stretch of the legs."

"I couldn't very well let the two of you wander off alone," Jaryd answered. "I have a favor to ask first, though."

"What favor would that be?" Sebastyn inquired.

"I'd like your permission to warn Dyrileah and her people."

"That might get a little interesting," Sebastyn mused. "Suppose I said no?" Jaryd's jaw firmed. Sebastyn chuckled. "My question was rhetorical. You have my permission on one condition."

"What condition would that be?" Jaryd wondered.

"That I have your permission to accompany you," Sebastyn stated.

"Considering what happened on our last outing," Jaryd remarked, "why exactly would you want to do a thing like that?"

"I think it is about time I met Bardus Quirow."

"Not two full days ago, you had a crossbow bolt sticking out of your chest," Jaryd reminded him.

"I doubt I could manage handsprings," Sebastyn allowed, "but if you can refrain from sprinting the whole way there, I'll get by." The old sorcerer and the young archer grinned at one another, looking like nothing so much as a pair of naughty little boys.

"Perhaps I should come along as well," Bode suggested.

"I think," Father Vars put in hastily, "that your time would be better spent here, Bode. There is something I believe you should see and do that will help you"—he paused a moment as if searching for the right words—"prepare for what lies ahead."

"If you say so, Father," Bode said meekly. She shifted her gaze to Sebastyn and then Jaryd in turn. "Should you two blunder into trouble or cause any for Dyrileah, you'll have to answer to me." The gray-eyed beauty's tone had lost any hint of meekness, and then some, by the time she finished speaking.

"Yes, ma'am," Sebastyn and Jaryd echoed in near-perfect unison, taking their turn at sounding meek.

Jaryd and Sebastyn waited until full dark before slipping out a side gate of the sanctuary. Even by the roundabout route they chose, an hour's walk found them knocking at the front door of the Quirow townhouse in the Elsacian Quarter of the city. Tamyra answered the door. The twelve-year-old took one look at Jaryd and then stepped quickly across the threshold to fling her arms about his waist.

"You shouldn't be here," Tamyra told him.

Holding his styaxe in his left hand, Jaryd stroked her hair gently with his right. "I know. I'm sorry. I need to speak with Dyrileah or your father. It is important."

Tamyra stepped back a bit and appeared to take note of Sebastyn for the first time. Her eyes widened at the sight of the sorcerer's stave he bore. "Who is he?"

"A friend, Tamy," Jaryd said quietly. "Please, trust me."

Tamyra stepped back and beckoned the pair of them inside. "They're both in the kitchen," she informed them.

Upon entering the house, Jaryd leaned his styaxe against the hall tree standing in the corner of the parlor. Sebastyn held on to his stave.

"What is your name?" Tamyra asked of the sorcerer.

Sebastyn executed the same awkward-looking bow he had when Jaryd first introduced him to Dyrileah, bending over an extended left leg. "I am Sebastyn Card, my lady."

Tamyra's big brown eyes, so like her elder sister's, went wide as saucers. She looked at Jaryd. "What have you been up to?"

"I'll explain," Jaryd promised.

"You'd better," Tamyra warned. She looked at Sebastyn. "Are you really Sebastyn Card?" At the old sorcerer's nod, Tamyra opined, "I thought you'd be taller."

"When I was your age, young lady," Sebastyn said confidentially, "so did I."

Bardus Quirow sat at the kitchen table, a steaming mug of tea before him. Ester and Dyrileah stood at the counter, aprons about their waists, drying dishes, facing away from the door.

"Visitors, Patua," Tamyra called as she led Jaryd and Sebastyn into the room.

"Friends," Jaryd said quietly, "if you'll have us."

At the sound of his voice, Dyrileah whirled about. "What are you doing here?"

Before Jaryd could respond, Sebastyn stepped in front of him, raising his right forefinger to his lips in an imperious gesture for silence. Taking two long steps across the kitchen floor, he pointed the same finger at a jade carving sitting on a shelf at the back of the room. When he was certain both Bardus and Dyrileah had taken note, Sebastyn held aloft his stave and slowly moved his right hand, tracing a circle from left to right in the air before him. He lowered his stave. Dyrileah gasped, covering her mouth with the fingers of her right hand. Bardus said nothing, but his features tightened with anger.

"Attend," Sebastyn rasped in a throaty whisper that sounded nothing like his usual mellow tone. He raised his stave a second time; the fingers of his right hand flickered. Lowering his staff, the white-haired sorcerer spent the next few moments stalking about the kitchen. If Jaryd didn't know better, he could have sworn the old man was sniffing the air. Finally, Sebastyn straightened and leaned on his stave. "That's done it. We can speak freely the now, at least in this room."

"Will someone explain what just happened?" Jaryd requested.

"The jade carving is a magic device," Sebastyn related. "Called a vox, it is a vile thing used for eavesdropping. Normally such a contraption would be readily detected by anyone with the capability to invoke the Yir." Sebastyn paused and bowed briefly to Bardus Quirow. "Or summon the One. The ward that enables this particular vox, however, has been inverted. This masks the weave, making it appear invisible. It isn't, of course, but to sense it, one must search in a particular manner." He glanced again at Bardus. "It is a matter of polarity."

"That carving allowed someone to listen to the conversations held in this room," Jaryd asked, testing his understanding, "from some remote location?"

"It would appear"—Bardus Quirow spoke softly, but there was no mistaking the steel in his voice—"that Rysah Kudreau has much to answer for." Kudreau had presented the jade carving as a regard gift to the Quirows some time back. Jaryd and Dyrileah shared a look of understanding.

"I think that answers your question at least," Jaryd stated, speaking to Sebastyn. He slipped the Fey talisman out of his shirt for all to see. "If you knew that your adversary was in possession of a talisman but were uncertain of its properties, might you not think it best to attack him with a heartstone-tipped weapon just in case?"

Sebastyn nodded. "Sounds logical. Who is Rysah Kudreau?"

"A dead man," Bardus growled in a voice that brooked no further discussion, "if his answers do not suit better than his actions of late."

"Bardus," Ester Quirow exclaimed, "the children!"

Bardus glanced at Dyrileah. Apparently satisfied with what he read in his eldest daughter's eyes, he rested his gaze on Tamyra. "Our daughters, Ester, are both mature enough to hear the truth and strong enough to bear its weight." He looked next to Sebastyn. "We are in your debt, sorcerer. Will you honor us by giving your name?"

"He's Sebastyn Card," Tamyra blurted.

"Are you indeed?" Bardus inquired mildly.

"I am," Sebastyn replied simply. "And you must be Bardus Quirow."

Bardus nodded. "My wife, Ester."

Sebastyn bowed once more to the both of them in that odd Elsacian manner, saying, "May the Light fill this house and bless all who dwell within."

"You are welcome here, Sebastyn," Ester Quirow responded

with a formal curtsy, sweeping her left leg gracefully in front of her right as lithely as any girl.

"I don't wish to be abrupt," Bardus said abruptly, "but why have you come?"

Jaryd conveyed the information Hexus Rygg had provided concerning the raids planned by the city authorities to round up known witches and accomplices. Bardus listened impassively and then asked, "Why should we believe you?"

"Bardus," Ester chided, genuinely angry.

Bardus calmly raised his hand in a placating gesture. "I want to hear Jaryd's answer."

"I don't expect you to believe me," Jaryd replied. "I expect you to consider that whatever the cost of accepting our warning and acting upon it should it prove false will pale in comparison to doing nothing if it is true."

"Clever. A lawyer's answer." Bardus shook his head. "I'd hoped for better."

"I owe you an apology," Jaryd said to Dyrileah. "This is the least I could do to make amends. You were right about me. I was jealous. I spoke out of spite."

"I meant to tell you about Rysah." Dyrileah took a step toward him. "I never expected—that is, I never intended…I didn't know how."

"It doesn't matter, not anymore," Jaryd avowed.

Dyrileah regarded him silently for a moment. "I can see from the look in your eyes that it does matter." She tossed her head. "I cared for him. I always have. But I've never loved anyone the way I love you. When I saw you that day in the park, I knew. I was so ashamed, I couldn't—"

Closing the distance separating them, Jaryd took her hand. "What do my eyes tell you the now?"

She lifted her gaze to meet his, her eyes searching. She smiled slowly and flung herself into his arms. "Beloved," she cried.

"Beloved," Jaryd affirmed. "Can you forgive me?"

Dyrileah nodded. "If you will do the same for me."

"Ahem," Sebastyn rumbled. "Excuse me." The sorcerer turned to Bardus Quirow. "What will you do?"

"We have been expecting something like this for some time," Bardus responded. "We have established certain contingencies. It will be necessary for some of us to go into hiding, while others will leave the city altogether, at least for a while. Your warning is timely. We are indebted to you for it as well."

"What will happen to you?" Jaryd queried Dyrileah.

Rearing back in his arms slightly, she said, "I will be among those leaving the city."

Jaryd frowned. "I don't suppose you will tell me where you're going?"

Dyrileah shook her head. "I don't suppose you'd care to come along?"

"Dyrileah," Ester said warningly, "that is not your decision to make."

"Don't worry, Mistress." Jaryd glanced briefly at Ester Quirow before gazing once again into her daughter's luminous brown eyes. "I can't. Turns out I'm going to be leaving the city too."

"To do his bidding?" Dyrileah cast a level look at Sebastyn Card.

"I owe him my life," Jaryd interjected gently, "and I believe he is trying to do right."

Dyrileah shook her head and hugged him tightly.

"Would you consider changing your travel plans?" Jaryd inquired.

"I can't," Dyrileah said softly, miserably. "I have—"

"Obligations," Jaryd overrode her sadly. "I know. We never did have much of a chance, did we?"

Dyrileah pressed her fingers against his lips. "Don't say that. Can you tell me where you will be?"

Kissing her fingertips, Jaryd replied, "I don't know where we're bound. At journey's end, I'll be going home to Greystock Village in the Three Rivers. Greystock isn't a very big place, but it isn't hard to find either, and the mail runs regularly. I'll be easy to locate should anyone be interested in looking me up."

"Jaryd..." Dyrileah's voice trembled as she spoke. "I don't know if I can do that."

"Don't decide the now." Jaryd's voice tightened. "I don't expect any promises. Just please don't decide tonight."

Dyrileah pressed her face into his chest and said nothing.

"We'll need to leave soon," Sebastyn announced quietly. "The entryway parlor is a safe place for you two to say a proper good-bye. I'll need to speak with Bardus here for a few moments. Make the most of them."

Jaryd led Dyrileah down the hall to the small parlor just off the front door. "I'm sorry," he said. "I never should have—"

Dyrileah silenced him with a kiss as fierce as it was tender. Finally breaking it off, she looked into his eyes. "I love you."

Jaryd smiled. "I love you too."

Dyrileah smiled back. "I heard about what you did today."

Jaryd's smile took on a rueful cast. "I nearly made a muck of it."

"But you didn't, did you?" Dyrileah's eyes shone. Running her fingers through his hair, she remarked, "You may still have hay in your hair, farm boy, but there is nothing but strength and kindness in your heart. I knew that the first day I met you, talking to chairs."

"Tables, actually," Jaryd corrected her. "Chairs are much less understanding."

Dyrileah's smile faded. "How is Bode?"

"She's strong," Jaryd responded, his own features sobering. "She'll be all right. She's decided to accompany us."

"Give her my love," Dyrileah said.

He kissed her then, a long, deep kiss. As their lips parted, Jaryd reached into the pocket of his tunic and extracted his grandmother's necklace. Sebastyn had used a bit of sorcery to mend the chain. "I'm hoping you will accept this to remember me by."

"I need no bit of jewelry to do that, Jaryd Hume," Dyrileah vowed. After a moment, though, she spun about and lifted her hair out of the way, insisting that he place the necklace about her neck himself.

46

New Hope

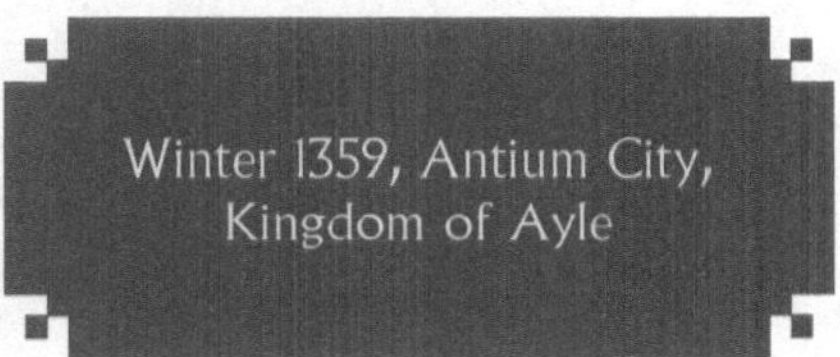

As soon as Jaryd and Sebastyn departed, Father Vars led Bode deeper into the sanctuary, down a winding staircase that descended into a torch-lit chamber with rock walls and a packed earthen floor.

"We are beneath the chapel," Father Vars explained, "in the oldest part of the sanctuary complex. Do you see that red stone arch?" He pointed.

Bode saw a gracefully formed arch about eight span from floor to the bottom of the inner curve and about ten span or thereabouts in overall height. The arch was freestanding, more like a piece of statuary than any form of structural support, and appeared to have somehow been hewn from a single piece of red stone.

"This has been hallowed ground for centuries," Father Vars continued. "No one knows how old the arch is or the means by which it was fashioned. It is a talisman of ancient origin."

The old prelate took Bode's hand in his. "If you stand beneath it and invoke the Yir..." Seeing the expression on her face, Father Vars patted her hand and smiled apologetically. "Or should you summon the One, you will see four visions, four brief glimpses of your personal future. They will likely be transient images only. Sometimes they are easily interpreted and sometimes not. They will happen, Bode, perhaps not in the order you see them, and there is no telling exactly when, but they will occur in your lifetime. That is certain."

Father Vars's eyes radiated kindness and understanding. "You have been sorely tested of late, ripped from your moorings. A glimpse into the future might give you some solace or some direction." He sighed. "Or it might not. I thought perhaps this," he indicated the arch with a wave of his hand, "might be something for you to consider. I will leave you the now. You know the way back to my chambers?"

Bode nodded.

"Come see me after. Should you decide to use the red stone talisman, remember only to summon the One. There is no need to perform any act of magic. Remember also never speak to anyone about what you see. To do so disturbs the balance of things, and the results of that are never beneficial. I cannot tell you where wisdom lies in this, my child. I do not know if it is better for you to make use of the talisman or not." He squeezed her hand reassuringly. "Follow your heart and whatever you decide will be for the best."

So saying, the Axton left, climbing back up the stairs with an alacrity that defied his age.

Bode stood before the red stone edifice for a long moment after the sound of Father Vars's steps faded into silence. Squaring her shoulders, she stepped beneath the arch and summoned the Power of the One. The images that danced before her eyes were fleeting but vivid. Bode knew she would never forget them.

The first brought her sorrow, the second joy, and the last she did not understand at all. The third vision changed everything. Bode lay in a field of snow; a man bent over her, a young man with wide, muscular shoulders. He wore a battered Three Rivers watch cap, and a woolen scarf wrapped about his mouth partially obscured the lower portion of his face. She could make out his features well enough, however, especially his eyes; green they were with flecks of gold in the depths of them and so dear to her she would have known them anywhere.

The vision could have but one meaning. As impossible as it seemed, Mat Bayrd was alive, and she would see him again at least once more.

Glossary of Terms

Term	Sounds Like	Definition
All Father	all fa-ther	Deity worshiped by those of the Penitent faith; the primary religion of the Tieran Empire and the kingdoms of Ayle, Syrdis, and Wystros.
Altair	al-tare	Kingdom located on the northeastern shore of the Middle Sea.
Antium	an-tee-um	Capital city of the Kingdom of Ayle; located on the eastern flank of the Donn Narrows (see Myr Sea).
Ayle	ail	Kingdom located on the north-central shore of the Middle Sea; also adjacent to the northeastern shore of the Myr Sea. The Ayle are long-term allies of the Tieran Empire.
Almyr	al-mir	Deity also known as the Mother Goddess or the Trascera Mother: worshiped by the Elsacians.
altyrn	all-tern	Tieran junior officer rank; typically a company commander.

Term	Sounds Like	Definition
Askante	ah-skhan-tee	Specialized light infantry raised by the Gracci faction during the War of Houses. Askante carry a clutch of javelins (throwing spears), a round, bronze-faced shield for defense, and the kante, a long-bladed, short-hafted thrusting spear. Well-conditioned and highly mobile, they have a reputation as tough fighters.
axton	axe-tun	Title given to a senior priest within the Penitent faith.
Aylitic	a-lih-tick	Primary language of the Ayle; also one of the most prominent tongues used for trade and commerce throughout the Middle Sea region, especially in lands north and west of the Middle Sea.

Term	Sounds Like	Definition
baelryc	bail-rick	Hand-and-a-half hilted bastard sword preferred by Kylgahran Highlanders: typically two and a half span in blade length, for most men about the same distance as from shoulder joint to fingertip with their hand and arm fully extended. It is a straight-bladed weapon, and the tip of the baelryc is formed into a symmetric, double-edged point. The leading edge of the sword is razor-sharp over its full length. About a span from the point, the back side of the baelryc blade gradually thickens to a blunt, rounded edge, which extends back to the hilt. Most hilts feature a simple iron cross-guard. The blade itself is made of watermarked steel, called so because the repeated hammered folding and quenching of the base iron mixed with charcoal during the forging of the blade leaves ripples in the finished steel that resemble a water mark.
Bandehar	ban-dee-har	Kingdom located at the southeastern extreme of the Middle Sea region along the shores of the Olyth Ocean to the east and the Saeryc Ocean to the south.

Term	Sounds Like	Definition
beagle	bee-gul	Slang term that Tieran Marines, seagoing heavy infantry, use in reference to their regular infantry counterparts.
briny	bri-nee	Slang term that Tieran Regulars, heavy infantry, use in reference to their marine counterparts.
Brynnai	brin-eye	Of or pertaining to the Brynnai faith: primary religion of the Kylgahran and their forebears, the Sea Isle folk; the Brynnai believe in a Creator, the One God, and the Four Fates, who act as intermediaries (see Four Fates).
caestor	kay-stor	Mid-level Tieran bureaucrat; an administrator; duties vary; sometimes assigned as a school supervisor.
Cartsys	kart-sis	Mainland north of the Middle Sea; an Aylitic word that means "homeland"; bordered on the west by the Maeryc Ocean and on the east by the Olyth Ocean; the northern extremes of the Cartsys encompass the Lands of Snow, north of the Torean Mountains, a vast hinterland about which little is known.

Term	Sounds Like	Definition
chieftain of Lairds	chief-tan	Principal executive of the Kylgahran Council of Lairds; elected by vote of the council members to a term of six years, the chieftain is primarily a battle leader.
compaglium	com-pag-lee-um	Tieran word for a temporary fortified encampment usually surrounded by a combination of trench and staked, wooden palisade.
Confederation of Clans	con-fed-er-a-shun of klanz	Governmental structure of the Kylgahran clans; an association of clans ruled by the Kylgahran Council of Lairds, headed by the chieftain of Lairds.
Confederation of Sorcerers	con-fed-er-a-shun of sor-ser-erz	Organization of sorcerers within the Tieran Empire. Most large cities have a corresponding confederation; the Confederation of Tyne (capital of the Tieran province of Quistyn del Aurus) is an example.
Cos	koss	Syrdisian city located on the banks of the River Sayx in the northwestern reaches of the kingdom.

Term	Sounds Like	Definition
croix	kroy	Primary weapon of Tieran regular infantry and marines: a thrusting spear, the croix measures eight span in length, about the distance the average soldier can reach up to standing flat-footed with one arm fully extended over his head. A croix spearhead is one-and-one-quarter-span long, triangular in shape, with a pyramidal cross section made of pressed steel. Affixed to an ash wood shaft, the spear point is counterweighted by a steel spike one-third of a span in length riveted to the butt of the weapon. The croix can be thrown effectively but is intended almost exclusively for use in close combat.
cutter	kuh-ter	A fast, midsized sailing ship; typically features a two-mast hermaphrodite sail configuration utilizing a mix of both square and lateen-rigged courses; cutters are highly prized by merchantmen and smugglers alike for their speed and maneuverability.

Term	Sounds Like	Definition
Danos	da-nos	Island nation south of the Morro Peninsula. The Danoans often serve as mercenaries and are among the favored auxiliaries of the Tieran Empire. The Danoans are famed archers, and the fearsome Danoan longbow is dreaded on battlefields throughout the Middle Sea.
Drach Orckens	drak or-kenz	An order of Penitent monks; a warrior society, the Drach Orckens provide armed escort to pilgrims and church officials traveling between religious sites. Renowned for their skill as metal workers and vintners, the Drach Orckens also lend money. The Penitent faith frowns on usury, but the Drach Orckens charter specifically allows the practice. The Drach Orckens are a close-knit, secretive society, supposedly in control of vast wealth, and rumors abound concerning them. Sorcerers are said to be among their ranks and, it is whispered, witches too. Their sigil is the rune symbol throi, also known as the death's head.
dymena	deh-min-ah	Proper form of address for a female Elven noble.
dymenu	deh-min-ooh	Proper form of address for a male Elven noble.
Elfan	El-fan	Male elf.

Term	Sounds Like	Definition
Elfin	El-feen	Female elf.
Elsacian	el-say-she-un	Ethnic minority within the Kingdom of Ayle, living principally in the major cities such as the capital, Antium: Elsacians originally hail from the portion of the Basyr Peninsula now known as the Tieran province of Quistyn del Tagus. Elsacians tend to be fair-skinned and blond-haired with a distinctive cast or tilt to their eyes.
Enduyi	en-doo-ee	A breed of horses favored by the Elves of Ilyria; famed for their speed and agility. Typical coloring varies from black to brown, including roan, with manes usually of black or brown.
esquire	es-quire	A class of lesser Kylgahran nobles; landowners who can claim at least four quires or one quadrant of land or the equivalent in property (see Quadrant).
Fey amulet	fey am-u-let	Magic talisman in the form of a circular disk crafted of pellinwahr (an iron alloy) characterized by the rune symbol Fey emblazoned on the surface of the medallion. Fey talismans are reputed to ward against all forms of adverse magic that intend to do the wearer harm.

Term	Sounds Like	Definition
Four Fates	for fates	According to the Brynnai faith, the Four Fates are immortal servants of the Creator. They see His will is done. There are two brothers, Ryx, who stands for courage, and Tal, who champions justice, and two sisters, Eym, who represents liberty, and Lyn, who embodies the spirit of love.
Glavius	gla-vee-us	Tieran infantry sword; double-edged, blade length of two span, with a symmetrically shaped triangular point. Forged of pressed steel, the Glavius is a heavy short sword nearly three fingers in width at the base of the blade. The Glavius will cut readily enough, but it is principally a stabbing weapon.
Glaylic	glay-lick	Native language of the Kylgahran and their antecedents, the Sea People (People of the Sea Isles).
Greymark	grey-mark	Ancestral hold of Clan Ard Ryan (see Hold).
Greystock	grey-stalk	Village nestled round Deben Bay on the northwestern coast of the Myr Sea in the Tieran Territory of the Three Rivers.
Gyft	gift	Name given to the ability to invoke (utilize) the power of the Yir (that is, the ability to do magic).

Term	Sounds Like	Definition
Gyft Ryll	gift rill	Special schools within the boundaries of the Tieran Empire and the Kingdom of Ayle devoted to developing the ability to use the power of the Yir; in addition to instruction in working directly with the Yir, Gyft Rylls offer a wide range of education in subjects including history, medicine, language, and mathematics.
hacker	haa-kur	Slang term Highland sailors have ascribed to the Kylgahran cutlass or sea sword; basically a pared-down version of the Kylgahran baelryc adapted for close-quarter fighting, including a "caged" or "basket" hand guard in lieu of the simple crossbar guard of the full-sized baelryc.
heartstone	hart-stone	A gray, glassy stone capable of being knapped like flint into various tools and weapons, arrowheads, spear points, and such. Heartstone possesses a peculiar property in that no sorcerer or witch can use magic to ward against it as a weapon.
Henfyrd	hen-feared	Large town in the Tieran province of Quistyn del Aurus; located on the east bank of the River Wyst at its juncture with the Middle Sea.

Term	Sounds Like	Definition
Highlands	hi-landz	Traditional home of the Kylgahran (see Kylgahra) Clans, the term refers to the rugged combination of hills and narrow, ridge-topped valleys that lie between the Tylcairn Mountains and the Cartsys west coast of the Maeryc Ocean.
hold	hold	Kylgahran term referring to the principal residence of a clan laird; typically a fortified dwelling.
housecarls	hous-karlz	Designation given to a class of warriors within the Kingdom of Syrdis; the housecarls are traditionally heavy cavalry; the most vaunted arm of the Syrdisian military.
Ilyria	ill-ir-ee-ah	Island homeland of the Elves; a chain of islands in the Maeryc Ocean south and west of the Cartsys mainland.
Ilyrian	ill-ir-ee-ahn	Language of the Elves; an ancient tongue widely spoken throughout especially the southern portion of the Middle Sea region.
invoking the Yir	in-vo-king the yea	Process by which a sorcerer accesses the power of the Yir, the source of sorcerers' magic. Invoking the Yir by a sorcerer corresponds to a witch's summoning of the One (see Summon).

Term	Sounds Like	Definition
jaltryn	jall-trin	Padded leather arming jacket worn by Tieran soldiers, infantry and cavalry alike, beneath their chainmail armor.
keppi	keh-pee	An Elsacian dress featuring a snug-fitting bodice and a full skirt.
kernyl	ker-nel	Tieran army officer rank ascribed to each regimental commander.
Kios	kee-os	Kingdom located just north of the Basyr Peninsula. Eastern neighbor and long-standing foe of the Kingdom of Ayle.
Kylgahra	kill-gar-ah	Traditional home of the Kylgahran (see Highlands) Clans, the region encompasses the rugged combination of hills and narrow, ridge-topped valleys that lie between the Tylcairn Mountains and the Cartsys west coast of the Maeryc Ocean; a Glaylic word meaning "highlands."
Kylgahran	kill-gar-ahn	Of or pertaining to the people of Kylgahra.
Kylgahran Clans	kill-gar-ahn klanz	Familial groupings of the Kylgahran people; the government of Kylgahra is based on the clan structure; each clan is ruled by a laird (see Laird).
kylo	kee-low	Standard Tieran measure of distance; one kylo is composed of sixteen hundred paces (see Pace, Span).

Term	Sounds Like	Definition
kyrobi	ky-roh-bee	A broad, brocaded belt of waxed linen worn by women in lands all around the Middle Sea.
laird	lehrd	Ruler of a Kylgahran Clan; the equivalent of an individual clan chieftain. Lairds are not absolute monarchs; the extent of their authority is shaped by years of precedent and tradition. No clan will tolerate a tyrant; lairdship of a clan is inherited, passed down to the eldest child of the current laird regardless of sex. About half of the Kylgahran lairds are, therefore, female; each laird automatically ascends to a seat on the Council of Lairds, the ruling body of the Kylgahran Confederation (see Confederation of Clans).
Lands of Snow	landz of sno	A great wilderness extending north of the Torean Mountains; home to a number of tribal folk who, in the past, have sometimes moved south to raid or even invade the lands surrounding the Middle Sea.
legio	leh-gee-oh	A Tieran term referring to an army barracks, typically associated with a permanent military installation (see Puglium or Stadia).

Term	Sounds Like	Definition
Lynium	leh-nee-um	Primary language of the Tieran Empire; spoken in all provinces and territories of the empire. Also one of the most prominent tongues used for trade and commerce throughout the Middle Sea region.
Maeryc Ocean	mair-ick o-shun	The great ocean extending west of the Cartsys mainland.
Mayne	main	Legendary city-state, once the jewel of civilization in the Middle Sea region, long fallen into ruin. The exact location of the once-renowned city-state is unknown. The prevailing view is that Mayne was most likely located somewhere in the northeastern portion of the Morro Peninsula. A minority view contends the site must have been much farther north.
Middle Sea	mih-del see	Large body of saltwater bordered by the Cartsys mainland on the north and the east and by the Morro Peninsula to the south. The Middle Sea opens into the vast Maeryc Ocean to the west.

Term	Sounds Like	Definition
Morgyn	mor-gin (hard g)	Breed of horse favored by Kylgahran clansmen. Mountain-bred, the Morgyns are medium-sized, swift, and surefooted. Not as fast as the elegant Enduyi horses favored by the Elves of Ilyria or as powerful as the Panyir chargers of Roi, the Morgyns combine a good turn of speed with incredible endurance. They make excellent cow horses. Typical coloring varies from brown to gray, often dappled with manes usually of black or gold.
Morro Peninsula	mor-oh	Territorial heartland of the Tieran Empire; a large peninsula that lines the southern shore of the Middle Sea.
Myr Sea	mihr see	Also known as the Inland Sea; a body of saltwater shaped roughly like a giant thumb angling mostly north and west; the base of the thumb, the southeastern terminus, connects with the much larger Middle Sea through a channel known as the Donn Narrows. The Myr Sea is bordered along its northwestern coast by the Tieran Territory of the Three Rivers; the Tieran Province of Quistyn del Aurus occupies most of its southwestern shoreline, while a portion of the Kingdom of Ayle lies along the eastern shore of the sea south of the river Poe.

Term	Sounds Like	Definition
Myrl	mehrl	Kingdom located on the eastern flank of the Middle Sea, bordered by Relwyn to the south and Altair to the north.
nithing	nih-thing	A Tieran term meaning of no consequence.
Olyth Ocean	oh-lith o-shun	The ocean extending east of the Cartsys mainland.
pace	pace	Standard Tieran measure of distance; one pace is composed of three span; corresponds to the approximate length of an average man's full stride (see Kylo, Span).
pallester	pah-les-ter	Tieran term for a parade ground located within a military installation such as a puglium or compaglium.
pellinwahr	pe-lin-wahr	An Elven word referring to a metallic alloy of iron; looks like black iron but is less dense. Pellinwahr is a material often used in the manufacture of magic talismans.
Penitent faith	pe-neh-tent faith	Dominant religion throughout the Tieran Empire and the kingdoms of Syrdis, Ayle, and Wystros. Penitents worship a deity known as the All Father, the Creator and bringer of Light and Life (see All Father).

Term	Sounds Like	Definition
pressed steel	prest steel	Steel composed of charcoal-laced iron formed by repeated folding and hammering of the base metal during forging; pressed steel is the standard for Tieran military-grade weaponry; also called layered steel.
puglium	puh-glee-um	A permanent Tieran military installation typically including barracks, stables, a hospital, baths, various workshops, and storage facilities. Also known as a military campus.
quadrant	kwah-drant	A Kylgahran term pertaining to a property holding equivalent in size to four quires (see Quire).

Term	Sounds Like	Definition
questing charm	qwe-sting charm	A magic talisman capable of guiding a bearer to the person for whom the charm was conjured. No ability to invoke the Yir is necessary to make use of a questing charm. Questing charms may be fashioned from most objects, especially those that have been in close, personal contact with the individual sought. Questing charms usually work only on sentient beings, although a form of questing charm can be fashioned from a part of a thing, a page torn from a book or a sliver shaved from a wooden item, for example. Inanimate objects may be enchanted to emit a telepathic beacon, but only someone with the ability to invoke the Yir would be able to detect the telepathic transmission. Iron will not serve as a questing charm, and neither will some gemstones (see also Seeking Charm).
quire	kwy-er	A Kylgahran term denoting a square plot of ground measuring four hundred paces on a side.
quistyn	kweh-sten	A word in Lynium, the language of Tier, meaning an imperial holding. The formal designation for all Tieran provinces begins with the words "Quistyn del."

Term	Sounds Like	Definition
regenerative talisman	re-gen-er-a-tive tal-is-man	Subset of magic talismans (see Talisman) with the capacity to regenerate. If placed in close proximity to a mundane object with matching physical properties, a regenerative talisman will transfer its magical properties while retaining its own. The time required varies, but regenerative talismans all have the capability to replicate provided the targeted mundane object is a close enough physical match to the talisman. Sorcerers' staves and seeking charms are examples of regenerative talismans.
regent	ree-gent	Tieran Army officer rank above altyrn and below kernyl. A regent typically commands two companies. Five regents are usually assigned to each regular army regiment. Of the five, one is normally a senior regent (see Regent, Senior), typically the regiment's second-in-command.
regent, senior	ree-gent, sen-ee-or	Tieran Army officer rank just below that of kernyl. A senior regent is usually second-in-command of a regular army regiment.

Term	Sounds Like	Definition
regiment	reh-jah-ment	Principal Tieran Army operational unit composed of ten companies of one hundred soldiers, not including officers, for a total of one thousand troops. Each regular army regiment is designated by both a name and a number ranging between zero and one hundred; examples are the 5th Minoa, 6th Gemina, 10th Accer, and 33rd Regulus. The combination of name and number is unique, although both name and number are reused; examples include the 12th Minoa, 6th Accer, and 5th Regulus.
regular	reh-gu-lahr	Designation given to professional Tieran soldiers. Regulars enlist for a period of twenty years. At the end of their twenty-year enlistment, they have an opportunity to either retire or to reenlist for an additional five years. The five-year reenlistment bonus is substantial, a single lump-sum payment equivalent to three years' pay. Tieran regulars are heavy infantry. Their principal weapon is a thrusting spear called the croix (see Croix).

Term	Sounds Like	Definition
Relwyn	rel-win	Kingdom composed of a confederation of tribes located northeast of Roi. The Relwyn are fierce warriors and perennial foes of the Roi. While no formal alliance exists, the Relwyn have long served as mercenary auxiliaries in the armed forces of Tier.
Roi	roy	Kingdom occupying the lands just east of the Tieran Empire on the Morro Peninsula. The warlike Roi are the most venerated and powerful foes of the Tieran Empire.
Saeryc Ocean	sair-ick o-shun	The southern ocean, extending south of the Morro Peninsula.
sajar	say-jar	Tieran noncommissioned officer rank. In Lynium, the language of Tier, sajar literally means the leader of twenty. In a regular army regiment composed of ten one-hundred-man companies, five sajars are assigned to each company. The senior sajar in each company has the rank of sajar first.
scralyng	scray-ling	A Kylgahran term denoting a person of low regard and questionable heritage.
Sea Isles	see eyelz	Island kingdom located in the Maeryc Ocean to the west of the Cartsys mainland; ancestral home of the Kylgahran.

Term	Sounds Like	Definition
seeking charm	see-king charm	Regenerative magic talisman (see Regenerative Talisman) capable of identifying individuals with the ability to invoke the Yir. Held in the hand of someone capable of invoking the Yir, seeking charms emit a soft blue light. Seeking charms may be fashioned from a wide variety of materials. Iron objects and some gemstones will not serve (see also Questing Charm).
Sircassian League	sir-cas-see-an	Originating in the Kingdom of Bandehar, the Sircassian League is a highly trained, superbly skilled band of assassins available for hire to anyone with the will and the coin necessary to make use of their unique services. Sircassians also serve as bodyguards, spies, and thief takers.
spada	spay-dah	Tieran cavalry sword; single-edged, blade length of nearly three span, with a symmetric leaf-shaped point. Forged of pressed steel, the straight-bladed spada is primarily a slashing weapon designed for use on horseback.
span	span	Standard Tieran measure of distance; one span represents the distance from the crease in an average-sized man's elbow to the base of his middle finger (roughly equal to one English foot). Three span comprise a pace (see Pace, Kylo).

Term	Sounds Like	Definition
stadia	stay-dee-ah	A Tieran school for officer training, more common than a military academy.
stone	stone	Standard Tieran measure of weight (roughly equal to four English pounds).
Suffolk Islands	su-folk eye-landz	Island nation located in the Maeryc Ocean north and west of the Cartsys mainland.
summoning the One	suh-mon-ing the one	To summon the One is the Wcyken's version of invoking the Yir (see Invoking the Yir). The One or the Power of the One is the source of magic utilized by practitioners of witchcraft (thought by many to be the same source as the Yir).
Syrdis	Sir-dis	Kingdom occupying and extending north from the Cambrian Peninsula located at the northwest terminus of the Middle Sea. Syrdis is one of the old kingdoms, often at odds with indigenous tribal peoples to the north and northwest, and an on-again/off-again adversary of the Kylgahran.

Term	Sounds Like	Definition
talisman	tal-is-man	Magic device capable of utilizing the Yir to perform one or more various functions. Some talismans are capable of greatly amplifying the power of the Yir fed into them, enhancing the ward cast through their use. Sorcerers' staves are one example of such. In modern times, few retain the knowledge to produce talismans. Those with such knowledge tend to guard their secrets closely. Over time, talismans have become increasingly rare and arcane.
telemosis	teh-le-mo-sis	One of the four basic forms of magic that comprise the Yir; involves the transformation of energy from one type to another. Telemosis is used to generate sorcerers' fire and, for the truly skilled, the more sinister and deadlier balefire.

Term	Sounds Like	Definition
telestasis	teh-le-stay-sus	The most exotic of the four basic forms of magic that comprise the Yir and the most controversial. Telestasis pertains to altering the properties of matter or, more specifically, infusing the power of the Yir into matter, changing its nature or condition. Perhaps the most basic application of telestasis is the transformation of water into ice. It is widely believed that in earlier times, during periods of High Magic, telestasis served as the principal form used for the manufacture of talismans. Some think telestasis, the so-called fourth state of magic, is not a form at all but rather a catalyst, a necessary element in the use of all three of the other basic forms but not a separate form in its own right. After all, employing telemosis to extract heat from water also produces ice. The argument is that no proof currently exists of a purely telestatic application. A few believe telestasis is actually a conduit to the realm of Spirit, a means of bridging the gap between the material world and the ethereal plane. This, of course, is heresy, at least per the tenets of the Penitent faith.
Tensys	ten-sis	Syrdisian city; located on the west bank of the River Wyst at its juncture with the Middle Sea.

Term	Sounds Like	Definition
Three Rivers	three reh-verz	A territory of the Tieran Empire located along the northwestern coast of the Myr Sea, bounded by the Escalon Plateau to the north, the Syrus River to the west, and the Poe River to the east.
Tyne	tine	Capital of the Tieran Province of Quistyn del Aurus, located on the western flank of the Donn Narrows (see Myr Sea).
vyldeen	vil-deen	A member of the Elven nobility.
Vyrland	veer-land	Large Island nation in the Maeryc Ocean north of the Sea Isles; populated by fierce, warlike seafarers who regularly raid all along the west coast of the Cartsys mainland as well as the Suffolk Islands and the Sea Isles.
Wycken	wih-ken	Of or representing the community of witches. It is said that becoming a witch is to be of the Wycken.
wysoi	wih-soy	Liquor distilled from fermented wort (as that obtained from corn mash); a favored beverage of the Kylgahran.

Term	Sounds Like	Definition
Wystros	wis-tros	Kingdom occupying the Hynde Peninsula, which extends westward into the Maeryc Ocean just west of the Middle Sea. Wystros is one of the old kingdoms, a traditional foe of the Syrdisians, and a longtime ally and trading partner of the Kylgahran, especially the Southern Clans.
Yir	year	The source of sorcerers' magic on Trascera. The power of the Yir, also known as the Hidden Source, is divided into four basic states or forms: telepathy, telekinetics, telemosis, and telestasis. Some believe the power of the Yir and the magic used in the practice of witchcraft, known as the Power of the One, are indistinguishable; both drawn from the same Hidden Source. Others believe that the differences, though subtle, are distinct and that the two forms of magic are separate both in substance as well as practice (see Summoning the One).

Acknowledgments

I would like to express heartfelt thanks to the following:

1. Julie Atchley and Heather Sanchez for help with the social media stuff. I would have been lost without you

2. Lori Bradford for continued support and guidance

3. The staff at Wheatmark, Inc. without whose expertise and patience this book would not have been possible

4. Rebecca, my wife, my companion, most loving and steadfast

   And to all who give of their time to read the thing

Until next time,

Randy Ellena
Fresno, CA

About the Author

Raised on a small farm in the central San Joaquin Valley, Randy Ellena graduated from California State University, Fresno in May of 1981 with a Bachelor of Science degree in electrical engineering, launching a thirty-two-year career as an engineer working mostly in the aerospace industry.

Randy earned a Master's degree in electrical engineering from the California State University, Long Beach in December of 1985 and went on to complete an Engineer's degree at the University of Southern California in May of 1994. The bulk of Randy's career was spent working as a communications system engineer in the area of satellite and space applications. Randy retired from Boeing in June of 2013 as a chief engineer for Boeing Satellite Systems located in El Segundo, California.

Upon retirement Randy moved back to Fresno where he now lives with his wife Rebecca and eight cats (it's a long story). Randy writes primarily to give himself something to do between trimming hedges, mowing the lawn, and cleaning cat pans. He is busy scribbling away at The Trasceran Chronicles, a fantasy anthology comprised of two distinct but related series of novels *The Kylgahran* and *The Tierans*, both set in lands surrounding the Middle Sea on a two-mooned world called Trascera.